CODEX

THE SERPENTS OF CAESAR

BOOK II

T.R. BURGESS

EQUUS HOUSE BOOKS

CODEX: THE SERPENTS OF CAESAR: BOOK II

Copyright © T.R. Burgess, 2024

The moral right of T.R. Burgess to be identified as Author of this work has been asserted in accordance with the Copyright, Designs and Patents Act 1988.

A CIP catalogue record for this book is available from the British Library.

ISBN: 978-1-7391298-3-5 (Paperback)
ISBN: 978-1-7391298-2-8 (eBook)

Book Cover Design by ebooklaunch.com
Typeset by ebooklaunch.com
Europa map by Pixeleiderdown
Gallia Narbonensis map by Gianpiero Mangialardi
Website by SPRK Design

First published in Great Britain in 2024 by
EQUUS HOUSE BOOKS
www.equushousebooks.com

For Robyn, my dear friend and writing buddy.

With love and gratitude.

THE SERPENTS OF CAESAR SERIES

Signum

Codex

Inferno

For more information please visit: www.trburgess.com

Map: Western Empire (detail)
850 Ab Urbe Condita,
from the Founding of Rema (AD 97)

Map: Gallia Narbonensis (detail)

*The brave and the bold cling to hope
even in the face of disaster…*

Tacitus, *The Histories*

The story so far…

Legend claims that a map of a lost Alpine pass is hidden in Iolia's Temple of the Flame and protected by the sign of the serpents.

In an alternate first century world, the city of Rema – founded when Remus killed Romulus – has prospered and grown. The Reman Empire extends in all directions, crushing and displacing those who were there before it.

Descendants of the Ambrone tribe live far from their northern homeland on the island of Iolia – now part of the Empire. When Ambrone descendant and Praetorian Guard Verendus returned to Iolia, he found his old adversary, Prefect Galenius, in charge of a new military unit. As his suspicions grew that the prefect's presence on the island was part of a conspiracy to overthrow the emperor, Verendus received a message from the temple's High Priestess imploring him to deliver a box to a fortress on the mainland. Believing the box to contain vital evidence of the conspiracy, Verendus agreed. He had not expected to be accompanied by a runaway hand-maid. Despite his attraction to Corinna, he does not trust her and has yet to discover why she fled the temple.

On reaching the mainland, Verendus learned that Galenius had become sole-prefect of the Guard and was more powerful than ever. Hoping to find proof of his treachery, Verendus opened the box. Within was a codex, an ancient book, secured by a serpent clasp. If this was the sign of the serpents, then the legendary map might be inside.

Now, determined to protect both the codex and Corinna, Verendus is on the road again…

THE SIGN OF THE SERPENTS

Many years ago, people of the Ambrone tribe left their northern homeland and trekked south across Europa in search of new land. Rema's legions pursued them, killing and enslaving thousands, pushing the tribe ever east towards the Alps where the last of the Ambrones fled into the mountains and disappeared. It is told they discovered a path through the Alps; a path no one has found since. According to legend, a map of the Ambrone tribe's route through the mountains is hidden in the Temple of the Flame and protected by the sign of the serpents.

Imperial security is a serious concern. An army could march on the imperial capital via an unguarded pass; therefore, all known Alpine passes are garrisoned and patrolled. Should this legendary map fall into enemy hands, the consequences would be grave indeed.

Chronicles of Imperial Rema

by Marcus Vedius Verendus

CHAPTER I

Gallia Narbonensis
850 Ab Urbe Condita
from the Founding of Rema (AD 97)

The next milestone came into sight, a stout pillar standing taller than a door, the carved place names bold in red paint. Commendator Ericus Vedius Verendus read the distance to Avennio and swore under his breath. They should have reached this marker yesterday.

He adjusted his seat in the saddle and rested a hand on the scuffed leather satchel that hung across his chest, pressing his fingers against the hard edges of the box within. Despite the warmth of the morning, the thought of what was inside that box sent a chill down his spine.

In a matter of days his world had been transformed, as though a storm raged, displacing everything in its path. He had done as ordered and carried the box to the fortress of Castellum Alba, only to find there was no safe place for it there. A new refuge must be found – and swiftly.

He endeavoured to shut out the rumble of the wagon and the chatter of the auxiliaries, and concentrate on the road ahead. He couldn't turn back. The auxiliary troop and its *decurion* commander were on official business, and he was under governor's orders to oversee that business. Once they reached Viorum he would discharge his responsibilities, consign the box to a suitable vault, and go his own way. That moment couldn't come soon enough.

Verendus glanced behind, but the wooden-roofed wagon and the auxiliaries riding beside it obstructed much of his view of the road. How long before the Praetorian Guard picked up his trail? Hard to tell. Vigilance was vital.

He reassured himself that even in the civilised province of Gallia Narbonensis, news only travelled as fast as the dispatch rider. For now, he must build distance between himself and Alba, give no cause for suspicion, and put up with the prattling auxiliaries. The men of the first *turma* of Fourth *Brittonum* were no exception to the griping and inane banter peculiar to close-knit units. Bonded through training together and living together, sharing barrack rooms in the fort and tents on campaign, they squabbled like feral children, but would unite as one to flatten any outsider who dared to cross a comrade.

Yesterday, Decurion Bretorus had led his troop through the narrow streets of Alba, past crowds of cheering bystanders. Mail shining, harness pendants jingling, the auxiliaries rode in pairs, following the White Horse Standard.

It hadn't taken long for the gloss to fade. Flushed-faced, stinking of sweat, and dusty from the road, they grumbled about the wagon and the extra pack-mules trundling along in their midst. And though the pothole-ridden track north from Alba was behind them, and level terrain beckoned, the grumbling continued. Decurion Bretorus, grim beneath his crested helmet, was no better. Since passing Alba's gate, the troop's commander had maintained a frosty taciturnity, his sole utterances moans and reprimands.

Verendus didn't bother to point out that the journey from Alba had been hindered from the outset when Governor Peronius insisted the turma delay departure to attend the funeral of Minister Dalcamus. Verendus was in no position to protest. The irony that he'd caused the minister's death, and had thus brought about the delay, wasn't lost on him. Regrettable, but Dalcamus knew too much.

Morning haze in fields beside the road evaporated in the sunshine. The day would be warm. A flock of white birds rose and melted into the blue. Save for a cluster of storehouses, and a squat, single-storey villa surrounded by outbuildings, the plain extended like a green lake. Ahead, the Via Aurelia stretched straight and pale, a silky ribbon of possibility compelling him and his stallion, Plum, onwards. Documentation permitting, one could travel hundreds of miles along these wide consular highways with their paving of flat stones set in concrete. On across Europa without leaving this network of imperial arteries, this vast web connecting the provinces with Rema, the heart of the Empire.

A row of chained slaves filed from a roadside field and jangled along the verge, shaven-heads bent, backs bowed beneath stacks of timber. An overseer followed, a broad-brimmed hat pulled low over his brow, one hand poised at his belt where a whip coiled like a brown snake. A boy leading a mule laden with axes and a bundle of branches brought up the rear.

The verge narrowed. Without a backward glance, the procession diverted onto the road.

Bretorus swore. 'Idiots! They have no right to use this road.'

Verendus left the decurion shouting rebukes and overtook the fettered line. Keep moving. Let them argue. Every step was a step nearer to Viorum.

An auxiliary began whining for a break. Two more added their voices to the plea. Verendus ignored them. The stopping place would be his decision, and he had somewhere in mind. The auxiliaries must wait. His self-imposed mission was to deliver the box to Viorum, not play wet-nurse to a gaggle of raw recruits on a mundane provincial tax collection. And this was the easy stage of the journey. The risk of a bandit attack would increase once the turma was carrying the taxes.

Movement on the bank of a stream caught his eye. A tall, thin figure sheathed in grey. Verendus tensed, almost snatched a spear from the quiver strapped to his saddle. But it was only a heron rising and flapping out of the mist. Silently, he scolded himself. There were no reports of bandits on this stretch of the highway.

His fingers strayed back to the box. He should never have opened it. Even the recollection of sliding the lid to reveal a gleam of metal was unsettling. Closer inspection had shown the metal to be a golden strap wound about a codex, a book small enough to fit in his palm. Then he'd turned the codex over and curiosity had ceded to unease. The strap was fastened with an ornate clasp, almost as large as the book, and circled by two ruby-eyed serpents, each swallowing the other's tail.

But he would soon be rid of the codex. At Alba, he'd thought himself so clever when he deposited a substitute box in the vault. What a fool he'd been. The ruse had roused the suspicions of Minister Dalcamus. When Prefect Galenius Dax learned his informant at Alba was dead, an investigation would commence. Soldiers of the Praetorian Guard, perhaps even their ruthless agents the *Speculatores*, would be dispatched to Alba. They would discover that the turma had departed for Viorum, and the search for evidence would have direction.

Verendus rubbed Plum's ears. Gods below, it was humid. On a mission, the fear of being captured by the enemy – of being tortured and killed – was a nagging dread. Fear of being caught by his own comrades was a new terror.

Again, he glanced at fields bordering the road. No living thing except a trio of cows sheltering under a tree, a cloud of flies buzzing around their heads. He pulled a cloth from inside his cuirass, swapped the reins from one hand to the other, and wiped his palms before untying the straps of his helmet and easing it off. Neat inside was a metal loop. He flipped it up and hung the helmet from a saddle-horn. There was no cooling breeze.

He must hold his nerve. With Fortuna's favour, he would deposit the box in Viorum, consult Tribune Aquinus, and be on the road again before Prefect Galenius heard a thing. With the Iolian Gap purported to be blocked and the harbour inaccessible, Galenius was stranded on Iolia. But for how much longer?

Verendus took comfort that his letter setting out concerns over the volatile situation in Iolia – the fire at the Officers' Club, the massacre of Parhels in Regia Square – should have reached Tribune Aquinus. The tribune was more than chief of the Gallia division of the Praetorian Guard – he was a friend. And just as well. Trusting in the wrong person could have dire consequences, and Verendus had no proof of Galenius' treachery. Speak out of turn and those he cared for would suffer.

It was no longer possible to report to the Castrum Remana, headquarters of the Praetorian Guard in Rema. Hopes of confiding in Prefect Secundus, of stating concerns that Galenius was plotting against the emperor, had come to nought. With the quiet sinistry of parasites invading a beehive, Galenius and his allies were infiltrating the Guard, eliminating all who opposed them. With Secundus in prison, and the imperial capital in a state of turmoil, setting foot in Rema would be unwise. Associates and sympathisers of the former prefect were being rounded up. And the name Verendus might be on the list.

But he could take his concerns to Viorum. Tribune Aquinus would help. Though first the taxes must be collected from the town of Combarus. He had little choice. Governor Peronius had left him in no doubt that failure to collect the taxes would be punished. Gallop off and the auxiliaries would pursue him. He could not afford to alienate the governor, nor could he leave Mos – it wouldn't be fair on the boy. He couldn't leave Corinna either. When Magistra, High Priestess of the Temple of the Flame, had entrusted him with the box and its precious contents, she had also entrusted Corinna. He was responsible for her now. And besides, he needed her help.

In the recess of his mind, the small voice of caution stirred. *Only that?*

The voice was right; it usually was. Corinna was a distraction. Even though he couldn't see her, she was distracting him. He pictured her finely cut features; the green eyes so characteristic of Enneans. Regiments were theatre enough without the addition of women. Yet, at his own insistence, Corinna and her two attendants were in the wagon. Slaves included, the procession numbered forty-nine.

The wheels of the wagon jarred and squeaked on a rough patch of road. A mule brayed angrily and several horses neighed in response. It was time for a break. They were nearing the junction Verendus had chosen as a stopping place; gods willing, they would arrive without incident. There was a booth selling hot food – that should cheer the auxiliaries. And spotting the yellow awning, he raised his hand to signal a halt.

You're wasting time, said the small voice. Having no good answer save that the auxiliaries and their horses needed rest and water, Verendus dismounted. After checking Plum over he left the stallion in Mos' care, and told Decurion Bretorus to question the man in the booth. If there had been trouble on this road recently, he would surely know of it.

Opposite the junction, where cooking fumes spewed from the roadside booth, stood a square-shaped temple built of wax-hued limestone. A porch had been stuck to the front like an afterthought, its door open to the elements to signify that somewhere in the known world, the Empire was at war.

Verendus crossed the verge and passed the stone altar. He didn't really believe the gods divulged divine wisdom via a lump of offal, did he? Probably not. Maybe…

Waste of time, said the voice.

Decurion Bretorus had made the offerings and auguries before departure. *Twice.* The first chicken's liver was blotched with disease. A bad omen. Governor Peronius had demanded a second sacrifice.

Though the bad omen was disconcerting, Verendus couldn't delude himself that he was at the temple on regimental business. This was personal. He was slipping back into superstitious ways. Magistra had warned him to tread carefully and had entreated the god Janus to watch over his journey. Now, further guidance was required and Janus might provide this. For a price.

Waste of time, waste of money, mocked the small voice, sounding exactly like Father. How the old man would have tutted.

Verendus reached the porch. With the feeling he was being watched, he turned. Eldoran, silver-haired Ennean of the

Nemusi tribe, was standing in the shade of a chestnut tree where his horse had drawn the interest of several auxiliaries. Built for speed, the gelding was compact and beautifully proportioned; the lightest prick of the spur would set it galloping. Not that the Nemusan wore spurs on those fancy, knee-high leather boots.

He met Verendus' eyes and nodded. Again Verendus felt the stab of antipathy he'd experienced on first seeing the Nemusan. Unable to rationalise his reaction, he set it aside and walked over.

At his approach, the auxiliaries stepped back and he was face-to-face with the creature. The gelding regarded him with dark, contemptuous eyes. Verendus lowered his gaze and whispered in the tender tone reserved for lovers and horses. Curious, the gelding extended a graceful neck. The proud head with alert ears, large eyes, and concave nose was as perfect as the statue on Father's desk. He longed to make a sketch. With a slow hand, he stroked its muzzle and took the opportunity to examine the bridle. The simple snaffle-bit would offer less control than the curb-bit in Plum's mouth. The saddle was plain, too, and lacked the four corner horns of a cavalry saddle, which provide grip and security while freeing a rider's hands for combat.

Perhaps the Nemusan had no need of such props. Mystery shrouded him. He was far from his northern homeland and had claimed to be travelling to Rema. The abruptness with which he had abandoned that destination and decided to accompany the turma to Viorum seemed at odds with his air of quiet diligence. He'd mentioned a business meeting in Viorum; Verendus wasn't convinced. For all he knew, the Nemusan was tailing him – albeit in an obvious way.

The auxiliaries slunk off. Verendus resolved to remain on his guard and did not follow. 'Fine horse,' he said. 'Has he a name?'

'Matara. It means spear, for he is swift and graceful.' Eldoran brushed an invisible speck from the bridle. 'Is it your intention to make camp before we leave the highway?'

'Why?' asked Verendus. The agenda was not open for discussion.

'I have spoken with the man in the booth. Two days ago, a farmer taking a bullock to market was ambushed on the old north road. The bullock was stolen, and the farmer left for dead. Travellers found him and carried him to a nearby villa where he died of his injuries. He spoke one word before he died.' Eldoran lowered his voice. 'Barbarians.'

Barbarians? This was troubling, though not a concern Verendus wanted to share. If common highway thieves had attacked the farmer, then surely he would have said *bandits*.

Over at the booth, Bretorus was questioning the cook. It would be interesting to see if the decurion received the same account. Some of these rustics were prone to embellishment and the turning for the old north road was just a few miles away.

It was the only road to Combarus.

CHAPTER II

Verendus crossed the threshold into the cool, candlelit chamber of the Temple of Janus. Aromatic camphor trails of incense smoke hung in the air. With its gleaming walls of coloured marble and offerings of wildflowers arranged upon a side table, the room held the expectant atmosphere of a theatre set. It wouldn't have surprised him if a chorus of masked actors had come dancing out from behind a column and burst into song.

The studs of his *caligae* boots click-clacking to disturb the peace, he approached the huge bronze statue at the room's centre and stopped beside it. The two-faced god was dressed in a toga of fine wool, and so tall that the laurel-crowned head almost scraped the ceiling. In one hand, the statue held a traveller's staff carved from a gnarled branch. In the other was a key, which could open any lock. The god's younger, smooth-faced countenance stared impassively at the temple's east wall: the direction from which Verendus had come. He turned to the bearded profile. This looked west: the future into which he was heading.

Magistra had warned him his path was clouded. In a desperate attempt to clear that path and keep his identity secret, it seemed she had paid with her life.

Footfalls echoed. It was time to ask for guidance.

A priest with snowy hair and beard as white as his immaculate toga stepped from the shadows. 'Janus sees all that has passed along the road,' he said. 'And all that shall pass.'

'In his graciousness he has helped me before,' Verendus replied.

The priest raised a wispy eyebrow. 'Do you wish me to intercede on your behalf?'

That settled it. Janus could set him in the right direction. Verendus opened his purse and handed over a coin. 'I need guidance.'

'Then I shall entreat Janus to light the way.'

The priest snapped his fingers, and two acolytes in brown tunics appeared. Clearly, they had anticipated the request as between them they carried candles, dishes, two miniature amphorae, and a silver knife. A third acolyte arrived bearing a wicker cage, the dove within scratching its protest.

Verendus followed them outside to the altar in front of the porch. Across the side road, at a respectable distance from the temple, the turma had taken over the verge. Despite the relentless clanking, and drone of voices as auxiliaries fetched food for themselves and their horses, the priest didn't seem to notice them. He adjusted his toga, pulling it up to draw a fold of fabric over his head, and murmured what might have been sacred words of invocation – or merely incoherent nonsense. An acolyte opened the cage and the dove fluttered and tried to flap free. A bad omen already; the gods preferred their conduits to remain calm.

Undeterred, the acolyte clasped the dove, lifted it from the cage, and held it on the altar. Still murmuring, the priest selected an amphora and sprinkled a few drops of wine onto the altar and then over the bird. Taking the second amphora, he repeated the process. A waft of incense scented the air. Verendus coughed. That was probably a bad omen too.

Thankfully, the priest gave no indication he'd been distracted. He picked up the knife. '*Ave*, Janus.' Bending over the bird, he slit its throat.

A twitch, a spurt of blood, and the neck flopped limp.

The priest turned the bird over and sliced through the bloodied feathers into its breast. He fished out the innards and a sour smell emanated. Using the knife, he deftly separated the tiny liver from the red slop on the altar. Lips pursed, head shaking, he bent closer and cut the liver. For a moment, all was quiet. Even the auxiliaries ceased their prattling. The priest sighed at the pattern of flesh revealed within. He straightened and hooked up the liver with the curved tip of his knife.

Verendus peered at the crimson scrap. It appeared healthy.

An acolyte proffered a dish of black powder and a candle. The priest held the liver over the dish and let four drops of blood discolour the powder, which he lit with the candle flame. The powder fizzed and a curl of acrid smoke drifted up.

Verendus caught his breath. 'Well?'

'If you are worthy, a sign shall arrive by dusk.'

None the wiser, Verendus thanked him and crossed to the verge, the words *waste of time, waste of money*, resounding in his ears. Horses stood cropping grass and flicking their tails at flies. Most of the mounts were the small greys native to the local marshlands, but there were several sturdy crossbreeds amongst them. The auxiliaries were a mixed bag too: recruits from Britannia cutting their teeth alongside battle-hardened Celts and Carthaginians.

Before departure, Verendus had joined Bretorus to inspect the men. Each trooper, smart in blue tunic and suede calf-length breeches, wore a short-sleeved mail shirt and a neck-scarf to minimise chafing from the cavalry helmet's deep protective nape-guard. A lightweight oval shield and a quiver of throwing spears hung from every saddle. In addition, each man carried a *spatha*: the long, double-edged cavalry sword designed for hacking at an enemy from the saddle. With a blade sharp enough to cleave helmet and head, yet heavy enough to smash a skull, it was a powerful weapon.

While the decurion's check of tack and uniforms had been elementary, Verendus had made a more personal enquiry, chatting with those he knew and asking the name and rank of those he did not, noting each on a wax tablet to ensure he remembered.

A bout of sickness in the First Turma had necessitated the transfer of four troopers from the Second to make up the numbers. Governor Peronius had insisted on choosing these men and, to Verendus' consternation, the brute Murvaro was among them. The scowl on the auxiliary's face made clear that the death of his comrade at Alba would be avenged. It made no odds that Verendus had acted in self-defence. The death would be neither forgiven nor forgotten.

Telling himself that he would have to watch his back, Verendus had moved on along the line. Five auxiliaries were new to soldiering and little older than Mos – boys in men's uniforms, smooth faces bleak with dread. How green they looked. Miserable too.

An ox cart clattered to a stop beside the verge, recalling Verendus to the present. He scanned the roadside scene, glancing from face to face, repeating the name of each auxiliary in his head as he went. Most had removed their helmets, making it easier to tell them apart. A few wore caps, stiff leather things designed to accustom them to the weight of a helmet, though the caps were nowhere near as heavy. A bareheaded lad, queueing at the booth where a dour-faced man fried sausages over a charcoal burner, was turning pink. Verendus searched his mind for the name. Tadius – that was it. One of the new lads.

Beside the booth, a pedlar hawking trinkets and potions had attracted attention with *treasures from the farthest corners of the Empire.* Verendus strolled over; there may be something for Corinna. Yesterday morning, in the yard before departure, she had flinched when she saw him armed and attired in full uniform. Had that involuntary movement not betrayed her, her eyes would have done. He'd wanted to reassure, but she was mounting the step at the back of the wagon and the yard was busy with auxiliary troopers loading kit and readying the horses. And then Mos, ungainly in his new mail-coat, had clanked from the stables to say he'd packed the carrier pigeons into their baskets.

A flower-shaped brooch inlaid with rosy enamel caught Verendus' eye. He picked it up, turning it as he held it to the light. The finishing was poor, the settings inadequate. He put it down and perused the bracelets and pendants. These so-called treasures had travelled no more than ten miles up the road.

'Guaranteed to ward off the Evil Eye,' said the pedlar, dangling a lucky phallus talisman before new lad Marinus.

'No.' Marinus held up a string of turquoise-coloured beads. 'I can't afford both.'

The lanky auxiliary beside him frowned at the beads. 'They're not worth it, mate.'

A third auxiliary who had been observing the exchange, cleared his throat with a self-important gurgle and leaned in.

'Quite so, considerably overpriced. You'll find better in Viorum.' Auxiliary Strabo, commonly known as Slug, turned. 'Isn't that so, Commendator?'

Verendus didn't know the misnomer's origin, though it suited the obsequious little shit. In common with several other auxiliaries from Britannia, he sported a moustache, which drooped mournfully on either side of his downturned mouth. A curious addition to an unremarkable face.

Verendus ignored Slug, and said, 'Are they for your girl, Marinus?'

'Yes, sir.' The flame-haired auxiliary's Latin had a Britannic burr as rough as cheap wine. He ran the beads through his fingers. 'Don't know when I'll give them to her. She's back home in Britannia.' He blushed. 'Sir, permission to speak freely…'

'Go ahead.'

'Well, sir… there's a rumour the Ninth Legion has left Britannia and sailed for Germania.'

'Quite so. That leaves Britannia vulnerable,' Slug said, interrupting, and the two younger auxiliaries nodded. 'There won't be enough troops to oversee the province.'

They were right. The posting of Legate Sentorus and his troops to restore order at Third Legion *Gemina*'s base in Germania would strain resources. The relatively new province of Britannia was still settling under Rema's yoke. Sentorus' contribution in striving for stability had been fundamental, and yet his presence in Germania took priority now. Verendus formed a careful response. 'Legate Sentorus will be back in Britannia before the autumn. It is not for us to question the will of emperor and Senate.' A vague answer, but this was no time for honesty. 'Have you decided, lad?' he asked, conscious of the pedlar – mouth agape – looking on.

Marinus stared at the beads. 'They're her favourite colour.'

'Best choose those then.'

Verendus walked on, past auxiliaries preparing for the off. On departure from Alba, the azure-blue shields with their decoration of golden ivy had been proudly displayed. Now they were being packed away. The auxiliaries worked in pairs, one holding open the leather cover, the other sliding in the shield. Once inside, the drawstring noose was tightened and the shield hung from two saddle-horns against the horse's flank.

Recently paid and grumbling about the regulatory deductions, apart from a few troopers lounging on the dry grass and playing dice, they looked a sorry lot.

Mos turned from watching the game and jumped up. He hastened over and held out a muslin parcel.

'Thanks.' Verendus had forgotten he was hungry. He unwrapped the bread and spiced sausage, then pointed to the booth. 'I hope this didn't come from that shack.'

Mos looked at the ground. 'No, Commendator.'

The bow-shaped brooch fastening the neck of his tunic was new. Mos had spent what little coin he had on one of the pedlar's *treasures*.

The boy glanced wistfully at the dice players.

'No!' said Verendus. Callow Mos would prove easy meat for that brute Murvaro who ran the game. The banter was the usual coarse, alcohol-fuelled fare seasoned with gripes about how the wagon was slowing the turma.

'Mind you,' said Murvaro, voice rising as he gestured at the wagon, 'I'd gladly ride in there and keep those women company. I'd give that Ennean bitch a good seeing to.'

Verendus threw the food aside. Cups and coins tumbling, he stamped through the dicers, grasped the knot of Murvaro's scarf, and pulled the burly auxiliary to his feet. Murvaro attempted to stand to attention, but wobbled, cap slipping as Verendus yanked the scarf. The three other auxiliaries rose smartly beside him.

'Name and rank,' Verendus demanded. He knew, of course, but wanted the satisfaction of seeing the man squirm.

'Septimus Murvaro, Auxiliary, First Turma, Fourth Brittonum, sir.'

Despite the crisp reply with no trip of the tongue over the recent transfer to the First Turma, it was gratifying that the arrogance in Murvaro's voice wasn't reflected in his eyes. Verendus resisted the urge to turn and look at the wagon. Corinna should be inside, would not have heard the comment. 'Auxiliary Murvaro,' he said quietly, tightening his hold, 'what was that about the Ennean woman?'

'Nothing, Commendator.'

'You had much to say about nothing. Another word and I'll have you strung up by your bollocks and flogged.' The shit smirked – he'd regret that. Verendus drew a deep breath and shouted in his face. 'Understood?'

'Yes, Commendator.'

'I'll be watching you.' He let Murvaro go and rounded on the auxiliary standing beside him. He'd noticed the new trooper earlier, queueing for food at the booth. Despite his sunburnt face, the lad was still bareheaded. 'First assignment, Auxiliary Tadius?'

'Yes, sir.'

'Piece of advice – give this reptile a wide berth.'

Verendus marched off. Everyone was staring. Decurion Bretorus, standing at the roadside with the driver of a cart, excused himself and hurried over. 'Something has displeased you, Commendator?'

'It's dealt with. Did the carter say anything of note?'

'No, sir. He's come from Avennio in the west and is heading for Alba. Says he's seen nothing out of the ordinary.'

Verendus asked what he'd discovered from his chat with the man in the booth, but the only fresh information concerning the farmer's death was that the weapon used was probably an axe. A Helutti weapon. This was bad news.

'There's no talk of the farmer being mutilated like that tax collector was.' Bretorus didn't elaborate; both knew the gruesome details of that horrific attack.

Despite the evidence, Verendus didn't want to believe that a horde of escaped Helutti slaves was murdering and mutilating unwary travellers. Again, he weighed the possibility that a bandit gang was disfiguring its victims to perpetrate the myth of a deadlier adversary. The theory wouldn't settle; there was too much evidence to the contrary. The tax collector's corpse in the crypt of the fortress of Castellum Alba had been mutilated with a savagery typical of Helutti barbarians. The kind of savagery he had witnessed in Grenorum. But he would not think about that.

Across the verge, Murvaro was straightening his leather cap. Attention back on Bretorus, Verendus said, 'Decurion, did you permit them to remove their helmets?'

'Yes, sir. It's a warm day.'

'Nevertheless, they will put them back on and take the covers from their shields. I want them ready for anything… unexpected.'

Bretorus saluted and marched off. At the roadside, the driver climbed onto his cart and prodded the oxen. The cart rolled away, and there, concealed from view until that moment, was Corinna. She was standing in the scant shade of a milestone, Plum's reins in her hands.

Verendus strode over. 'You shouldn't leave the wagon without an escort.'

She looked up. The din of the verge faded like a receding tide, and a minute must have passed before he attended to what she was saying.

'…and Dorcas upset poor Saffi. And it stinks in there with those pigeons. Dorcas opened the basket and one flew out. Don't look so cross. I caught it.'

He nodded and didn't say that he'd brought the pigeons so he could send word home to Iolia. Trust blabbermouth Dorcas to pry. He should have left the nosy slave at Alba.

The stallion pulled at the reins. 'Careful! He bites.' Verendus grasped the reins, taking control.

Paying no heed, Corinna rubbed the chestnut muzzle. Spellbound, the horse stilled its head and enjoyed the attention. 'Such a handsome boy,' she said, looking up. 'What's his name?'

Caught in the light of her depthless green eyes, Verendus could barely remember his own.

'You're staring,' she said.

He blinked. 'I can't take my eyes off you.'

Corinna dismissed the remark with a *pft* of disbelief and repeated her question.

'He's called *Plumeus* because of the blaze on his face. Plum for short. Despite his size, he's light as a feather.'

She stroked the white, feather-shaped blaze, and Plum nuzzled against her. Verendus slackened his grip and slid his hand along the reins in the hope Corinna's fingertips might stray to his. 'He yields as readily to your touch as his master would.'

'Shall I stroke your face?' she said, without the flicker of a smile.

'It would be a start.'

'I shan't risk it. No doubt you bite too.'

His blood surged. 'Can't promise I won't.'

She blushed and lowered her gaze. 'I keep dreaming that Magistra is in danger. I know she was afraid.'

Verendus studied her face, searching for a likeness with Attea, but his memories of Corinna's mother were hazy. He should tell her of his conviction that Attea and Magistra were one and the same, that Magistra was her mother. But if his fears were correct and Attea was indeed dead, it would be too cruel for Corinna to find and then lose her all over again.

She regarded him expectantly. 'I know Magistra asked something important of you. You took something from the Temple.'

She'd asked him that before. If she believed persistence would pay off, she was mistaken. Verendus unhooked his helmet from the saddle-horn and eased it on. 'Time we were moving,' he said, and secured the straps.

Corinna watched from the wagon as Verendus spoke to the men. He cautioned them over the road and told them to stay alert. Sun gleaming on the scorpion insignia of his cheek-guards, breeze caressing the red-feathered plume and lifting the folds of his scarlet cloak, he stood resplendent and terrible in the uniform of the Praetorian Guard.

He had been evasive when she asked about the Temple, about what he'd taken from there. She supposed that was the reason for their sudden departure from Castellum Alba; that this journey was more than an assignment to collect taxes. At Alba, Minister Dalcamus had searched his room. That search had ended in bloodshed – Dalcamus and an auxiliary were dead.

She'd only known Verendus a few days; already, it was clear that trouble followed him.

She turned away and closed the wagon door.

CHAPTER III

Thyme and lavender fragrant in the warm air reminded Verendus of home. This fertile valley of vines, ridged with terraces of almond trees and enclosed by rocky escarpment rising to limestone-scarred peaks, was much like Iolia.

He led the turma past the next milestone. The sun was high and traffic decreased as travellers sought shelter in the nearest *mansio* inn or dozed under a shady tree. Only the dispatch rider hastened, urged on by the auxiliaries as he galloped past. Even without the wagon, the turma could not have matched such a pace. Sustained speed required a regular change of horse, a service the mansio inns provided to men on official business. In a single day, with good conditions and the right documentation, distances of sixty miles could be covered. Even more *in extremis*.

Laughter erupted from the column. Verendus didn't need to turn; he knew it was Quintus. The governor's son had been joshing with the troopers since departure. His current sparring partner was second-in-command Perseo, honoured bearer of the turma's standard, and one of three troopers from the rebuilt city of Carthago on the north coast of Africa. At the next snort of laughter, Verendus and Decurion Bretorus turned.

'Shut it!' the decurion barked.

Perseo flinched. The standard swayed and slipped from his grasp. He gasped and grabbed the pole, grinning as he steadied it.

There was a collective sigh of relief. To let the standard fall was a terrible omen, presaging disaster not only for Perseo but also for the thirty auxiliaries following in his wake. 'Fucking ham-fist!' one of them shouted.

Bretorus muttered into his beard. From the off, he'd complained that the wagon was unwelcome, each misstep a result of its presence. Verendus determined to ignore him and press on to find the junction that would take them off the highway and towards the town of Combarus.

By mid-afternoon, the steady pace brought them to a wide verge where broad branched trees afforded some shade. The turma was a half-mile from the fork for the old north road, but the horses needed rest.

This verge had no food bar or temple, although a shrine had been painted on the boundary wall of a distant white villa. A low altar of stuccoed brick stood beside the wall. As Verendus signalled a halt, the auxiliaries reined in by the roadside and dismounted in a noisy rush to grab a water flask, stretch their legs, or take a piss.

Eldoran the Nemusan slid from the saddle, climbed onto a tree stump, and stared back down the road. Several auxiliaries wandered over to the shrine. Verendus followed.

The artwork was simple though expressive: a depiction of Bacchus god of wine and his attendant *maenads* making merry amid grapevines. Slaves carrying wine buckets and goblets appeared to float above the painted plane, their weightless feet dancing over a giant yellow snake, a smug creature that seemed content to be part of the celebration.

Verendus felt the edge of the box in his satchel. With their bared fangs and sinister eyes, the golden serpents on the codex within belonged to quite a different species.

As he turned from his contemplation, Decurion Bretorus hailed him. 'Would you consider making camp nearby, sir? We'll not reach Combarus tonight, but there's a mansio a quarter-mile on. It's a decent enough place.'

Quintus sauntered over. 'Be more comfortable for the women.'

More comfortable for you, too, thought Verendus – the governor's son needed toughening up. Fishing for sympathy, Quintus fiddled with the bandage around his neck. Two days ago Minister Dalcamus' scribe had attacked him with a stylus. The sharp nib had only grazed, but he was relishing the role of wounded officer.

'It's too early to stop,' Verendus said. Time lost to yesterday's delayed departure needed to be recovered.

Eldoran was still staring at the road. He was as keen-eyed as Enneans were alleged to be, for though Verendus' vision was sharp, he saw nothing untoward and nodded over the decurion's shoulder to where Eldoran stood. 'What's he seen?'

Evidently the Nemusan's hearing was keen, too, for he turned, and said, 'A rider approaches. He travels swiftly.'

Verendus' heart lurched. With a flick of his hand he summoned Mos and told him to ensure the women remained in the wagon.

He strode to Plum and remounted. Dust rose in the distance. Whatever was coming along the road, he knew it was coming for him. The Praetorian Guard? Its elite unit of Speculatores? Had they picked up his trail already?

He pulled a spear from the quiver. Fight or fly? One kick of his heels and he could gallop away across the field and into the wood beyond. No, he knew the answer. He would not abandon Mos and Corinna.

Right hand clasped around the spear shaft, Verendus watched the rider draw nearer. Praetorians hunted in packs; Speculatores tended to be lone wolves. He squinted at the advancing cloud, trying to distinguish more detail.

Armour glinted in the sunshine. This was no dispatch rider. He tightened his grip on the wooden shaft, the spear leaden in his hand.

'Warm day to be travelling fast,' said Quintus. 'A messenger?'

'A soldier,' said Eldoran. 'And there is a feather on his spear.'

'Then it is a message,' said Bretorus. 'Aye, it's Treseus. Bad news, I'll wager.'

Verendus thrust the spear back into the quiver and dismounted. Smiling troops rushed to the roadside. Auxiliary Rufus led the cheer as Decurion Treseus brought the horse veering to a halt and sprang from the saddle. Treseus winked at his younger brother, then saluted Verendus and handed him a tiny packet of folded linen.

Verendus checked his desire to open the message immediately and slipped the packet into his satchel. He signalled to Mos, standing attentively beside his pony. 'Fetch a wineskin.'

Treseus unwound the cord that bound the feather to his spear. Signifying haste, it marked him out as a messenger on urgent official business. 'Why are you playing messenger?' asked Verendus. 'I told you to keep an eye on the governor.'

'Governor insisted, sir.' He lowered his voice. 'Commendator, I've not so much come about the missive as...' He fell silent as Mos approached, wineskin in hand.

Bretorus seized the wine from Mos and stomped over. 'You'll not make it back to Alba before dark.'

'Thanks. I'm dry as the road.' Treseus unstopped the wine and took a gulp. 'But I'll not be returning yet. I'll continue with you to Avennio.'

'Very well,' said Verendus. 'Bretorus, prepare your men to depart.'

The instant Bretorus had marched out of earshot, Treseus said, 'Late last night, three soldiers of the Praetorian Guard arrived at Alba. They had a warrant bearing the seal of Prefect Galenius Dax. They asked the governor a lot of questions about who had visited in the past few days. Then they searched the vault and some of the rooms – including yours.'

Galenius must have received word that his informant at Alba was dead and had sent the Praetorians to investigate. Verendus checked that thought. Word could not have come so soon. More likely, Galenius had grown impatient waiting for news from his informant. The Praetorians had been sent to hurry things along.

Verendus had prepared for this. Before leaving Alba, he'd packed up most of his kit and personal effects save for a few items of no importance. The Praetorians would find nothing to incriminate him. They would, however, learn that a turma had recently departed for Viorum. Now their search had direction.

He peered at the highway. No sign of anyone approaching. But they would come, of that he was certain.

As he warmed himself with the thought that he was several steps ahead, a chill crept through him. In bringing that message, Treseus may have led them straight here. 'When did they depart?' he demanded.

'I set off afore dawn. Far as I know, they were still abed. The governor told them you were accompanying the turma as far as the old north road junction and diverting to Narbo Martius on personal business.'

'I see.' Verendus ran through the ruse in his mind, going over the route and calculating the time and distance to Narbo, and from there back to Viorum. If the Praetorians came after him, by the time they reached Narbo, he would be over a hundred miles away in Viorum.

'Don't know what they want with you, Commendator, but they didn't look the sort of men you'd want to cross. Is this about the death of Minister Dalcamus?'

'No…' Verendus thought quickly. He hated lying to his friend, but this was no time for truth. 'Just an indiscretion on my part involving a fellow officer's wife.' He shook his head and tried to appear contrite. Adultery in the officer corps was a serious transgression.

Treseus grinned. 'Well, this should get you out of their way. I've gone over and over it in my head.' Using the tip of his vine-stick, he scratched a row of figures in the dry earth. Brow creased in concentration, he stared at his drawing and nodded. 'If they fall for it and ride south to Narbo they'll look for you there… so, allow a day for searching. Then they'll double back and take the Via Agrippa north to Viorum.' He tapped the row of numerals, giving each a corresponding place name as the Praetorians made their theoretical journey along the highway. 'Could cost them ten, maybe twelve days, Commendator.'

Piecing the information together, Verendus pictured the main stopping points on the highway and how long it would take to reach each one. Yes, it might work. For now, he must leave the highway. The turma could head for Combarus Hill without him, make camp there, and be better placed for the morrow's journey.

'Of course, the Praetorians can go faster,' said Treseus. 'If they change horse at the *mansiones* that will knock days off my calculation.'

Verendus considered and then rejected this. Travel too fast and they risked missing him altogether. He smiled to himself. If the Praetorians rode to Narbo and failed to find him, there was a fair chance they would assume he had continued west on the Via Aquitania and gone deep into Gallia or taken the Via Domitia south into Hispania. They might continue along one of those highways and be hundreds of miles away before they realised he'd ridden north. Meanwhile, he could do what was necessary in Viorum and be on his way. Governor Peronius had done him a great favour.

Verendus felt a flush of shame for doubting the governor's loyalty. And then he saw the snag. There was a checkpoint coming up. The sentries at that checkpoint would inspect the turma's permit, and the details would be noted in their records. If, or rather when, the Praetorians arrived and questioned the sentries, it would be swiftly ascertained that the entire turma had headed north. As the Praetorians could cover more ground in a day than the wagon, they would catch the turma up.

He was about to voice this concern when Auxiliary Nonus approached to say the turma was ready to depart. With his sinewy frame and bland, youthful face he looked more like a palace serving-boy than the turma's best scout and third-in-command. Verendus thanked him and dismissed him back to the line of troopers. Nonus cast a curious glance at the numerals scratched into the earth and marched away.

'I don't think he'll say anything.' Treseus scuffed out the calculations with the toe of his boot. He opened his saddlebag. Leaning close again, he handed Verendus a scroll. 'Permit for the highway to Narbo Martius, courtesy of Governor Peronius.'

The governor had anticipated the snag. 'He's a sage man,' said Verendus, slipping the parchment into his satchel. With this permit it could work. All that remained was to tell Bretorus.

***

Ahead stood two checkpoint huts, one on each side of the highway. They were staggered at a distance of a hundred paces apart, the north road turning isolated on the stretch of road between them. Beside each hut, a wooden barrier closed off the road beyond.

Verendus' pulse quickened, and he suppressed an urge to touch the talisman at his neck for luck. Do nothing to draw attention. The white agate talisman, carved in the image of a horse-head, had hung above his cradle and protected him ever since. He could feel it cool against his skin – that must suffice.

Squaring his shoulders, he sat straighter in the saddle. This was just a formality. The turma had encountered no difficulty passing the previous barrier to gain access to the highway. But hours had elapsed since then. News could travel as swiftly as a dispatch rider's galloping horse. Had those Praetorians got a message here?

Before the checkpoint came into view, Verendus had ridden close beside Treseus and asked him to describe the three men who had been asking questions at Alba. In response, Treseus' eyes had grown large, his face more anxious sheep than usual. Even after a few moments of concentration, he could only manage a cursory description. Two of the men were tall and muscular – one fair of hair, the other dark. Both were tough-looking buggers. The dark one had done all the talking. The third man was dark, too, but younger and slighter. It wasn't helpful. Plenty of guardsmen fitted those descriptions.

He thought of Festinus riding east towards the Alpine foothills – he'd sent his friend into danger. Governor Peronius had made clear that failure to complete the tax collection would mean arrest – for him, and for Fes. It was no idle threat.

In the course of their questions, the Praetorians would discover that a highway permit had been issued to Fes. They might think that he was carrying the codex. Even if those three did not pursue him, other agents would be alerted. Fes would need his wits about him.

Verendus slowed to survey the surrounding countryside. Meagre cover. Dusty, open farmland on both sides; the distant white villa he'd noticed earlier. The checkpoint loomed ahead, the roadside undergrowth cut back to give the sentries a good view.

As he reined in beside Decurion Bretorus, voices resounded from the nearest hut. At least two, maybe three men in there. A granite-faced sentry stepped out; a skinny scribe, writing tablet at the ready, followed.

The sentry held up his hand. 'Halt!'

Decurion Bretorus saluted and announced the turma's destination as Viorum via the town of Combarus. The decurion carried all the turma's permits and took pleasure in presenting them for inspection. He brought a scroll from his saddlebag and passed it over.

The sentry wore a little bone whistle on a cord at his neck. His double-weave mail was girded with a wide belt and the pommel of a *gladius* sword protruded from a scabbard. He regarded Bretorus with the blank, indifferent air so natural to the officious and raised the whistle to his lips. He unfurled the permit and read slowly. The scribe stood beside and made a few notes on his tablet.

At last, the sentry returned the document with a nod. Verendus handed over his own permit. No one spoke. He rested a hand on his sword and focused on the sentry, watching for the twitch of misgiving or signal to the others in the hut that here was a fugitive wanted by the authorities. Whatever happened, flight was not an option. He would have to fight – impossible to calculate the odds. Many of the auxiliaries resented him for the fight at Alba that had left one of their comrades dead. If things turned rough, they might side with the sentries. He wouldn't stand a moth's chance in Hades.

The sentry frowned as he read. Verendus swallowed. Gods, he was parched. What was taking the bloody man so long? The scribe had stopped writing, but the sentry was still reading, scrutinising the wording with the zeal of a lawyer and sucking on the whistle like a new-born at the teat.

Across the highway, on the opposite side, stood a second checkpoint. A sentry, sturdy javelin in hand, stepped out and stared over. Gaze flitting between Bretorus and the two sentries, Verendus slid his fingers around his sword pommel. Cool as marble, the decurion sat stroking his beard.

The sentry looked up, let the scroll roll in on itself, and blew a short blast on the whistle. Verendus' heart skipped a beat. Two sentries stepped purposefully from the hut. He altered his grip, ready to draw the sword. Plumeus shuddered beneath him and gave a snort of impatience as a fly buzzed around.

The granite-faced sentry let the whistle drop from his lips. 'Here, Commendator.' He held out the permit. 'All in order.'

With regimental efficiency, the sentries opened the barriers. The turma passed through and took the turning onto the old north road. Verendus and Mos continued along the highway and through the second checkpoint. Without a backward glance, they kicked their mounts into a trot.

They did not need to ride far before the sparse roadside undergrowth thickened to woodland. After about a mile, Verendus reined in. The white villa was out of sight. No one was around. That villa had proved useful. He'd told Bretorus he had business there – a message to deliver for the governor. A reply was required. It might take a while, so rather than delay the turma, he would find the road north and catch them up.

Bretorus had made his displeasure clear, but assented with a grunt. It wasn't his place to question the governor's orders.

Mos exhaled with a *phew*. Verendus pulled a cloth from his cuirass, wiped his palms, and unhooked the flask that hung from his belt. All was going to plan. If questioned, the checkpoint sentries would consult their records and confirm that he had taken the highway for Narbo Martius. He took a long draw of the sour alcohol and offered the flask.

'No thanks, sir.' Mos sniffed the air as if trying to pick up a scent. 'What if those sentries come after us?'

'We'll muddy the trail.' Verendus dismounted. He found his drab *paenula* cape in the kit and put it on in place of his red cloak, which he folded into a saddlebag. He told Mos to do the same. Suitably camouflaged, he walked along until he chanced upon a deer track half-hidden in the undergrowth. He beckoned Mos. 'This way.'

Mos led the horses into the scrub; Verendus followed. He found a fallen branch, full with last year's desiccated leaves, and dragged it across the opening, concealing the narrow track. He walked behind Mos and the horses, scanning the rising ground, ensuring no trace of hoof or footprint remained. The track wound through a wood dense with thickets of the type of stunted oak that thrived in this part of the province, the sharp leaves scratching his arms. Pulling the paenula closer, he walked on.

Fine weather had dried the stony ground, but there was a hollow of deep shade where the muddy track needed to be smoothed over and hidden under dead leaves. The track straightened and climbed through rough, rocky ground. The trees thinned and there, in the distance before them, stretching from east to west across the horizon, stood a range of craggy peaks, children of the mighty Alps.

With no time to admire the view, Verendus remounted. As he settled into the saddle, Plum tensed, head alert, ears back. He stroked the stallion's neck and listened to the wind rustling and whining through scrub and branches. The wind strengthened, rose to a feral cry like the howl of a wolf, and then dropped, fading to a murmur.

It all happened so swiftly that Verendus wondered if he had imagined the sound. There were no wolves in this part of the province; the governor's rigorous hunting policy had pushed them back to the mountains. And yet something was out there. Plum had sensed it.

CHAPTER IV

Verendus heard the turma before he sighted it. The din of voices and jingling harness pendants guided him to the old road where troopers were watering their horses. If they were curious as to where he had been, none showed it. Treseus flashed him a smile of relief; Bretorus acknowledged his return with a peremptory nod and said that he had sent Auxiliaries Dexo and Nonus to ride ahead as scouts.

Verendus rode past the wagon. He didn't slow; Corinna was too much in his thoughts. When they reached Viorum he must bid her farewell. Why make that harder? Relationships were frowned upon in the Guard. Only the most senior Praetorians were permitted to marry, although a few of his comrades had done so unofficially and kept it quiet. Years ago, in the first heady days of their affair, he'd asked Drusilla to leave her husband and make such a union with him. Had promised it would be officialised when he'd completed his service.

She hadn't accepted. As a divorced woman, she would have no right to see her children. The affair continued, though he was away so often that he took his opportunities where he could.

No, he had nothing to offer Corinna. He checked Plum over, taking care to ensure the stallion's hooves were sound and the girth of the saddle was secure. On his way to fetch water, he told Bretorus to ready the turma for the off. There were still several miles to cover.

The old road cut through a limestone gorge to Combarus Hill, where its serpentine ascension slowed the wagon and thereby the progress of the entire troop. At first, Verendus welcomed the shade. But the light waned, leaving the steep way perilous. He pressed on, his anxiety that the turma wouldn't reach the summit before dusk, mounting with each new twist of the road. He kept this care private, though it was evident in Bretorus' harrying of the wagon driver that he shared this concern.

The scouts reported nothing of note. Nevertheless, Verendus scanned the dense woodland. Perfect cover for an ambush.

With each turn, the road grew steeper and narrower. Branches and brambles swished against the sides of the wagon. The wheels groaned and almost stuck in a patch of soft ground. Just when he was thinking he would have to order the auxiliaries to dismount and push, the ground levelled and opened out. They had made it to the top.

The sun was sinking towards the horizon when Verendus slipped from the saddle and stretched. In a wood, where the summit dipped like a shallow bowl, past wayfarers had made and maintained a clearing. A ring of scorched stones marked the boundary of a fire. He crouched beside and crumbled ash, cold between his fingers. 'Bretorus, have your men set camp. And a watch. We don't want any unpleasant surprises.'

'Will you choose the watchword, Commendator?'

Verendus considered. *Deliverance.* No, the word held significance for him, but it was unlikely to stick in the mind of a bored trooper. Something choice from his stock list of filth seemed inappropriate – perhaps it was the thought of Corinna overhearing. He settled for something more subtle. 'Camels' hump.'

Bretorus remained stony faced. 'Thank you, Commendator. Camel's hump,' he replied, altering the inflexion, as Verendus guessed he would.

On Bretorus' signal, Auxiliary Adarius sounded the cavalry trumpet and Perseo planted the standard in the ground. As troopers lined up to receive orders, Verendus stole to the edge of the clearing where the incessant thrum of cicadas filled air sweet with pine and rosemary. He sat on the sloping ground and pulled off his helmet, rubbed his chin where the straps dug in, and ran a hand through his hair. He untied his neck-scarf and unfolded it across his lap. Now he had the opportunity to open the missive, reluctance stalled his hand. It may be bad news.

The light was fading. If he didn't read it soon he'd have to wait until his tent was ready and the lamps were lit. With a glance to ensure no one watched, he opened the linen packet and found a tiny tube formed from a hollow plant stem. He unhooked the camping knife from his belt, flicked out the slender awl, and poked it in the end of the tube. The missive popped out of the other end and landed in his scarf.

He uncoiled the parchment ribbon to reveal a line of letters, one long word with no apparent meaning. It wasn't from his friend Decanus Carbo. This was Jae's rounded script. His heart squeezed. This would be bad. Last month, when they parted on the shores of Iolia, he'd told Carbo to go to Naeos' house. Carbo was a stubborn sod but, thank Jupiter, he'd done as asked. The last missive, from Naeos' daughter Jae, confirmed that she was caring for the wounded *decanus*. Was Carbo too poorly to send word? Had he worsened?

With mounting unease, Verendus brought a strip of charcoal and the *scytale* stick from his satchel and aligned the first letter with a notch in the wood. He wound the spool around the tapered stick, eliminating the random letters that Jae – with her identical scytale – had used to plug the gaps. A new, shorter column of letters ran the length of the narrow stick. He saw the letter C, grabbed the charcoal, and underlined it.

Soon all the relevant letters were underlined. He flattened out the parchment and separated the underlined letters into words. A few more minutes of concentration and he had the meaning. But it wasn't C for Carbo. It was a G.

GAP-CLEAR-HARBOUR-OPEN-MAGISTRA-DEAD

Dear gods, Corinna was right to be worried. Magistra, High Priestess of the Temple of the Flame, was dead. Jae's missive gave no clue as to how, but he suspected Galenius' involvement. That he – Verendus – was not in custody already, confirmed his belief that Magistra had died under interrogation without disclosing his name. But bit by bit, Galenius was piecing it together – he knew Magistra had sent a box to the fortress of Castellum Alba and was determined to get his hands on the contents. But why? Whatever the reason, the codex must be kept from his treacherous grasp.

Verendus pictured Magistra from before her life at the Temple, when she was simply Attea. A different time, a different place. A golden stretch of sand materialised in his mind and he was a child again, walking along Shell Cove, his small hand warm within hers. How special her brief time in his life had been. Corinna had never known that love.

'Something wrong, Commendator?'

'Mos!' Verendus closed his fist around the parchment. 'Where did you spring from?'

The boy straightened to attention. 'Your tent's set, sir. Is there a message?'

'From Jae…' He hesitated, he would be the one to tell Corinna of Magistra's death. He kept it brief. 'The harbour has reopened.'

'But that's good… isn't it?' Mos wiped his nose with the back of his hand, thought better of it, and found a rag in the sleeve of his tunic. As though picturing the scene, he gabbled away. 'Ships can bring supplies. Father will surely find work at the port.'

'Indeed. They'll need people like him to oversee things.' Verendus slipped the scytale stick into his satchel. The Gap was officially clear. Ships could sail again. There was nothing to keep Galenius in Iolia now.

'Oi, Mostus!' Murvaro's voice boomed across the camp.

Mos winced. Scrunching the rag into a ball, he said, 'Wish I could throttle Murvaro like you did this morning.'

'Off you go,' Verendus said. 'Or he'll be throttling you.'

Verendus didn't follow. He twisted the slender ribbon of parchment and watched the sky deepen from orange to red. Poor Magistra. She had hinted that safeguarding the codex might thwart the conspirators in Iolia. He couldn't see how. Though he would keep the codex safe – safe from Galenius. The unrest in Iolia could be one move in a plot to overthrow Emperor Flavio. A plot that could plunge the Empire into civil war. The Gap was clear. Did that mean Galenius had completed his plans on the island and was ready to move to the next stage?

Whatever happened, Verendus' oath of loyalty was to the emperor. He must protect his Caesar – however cruel or vacuous the man might be.

As for his father, Verendus could only hope he hadn't been arrested. Jae would surely have sent word if he had. Even if the Praetorians didn't establish a connection between Father and Magistra, a search of the villa might uncover the Chronicles he wrote – and Marcus could be very critical of the authorities.

The breeze strengthened, whipping through undergrowth and stirring the dusty earth. Verendus rose and went to find his tent. Time to make a start.

The tent was divided in two: the sleeping quarters curtained off at the rear, and a folding desk and stools at the front. Verendus sat and opened his satchel. He found a sheet of parchment and his drawing kit: a slim leather case crammed with styli, pens, and strips of charcoal. From this, he took a metal pen and an inkpot and set them on the desk. He brought out the box that Magistra had given him. For a while he sat staring at it. He would do this. For Magistra.

Galvanised, he untied the cord, unwrapped the cloth, and peeled away the calfskin binding to reveal a box of unvarnished pine. He slid back the lid and packing straw sprouted through the opening. He brushed it aside and lifted out a silk pouch. Magistra had told him not to open the box. And he would have respected her wishes, really he would, if things had gone to plan at Alba.

The tent flap twitched. Only the breeze. He opened the pouch and pulled out the codex, the leather-bound book small enough to fit in the palm of his hand. The codex was secured by a clasp, almost as large as the book. It was convex like a shell, smooth save for two deep lines engraved in the metal.

The clasp was ringed by two golden serpents, each swallowing the other's tail, joining as one to form a circle, their ruby eyes glimmering in the lamplight. The artistry was exceptional, every scale of the taut bodies incised in skilful imitation of snakeskin.

He turned the codex ninety degrees. Now the serpent heads were at the left and the right of the circular clasp, the bulbous heads in the same position as the nodes on a *phixus*: the sign of the serpents and, he suspected, an Ennean sign. Though whether common to all nine Ennean tribes, or unique to one, he couldn't say.

At Alba he had felt compelled to draw the codex, as though in doing so its power over him might diminish. It remained just as sinister. Magistra's words whispered in his head. *If the Empire should fail you, if you cannot do as I ask, then seek out the Ennean, Landren of Lignora. He will know this thing for what it was.*

If the clasp or the codex had once served another purpose, he was no nearer to discovering its secret. It was said that his Ambrone forebears discovered a path through the Alps; a path no one had found since. Legend claimed that a map of the so-called Ambrone Pass was hidden in the Temple of the Flame and protected by the sign of the serpents. If these golden snakes were the legendary serpents, he had yet to find anything within the codex that resembled a map. He drew in his breath; he would not give up that easily. Landren of Lignora was a last resort.

Corinna had agreed already to translate the codex. Not that he'd mentioned the codex, only that he had some archaic writing which he needed translated. She was safer not knowing the details.

Magistra had insisted that the codex be stowed away, so perhaps it contained information that could assist the conspirators. With Fortuna's favour, Corinna's translation would yield a clue. There must be something important. So important that soldiers had pursued him to Alba. Was Galenius searching for a map of the Ambrone Pass? And, if so, why?

The worn leather cover was bound by a band of gold decorated with hundreds of indentations like a ribbon of fine lace. There was a tiny keyhole, but Verendus didn't have the key. He brought the set of miniature tools from his satchel and selected the lock-pick: long, slender as a darning needle, with a flat stub at one end. Angling the tool into the space, he probed the keyhole, slotting it in as far as possible. He pushed the stub end and felt something yield. He turned it slowly. A click and the lock sprang open.

He lifted away the band with its repellent clasp and opened the codex. Not at the place denoted by a length of ribbon, but at the beginning. Everything would be scrutinised. Although Verendus had scoured the pages the first time he opened the codex, he searched again, turning leaf after parchment leaf until he reached the end.

Still no map. If the legend were true, the map must be inside. He looked again, checking for any indication that a page had been torn out.

Nothing.

He turned to the beginning. The words were barely legible, which made his task all the harder. The letters were Graecian, a language he'd learnt to read and write as a boy. However, the words were a phonetic form of Ambrone and he couldn't decipher anything.

At the head of the page was the letter *phi* enclosed in a gilded square. He picked up his pen, dipped the nib in the inkpot, and copied it down, struck again by the letter's resemblance to the detested phixus symbol. Even as the thought formed, he saw he had drawn a node on either side of the phi, making it into a phixus.

He ripped the abhorrent symbol from the parchment but didn't start again – the writing was too faded to make an accurate copy. He turned to the next page and smoothed the parchment sheet. Another gilded square, this time the letter alpha followed by a page of neat, clear writing. Carefully, he copied the entire page. Making no mark to show the turn of page, he copied another.

At the foot of the page was a drawing of a plant with star-shaped flowers. He copied this too; Corinna might know it. Yawning, he rubbed his eyes. This was taking longer than expected…

***

The scream woke Verendus. He opened his eyes and reached for his dagger. Stumbling to his feet, he knocked over a stool. Once he was satisfied nobody else was in the tent, he clicked shut the lock of the codex and slipped it inside his satchel.

Stealthily, he drew back the tent flap. Outside, two auxiliaries were pitching the last of their tents. Cooking fires scented the air with wood smoke and boiled ham. Those not preparing dinner sat drinking from wineskins or cleaning and polishing kit.

A thwack, another scream. No one took any notice. Thanking the gods that he was not the one receiving the flogging, Verendus sheathed his dagger. He returned inside and righted the stool. He sat at the desk and stared at the parchment copy. Please, gods, let there be some clue in these strange words.

He was rolling up the parchment sheet ready to take to Corinna, when Decurion Bretorus reported. By the look of his sour expression and apologetic gait, there was a problem.

Verendus fetched a wineskin and two cups, but the decurion shook his head and explained in his dry, measured tone that Auxiliary Tadius was missing. 'It appears he's run away, Commendator. I've sent scouts to search.'

Verendus pictured the bareheaded auxiliary with the pink, sunburnt face. He'd spoken to Tadius this morning, had advised him to avoid that reptile Murvaro. 'He's one of the new lads. Isn't one of your more experienced troopers responsible for keeping an eye on new recruits?'

'That would be Auxiliary Portoc, sir.'

It would be. That chubby-faced auxiliary, better known as Piggy, had as much sense as a turnip. 'From the racket just now, I presume you've given Piggy a good flogging.' Verendus poured some wine, filling the cup without diluting it. He took a swig and, recalling a story of how the decurion's heavy-handedness had resulted in the breaking of not one, but two vine-sticks on the back of a defiant trooper, said, 'I hope you weren't too hard on him, Decurion. He must be able to ride in the morning.'

Verendus picked up the parchment roll and something slipped out. Before he could retrieve it, Bretorus bent and plucked a scrap from the floor. He held it in his fingertips and frowned at the drawing of the letter phi which had become a phixus. Verendus managed not to snatch it back. That parchment should have been destroyed.

'Looks like a phixus,' said Bretorus.

'You know it!' Verendus forgot his irritation.

'It hails from these parts, Commendator. Ages past, there was a tribe in the Alpine foothills that worshipped a snake god. The tribe's long gone but occasionally, out on a trek, I've seen their sacred phixus carved on a standing stone or painted on the wall of an Alpine cave. The locals call it the sign of the serpents.' He put the parchment scrap on the desk. 'You unwell, Commendator?'

'I'm fine. Tell me, have you seen the phixus recently? Has anyone else asked you about it?'

The decurion scratched his beard. 'Funny you should ask. It was back at Alba, Eldoran the Nemusan was asking about the murdered tax collector. I'd already told him the man was butchered Helutti fashion, but the Nemusan wanted to see for himself. On Governor Peronius' orders, I escorted him to the crypt.'

Verendus nodded, he could see where this was leading.

'Well, he took his time looking the corpse over,' said Bretorus, 'but didn't say if he agreed with my theory about the Helutti slaves.'

The theory was plausible. Verendus didn't recall the incident, though Bretorus reckoned that several years ago, following an uprising in an Alpine mine, fifty or sixty Helutti slaves had escaped into the mountains. Such incidents weren't unusual, especially amongst captives not yet broken to slavery. Slaves from the same tribe, confined together and speaking in a tongue unknown to their captors, might readily plot an escape. Though even if they succeeded, most were recaptured.

However, these Helutti had found a refuge in the mountains and disappeared. Why, after years in hiding, had they left that refuge and strayed into this stretch of the province? They were taking a considerable risk. As a deterrent to others, recaptured slaves were routinely crucified on crosses set along the highway.

'If the uprising was several years ago,' Verendus said, 'other fugitives have no doubt joined them.'

'Aye, there could be a few hundred.'

'And the phixus?'

Bretorus glanced at the parchment scrap. 'We were leaving the crypt when the Nemusan stopped abruptly, drawing in his breath like he'd been stung by a wasp. He was beside one of those arches, the big one with the fancy gates, with tombs and urns inside. He pointed through the bars at the nearest tomb. There were symbols carved on it, stars and moons, that sort of thing. He was pointing at one symbol in particular. Then he turned and asked if I'd seen the phixus before. I never knew phixus was its name but, like I said to you, I've seen it before.'

'How did he react?'

Bretorus sniffed. 'He nodded in that haughty way of his.'

Verendus could picture it. 'He knows more than he's letting on. I think he shares our concern that the Helutti are responsible for the attacks. So stay alert. I don't want the turma to become another casualty on the old north road. The morrow's journey will not be easy.' He set the scrap of parchment to the flame. 'And, Decurion, let's keep this conversation between ourselves.'

CHAPTER V

Corinna took the little mirror from her bag and checked her reflection in the polished surface. Her eyes were red and puffy from weeping. She had tried to distract herself, but concentrating on the translation for Verendus had given her a headache, and she was only part way through the roll of parchment. She pinched colour into her cheeks and put away the mirror. She shouldn't have taken it. Now Magistra had no need of the mirror, perhaps it didn't matter.

Despite the nightmares of blood and shadows, it was hard to believe that Magistra was dead. She'd made life at the Temple difficult and yet, when it mattered, had acted with great compassion. Such kindness could never be repaid.

Verendus couldn't – or wouldn't – say anything about the circumstances of her death, and his eyes had filled with tears. Left to draw her own conclusions, Corinna decided that following the death of Centurion Torvius, there had been a thorough investigation at the Temple. Magistra would have been questioned by the Praetorians. May have lied to protect her.

It was all conjecture, Corinna had no proof. Nor could she share her theory with Verendus. He must not discover she had killed Torvius. As a Praetorian officer he would be duty bound to arrest her.

She wrapped on her cloak. Verendus had told her not to leave the wagon without an escort, but she needed air and the peace of her own company. Outside, the clearing was filled with rows of small tents stitched from squares of leather that stank of goats and sour oil. A trumpet sounded and four auxiliaries marched by to take over the watch. Just as her life of service at the Temple had been regulated by the toll of the bell, theirs was ordered by the blare of the trumpet.

Supper over, a few auxiliaries sat huddled beside a campfire, warming hands or cleaning kit, their voices hushed, barely audible over the clinking of metal and the snickering of horses. After their earlier chatter, the quiet was unsettling. The slave Dorcas reckoned they were sulking because one of them had been flogged.

Beside the wagon, at the centre of the site, stood the larger tents for the officers. A wide walkway divided them from the auxiliaries and a line of tethered mules and horses. Eldoran's tent was a short distance apart. He was standing outside, observing the scene with a bemused air, as though watching a play he couldn't grasp the meaning of.

Only a few days had passed since their visit to the Atrox Tower – it felt like months. She had confided in him, told him of her dream to find her father. Eldoran had been kind, had said he was meeting a Lignoran called Landren and would ask his opinion about the ring that had belonged to her father.

But something had altered. She was conscious of a growing coolness, a sheet of ice thickening between them, which he sometimes watched her through, though he no longer smiled when she met his eyes. Would he keep his word and help her?

For now, Verendus was her priority. When she'd questioned him at the roadside about Magistra and the Temple, he had been evasive. In an attempt to disarm him into saying more, she had flirted with him. A mistake, for he had flirted back and she shouldn't encourage his attentions. If only he would confide in her. Couldn't he see he was making her suspicious? That battered satchel of his – the codex was probably inside. He'd claimed to have gone to the Temple on Magistra's bidding. Had she given him the codex, or had he stolen it as Torvius had tried to? It seemed the Praetorians had blamed Magistra for its loss and executed her. That would explain Verendus' distress.

This evening he had given her a roll of parchment together with pen and ink, and asked her – very courteously – to translate what was written there. She supposed the writing was his. The ink looked fresh and the words were written in a bold hand. Between each line was a space to write the Latin translation.

Initially, she'd wondered if he'd copied the text from the codex, but the translation suggested a catalogue of herbs and their medicinal uses. There was even a drawing of a plant with little star-shaped flowers. Why did he want a translation of a herbal?

It occurred to Corinna that she was familiar with only one page of the codex: the page that was recited at the start of the divination service. She had assumed the mysterious book with the serpent clasp was full of such divinations – but perhaps not.

She returned to the wagon to resume her task. It gave her something to do. Though she was not sure why, she felt that in doing this, she was carrying out Magistra's wishes. And, if she helped Verendus, when they reached Viorum she'd persuade him to arrange for her to meet the Lignoran named Landren. That way, she wouldn't need to rely on Eldoran's help.

Until then, each mile of the journey was taking her further from Iolia's Temple of the Flame and the soldiers hunting Torvius' killer. But they would follow. Of that, she was certain.

The words of the Temple Seer rang in her ears: *Thrice Fate's wings will touch you. One will break. One will bind. And one will kill.*

The prediction was coming to pass, albeit in reverse order. Fate's wings had killed, but her own hand had struck the blow and Centurion Torvius was dead. It was self-defence, she'd had no choice. The prediction must come to pass.

At Alba, the second feather had appeared a few moments before she met Eldoran. Soon Fate's wings would touch her a final time and the third feather would appear. The feather that foretold *break*. A break from the past and all that bound her? The breaking of a vow or of a heart? Corinna did not know.

The Commendator was working again. Wax tablets and scrolls of parchment covered the desk. Mos lit another lamp for him, fetched a bucket from the kit, and went to check on the horses.

Once the taxes were deposited in Viorum, perhaps then they would return to Iolia. He'd only had a few days at home, had missed the Equinox Festival. Biggest festival in the Parhel calendar and he'd missed it. He kicked at the ground, sending up a shower of grit. No good asking the Commendator when they would return – may as well ask how long a length of rope was.

At least Saffi was with them. Mos walked the long way around, whistling a lively tune as he neared the wagon in the hope she might hear him and look out. It was no use. The rear door was closed – no sign of Saffi. One of the pack mules was there. Someone had tethered it there to unload kit and forgotten about it. Mules were always being taken for granted, even though they were strong and tough and didn't eat as much as the horses.

Mos patted the mule and led it to the horse-line beside a stream at the edge of the camp. He tethered it with the others and found Plum and Pepper further along. Mos filled the bucket with water and carried it over. Auxiliary Murvaro and two new lads – one tall and thin, the other spotty with red hair – were there already, moving along the line, checking each animal as they went. Mos kept his head down.

'Oi, runt!' Murvaro beckoned him.

Mos traipsed over. Why couldn't they leave him alone?

'Show these two idiots what needs doing,' said Murvaro, shoving an empty bucket at him. It knocked against the full one, sloshing Mos.

'Yes, sir.' He didn't argue. Didn't want to end up in the stream.

Murvaro marched off. There was a moment of awkward silence as the two auxiliaries sized Mos up. He stared back and determined to take charge. He was the Commendator's attendant; he would not let the new lads bully him. 'I'm Mostus,' he said. 'Murvaro's even grumpier than usual.'

The tall auxiliary nodded and introduced himself as Cico. The other one, who was called Marinus, explained that Auxiliary Tadius had run away. Softly spoken, with a thick Britannic accent, it was difficult to hear what he said. Mos had to concentrate to understand.

'Keep it to yourself,' said Marinus, glancing at the tents and lowering his voice even more, 'Tadius lost most of his wages dicing. And, well, we've just been paid. He's up to his eyes in debt to Murvaro. If he doesn't come back, Murvaro won't get his money.'

Mos wasn't surprised. Only this morning the Commendator had warned Tadius to avoid Murvaro.

Mos helped Cico and Marinus to check the line of mules and horses. He could have done it quicker on his own. The two auxiliaries were willing enough, but they kept joshing each other and whispering in what Mos supposed was their native tongue. Surely they knew that was forbidden when in uniform. The Commendator would have reprimanded them, told them to speak Latin. Mos gave a disapproving glare and said nothing.

By the time all the beasts were fed and watered, the moon was high and the camp was bright with lanterns and cooking fires. Auxiliaries were settling down for the night. A few sat drinking outside their tents, three-man units with one experienced trooper to keep the other two in check.

Cico and Marinus thanked him and hastened off. Whistling softly, Mos walked back past the wagon. The rear door swung open.

'Hark at you.' The slave Dorcas peered out, a piss pot in her hand. 'Tuneful as a sick crow.' She raised the pot. 'Shoo, go away. People are trying to sleep.'

Still whistling, Mos strode on.

REMA

850 AUC (AD 97)

Following the assassination of Emperor Domitianus, rank-and-file Praetorians were eager for revenge. With their backing, Titus Galenius Dax built a case against joint-prefect Titus Petronius Secundus and imprisoned him on suspicion of conspiring against the late emperor.

Emperor Flavio, who had succeeded his father as Caesar, proclaimed Galenius sole-prefect of the Praetorian Guard. With his hold over the Guard cemented, Galenius further ingratiated himself with the young emperor.

As demands grew for the instigators behind the assassination to be punished, Galenius assured Flavio and the Praetorians that justice would be done. Officers who did not meet with Galenius' approval were ousted or conveniently disposed of. Civilian associates and sympathisers of Secundus were arrested and taken to Praetorian headquarters at the Castrum Remana for questioning. Fear gripped the imperial city, neighbour watched neighbour, everyone a potential spy.

The purge had begun.

Chronicles of Imperial Rema
by Marcus Vedius Verendus

CHAPTER VI

Despondency darkened the new morning. The scouts found no trace of Tadius, and word of their failure spread swiftly through the camp. The men had looked a sorry lot yesterday; today, even second-in-command Perseo was quiet. Drill over, Verendus stood on the mound at the edge of the clearing with him, going through the day's route. The dark-skinned auxiliary nodded and chewed his lip as he mulled over the information.

Beside him, Bretorus glowered at the view. 'If I could have one more hour, Commendator.'

'Your trooper's gone into hiding,' said Quintus, strolling over and sparing Verendus a reply. 'Tadius won't have gone far. Probably holed up in a barn. However, if I don't deliver those taxes to Viorum and return to Alba by the *ides*, my father will put this whole turma on report.'

Bretorus conceded with ill-concealed disdain – he would not argue with the governor's son. His eyes strayed back to the view.

Verendus followed the decurion's sightline. Nothing save for trees, scrub, and a pale road that cut through the valley. He doubted Tadius was holed up anywhere.

Yesterday evening, Mos had recounted the latest gossip regarding the trooper's disappearance. If Tadius was indeed in debt to Murvaro, it was little wonder he hadn't confided in the auxiliary designated to watch out for him. Piggy Portoc was Murvaro's closest comrade, one of the last men a desperate lad would turn to.

Verendus kept the thought to himself. This was his chance to speak out, to insist that the search continue – but further delay could be costly. It could mean the difference between reaching Viorum and seeking the help of Tribune Aquinus, or the Praetorians catching up with him and the codex.

A crow cawed and was answered by another and another. Something felt wrong. And then he saw it, a distant speck moving along the road, drawing nearer. The small voice of caution stirred. This was going to be trouble.

Slipping his thumb between his forefingers, he made the sign against evil and sent Perseo to fetch the sharp-eyed Nemusan. Oblivious, Quintus gabbled on about the taxes.

Eldoran arrived and frowned at the speck in the valley. 'Verendus, please accompany me.'

By the time Bretorus and an escort of three auxiliaries were ready to ride with them, the speck materialised into a horse with a blue-cloaked rider.

'Seems Tadius has come back,' said the decurion. 'He won't be sitting on a horse when I've finished with him.'

Bile rose in Verendus' throat. In his days with the Third, he had twice stood beside the other officers, reluctant witness to the punishment of *fustuarium*, an extreme form of discipline meted out to deserters. Such cruel brutality to beat a comrade to death for an act which, for many, was blind panic. Tadius was just a lad, homesick and afraid of what Murvaro would do to him. Now he was returning to a fate worse than the beating he'd fled. Stickler Bretorus would probably insist on following regulations and, as they rode to intercept the auxiliary, Verendus braced for an argument.

The track made a winding descent through woodland. The trees thickened, shrouding the way in a dappled robe, and they lost sight of the rider. Verendus nursed the hope that Tadius had changed his mind and fled. The clip-clop of hooves told him that wasn't the case.

The road straightened, the trees thinned, and the horse reappeared. There was something unnatural in the rider's posture. And, as the distance between them decreased, he saw what he had feared all along. The auxiliary was dead.

Alert to the danger that the perpetrators could be hiding in the roadside woodland, Verendus reached for a spear.

'No need for caution. Whoever did this has not stayed to observe,' said Eldoran. 'Tell your men to remain here.'

As he rode off, the three auxiliaries leaned forward, whispering to each other and craning their necks for a better view. Verendus told them to shut up and wait there. He took a deep breath and followed Quintus and the decurion.

Eldoran gave a low whistle, called to the mare, and caught the horse without difficulty. Bretorus drew up alongside and pulled off the rider's hood. Auxiliary Tadius' sunburnt face stared back at them, eyes bloodshot, mouth wide in a silent scream. The cloak slipped, exposing the mutilated, naked body.

Quintus gasped, turned abruptly, and vomited.

Verendus tightened his grip on the reins. He'd trained Plum not to be alarmed by the smell of blood, but he could feel the stallion's unease.

Flies crawled over the auxiliary's body, swarming at the stubs of the severed limbs. The arms had been amputated at the elbows; the legs severed at the knees and tied to the saddle-horns. In common with the tax inspector's corpse at Alba, the auxiliary had been mutilated with savage yet meticulous cruelty. Unlike the tax inspector, the auxiliary's head remained firmly attached to the body. From the moment of capture, the intent was to set him back on the horse. Then, whoever found the auxiliary would see the bruised face contorted in terror and the blood-shattered, staring eyes.

Mindful to avoid the dead eyes, Verendus averted his gaze. The reek of stale blood stung his throat and wrenched him into the past, back to his time as a junior tribune in Germania, to that day when he'd overseen the inspection of a legionary scout's dismembered corpse. His order had sent the scout across the river where the poor sod was captured. The Helutti butchered the scout, tied his body to a raft, and sent some of him back. The arms had been cut off; the legs were no more than stumps roped to the planking. The agonised horror wrought on the man's face impossible to forget. Other officers had reassured Verendus it wasn't his fault. These things happened; would happen again. And they did. Though he never got used to it.

'Poor lad.' Bretorus removed Tadius' identity tag and tucked it in his own belt. 'I've seen this before, when I was stationed on the Germanian border.'

'The Helutti tribe specialises in it,' said Verendus.

'Those fucking barbarians should have been wiped out after Grenorum.'

Eldoran paused from examining the rope. 'Why, Decurion? The Helutti's intent was not one of conquest. The tribe's objective was to warn imperial troops not to cross the river and encroach its territory.'

Bretorus spat and didn't reply.

Quintus, his face as pale as a wax mask, looked over. 'It can't be Helutti, they're a Germanian tribe. Germania's hundreds of miles away...' He caught his breath. 'Gods above, someone's cut off his prick!' He slid from the saddle and retched again.

Talk among the auxiliaries waiting along the road rose to a discontented drone.

'It's Helutti handiwork.' Verendus tried not to look at the dark hole that gaped like a toothless mouth where the genitals should have been. 'Helutti rarely decapitate scouts. They want us to see the man's terror. Most other northern tribes take the head but leave the limbs.'

'Must be those escaped slaves,' said Bretorus.

'Why risk leaving the mountains?'

'That question has been troubling me,' said Eldoran. 'Something may have disturbed them.'

'Speculation won't avail us.' Bretorus brushed aside a fly. 'I'll cover him up. The men grow restless.'

'Have them bury him in the woods,' said Verendus, with an eye on the auxiliaries. 'And swear them to secrecy, bribe them if you must. I don't want the turma unsettled.'

***

Despite his precautions, the name Helutti murmured through the ranks. Overnight rain had left Combarus Hill slippery with mud, and time lost by the delayed departure increased as the road deteriorated. At mid-morning, Verendus calculated they had fallen behind pace. If the light failed early, the troop would have to negotiate the old road at dusk.

At midday, he permitted a brief respite. While others ate, he stared at the blur of distant mountains. He hadn't seen the phixus for ten years – not until his return to Iolia last month. If Bretorus was correct, and the phixus originated here in the province of Gallia Narbonensis, that might explain its presence in the crypt at Castellum Alba. After all, it was an ancient symbol of endurance.

So why had he seen it on the trunks of oak trees in a sacred grove hundreds of miles away in Germania? Coincidence? The explanation wasn't satisfying. That the emblem of an extinct Alpine tribe was carved not only on trees in a Germanian grove, but also on caskets in Alba's crypt seemed ominous. That it was now the emblem of the Iolian Watch was a coincidence too far.

What was it that Father said about chance? *Two is coincidence, three's a pattern. Find the link.* Verendus nodded. There was a link all right. Something that connected the three. Or rather, someone. *Titus Galenius Dax.*

Ten years ago, Galenius had been one of the officers who inspected the Helutti grove at Grenorum. Before becoming prefect, he'd visited Alba. Earlier this year, he'd endorsed the formation of the Iolian Watch. Had he chosen the phixus as the symbol of the Watch? Probably.

Verendus couldn't grasp the reasoning behind such a choice, but it was surely a factor in the Praetorian Guard Prefect's designs on the Purple. Galenius was a meticulous planner and, in his bid to overthrow Flavio, would have allies and informants among the emperor's advisors. Moreover, he had doubtless secured the support of key officers both in the Guard and in its elite unit of spies and assassins: the Speculatores, Serpents of Caesar. Thanks to that unit's inherent secrecy Verendus knew hardly any of his comrades, let alone whether they supported Galenius.

Of course, to have any hope of success, Galenius and his co-conspirators would need the backing of several legions and the coin to maintain such an army. Not to mention a fleet of warships. Though perhaps they already had a fleet. Corinna said the Seers at the Temple of the Flame had warned about hostile ships. She claimed to have seen them out at sea, the phixus symbol on their sails.

Verendus strode to the wagon and called for her. The door opened and she looked out, expression watchful. He offered his hand, but she jumped down to stand beside him.

'Have you completed it?' he whispered.

'Here.' She fished inside the sleeve of her tunic and gave him a roll of parchment. 'I wrote the translation under each line as you instructed. May I ask why you require a translation of a herbal?'

He unfurled the parchment to reveal the drawing of a plant with star-shaped flowers, which he'd copied from the codex. Casting his eyes over her neat lettering, he skimmed through the translation – a tonic for healing nervous disorders.

Disappointment smote him. He dropped the parchment into his satchel and brought out the copy he'd made of the next two pages. 'Will you translate more?'

While she concealed the parchment in her sleeve, he rummaged in his satchel. Finding what he sought, he took her hand. She regarded him warily, though her hand remained. He placed five grassy tufts in her palm. 'You know about plants. What's this?'

By the look on her face, the seeds were unfamiliar. Nevertheless, she made a careful inspection, smelling the tufts and prodding them with her fingertip. 'Tarnas seeds,' she said, at last. 'The plant's roots can be infused to make a tonic. Where did you find them?'

'Tarnas. Is it native to these parts?'

'No, the north. Belgica and Germania Inferior.'

'How about the Alps?'

'On the foothills, perhaps. Where—' She broke off as Mos hastened over.

He held out a small round loaf filled with cheese. 'Your food, Commendator.'

Verendus raised a hand. 'I've no appetite. Haven't you anything to do? Go and see if your dozy friend Hostus needs help with the water.'

He watched Mos trudge off and turned to Corinna. She met his gaze, concern in her eyes. 'You haven't told me where you found the seeds. What's happened? Dorcas told me an auxiliary was horribly butchered.'

'She's a bloody blabbermouth,' Verendus said. 'Look, there's nothing for you to fear. The auxiliary ran away and was killed by bandits.'

'Poor lad. Is that why you rode off with Mos yesterday? Were you searching for him? You were gone a long time.'

'I'm flattered you missed me.'

'I never said that,' she replied with a toss of her head, which wasn't fooling anyone.

'It was business, actually – a message to deliver for the governor,' he said, repeating the lie he'd told Bretorus. If one must lie, be consistent.

She turned the seeds in her palm. 'Is this about the bandits?'

'Decurion Treseus checked the auxiliary's body. He found tufts snagged on the cloak but couldn't identify the plant, though he's lived here many years.'

Corinna cringed but didn't drop the seeds. She held up a tuft. 'See, the tiny barbs catch on clothing and animals.'

Verendus nodded. Whoever killed Auxiliary Tadius had ventured west from the colder climes of the mountain foothills. He pressed her hand in his. 'Put the seeds somewhere safe.'

***

After a swathe of vine-covered farmland, the rising track wound through rocky outcrop and all but disappeared beneath weeds as Nature reclaimed the crumbling causeway. Stunted trees clung to rugged flanks, forming thickets between the boulders. Amid the scrub, a small, domed hut stood as stark as a forlorn sentry. No sign of a resident shepherd or his flock.

On the horizon, the granite range of little mountains rose, hemming in the narrow vale. With each passing mile, Verendus' confidence grew that the three Praetorians were well on their way south to Narbo Martius.

There was no room for complacency. The turma's pace had slowed, and he was beginning to doubt they would reach the town of Combarus before dusk, when Bretorus shouted, 'Halt!'

A horse had gone lame. Verendus dismounted, stiff from so long in the saddle. He stretched, rolled his shoulders, and went with the decurion to assess the injury. Eldoran the Nemusan was there, massaging the left foreleg. Jaw trembling, Auxiliary Marinus held the bridle.

At Verendus' approach, Eldoran shook his head. 'The horse cannot be ridden.'

Bretorus patted the gelding and bent to inspect its leg. 'Doesn't look too bad. Let's see what the medic reckons… Oi, Callenus!'

The wiry Graecian slung a drum-shaped dressing-box across his chest and jogged over. In deference to town medics he wore a red sash over his grey tunic though, according to rumour, the man wasn't a fully fledged medic but an orderly covering the post.

The governor's son Quintus followed, the apprehension creased on his chiselled countenance incongruous with his usual pleasant vacancy. 'How much further to this damn town? We don't want to be stumbling along this track after dark.'

'There is unease here,' said Eldoran, before Verendus could reply.

'The scouts haven't reported anything,' Bretorus said. 'Marinus, buck up, lad. Ride Tadius' horse. He's no need of it now.'

The Nemusan's instincts had been right about Tadius. Verendus leaned closer. 'What sort of unease?'

Eldoran lowered his voice. 'Someone follows. They are not yet close; we should outpace them. But we must make haste to reach Combarus while the light lasts.'

Verendus left Callenus bandaging the foreleg and hoped the man wouldn't be required for anything more serious. He peered through overhanging branches at a sky that sagged like the sallow underbelly of a sow. He couldn't locate the sun's position. Yesterday, in his determination to cover as much ground as possible, it had been a close thing to reach the campsite in the daylight. Today angst churned his stomach, reinforcing this resolve. He touched the horse-head talisman, but felt no better. The Nemusan was right: they must pass the gates of Combarus before nightfall. He beckoned the decurion and told him to alert the turma.

They remounted and rode on. Eldoran had strung his bow and carried it ready before him. Bretorus dropped back, riding along the line as he spoke. 'Attention, lads! Yes, that includes you, Slug. Shut your big, ugly mouth or I'll shut it for you.'

Piggy Portoc sniggered and caught the sharp smack of the decurion's vine-stick across his thigh.

'Listen!' barked Bretorus. 'Bandits follow. For now, we maintain pace. Let them think they have us on the run. On my word, we turn and rout. Give the fuckers a taste of their own medicine before we round them up. Understood?'

'YES, SIR!'

'Stay alert.'

The auxiliaries urged on their weary horses. Shadows lengthened, merged into darkness. Cloud smothered the moon. Eldoran disregarded Bretorus' protestation that it would draw attention, and insisted all lanterns be lit. Verendus ruled on the Nemusan's side and reminded the men to be vigilant.

Brisk through the thinning trees the wind rose, swirling dead leaves and rattling branches. Something was out there. In the flickering lantern light, broad-trunked trees took human form, their branches wizened limbs reaching out. An army of giants lurking in the shadows.

The cry of a fox curdled the air. Verendus gave Plum a reassuring rub. The stallion was making his agitation clear: ears flat, he chafed at the bit.

The track descended to a gully enclosed by sloping banks of stone, the way just wide enough for the wagon. Another cry. Louder, deeper, and very close. The distinctive howl of a wolf. The same wolf he'd heard yesterday? Hard to tell. Again, he questioned his decision to bring the women. Again, he dismissed the vexation.

It came thudding back when Eldoran leaned across to say, 'They are coming.'

Verendus drew in his breath to speak. The response died on his lips. At the bend of the track, where wizened oaks formed a thicket that covered the slope, a branch creaked. A flurry of wood pigeons clattered into flight.

A horse neighed and veered out of line. 'Stupid birds!' snapped an auxiliary, fighting to regain control. Then he gasped, and grasped at the haft of an axe that sliced his mail and lodged with a bloody spurt in his stomach. He tumbled from the saddle and was kicked in the head by the startled horse.

Eldoran loosed his bow, sending an arrow into the thicket. A screech confirmed he had found the mark.

'Halt!' Bretorus cupped a hand to his mouth. 'Shields up! Protect the wagon.'

Adarius blew a strident blare on his trumpet. Auxiliaries massed to form up, the gilded acorn motif on their shields gleaming in the lamplight as they pushed for space around the wagon. Verendus and Eldoran took their places beside them.

With a choking scream another auxiliary hit the ground, his skull split by an axe. Verendus flinched, almost slipped from the saddle. He couldn't see the attackers, but they were no mere bandits. These were Helutti, he was certain of it. He gritted his teeth, steeled himself. This was no time to lose his nerve.

He weighed his options. The turma could either retreat or go forward. They would never get the wagon up the steep banks that hemmed the track. It's a trap, he thought. They'll pick us off like birds on a limed branch. Or rather, the troopers would be picked off. Officers would not be dispatched so swiftly; the Helutti would try to take him, Quintus, and the two decurions alive. In Germania he had seen what Helutti did to captured officers. That filthy, bloodstained slab; the trussed corpse that had once been a man. Memories flooded back, chilling him to the core.

Hooves pounded, jerking him into the present. He glimpsed a flash of silver amid trees on the opposite slope, and a horse crashed from the undergrowth and slid down the bank. It was the scout, Auxiliary Dexo. He skidded to a halt beside Bretorus.

'Report,' demanded the decurion.

'Barbarians! They're following us. Maybe fourscore, could be more. Clear ahead, sir.' Dexo winced as an axe hurtled past his shoulder and thwacked into the side of the wagon. The mules brayed and pulled at the reins.

In the confines of the gully sounds amplified, clashed. 'Dex!' Verendus shouted to be heard. 'What's the terrain?'

'A clearing fifty paces north, sir. Nonus is checking east.'

A clearing. It was their best hope. 'On me!' Verendus shouted, and led the way.

The banks steepened and closed in. An axe flew past his helmet and clanked, sparking, on the stone bank. He kept his shield high and spurred Plum. Into the turmoil came Father's voice, low but distinct in his head. *Choose your ground. Don't do what the enemy wants you to do.*

'I'm not,' Verendus said aloud. But where the hell was the clearing?

A glance to ensure the turma was keeping pace, and he pushed through a thicket. Twigs and trailing brambles lashed his face. He swiped them aside, pushed on, and emerged in a wide stretch of open ground surrounded by woodland. 'Close up!' he shouted. 'Stake the lanterns and circle the wagon.'

The auxiliaries followed, pushing through the undergrowth. Perseo planted the standard in the ground. 'Fourth Brittonum!'

'FOURTH BRITTONUM!' Auxiliaries echoed the call.

'Shields up. Form a circle.'

Noise everywhere, rising, crashing, a great wall of sound. Bretorus shouting orders from within the circle; auxiliaries griping as they jostled for position; horses neighing, snorting, and stamping the earth.

'Hold the circle!' yelled Bretorus. 'Spears ready. Steady, lads. Steady! On my command…'

CHAPTER VII

At the boom of the first drumbeat, Mos touched the sun pendant that hung at his throat and clutched his shield close. The pendant was his mother's. She'd given it to him when he left Iolia. Said it would protect him.

The Commendator and Plum were on his left; Auxiliary Hostus on his right. This was it. They would make a stand. There was nowhere to run.

The Commendator adjusted his seat in the saddle and looked across. 'Remember, Mos, whatever is out there, you stick by me, and we do as we practised. Understood?'

'Yes, sir.'

'Good lad. I know you won't let me down.'

The drums grew louder. Must be close. What in the name of Jupiter was stomping through the forest? Whatever it was, it was getting nearer.

Mos smelt them before he saw them, a stink like the rancid reek of the Portula Canal glue factory. The beat slowed, deepened. From somewhere high up, a howl resounded. The Commendator pointed across the clearing to the enclosing bank. High on the bare ridge stood a cloaked figure with the head and antlers of a mighty stag. Beside it sat the largest wolf Mos had ever seen.

No one moved. It seemed no one dared to breathe. Men and horses frozen with dread.

With a shout of defiance, an auxiliary flung a spear. Sailing high, it sped through the air, rising towards the ridge where the antler-headed figure stood bold, motionless, as though shielded by the gods. Mos watched, willing the spear on.

It lost momentum, plummeted into the side of the ridge, and buckled.

The stag man raised his arms and bellowed. His cry was answered by a low rumble like the merging of fierce voices. Out of the shadows they marched, a dark noose tightening.

The blur focused, took shape, and row upon row of bearded faces appeared, the whites of their eyes shining in the half-light.

Mos swallowed hard. These were the Helutti. The Germani tribe had left its mountain lair and was closing in, nearer and nearer. The Helutti were here in Narbonensis. It wasn't a story. It wasn't made up.

Pepper shuddered. 'Easy, Peps.' He patted the pony's neck.

Branches crashed. A horse, its grey flanks streaked with blood, tore from the bushes and skittered before the horde. The reins hung loose, the rider bouncing in the saddle like a rag doll. Trapped between the two forces, the horse raced around the cordon. The rider juddered, would surely fall.

'It's Nonus,' someone shouted.

The horse slewed to a halt, the rider swayed, and Mos was looking straight into his swollen face. It was Auxiliary Nonus, the turma's scout, no mistake. His head jerked and slumped; blood dripped from his open mouth. Where his forearms should have been, there were two bloody stubs. His legs had been hewn at the knees, his thighs roped to the saddle-horns.

Acid scorched Mos' mouth. He spat it away, and yelled, 'Fucking barbarians!'

The grey horse startled and darted away.

Beating a harsh rhythm on their small, round shields the Helutti advanced. Most were bareheaded, their hair tied in long braids. A few wore ill-fitting helmets. Some had body armour: jerkins of chainmail over leather tunics. The better equipped ones also wore furs: wolf-skins or fox pelts draped around their shoulders. And all carried an axe or a double-headed pick.

'Mos! Spear!' barked the Commendator.

Holding the shield in his right hand, Mos pulled a spear from the quiver with his left and passed it over. They had done this before, in drill and in combat – a smooth, wordless exchange. Only now, Mos couldn't stop his hands from shaking.

The battle cry, which had started as a rumble, swelled to an angry storm.

'Launch!' Bretorus bawled above the din.

The noise rose – louder and louder. A ferocious roar erupted and the Helutti charged.

Eldoran loosed his bow and the foremost warrior fell, pierced through the eye by a white-feathered arrow. A cry of rage from the men behind and then they trampled over the body and surged on. More followed, hollering in their fearsome language.

The Commendator hurled his spear. It thudded into a warrior, slicing through his leather tunic. Mos grabbed another spear and slapped the shaft into the Commendator's outstretched hand.

A whirr like an enormous cicada droned from the undergrowth and a line of Helutti rose and stepped forward, each rotating a short length of cloth.

'Slingers,' shouted Eldoran, loosing another arrow.

A hail of stones whizzed over the Helutti and clattered on the auxiliaries raised shields. A stone clanged against the crown of a helmet and the auxiliary crashed to the ground.

Eldoran answered with arrow after arrow. But although he was swift and found his mark, he couldn't keep them at bay. The auxiliaries, struggling to control their terrified mounts, hold shields, and launch spears, flailed feeble as puppets.

The Commendator yelled for another spear. The cries of man and beast reverberating through his body, Mos grabbed a spear from the quiver and held it out.

As the Commendator snatched the shaft, a mound of grey fur bolted from the horde, bounded over a body, and loped nearer. Pepper reared. Mos jammed his legs hard against the saddle-horns. Fangs bared, fur bristling, the big wolf snarled.

Mos stared into the yellow eyes.

The wolf leapt at him, squealed, and twisted in the air. Then it dropped, the Commendator's spear impaling its neck.

Mos exhaled, handed over the next spear, and reached for another. The last one. As he grasped it, a tanned, dark-bearded man who looked more local bandit than Helutti warrior, thundered towards him. With no time to think, Mos launched the spear. It soared over the man's head and plunged into the shadows. Useless.

The Commendator swore and pulled a spear from his own quiver. Axe raised, the man ran on. Mos switched the shield to his left hand, drew his sword, and hacked, cleaving the air in a reckless scythe. He swayed, almost fell. The man dodged and stumbled sideways into Plum. The stallion lunged and sank its teeth into the man's face. He screamed, raising his shield, too late to protect his ruined nose. The Commendator buried his spear in the man's gut and drew his spatha as another warrior charged in. A flash of steel, a mist of blood, and the Helutti dropped to the ground.

A dreadful whinny drowned Mos' cry of triumph. In the tail of his eye, he glimpsed an auxiliary grappling with the haft of a pick that pierced his thigh and pinned him to the saddle. As the horse bucked and broke from the circle, a Helutti warrior snatched up a discarded spear and sprinted on. Using the spear like a lance, he stabbed the point into the horse's chest and the beast shrieked and collapsed.

Warriors closed in. The horror hidden from view, a part of Mos' mind looked on, playing out the agony as they hacked at the auxiliary. Screams pitched and died.

'Hold the circle,' shouted Bretorus, shoving forward to seal the breach.

The circle was slacking, a gap opening between Mos and the Commendator. A mule brayed. Mos glanced behind at the wagon. The driver sat rigid in a pool of blood, an axe wedged in his chest. As the mules strained against the brake, the wagon's front hatch opened and Corinna climbed through. Gods, what was she doing?

The wagon lurched and rolled on. The Helutti cheered and stormed towards it.

Eldoran pulled a lantern pole from the earth and launched it into the fray. A warrior fell, his face drilled by the spike at the end of the pole. The lantern smashed into a shower of sparks. Clothes aflame, a Helutti warrior ran wailing through the horde and collided with another. Mos whooped as fire consumed both in a stinking blaze.

'Close up!' yelled Bretorus. 'Close the circle.'

Auxiliaries hastened to re-form around the wagon. Mos tried to manoeuvre; Pepper wouldn't budge. A blade whooshed. Mos raised his shield in time to fend an axe blow coming in on his right. Wood splintered. The force of the impact jarred, vibrating through him. A pot-bellied warrior with a fox pelt over his armour tugged at the axe. Wobbling and rocking in the saddle, Mos clung on. That bloody axe was stuck in his shield.

A pale fold of skin bulged between the fox-man's mail and tunic. Here was a chance. Mos gripped his sword hilt, let go his shield, and stabbed at the exposed skin. Fox-man knocked away the shield, jinked aside, and the blade cut the air. Grinning, Fox reached over his shoulder, drew a second axe from the harness on his back, and chopped.

Mos countered with his sword. The blow shook him and he was in the air, falling. He landed with a thud, started to rise, but his knees buckled. Legs astride, booted feet planted in the ground, Fox bent over him.

Fear walloped Mos. He raised the gladius – only a jagged stump remained. His heart turned to ice. Gods below, he'd had it now.

Fox grunted. Voice mocking he hefted the axe, taking his time, eyes narrowed, mouth twisted in contempt as though it was beneath him to kill such a pathetic creature.

Deep inside Mos, something snapped. Enough. He was no worm. He thrust the broken sword into Fox's foot. The jagged metal pierced the leather boot and crunched through bone. Fox yelped and stooped to pull it out, his big hand closing around the sword hilt. Mos staggered to his knees and yanked his dagger from the scabbard. With all the strength he had left, he drove the dagger up into the fleshy throat.

The blade slid in. Blood sprayed, splattering hot over Mos' face. Fox deflated with a whine, his eyes rolled up into his head, and he toppled forward.

Mos recoiled, ducked aside, and the night swallowed him.

Corinna opened the hatch at the front of the wagon. The noise, which had seemed loud beyond measure when she was inside, rose and clashed. Air thick with the earthy smell of blood took her breath. She froze, staring at the chaos, desperate to return to the dark sanctuary inside the wagon. As she'd feared, the driver was dead, slumped sideways where he sat, an axe embedded in his chest. She'd heard the sickening thwack, felt the wagon shake. She'd trembled in the darkness and prayed, but it had made no difference.

The mules brayed and strained against the brake. The wagon jerked and moved forward: a jolting, erratic progress. If she didn't stop it now, the mules would drag it into the fray. She must take over the reins, if only she could make her body obey. Noise shook through her. A line of auxiliaries stood between the barbarians and the wagon. Verendus was there, sword in hand. She mustn't look. A sea of bearded faces, eyes bright in the lantern light. She must not look.

Someone grabbed her arm. She startled and turned, struggling to break free and raising a hand to strike back.

'Get inside!' Dorcas shouted, pulling Corinna's cloak.

The wagon lurched. Corinna fell against her, and they tumbled backwards into the wagon. Dorcas screamed as she hit the floor, and screamed again as Corinna landed on top of her. Without checking if the slave was injured, Corinna clambered up and climbed back through the hatch. In a flash of clarity, she knew she could jump down and leave the wagon. From the moment she'd opened the hatch, Dorcas had tried to stop her, whining and pleading, until Corinna silenced her with a slap. She could leave the bleating slave to her fate, but Saffi was in there, too.

Corinna edged towards the driver. The narrow wooden seat was slick with blood. Blood covered the driver and pooled around his feet. At least he had slumped forward; his face was hidden. As she reached for the reins, the wagon lurched again. She put out a steadying hand and fell against him. He was still warm.

Corinna flinched and tugged the reins, but couldn't wrench them from his dead grip. Remembering the knife on her belt, she drew it. Hand trembling, she sliced through the leather. As she took hold of the shortened reins, a mule bucked. A shriek of wood. She slipped, almost fell. She gripped the edge of the seat and rocked to her feet. If she didn't calm the mules the brake would snap.

Using her weight as a counterbalance, she pulled the reins. The barbarians roared and charged at the wagon. Corinna clung on, drawing tight the reins as the wagon shuddered and juddered to a halt.

CHAPTER VIII

After the darkness, the moon appeared brighter, lighting a way for the fleeing Helutti. Verendus didn't pursue; the turma was in no state to manage a rout. A stench of blood, sweat, and the sewer stink of torn bowels poisoned the air.

He rubbed Plum's warm neck and watched Eldoran step quietly through the carnage, ensuring with a stab of his long knife that every fallen Helutti was dead. Murvaro followed, checking the bodies and no doubt helping himself to any loot.

The wind strengthened, scattering clouds, though the breeze brought no freshness. Verendus unstrapped his helmet and eased it off. Even as he pushed back his damp hair, he realised his fingers were sticky with blood. Thank the gods it was Helutti blood and not his own. There had been so many of them. An impressive force – about one hundred – mixed, too. Local fugitives had joined them, increasing the number. They probably had a new refuge in the hills and—

'Verendus!' The Nemusan stopped beside Plum and looked up. 'Verendus, help me move this body.'

Noise, which had been there all along, crashed over him like a wave engulfing a resurfacing swimmer. Men groaning, horses neighing, rapid-snap orders, and pleas for aid. A tide of misery surging to immerse him.

'Verendus!'

'I heard you.' Couldn't a man have a moment's peace? He slid from the saddle and dropped with a thud, his legs weak, the ground unsteady. He retched and spat away the bile. With careful steps – the ground seemed to creak – he crossed to where Eldoran crouched beside the body of a Helutti warrior, a fox pelt over his mail. A patch of white fabric poked from under the bloodied armour. Verendus dropped to his knees beside the Nemusan. Together they shoved and rolled the warrior's body away. Mos lay beneath.

A slick of blood covered the boy's face; his eyes were closed. Verendus tore at the straps of the helmet and eased it off. He probed Mos' neck for a pulse, pressing his fingers behind the left ear. *Please…*

Verendus drew in his breath. 'He's all right.'

'I did not doubt it,' said Eldoran.

Rising swiftly to his feet, Verendus looked around. 'Where's the medic?'

'Endeavouring to save Rufus' leg.' The words fell cool and even. 'I shall keep watch.' Eldoran rose and walked away.

Verendus fetched some rag and a water canister from the kit. As he washed away the blood, Mos opened his eyes and tried to sit.

'Steady.' Verendus set a restraining hand on his shoulder. 'Mostus, look at me.' The boy's eyes had the bewildered glaze of a sleepwalker woken in a strange place. He helped him to sit, then unhooked his flask. 'Drink. Slowly.'

Mos guzzled, coughed, and took another glug. He glanced around. 'Pepper?' His voice choked on a sob. 'Where's Pepper?'

'Right here, cropping grass.' Verendus handed over the rag. 'Clean yourself up, then check the horses. And don't wander about unarmed. Fetch another sword from the kit.'

He left Mos clutching the rag and ran to the wagon. The door was open. 'Corinna?' He peered inside. 'Corinna?'

Fear smote him. She wasn't there. She wasn't anywhere. Dorcas and Saffi sat cowering on the grass. 'Where is she?' he demanded.

Saffi jumped to her feet, fled into the wagon, and slammed the door.

Without looking up, Dorcas shrugged.

Bending, he grabbed her by the shoulders and shook. 'Where is Corinna?'

Dorcas struggled. 'Don't know...'

'Make yourself useful and help the wounded.'

He released her and snatched up a lantern. He hastened to the front of the wagon and almost stumbled over someone who was squatting on the grass, setting out tools. Auxiliary Gallus looked up and regarded him through half-closed eyes. Tanned face swarthy in the lantern light, he wore the nervous expression which had earned the nickname Mole. A second auxiliary – by the enormity of the feet it could only be Hostus – lay underneath, swearing as he assessed the damage.

Verendus walked on, picking a path through the stinking corpses, past buckled spears and discarded shields, and around the body of a horse steaming in the cold air.

At last he found her, kneeling in the dirt and tucking a blanket about an auxiliary. Relief rendered him speechless. He touched her shoulder, and she startled and turned. Blood soaked her cloak. 'Corinna,' he gasped, finding his voice.

'I'm not hurt.'

'You saved the wagon...' Proud yet furious, he couldn't say more. He bent to the auxiliary, but the lad didn't stir. Light fell on the raised leg. The limb had been hacked at the ankle, and the rough stump of a severed and bloody bone protruded. The auxiliary's foot, encased in its *caliga*, lay flaccid on a rolled-up cloak. Skin, sinew, and a single bootstrap all that remained to attach it to the leg.

'I can't stop the bleeding,' Corinna said.

Verendus knelt beside her and tightened the tourniquet she'd made from the auxiliary's belt. 'You've done well. Stay with him.'

Nearby, Auxiliary "Slug" Strabo was heating cauterising oil for the amputation. He was shaking and muttering and his short hair was matted with blood. As Verendus approached, he looked up. 'Commendator, I was just—'

'Good. Soon as you're done here, get that cut seen to,' said Verendus, and walked on. The smell of hot oil and the thought of the exposed flesh it would seal brought the bile back to his throat.

At the edge of the clearing, a loose horse grazed beside a row of blanket-covered bodies. Caligae-shod feet jutted from under the first shroud. A tall man. Gods, he hoped it wasn't Treseus. No, there he was, crouching beside the prone body of his brother Rufus, comforting him while the medic stitched. Quintus, ashen-faced, looked on. Verendus sent him to keep watch and went in search of Bretorus.

He found the decurion tending to Auxiliary Adarius who still wore the cavalry trumpet about his neck.

'Report,' said Verendus.

Decurion Bretorus snapped out a salute. 'Sir, of the troop: five dead, seven injured, one critical.'

Worse than he'd feared. Having no suitable answer, Verendus knelt beside Adarius. His left arm had been tied with a scarf and bandaged. Despite the decurion's attention, the wad of dressing was sodden with blood.

'Sir…' Adarius stopped fiddling with the trumpet strap and attempted to rise.

'As you were.' Verendus grasped the auxiliary's right hand, the rough skin clammy. 'It's just a scratch.'

'It fucking hurts, sir.'

'It's bad,' whispered Bretorus. 'The medic's with Rufus. Poor lad's conscious.'

Verendus nodded; he could hear him screaming. He took the first-aid kit from his satchel and set out what he needed. He cleaned the gash with refined alcohol borrowed from the medic's kit; Adarius slouched and wheezed through clenched teeth.

'Passable stuff this.' Verendus inhaled the alcoholic fumes. 'We'll have a drink afterwards.'

As he threaded the needle, light touched his hands. Corinna brought the lantern closer. 'Eldoran is caring for the injured auxiliary. May I help here?'

Bretorus baulked. 'You're not a medic. Best you go back to the wagon, my lady.'

'I'm more use here,' she said. 'I've worked in a dispensary. I've read Celsus and Dioscorides.'

'Theory's no use.'

She brought a glass vial and a little metal cup from her bag. 'I can ease his pain.'

'Do it,' said Verendus.

Corinna un-stoppered the vial, poured a few drops into the cup, and a whiff of aniseed sharpened the air.

'That's enough,' said Verendus, and added a little liquor from his flask. *Somniferum* was a perilous drug distilled from the potent sap of Morpheus Poppies. He'd seen men go mad from too high a dose.

Adarius drank without question, settled back, and closed his eyes. The balding auxiliary's arm was as hairy as a hog, the exposed muscle quivering like the torn flesh of a wounded animal. He winced as the needle went in. Verendus knotted the thread and inserted the next stitch, working quickly until he had closed the flesh in a line of neat stitches. He tied two scarves together to make a sling and told Corinna to fetch more water. In the moment of quiet that followed, he realised Rufus had stopped screaming.

'Nice work, Commendator,' said Bretorus. 'Poor lad's exhausted. I don't hold with her giving him Ennean stuff.' He frowned at the wagon. 'Our pack-mules have gone. They were tied to the wagon.'

Verendus stood. In his haste, he hadn't noticed. Each of the turma's three units had its own pack-mule to carry large supplies like tents and cooking pots. All three had gone, along with their loads. The lame horse had gone too.

'Thieving Helutti bastards must have broken through the line and stolen them.' Bretorus spat on the ground. 'That's the last we'll see of those gutless slaves, too, I'll wager. They all scarpered when Nonus' horse was running round the circle.'

Auxiliary Nonus was the turma's rising star; now he was dead. 'He would have made a fine decurion. He was a good man.'

'They all were,' said Bretorus. 'We shouldn't have brought the women. If it weren't for that bloody wagon slowing us, we could have outrun the bastards.'

'Not in this light.'

Decurion Treseus staggered towards them, his face streaked with tears. 'Commendator, we did our best...' He pressed his head against Verendus' shoulder and wept. Verendus held him there, waited; he didn't know what else to do. That made six dead; seven if you included runaway Tadius. Almost a quarter of the turma's troopers.

When Corinna returned with the water, he left Treseus in her care and continued his inspection until he was back where he had started, beside Plum.

Eldoran hastened over. 'I could not save the auxiliary's foot, though with care he should live. The Helutti will regroup and return. We cannot linger.'

'I know that.' Verendus strapped on his helmet.

With no time to cremate or bury, he told the auxiliaries to load the bodies onto the wagon. He would not leave them for the Helutti to defile. Auxiliaries stripped the dead horses of their tack, and a hasty reordering ensured everyone had a mount. Callenus the medic, and anyone unfit to ride, clambered into or onto the wagon, until it seemed the mules would not take the strain. Despite their injuries, Adarius and Slug Strabo insisted on riding. Verendus didn't overrule; such fortitude set an example to the younger troopers.

Verendus led the way. Somewhere nearby was a river. If they could cross before the Helutti regrouped, they might stand a chance of reaching the town of Combarus. The alternative was too grim to contemplate.

Resolutely they forced through the dark wood. A low grumble rose and followed. Verendus turned, and the knot in his stomach tightened. The wagon was falling behind, jarring and bumping over the rough ground, the Herculean bulk of Auxiliary Hostus filling the driver's platform.

'Keep up,' yelled Verendus. At every shift in the shadows he tensed, ready to face another attack. With every rush of sound, his heart leapt in anticipation that the river lay just past the next line of trees. But it was only the wind rustling the overhanging branches. Blessed Jupiter let the repairs hold until Combarus. Just a bit further. Keep going.

Then, even as he feared he had led the turma in the wrong direction, he glimpsed movement beyond the trees. *Water.* The chance of salvation shimmering in the moonlight. 'Slow!' he shouted, though he urged Plum on to reach the bank. 'River ahead.'

He emerged from the undergrowth, the stallion's hooves clip-clopping on the slope of pale stone that bordered the water. Verendus stared in disbelief, trying to get his bearings. This was wrong.

Quintus reined in. His eyes were shiny and he was breathing hard. 'Where's the bridge?'

'Ten miles upstream.'

Decurion Bretorus slewed to a halt and swore. 'We'll never get that bloody wagon across.'

Exhaustion flooded Verendus. Ahead stretched fifty feet of coursing water. The expanse gaped like five hundred.

'We might ford it there, before that bend,' said Eldoran, halting beside them. He raised his lantern and pointed downstream to where the bank was wider, with an expanse of low, flat rock and the carcass of a fallen tree that checked the current.

'Come!' Without waiting for an answer, he dismounted and led his horse the short distance along the bank.

'The river could be twenty feet deep,' said Bretorus.

'We don't have the luxury of choice,' Verendus said, and followed.

Eldoran unhooked a coil of narrow rope from his saddle, tied it about his waist, and tossed the slack to Verendus.

'I shall cross first.' Eldoran led his horse over the flat rock and into the shallows, his lantern bobbing on its pole. 'Stony underfoot,' he called over his shoulder.

Preferable to mud, Verendus thought, and uncoiled more rope. A third of the distance across now, the Nemusan was waist-deep in churning water.

Hope flared. They might ride across – providing it got no deeper. There were trees on the opposite bank where Eldoran could secure the rope. A lifeline across the river. There wasn't time to organise a system of rafts to float stuff across. Wet kit was the least of their worries. Closer now, pulsating through the forest, the beat rose.

'They're coming,' said Quintus.

Verendus shoved the rope at him and hailed Bretorus.

He was helping the decurion to select the ablest riders when Quintus said, 'He's made it! Eldoran's across.'

'Thank the gods!' Verendus pointed to a stout tree trunk and told Quintus to secure the rope around it. Thanks to the Nemusan, they had a line across the water. The opposite bank was steeper, it would be a slog for the wagon. He couldn't worry about that now. One step at a time.

Verendus hitched up his cloak and led the chosen riders into the water, following the silken rope. It didn't look strong enough. He reassured himself that it was Ennean rope, the finest money could buy. If only it looked thicker.

He glanced behind. Bretorus, muttering as he followed; horses wading tentatively through the water, the forms of their riders unsteady in the lantern light; the wagon and the remaining auxiliaries lined up on the bank, waiting to cross.

Two strides and the water covered Plum's hocks. Cavalry trained and accustomed to Iolia's beaches, the stallion didn't fear water, but moonlight and shadows rippled the moving surface with menace. Verendus gripped the reins. 'Steady. Steady, boy.'

Cold water lapped at his feet, shocking him to a heart-thumping state of alertness that quickened his breathing and dried his mouth. The beat intensified, closing in. An image of the Helutti grove at Grenorum sparked unbidden in his mind. The great stone slab, the decomposing body of a legionary officer tied upon it, a glittering trophy of shields, helmets, and mangled spears piled beneath. And all around, the ring of gnarled oak trees, a phixus etched into every trunk, so distinct it might have been carved that very day.

Verendus concentrated on the river. *Jupiter Maximus, Jupiter Maximus*, must get across. He longed to spur Plum, crash through the water to the far bank and gallop away.

He inhaled slowly; he would not let fear better him. A few more paces and water covered his knees. He looked from bank to bank, calculating the distances in his mind's eye. He'd come far enough – for now. This would be the place. Any further was too great a risk.

With the decurion's help, he positioned the selected riders on either side of the rope: one line close beside it and the other a short margin away so the wagon could pass between them. There weren't enough riders to cover the river's entire width, but there were two lines of five ranged across the deepest point, the first to break the current, the second to recover anyone swept away by it. In theory, anyway. In reality, the chances of rescuing anyone were slim. By the look of the terrified faces around him, the auxiliaries knew this too.

Murky water sloshed his thighs. He couldn't hear the drums above the rush of water; intuition cautioned him they had not fallen silent. If the Helutti attacked now, with half the troop in the river… He quashed the thought. 'Decurion, carry on,' he said, turning Plum.

Verendus rode back, splashing through the lines, calling encouragement as he passed. Give the lads hope, show them he wasn't afraid, though his heart raced, pounding hard against the walls of his chest. He reached the near bank and beckoned Perseo. 'You first. Take the standard across. The sight will embolden the troop to follow.' He told Mos to go next. 'Lead the way for the wagon.'

The boy stared stupidly, then saluted and set off. With the consolation that he was sending Mos as early as possible, he ordered Adarius and Strabo to follow. Both were injured, it was better to send them across now, though he could tell by their disappointed faces that they wanted to remain and help.

Verendus rode to the wagon. A compulsion to open the door and check on Corinna seized him. No. He must not indulge his anxiety, must stay in control. He slapped the side of the wagon, and shouted to Hostus, 'Drive!'

It would be a labour of heroic proportions to drive safely across the river and up the bank. Mighty Hercules, champion of impossible tasks, watch over us.

Hostus lashed the mules into the water. Verendus waited on the bank with the last of the troop, a bedraggled few clustered in the lantern glow. The light no longer seemed prudent. 'We'll manage without these,' he said, extinguishing his own. The auxiliaries followed his example and darkness closed in. Verendus slung his cavalry shield over his back and told the others to do the same. Designed to be light in weight, the birch wood and leather shield might not stop an axe blow, but it afforded another layer between spine and blade. And even the impression of protection could impart a little confidence.

Drums thudded, growing louder. Quintus puffed out flushed cheeks, and said, 'Did you hear that?'

'I heard it,' said Decurion Bretorus, returning to stand beside them.

Verendus kept his attention on the river. The wagon was nearing the mid-point, water rising, covering the wheels. The mules brayed and refused to move. Again Hostus cracked the lash, urging them on.

As they passed the mid-point, the mules pulled hard, straining for the far bank. Mos must be almost there. 'Bretorus, lead the men across. You next, Quin. Go!'

Eager to follow, Plum pulled against the bit. Verendus steadied him and remained on the bank, watching the horses wade through the shallows. Thanks to months of rigorous training all the auxiliaries could swim, but armour which protected on land was a deadly liability in the water. There wasn't time to remove it. Given the choice between the risk of falling in and the reassurance of a defensive layer, the auxiliaries were better off wearing their mail.

The last horse entered the protective channel. Verendus whistled to signal the lines to turn and follow. As he rode towards the water, a roar shook the air. An axe struck the ground beside them in a burst of gravel. Plum skittered. Sling stones raining like hail, Verendus spurred the stallion into the river.

Ahead, the smaller mounts were up to their necks. One was lagging, the gap widening between him and the two riders in front, a bay and a grey. Plum closed in on the straggler. Stones hurtled around them and the water spat like a boiling pan. He was almost neck-and-neck with the straggler when the bay horse in front of them squealed and stumbled, launching its rider into the river. The man screamed and disappeared beneath the surface.

It seemed he must be lost, but he thrashed to the surface and grabbed a saddle-horn. At the same moment, grey's lanky rider slowed and turned his head towards the commotion. Then he flinched, dropped sideways into the water, and was gone. The grey floundered on.

Instinctively Verendus veered after the bay horse, realising as he did that it was a bad idea. The rider made no attempt to remount, but clung to the saddle-horn as the current swept horse and rider downstream.

The straggler got to them first. Auxiliary Gallus raised his shield in one hand and lunged for the stricken rider with the other, reaching out, almost there. Something clattered against the shield rim. The distinctive plink of stone on metal. He screeched and recoiled in a spurt of blood.

Verendus drove Plum nearer and, in a few strides, drew level. Gallus' right eye was a bloody mess. He swayed in the saddle, touched his face, and groaned.

'Ride on,' shouted Verendus. 'Go!'

Gallus splashed away; Verendus almost followed. The bay horse was gone. He saw it flailing towards the bend in the river where the sparse branches of the fallen tree poked from the water. Beyond, the current was stronger. A point of no return. He'd never reach the rider in time. He glanced back. On the ridge of the shore, fuzzy in the gloam, the man in the antler headdress was goading his horde down the bank to the water's edge.

As Verendus unhooked the shield from his back, pulling it over his shoulder to cover his exposed left flank, a stone whizzed down, clipping the side of the helmet and scraping the cheek-guard. Light flashed across his vision. Plum shied, hooves skidding on the riverbed. Verendus thrust out his shield arm to steady himself. A whoosh of air, a thud, and an axe clanged against his shield, slamming it hard against his arm. Pain seared the limb from fingertip to shoulder. He braced, but his arm sagged and his hold faltered. The shield was slipping. So was he.

Strength borne of experience and years of training kicked in, bestowing a precious reserve of inner steel that mastered his panic. He pressed his thighs into the front saddle-horns and clung on. Thank Minerva, the axe had struck the iron shield boss and ricocheted. He regained his balance, blinked away spray, and peered around the rim of the shield. His heart lurched – the bay horse had vanished. 'Auxiliary!' he shouted. The word drowned in the gushing water. He raised the shield as a stone impacted. 'Auxiliary! Auxiliary…'

Metal glinted in the moonlight and a volley of spears from troopers on the far bank soared overhead to check the Helutti slingers.

Verendus shouted again, heard an answering cry. Using his knees, he manoeuvred Plum towards the sound. Someone in the water, the crown of a helmet just visible in the froth. No sign of the horse.

Telling himself to focus on the auxiliary, Verendus rode closer. Never take your eyes off a man in the water: he could be swept away in the blink of an eye. The way that the auxiliary was thrashing around, the river might claim him at any moment.

Verendus drove Plum on. The current was less fierce here, checked by the fallen tree. Slip beyond and the force returned with renewed vigour.

The auxiliary was wedged against the trunk, clutching a branch with one hand and groping the water with the other.

He was shouting one word, over and over. And, as Verendus neared, he realised it was the name of the trooper who had fallen from the grey.

'Cico! Cico!'

'He's gone.' Verendus dropped his shield and reached out.

'I saw him,' cried Auxiliary Marinus, his thick Britannic accent unmistakable.

'Grip!' screamed Verendus, stretching further.

The lad didn't move. Verendus grasped his tunic and tugged. He urged Plum on, dragging Marinus through the swirling water and out onto the bank.

CHAPTER IX

The gods were merciful and the Helutti did not pursue the turma across the river. And just as well. Although Verendus and Decurion Bretorus hammered their fists on the gates of Combarus, several minutes passed before a man peered over the rampart to demand what the ruckus was. Even then, the decurion had to produce the dictate confirming the troop's entitlement to collect the taxes before the order was given to open the gates.

Verendus ushered everyone inside. Satisfied that the big locking-bar was in place and the gate secure, he dismounted and checked Plum. The stallion was steaming, and his mouth and flanks were flecked white with sweat.

Mos trudged over. He looked exhausted, but there was little point telling one of the auxiliaries to do the rubbing down and watering – the boy would only fret that the task hadn't been done properly if he hadn't completed it himself. Verendus left Plum in his care and remained with Tribune Quintus to question the gatekeeper.

The old man bowed low. 'Sirs, begging your pardon,' he said, grey head nodding, 'we're more careful nowadays. We've had to be. Been some dreadful goings on in Combarus Forest.'

'What sort of *goings on?*' Verendus pulled off his helmet and water trickled out. He ran his finger around the dent in the metal where the sling stone had clipped the side. Unlike a cavalry helmet, the Praetorian helmet did not cover the wearer's ears. A mere thumbnail lower and the stone would have struck his ear and plunged him into the river with poor Cico. It didn't bear thinking about.

Still nodding, mouth open, the gatekeeper watched the process, and said, 'Cries in the night. Howls. Terrible they were. As loud as in the cruel winter, though that were nigh on fifty years ago. Long afore you were born. I were a lad then, but I well remember. So cold the river froze and the snow lay deep for many a day. Wolves came from the mountains – hungry, bolded by the freeze. Their howls were nowt to these cries. Fell enough to chill the staunchest man's blood. We let things be at first. But, and this is like the wolves all over—'

'Fuck the wolves!' Verendus grasped his sword hilt and the gatekeeper cowered.

'The old boy's trembling like a tart's tits.' Quintus grinned. 'Calm yourself, man. Get up. On with the story.'

He accepted Quintus' hand and grunted to his feet. 'Well, 'twere like that, sir. Sheep missing. No one saw 'em taken. Five men went to search… 'Twere, let me think, three days after the ides. Ain't been sign of 'em since. So,' he said with an air of justification, 'we keep the gate locked and suffer no strangers.'

'Quite right.' Quintus patted the gatekeeper's arm. 'Why hasn't word been sent to the governor?'

'Begging your pardon, Tribune, a rider left four, no, let me think, five days past. Told to take the highway, he were.'

'Had we been forewarned we would have brought more men,' said Quintus. 'Seen the Helutti off for good.'

The furrows in the old man's brow deepened. 'Helutti? Ain't they a northern tribe? I know my history. They was the tribe that slaughtered Second Legion *Minervia* away in Grenorum.'

'Indeed.' Verendus shivered. His wet tunic stuck to him like a shroud. He would not think about Grenorum.

With a cry of, '*Salvete!* Salvete!' the town's magistrate came hastening to the gate. Flush-faced, his arms flapping, he resembled a cockerel disturbed from its roost. Two cudgel-bearing attendants followed, and stood scowling while the magistrate gave a brisk welcome speech that implied he was not at all pleased to meet the men who were here to collect the region's taxes, but felt obliged to observe the formalities. Speech over, the pompous little man puffed out his chest and demanded to know what Governor Peronius was doing about the bandits.

Verendus kept it brief. 'We're dealing with a gang of escaped Helutti slaves, which means they are desperate and dangerous. Ensure an adequate watch is posted on the ramparts and light more beacons.'

Determined to see his request carried out, Verendus oversaw the job. Quintus stood beside him, questioning and passing comment on everything, and an hour passed before it was done.

The magistrate had arranged accommodation at the local inn; Verendus told him they would make their own way there. Ahead, the street led into a cobbled square enclosed by tight-packed rows of tall houses. To his tired eyes they appeared to be living, animate beings, the top-heavy structures leaning to such an extent that each wooden edifice tapered towards the fountain at the square's centre like deformed plants straining for the sun. Across the square, a lantern lit a mural of a gilt-horned ram: *THE GOLDEN RAM* painted in yellow letters below.

'This must be the place.' Quintus pointed to the door.

Without reply, Verendus turned and strode to the fountain. He doused his head under a jet of water, letting the cold stream wash over him in the hope it would cleanse him of the night's horrors. It just made him colder and wetter. He shook himself and followed Quintus inside.

Subdued talk from the table nearest the door ceased as the locals looked up from their wine cups. Service as a Praetorian had accustomed Verendus to people's aversion and apprehension towards his uniform. Tonight, as he hung his cloak to dry by the hearth, even the fire spat and snarled like a chained dog.

The turma occupied three tables, their places chosen loosely according to rank. Two chairs remained at the head of the fireside table where troops stood smartly to attention as the two officers approached.

With a flourish of his hand, Quintus gestured the men to retake their seats. At the gate, Verendus had made a point of telling Bretorus they would all eat together. Troopers and officers had stood as one against the Helutti, and they would share a table now.

The stench of mud, sweat, and stale blood took Verendus' breath. He longed to go to his room, lie down, and close his eyes. No, get through this first. He made a covert headcount. The disparity between youth and experience had shifted. The Helutti had smelled the youngsters' callow fear and slain them with the ease of wolves taking lambs. Of the turma's five newcomers only flame-haired Marinus remained, seated on a bench at the next table and staring at the wall, a bowl of stew untasted before him. Verendus went over and clamped a hand on the lad's shoulder. Marinus flinched but didn't turn.

Verendus bent closer, and whispered, 'There was nothing you could have done. Cico would have been dead before he hit the water. We'll say no more about what happened afterwards. About how you ignored my order.' He tightened his grip and Marinus gulped. 'Disobey an order again, Auxiliary, and I'll thrash the shit out of you. Understood?'

'Yes, sir. Sorry, sir.' His freckled cheeks reddened.

Verendus let go and nudged Portoc who was next on the bench. 'Piggy, make yourself useful and show Marinus where you're bedding down tonight.'

Verendus found his place beside Quintus at the fireside table. Slug Strabo had bagged a seat next to Bretorus, all the better to suck up to the decurion. Dexo the scout had the next place; Perseo, the standard-bearer, sat opposite. Beside him, bigmouth Murvaro and his flaxen-haired comrade Hostus regarded Verendus with the contempt of a pair of petulant camels scrutinising a herder with a long stick. A swift reshuffle to replace the murdered Nonus had seen Murvaro promoted to third-in-command. The burly auxiliary's head seemed bigger than ever.

Verendus glanced around. Someone was missing. 'Where's Eldoran?'

'Keeping watch, sir. He insisted,' said Bretorus, as two steaming dishes of something resembling runny cement arrived. 'I instructed cook to keep yours hot.'

'Thank you, Decurion.' Quintus frowned as the serving-boy set a dish before him.

'And the injured?' asked Verendus. He prodded the mush with his spoon.

'Resting,' said Bretorus. 'Adarius and Gallus ate with us – they've just turned in. The medic did his best for Mole. Poor sod's lucky to be alive. Had that sling stone hit him square in the face, he'd be dead for sure. As it was, it clipped the rim of his shield and lost momentum.' He lowered his voice. 'Though he's not much use to the turma with only one eye.'

'Blind as a mole!' said Murvaro.

Verendus doubted that irony had been lost on anyone, though only Murvaro was crass enough to mention it. 'I won't write him off.'

'With respect, Commendator, it's not your decision. Or mine. Treseus and the medic are with him.' Bretorus went on to explain that the young auxiliary who'd lost a foot was weakening. 'The amputation almost did for him. He'll have to remain here.'

Verendus shook his head and water dripped cold down his neck. He was not prepared to leave anyone in the care of the local wise-woman. 'There's a military hospital in Avennio.'

'Yes, Commendator. If he lasts the night.'

Verendus sighed. Soon as he'd eaten, he would check on the patients. He stirred the overcooked mush, tasted it, and gagged. The meat had been boiled to a paste, impossible to tell from which unfortunate beast the slop originated. He set down his spoon and the stilted conversation around the table faltered. Grim-faced auxiliaries exchanged glances.

Hostus eyed the leftovers. 'You leaving that, sir?'

'You're welcome to—' The dish was snatched before he finished the sentence.

Verendus reached for his wine cup and pain shot up his arm. He flexed his left hand, stiff and discoloured since the impact of the shield, the signet ring digging into his swollen finger. He shifted the cup to his right hand, took a swig, and met the faces turned to his. The words of solace he struggled for choked and drowned. He beckoned the landlord. 'Bring more wine. And have one yourself.'

The drinks arrived. With the exception of Murvaro – preoccupied in polishing his knife – all the auxiliaries managed a weary cheer. Verendus concentrated on what needed to be done. He must check on Corinna. Thoughts of comforting her became thoughts of what he'd like to do to her, but the gatekeeper's tale of the lost messenger crept into his head and spoiled the fantasy. The gatekeeper reckoned the messenger left four or five days ago. Ample time for word to have reached the fortress of Castellum Alba before the turma departed. Unless the Helutti had him too.

He related the concern to Bretorus, and the decurion's dark eyes hardened. 'Not on the highway, Commendator. We patrol that stretch regularly.'

Several auxiliaries murmured agreement. Murvaro paused from picking his teeth with the tip of his knife and was about to speak when Slug Strabo assumed a look of authority, and said, 'Quite so. It's safer than the old road.'

'Shut it, Slug.' Murvaro stabbed the knife into the table. 'We don't get paid enough for stuff like this. Ain't so bad for legionaries, they get paid more and they don't have fodder deducted.'

'You'd let that miserable horse of yours starve if it wasn't,' said Perseo.

'It's dead,' said Murvaro. 'And my fucking slave scarpered.'

'It's time we had a rise,' said Slug, scratching his bandaged head.

Perseo nodded. 'Slug's right, we deserve a rise. Those fuckers butchered Nonus.'

Verendus drained his cup and didn't point out that the imperial coffers were rumoured to be empty.

'There's as much chance of a rise as there is of Slug getting laid,' said Hostus. He belched and scraped the dish. 'Those brutes were savager than that tribe we routed in the push over the Rhenus.'

'I'd sooner fight those fucking Saxtili barbarians than go through tonight again,' Murvaro said sourly.

Slug finished his wine and made a performance of dabbing his moustache with a corner of his scarf. 'The Hermunduri tribe is worse. They decapitate and stick the heads on trees. Then they chop off your prick and shove that in your mouth.'

'They'd never find yours.' Murvaro wiggled his little finger.

Auxiliaries laughed. Slug opened his mouth but didn't speak. Bretorus thwacked his vine-stick on the table, silencing the noise. Across the room, the locals turned and then looked hastily away.

'Helutti are worse,' said Perseo. 'They cut it off while you're still alive.'

This sparked a vociferous debate over which Germani tribe was the toughest. 'They'll be arguing all night,' Bretorus moaned into his cup. He turned to Quintus. 'With your permission, Tribune, I'll send a man back to Alba to inform the governor of tonight's ambush.'

'Good idea, Decurion. The Helutti must be hunted down. Father's given me authority to issue travel permits, and I'll write a missive asking him for reinforcements from the Second Turma.'

'Dexo can carry it, he's the fastest. If he takes the highway, rides hard, and changes horse at the mansio, he'll be there before dusk day after the morrow.'

Dexo grinned, his sharp face keen. 'Sir, I'll do it, easy.'

Bretorus leaned nearer to Quintus. 'Tribune, I suggest we await the Second Turma here.'

The suggestion was reasonable. The more troops that could be set against the Helutti the better. But it would entail a delay of several days. 'No,' said Verendus, and the table fell silent. 'We depart on the morrow and continue as planned. Treseus will take word to Alba.'

Bretorus flushed brick red under his beard and slammed down his cup, splashing wine over the table.

'As you like,' said Quintus, deaf to the ill-feeling. 'We'll leave in the morning. Make the arrangements, Decurion.'

His lips twitching, his hands clenched before him in impotent fury, Bretorus growled, 'Yes, sir.'

CHAPTER X

Above, at the back of the inn, was an oak panelled bedroom with a low ceiling that sloped mournfully into the eaves. A large bed occupied half the room, its carved headboard set against the one wall that reached to full height. With the window shuttered and the lamps extinguished, only the glow of a fire burning low in the hearth remained to push back the shadows.

Corinna closed the door and caught her breath; she wasn't used to feeling like this. She secured the bolt and took a moment to compose herself.

Saffi stopped whimpering. She threw off the bedcover and sat up. 'Who do you talk to?'

'The Commendator was checking we're comfortable.' Had he asked that? Corinna wasn't sure. In his blood-smeared armour with the red cloak wrapped about his shoulders, he had looked cold, exhausted, and as fierce as the day he found her hiding in the Belvedere yard. Then he'd smiled, a small half-smile, and she saw the man beneath the armour shell. Vulnerable, boyish, in need of a bath. His clothes smelt of the river, and his fair hair was streaked with dried blood. A raw bruise discoloured his left arm and his hand was swollen.

She had not expected to see him until the morning. They had stood mute, staring at each other, as if what needed to be said could be conveyed through thought alone. And then they both spoke at once, though she couldn't recall his words. He must have been satisfied with her reply, for he'd nodded and bidden her goodnight.

'That way he looks at you,' said Saffi, wrinkling her nose. 'A hungry look. I know his sort.' Voices and clanking pots resonated from downstairs. She glared at the floorboards. 'They are all down there, all the horrid soldiers. Drink and bicker, drink and bicker. I wish they shut up.'

With difficulty, for her hands were bandaged where the reins had blistered her palms, Corinna set the last paltry log on the fire. Flames rose to embrace it, casting light on the slave Dorcas, wrapped snug on a straw pallet under the eaves.

Saffi sniffed. 'Trust her to sleep.'

'It's late,' said Corinna. 'Try to settle. We are safe here.'

'How do you know? The Helutti are very terrible, very cruel to my people. Almost as cruel as men of the Empire.'

'Go to sleep.'

'I am not tired. I will tell you of the men of the Empire, I want you to know what happen, know what is true.' Saffi retrieved the bedcover and hugged it around herself. 'Two years past, soldiers of the Empire cross the wide river and attack my village. We are Saxtili. We do not flee. Saxtili fight. My father was a great warrior, he led the defence. But the soldiers were many. Soldiers like your commendator.'

'He is not *my* commendator.' Corinna grabbed the poker and jabbed the fire. Sparks flared and died. 'It's hopeless. The wood's damp.' Her palms hurt even more, and she had failed to revive the fire. Soon it would die. There would be no work on Verendus' translation tonight.

'The soldiers come before dawn,' said Saffi. 'Very many of them. Some on horses, some marching, and all carrying torches of fire. They burn everything. People ran from their homes, but there was nowhere to run, nowhere to hide. So many people screaming and running, cut like crops and trampled where they fall. What happen to my mother, my sister…' she shook her head. 'My brother, he tried to protect me. A soldier much like your commendator stabbed him through the chest and kicked him aside like a dog. My dear baby brother. He was ten summers old.' She gripped the cover and stared defiantly from the folds. 'I think the soldier kill me next. I try to fight. But he was strong… too strong. He forced me down, pushed my face in the dirt, and pulled up my skirts. What he did hurt so much I think I die. I wish I did die.'

Corinna sank onto the bed. She had no words.

Mice scuttled through the rafters. Saffi cringed, and said, 'I scream and scream, and I hear my sister screaming. I could not help her.' She tugged the end of her stubby braid. 'Before slavers cut my hair it was long, to my waist. That pig held my hair. When he had done with me, he put his mouth close to my ear. His breath stink of bad fish. He said, "Beautiful hair" – said it in the tongue of my people. Then he called his friend over.' She inhaled with a hiss. 'It is not a nice story, no?'

'No…' Corinna slumped. The air had been knocked from her lungs. Meeting the girl's eyes, she saw her own anguish mirrored there and remembered Centurion Torvius at the Temple, what he had tried to do.

'The soldier sold me to the slavers. Those crows follow the soldiers. They chain us together and herd us like cattle through the forest. We come to the river. I see their big boats waiting there and I am frit. I see the big cage in the belly of the boat and am more frit. That cage stink of death.'

Corinna put her arms about the girl and rocked her gently.

Saffi jerked free. 'Does your commendator make you lie with him? Is that what he asks you tonight? The Empire is full of brutes, even at the Temple. Many, many, many!'

'Shush! You'll wake Dorcas.'

Saffi frowned at the eaves. 'She snores like a fat sow.'

'What do you mean, even at the Temple?'

'In the courtyard is a balcony. Many plants. Easy to climb up and hide.'

A nameless anxiety prickled. Corinna plucked at the bed-cover, pulled a thread. 'Did something happen while you were hiding?'

'Often I hide there, often I hear things. This day I see something.' A smile rippled her thin lips. 'A warm day, the shutters are a little open. I look in and I see them.'

'Who?'

Taking her time, Saffi plumped a pillow. Feathers came loose, dust rose. She brushed the feathers aside, and said, 'Magistra and a man. Naked on the bed. But not like beasts in the field. No, she was on him.'

'Are you certain? You said it was warm.'

'You say I dream it? No. I see them.'

'The man…' Corinna clutched the bedcover. 'Did you recognise him?'

'I do not see his face, but he was Guard. A red cloak like your commendator's was on the chair. Maybe it was your commendator.'

Corinna rose and prodded the fire. Torvius. Surely it was Torvius. He had spoken of the sign of the serpents, and the snakes on the codex clasp might be those serpents. Somehow the Praetorian Guard centurion had gained a hold over Magistra and attempted to take the codex.

That horrible night in the Belvedere library before Torvius attacked her, his guard, the vile Nevoso, had mentioned an appointment that evening. For a heartbeat, Corinna had thought they would leave immediately. But no…

She tried to remember. Who had Torvius been going to see? A prefect? Yes, that was it. She couldn't recall the name, but maybe Torvius was taking the codex to him.

Corinna shuddered, glad Torvius was dead. Despite Saffi's assertion, Magistra could not have been with Verendus. He'd been a year in Germania, had crossed over the river to Barbarian Germania. What had he done there?

GERMANIA INFERIOR

850 AUC (AD 97)

On arrival in Germania Inferior, Legate Paullus Regimius Sentorus marched first to Noviomagus, home of that province's most northerly legion, the Tenth Gemina. Assured of their allegiance he continued to Auster Grenorum, base of Third Gemina, south of the infamous battleground.

Sentorus restored order and arrested the instigators of the revolt. Five executions followed, the bodies exhibited outside the camp so all might see Reman justice had been done. Sentorus paid the troops their overdue bonus from his own funds. The colours were reinstated; the oaths retaken in his favour.

He berated the soldiers for their lack of discipline. Rema, he said, was relying on them to defend the border, not squabble among themselves and let the barbarians in through neglect. He reminded them how, ten years ago, Saxtili treachery had led the Second Legion into the Helutti's trap. As a senior tribune in Third Gemina, he had been sent to inspect the aftermath. Men wept as he recounted the gruesome scene and told of the courage of Second Minervia, his beloved brother among the fallen.

Fired by tales of vengeance, spurred by the promise of reward, the men were his to command. A new, strict regime in place, the soldiers grumbled; none openly challenged it. With men selected from Germania's northernmost legions and auxiliary forts, and the Ninth Hispana recently arrived from Britannia, Sentorus augmented his own force of a thousand troops to form a new le-gion, which he gave the number Twenty-Four and the title: Ger-manica. He established a system of local recruitment to replenish the depleted legions, and gave the order to ready the troops.

Sentorus sacrificed a white bull to Mars Ultor the Avenger and turned his hand to conquest.

Chronicles of Imperial Rema

by Marcus Vedius Verendus

CHAPTER XI

At first light, on a clearing outside the walls of Combarus, Decurion Bretorus led a cremation service for the slain troopers. Verendus and Quintus stood slightly apart from the men of the first turma of the Fourth Brittonum. Though all of those present were soldiers, in grief the turma closed ranks, widening the gulf between trooper and officer. Antipathy radiated from the huddled group, warning Verendus not to intrude. They were the non-citizen auxiliary troopers, but he felt like the outsider.

As the trumpet rang out, he hardened his face; he would not mourn before the men. To distract himself, he glanced from trooper to trooper – Murvaro and Hostus solemn and dry-eyed, Piggy Portoc staring at the sky, Slug Strabo holding up Marinus who was sobbing and trembling and muttering under his breath. In spite of their grief, each man had cleaned and polished away the filth and the blood of yesterday and their armour gleamed in the low sunshine.

In common with many such gatherings, after the service there was a collective reluctance to leave. Men reminisced; someone passed around a wineskin. Verendus left them to it. Incense smoke and the reek of burning flesh thickened the air with a sickly sweetness. He blinked away tears and did not look back. It would be a long day. Dreams of blood and stones raining from the sky had woken him in the night. Unable to settle, he'd risen early and copied another page of the codex. Now, it was in his satchel ready to give to Corinna for translation.

On nearing the main gate he saw Eldoran sitting on the wooded rampart, a bow in his lap. Verendus hailed him. 'I trust you weren't up there all night.'

Eldoran slung the bow on his back and climbed down. 'No. I do not believe the Helutti followed us across the river.'

'Perhaps they'll keep away until reinforcements arrive.'

'Perhaps. What news of the patients?'

'Well enough to travel. The wagon's repaired. We'll leave as soon as the taxes are loaded.' Verendus walked on.

Quintus' generosity with his father's coin had been welcome. Galvanised by the promise of reward, the smith and his team had worked through the night to make the repairs.

In the yard outside the forge, Verendus and Decurion Bretorus oversaw the loading of the taxes. Though relatively small, the region's wealth was evident in the four coffers heavy with coin. Verendus appointed Auxiliary Strabo as guard and sent him in next. Then they assisted the wounded into the wagon, Callenus the medic staying close beside the stretcher bearing the young auxiliary, the stump of his severed leg heavily bandaged and reeking of dried blood.

The women followed, heads low, shrouded. He went to Corinna and gave her the next extract from the codex. She nodded and, without glancing up, slipped the scroll into her sleeve. Last night, standing at her bedroom door, she had gazed long at him. This morning she could not meet his eyes.

Verendus closed the wagon door behind her. She was as much a mystery to him now as she was when he'd found her hiding in the Belvedere yard.

The smith – a short, muscular man, almost as broad as he was tall – drove the wagon to the gate. 'Rolling sweet as an apple,' he said cheerfully, handing over the reins to Auxiliary Hostus.

The rest of the turma was mounted and waiting, Decurion Treseus at their head, a packhorse bearing the wrapped and bound body of his brother beside him. Quintus, who had avoided the entire loading process, arrived last, yawning as he rode across the yard. The magistrate hastened beside him, talking volubly.

Concerned that the magistrate would delay their departure with a speech, Verendus ordered the auxiliaries to strap on their helmets and uncover their shields. Strange to recall that just a few days ago, the turma had ridden through the narrow streets of Alba cheered on by an enthusiastic crowd. All Combarus could offer was old men, beggars, and a woman selling almond cakes.

'Locusts. Thieves,' yelled a man, and spat on the ground.

The turma ignored him and rode through the gates, bowing their heads as they passed their comrades' smouldering pyre.

On Verendus' insistence, the turma maintained strict formation. Eldoran volunteered to scout ahead; Verendus led the vanguard. Though they would not have to travel far on this stretch of terraced farmland, he wasn't about to lower his guard. With morning traffic steady on the old road such caution seemed excessive, but he took nothing for granted. Besides, it was good training for the auxiliaries.

As he glanced behind to ensure they were keeping pace, a nagging concern stirred. Why, after years in hiding, had Helutti slaves left their mountain refuge and strayed into this part of the province? He turned the matter over and reached the same conclusion Eldoran had mooted: something or someone had disturbed them from their refuge in the Alps. That might account for Legate Capito's unseasonal inspection of the mountain passes.

After the fields came woodland. Soon they would reach the checkpoint for the Via Domitia. Verendus dropped back in line, letting others pass. At every pothole in the old road his stomach lurched. Was it apprehension over the woodland ahead or the prospect of negotiating the checkpoint beyond? Probably the latter. If he had failed to throw the Praetorians off his trail, it was here, at the checkpoint barring the way to the Via Domitia, that they would arrest him.

At the rear of the column, he fell into pace beside Treseus who acknowledged him with a nod. Treseus glanced behind at the packhorse that bore his brother's body, and said, 'My parents will want him home. Arrange his funeral…' he added, explaining again his decision not to cremate Rufus with his fallen comrades. He met Verendus' eyes and immediately looked away, down to the mane of his horse, which he stroked absently. 'I know what some of the lads have been saying, Commendator, and I want you to know… the ambush yesterday, I don't blame you for what happened.'

The wind blew chill through the trees. Verendus resisted the temptation to ask who these lads were. A few more days and he'd be moving on, choosing his own path. For now, his sole ally in the auxiliary troop was departing; the next few days would not be easy.

'You go first through the checkpoint,' Verendus said. 'The turma will have more formalities. We'll only delay you.'

Together they rode through the line, auxiliaries lowering their heads and averting their eyes from the body as they passed. Ahead, the trees thinned and the checkpoint came into view. Beyond the barrier, the Via Domitia stretched far: east to the Alps, and west across the province where it would meet the Via Agrippa, which led north to Viorum and beyond, and south towards the coast.

On reaching the head of the column, Verendus raised his hand to signal a halt. He leaned across and squeezed Treseus' arm. 'Ride hard and fast, my friend. May the sun shine on your face and a fair wind blow at your back.' They exchanged a salute. 'Farewell.'

Treseus passed the checkpoint without incident. Efficient as ever, Bretorus presented the turma's highway pass to the waiting sentry. Verendus scrutinised the man's bland face for any hint of suspicion, but the sentry nodded, opened the barrier, and waved the turma through. Verendus peered along the road, but Treseus had faded from view.

Though the turma managed a steady pace on the highway, the sun was sinking low, glinting off the river that ran beside it. Quintus pointed to a picturesque town perched on the hillside and suggested they lodge there. Verendus overruled. The amputation yesterday had ignited a fever in the wounded auxiliary. Corinna and Callenus the medic were doing their best, but he wouldn't last another night without specialist care. They must reach the military hospital at Avennio before nightfall.

Verendus remembered a track, an old farm path that a travelling oculist had pointed out for the price of a cup of wine. The shortcut was still there, rough but adequate, the ground dry enough to accommodate the wagon. Decurion Bretorus argued it was unwise to leave the road, but Verendus prevailed.

The track cut through open countryside bountiful with vines and orchards, the pear trees bright with blossom. Distant villas sparkled like pale gems and the sunset-gilded battlements of Avennio materialised. The short cut had proved invaluable. Furthermore, they had avoided the Via Agrippa checkpoint.

Dusk nigh, bells ringing out across the valley, Bretorus, Quintus, and the medic escorted the wounded auxiliary to hospital. The troops bemoaned the order to set camp outside the walls, but the decurion was determined to keep them away from the bars and brothels within. Even when he returned with tents, equipment, and pack-mules to replace the losses, the mood remained sombre.

Verendus and Quintus paid for the replacements. Verendus thanked the gods that his own kit hadn't been taken, and retired to his tent to study the route. He sat facing the entrance, the leather flap tied back to let in light from the campfires and lanterns. He set his binder, chart, and a wax tablet on the folding desk. Outside, the auxiliaries were settling to their chores – a few cooking, some cleaning kit, most of them grumbling while they worked.

Mos lit a lantern and hung it up, casting a pool of light over the desk. Verendus yawned and stared at the chart. He ran an inattentive fingertip along the road of ink and attempted to calculate how far Fes would have progressed on his journey east to the Alpine village of Brigantium in search of Capito, legate of Twenty-Third *Victrix*. Capito could confirm whether troops of that legion – currently camped on Waterside Plain in Iolia – were genuine or another cog in Galenius' war machine. If they had taken over the nearby peninsula of Chiros, Galenius would have access to specialist military equipment.

With the tip of a stylus, Verendus scratched figures in the wax of a tablet. He couldn't concentrate. He'd sent his friend into danger. In the course of their questions at Alba, the three Praetorians might discover that a highway permit had been issued to Fes and send an agent to investigate. With Praetorian entitlement to a regular change of horse at the roadside mansio inns, any head start Fes had gained would be swiftly eroded.

There was one crumb of comfort: the Guard would underestimate him. Deep-rooted contempt and the conviction that all Saxtili were fools would make the Guard slack. Fes was wily as an old fox. If they were after him, he would know. He'd leave the highway and go to ground.

Reassured by his theory, Verendus went over the figures, adding them up in his head until he realised he'd drawn a phixus as though that was the answer. Using the stub at the other end of the stylus, he scrubbed it out. Strange to think that Galenius had seen the Helutti grove and yet chosen the phixus symbol for the Iolian Watch. Legate Sentorus had been there too. Did he share Galenius' obsession with that symbol, the sign of the serpents?

Verendus stretched and the cuirass pressed tight against his torso. Last night, after cleaning his armour, he had put it back on and slept sitting up in a chair, his sword strapped to his side. It would be a relief to undress. A long soak in a bath would be bliss. At present, that was as likely as Corinna coming to his tent and seducing him. He coiled the chart. 'I'm turning in.'

Mos was sitting cross-legged on the floor polishing a belt. He looked up, bleary-eyed. 'Yes, sir. I'll fetch water.' As he stoppered the polish, a figure in a hooded cloak appeared at the entrance of the tent.

'Corinna!' Verendus shut the tablet and jumped to his feet. Things were looking up. 'It's all right. Come in.'

She nodded to Mos and pushed back her hood as she stepped inside. Her hair was unkempt, tied in a loose braid; her eyes shiny as though she'd been crying. The past couple of days had been rough, and she was probably grieving for Magistra.

As though deciding that coming here was a mistake, Corinna stood silent. The bandages had been removed and her hands were clasped around a small jar. He couldn't see her palms to check if burn marks from the reins were healing. Afraid to upset her further, he withheld his protest that she should not have left the wagon without an escort.

She thrust the jar at him. 'Balm.'

Tiredness slipped like a cloak from his shoulders and he held out his shield arm. The bruising he'd suffered during the skirmish in the river had darkened to match the ink on his bicep. 'Will you check?' he said, taking the jar. 'I may have broken something.'

'You wouldn't be holding that jar if you had.'

He put down the balm. 'Mos, no hurry for the water.'

'Understood, sir.' He grinned and retreated outside.

Verendus closed the tent flap behind him.

'It's dark in here,' Corinna said.

'Is it?' he replied, doing nothing about it. This was too good an opportunity to waste. He fetched a wineskin, set two cups on the desk, and poured. He placed a stool beside her. 'Sit, please. Are your hands better?'

'Much. Though I haven't translated the piece you gave me this morning.'

'I hadn't expected you to.' Gods, she was on the defensive already.

Corinna remained standing, sipping wine and glancing past him to the back of the tent. The curtain was hooked open, revealing the low bed in the chamber beyond. She drew in her breath, but didn't speak.

'What is it, Corinna?' His hope that she was about to confide in him wavered, ceding to trepidation. 'You didn't come here just to bring me that balm.'

She turned the cup. 'What's happening in Germania? Men talk in loud voices, but they do not explain.'

Verendus was conscious of both relief and regret: this was not the root of her distress. No, he suspected that stemmed from the Temple, an incident so serious Magistra had placed her in his care. He wondered again if Corinna had been caught with a sentry. He couldn't bear to ask. She was watching him, waiting for his answer. He tried to reassure. 'There was unrest following the sudden death of Emperor Domitianus. Legionaries were angry, wanted a thorough investigation. Legate Sentorus is on his way to deal with them.'

'Then he has departed Britannia. I overheard the auxiliaries complaining there aren't enough troops left to oversee that province. Those with families there are troubled.'

'The need in Germania Inferior is greater,' Verendus said, though he supposed this posting could be the next move in Galenius' plot against Emperor Flavio. For such a plot to succeed, legionary support was essential. And Sentorus was the brother of Galenius' adoptive father. Nothing like keeping power in the family.

'You speak Germani. Will you be sent north?'

The question unexpected, he faltered. '…this rebellion involved our legionaries, not the locals. My language skills would not be relevant.'

'Are you often in Germania?'

Whatever gave her that idea? He kept his tone light. 'There are many dialects. Fes taught me Saxtili, he says my accent's terrible. Saffi wasn't impressed.'

Corinna rubbed her throat. The skin reddened to a rash as red as the wine to stain her skin. She was working up to something. Something he would not like. She stopped rubbing, and said, 'When we landed in Gallia you removed Saffi's slave collar... you spoke to her in a Germani dialect. Something you said upset her. What did you say? Was it about her hair?'

A strange question. Sensing a trap, he took his time, sipping wine as he remembered. He had crouched on the shore beside the slave girl and cut the leather collar from her neck. Yes, that was it. 'Something about the collar,' he said, studying Corinna as he spoke, trying to gauge her motives. 'It was one of those tight leather things with a ringed metal fastening. I thought it harsh she should wear it.'

Frowning, Corinna considered. 'Are you certain that's all you said?'

Verendus shrugged. He'd hardly spoken to the girl. Why must women make such drama from trivialities?

Corinna knocked back her wine and peered into the cup like a *haruspex* interpreting an omen. She looked up and her eyes bored through him. A cold splinter of dread pricked the pit of his stomach. Still glaring, she said crisply, 'Saffi told me about Germania.'

'Corinna, don't.'

'Why not? You served there.'

'It was war...' He heard tension in his voice. 'I won't speak of it.'

'War? An unprovoked attack on a Saxtili village.' She clanked down her cup. 'Saffi told me what the soldiers did to her. She was thirteen!'

Verendus flinched; Corinna may as well have slapped him. Images of a Saxtili village near Grenorum flashed into his mind. The fire and the blood. The stink of burning flesh. And the screaming, so much screaming. Hundreds of legionaries on the rampage, and he'd been powerless to stop the slaughter.

That was a decade ago. Corinna was talking about a different time, a different village, but the insinuation remained. If Saffi had been thirteen, then the raid on her village would have been two or three years ago. He knew nothing about it. The accusation that he'd been involved, coupled with the realisation that Corinna's opinion of him had sunk so low, filled him with cold rage. His words emerged as a whisper. 'Do not think that of me.'

Silent, she stared at him. 'I don't,' she said, at last, and slid his binder from under the wax tablet. 'What's this?'

Verendus exhaled. She'd accepted his word. Truly, the gods were smiling on him. Recovering his wits, he took the binder. At Alba he'd made a sketch of Corinna – the face drawn from memory, the body from imagination. There were other women in there too. He wasn't sure how she would react to his drawings of Drusilla, Nellis, et al, and didn't care to find out. 'Just a few sketches.' He secured it in his satchel. 'More wine?'

She nodded and tapped the parchment scroll. 'And this?'

'My chart.' He let her unroll it while he poured. 'I was checking the route.'

'It's beautiful. What are these numbers?'

'Distances between towns and forts.' He pointed to the miniature citadel that denoted Avennio. 'This is where we are camped.'

Leaning past him, she unfurled another swathe of parchment, moving the chart in a westerly direction, so close now that her body brushed against his. Unable to trust himself, he stepped back.

The chart was spreading across the desk. She furled the eastern side and moved on west. Nemausus, Tolosa, Lignora – home of the last Ennean tribe in the Empire.

Her braid of hair slipped aside revealing the perfect line of her neck. His heart quickened and a surge of desire coursed through him. Despite her coolness, he was convinced she had a heart of fire. The prospect was intoxicating. He had only to reach out.

She turned, lifted her hand, and the chart coiled and closed with a snap.

'What were you looking for?' he asked casually, she mustn't guess what was on his mind.

Her eyes narrowed. Conversely, he had the feeling that she was the one hiding something. 'I wasn't looking for anything.' She reached for the jar and scooped a dollop of balm. 'Sit down.'

He did as asked, catching his breath as she touched him.

'Does it sting?'

'No.' A tingling sensation warmed him. Her cold fingers glided over his skin, stroking, caressing, traversing his forearm, sending a shock of excitement down through his torso to his groin – but he would not tell her that. He inhaled air fragrant with lavender, focused, and said, 'With Fortuna's favour, we should reach Viorum on the morning after the morrow. It's a fine city. There's a new place near the Forum that I have on good authority serves the best seafood in this province.'

'Seafood? Viorum is miles from the coast.'

'I'm assured it's a place of quality. I would like to take you there. Yes?'

'You've more important things to do than amuse me,' she said, though an expression that may have been curiosity lit her face.

'I can't think of any. You're smiling. Say yes.'

'Maybe…'

As she put down the jar, a compulsion to catch hold of her hand and not let go seized him. He stood, towering over her. Corinna drew back, eyes wide in alarm.

Verendus swallowed his disappointment and told himself it wasn't he but the uniform that had startled her. He must remain calm. Must not make this worse. 'It's late,' he said gently. 'Come, I'll walk you to the wagon.'

CHAPTER XII

The mood in the camp was no better in the morning. Verendus consoled himself that every step brought him closer to Viorum and the Temple of Vesta, where he could deposit the codex. As soon as they arrived in the city, he would send word to Tribune Aquinus at the castrum and arrange a meeting – preferably on neutral ground. If Galenius was plotting against Emperor Flavio, the tribune would take steps to counter the threat.

There was Corinna to consider, too. He'd have to find somewhere safe for her. Governor Peronius had arranged for them to stay at a house he owned, but if the Praetorians picked up the trail that was the first place they'd look.

The turma passed another milestone, and he reckoned his confidence in reaching the city on the following morning was justified. If the turma upped the pace it might be possible to reach Viorum tonight, though that would mean negotiating the last mile or so in the dark.

Ahead, the road met the river's steady course and the auxiliaries began their usual grumble about stopping for a rest. Bretorus told them to shut up; Quintus raised his hand, and shouted, 'Halt!'

As Verendus turned to overrule him, Quintus apologised, and said, 'I need to stretch my legs and this looks as good a place as any.'

The auxiliaries reined in on a ridge beside the river. Murvaro dismounted and scrambled down the steep bank to the water. Several auxiliaries trailed behind, scattering loose stones beneath their boots.

Eldoran climbed atop a boulder. He scanned the view and pointed west to a distant aqueduct. Verendus followed his line of sight. As perfect as an architect's model, and built of the same pale limestone that lined the ravine, it spanned the river in a three-tiered colonnade of rounded arches, the bright blue water glittering beside sun-bleached banks.

On the bank below, auxiliaries shed their clothes and splashed into the river. Murvaro swam to an archipelago of flat rocks. He dragged himself out of the water, lurched to his feet, and strutted from one rock to another, whooping as he went. With luck, he'd slip and fall in.

Despite his assertion that he needed to stretch his legs, Quintus remained in the saddle. He turned his horse and, with a single trooper as escort, cantered up the vine-carpeted hillside. Any fears of a Helutti ambush seemingly forgotten.

Decurion Bretorus watched them depart, rubbing his beard and muttering like a disgruntled soothsayer. It surprised Verendus that the decurion hadn't accompanied them.

'Was told to wait here,' said Bretorus. 'There's a shrine in yonder wood. The tribune was struck with a desire to visit.'

'Indeed? He's in some haste.' If the idiot wanted to risk his neck, Verendus wasn't about to run after him. He glanced at the low sun and calculated how long he was prepared to wait.

The wait was briefer than expected. Auxiliary Portoc's solitary return confirmed Verendus' suspicion that Quintus had no intention of visiting a shrine.

Colour drained from Bretorus' face. He marched over. 'Where is he, Piggy?'

The chubby-faced auxiliary had the look of a boy caught sticky-faced in a peach tree. 'At his cousin's villa, sir. Spurius Decimius Peronius presents his…' He faltered, brow creasing as he tried to remember.

'Compliments,' snapped Bretorus.

'That's right, sir. We're all invited to dine. I was sent back to lead the way.'

'We'll not reach Viorum tonight,' Verendus said. Dinner was bound to escalate into a five-day binge. They should refuse the invitation and continue with the taxes to Viorum.

No, it wouldn't work. Without Quintus' signature on the documents the taxes could not be deposited, and he – Verendus – could not discharge his duty to the governor. With little choice in the matter, he accepted the invitation. It was up to him to ensure that first thing on the morrow, Quintus was back on the road.

Speculation revived the troops. All were hungry and most were damp from their swim. Of those who had gone in only Murvaro was dry, having used Marinus' tunic to towel himself.

Eldoran climbed down from the boulder and said he would continue to the city alone.

'The highway runs through the necropolis,' Verendus said. 'It will be dusk when you pass through. You should not travel unaccompanied.' An idea stirred and took shape. He could get word to Tribune Aquinus tonight. 'I must send Mos ahead to Viorum with a message – you can watch each other's backs.' Both knew that Eldoran would watch over Mos, but that went unsaid.

Verendus dashed out the missive, found one of the cylinders for diplomatic correspondence in the kit, and wound the parchment inside. He assembled a ring of stones, then placed parchment scraps and dry grass within. All rather time consuming, but the missive was for the tribune's eyes only. It must be sealed properly.

Verendus took the stick of red wax from his drawing kit and set it down ready. He regarded his signet ring, the Praetorian eagle carved into the square carnelian setting. Just as well it was this way around. His finger was still swollen, he couldn't have removed the ring to flip the setting over to the Vedius family emblem.

He found fire-steel and flint, and crouched beside the tinder. As he struck the steel across the edge of the flint sparks flared, sprinkling the dry grass. He set down his tools and, cupping his hands, breathed life into the glow. Working quickly, he dipped the wax into the flame, dripped a few red blobs over the ribbon ties on the document cylinder, and pressed the ring's setting into the soft wax to leave a miniature impression of an eagle. He stamped out the little fire and summoned Mos.

The boy was disappointed about missing dinner, though he cheered up when handed a silver *denarius* with the missive.

In addition, Verendus gave him enough coin for a respectable inn just inside the city walls where they had stayed before. He repeated the instructions and Mos trotted off along the road with Eldoran.

After tightening the girth of Plum's saddle, Verendus remounted and set off beside Portoc at the head of the column.

The auxiliaries followed, chattering about the prospect of a good dinner. The track ascended past vines and olive groves, through terraced fields and an apricot orchard bright with blossom, then cut a wide arc around a walled perimeter to where a slate-tiled hut stood beside the road. Iron gates barred the way ahead.

Verendus had a vague recollection that this land was part of an old estate, but not that Spurius or his family owned it. Spur rented a house in Viorum, though he spent much of his time alternating between the family's home in Rema and their holiday villa on Italia's west coast.

A sentry dressed in a smart brown uniform emerged from the hut. Recognising Portoc, he opened the gates and waved the turma inside. The track wound through woodland, past a grey-green lake with a waterside temple dedicated to Minerva, and emerged on the terrace of a palatial villa. Verendus had it on good authority that despite the family's apparent wealth, Spurius was heavily in debt. His father, low in funds following a questionable business venture, could not bail him out. Life was on the up if the prodigal son could afford such a stately residence.

Beyond the terrace, the view opened out over rolling hills of fields and woodland to the distant city of Viorum. Verendus discerned a pale stripe of road cutting through the green – the highway that he should be riding along. Tomorrow, he told himself.

The villa dated to the time of the Republic and had been enlarged in a style sympathetic to the original design. A cart piled with sacks and amphorae stood beside the open front door. Ladders, scaffolding planks, and lengths of lead pipe were ranged against the wall where two builders were mixing plaster in a great vat. Somewhere inside the building a hammer pounded. Aromas of paint, smoke, and roasting meat drifted on the warm air.

Auxiliary Portoc led them past the villa, through landscaped gardens ornamented with statues and fountains, to a vast clearing where three pavilions of blue and yellow striped canvas were staked in a row. At the far side of the clearing, a giant of a man in a bloodied apron was roasting a carcass of venison over a fire. Slaves were unloading a cart, stowing amphorae and hampers under an awning. It appeared the turma was expected.

As Verendus reined in at the clearing's edge, Quintus and his cousin came out of the central pavilion. Spurius Decimius Peronius welcomed Verendus with a regal flip of the hand and called him over. Though dressed modestly in tunic and breeches, Spur looked as sleek and groomed as if he'd passed the day at the baths. Since their last meeting three years ago, the senator's son had gained weight and his dark hair had acquired an artificial sheen.

He greeted Verendus with exaggerated delight and said he'd been hunting, which explained the clothes. 'Quin's been telling me about your encounter with the ghastly Helutti tribe. Haven't seen the buggers myself, but we're sheltered here in our little Elysium.' With a sweep of his manicured hand, he indicated the elegant pavilions. 'See, I'm living the simple life under canvas. Redecoration will take months.' He gestured towards the villa. 'I'm checking on progress. Crack the whip, banish delays. The estate's to be a wedding gift from Father. He's here, you know.'

'Here?' Verendus snapped to attention.

'Not literally here,' said Spurius, laughing at Verendus' reaction. 'He's in Viorum for a few days, lecturing at the *Ministerium*. Ensuring the new ministers are worth their salt.'

Verendus nodded, a plan forming. Spur's father was a senator of Rema. It would be useful to ask his opinion of events in the capital, perhaps secure his support.

Spur was still talking. '…this place is adequate enough, but it's frightful inside. Belonged to one of Domitianus' cronies – the décor is so last age.'

No doubt Spur's father was paying for redecoration. Despite his steely political repute, the senator was a soft touch where his only son was concerned. But where had he raised the funds?

On Spur rambled, barely pausing for breath as a slave brought water and towels so Verendus could wash his face and hands. Other slaves brought bread, olives, and silver goblets of wine. Verendus drained his cup and the day slipped away.

CHAPTER XIII

Corinna didn't know why the turma had stopped outside the villa on the hillside, although Verendus' solemnity when he knocked on the wagon door to ask her to dress for dinner implied something had displeased him. She asked if Saffi could accompany them, but he said, 'No. I'll fetch you at sundown, but Saffi will eat in the wagon.'

It had been Corinna's intention to work on the translation. The bumps and jolts of the road meant she could only work when the wagon was stationary, and it was easier on her eyes to have the door and shutters open. With the feeling it would be simpler to comply with his request, she changed into the green tunic he'd given her at Alba. Over this she draped the matching *palla*, pinning the mantle with a pair of brooches – one at each shoulder to keep it in place – as was the custom at the Temple. A small act of familiarity in this unsettled world.

Dorcas combed Corinna's hair and pinned it in a neat coil. At least the dinner was being held in one of the pavilions. It would spare her the ordeal of going inside the villa. She doubted Verendus understood her apprehension; such grand surroundings would hold no dread for him. His parents probably lived in a similar place; the entire village of her childhood home would fit within those stuccoed walls.

Corinna put on the jade earrings, her fingers trembling as she secured them. She would need a sniff of somniferum to steady her nerves. She wasn't hungry. Why must Verendus insist on involving her in his arrangements?

Outside, a man was roasting a carcass of meat over a fire. Shouts and laughter filled the air. Across the clearing, troops had pitched their leather tents and set larger ones for the officers at the centre near the wagon. Beyond stood the three huge pavilions.

As shadows closed around the clearing and lanterns were lit, a glimmer of anticipation roused the camp. Through the part-open wagon door, she saw a formidable figure in a white toga and caught her breath. Verendus passed through the activity of the little campsite with leonine grace, his toga impeccably swathed, the excess folds of cloth draped over his left arm. Noticing her, he quickened his step. The folds slipped, he almost stumbled. He stopped, gathered up the slack, and approached at more dignified pace.

He grinned. 'See, I'm rendered helpless by the sight of you.'

In spite of herself, Corinna smiled. 'Do you always travel with a spare toga?'

'Gods, no. But this thing cost a small fortune, and I didn't care to leave it at Alba.' He met her eyes. 'I didn't care to leave anything precious there.'

Telling herself not to be taken in by his charm, Corinna allowed him to lead her to the largest of the three pavilions. Laughter rang out; the din of several voices speaking at once. The other guests were already inside. She hesitated but Verendus led on, beneath a wide pergola and into an atrium. At the side, on a console table, stood a *lararium*. The intricately carved shrine resembled a palatial dovecote. It was lit with tiny lamps and inhabited by a family of exquisite bronze figurines set around an altar piled with raisins. Following Verendus' lead, she bowed respectfully.

'We leave our shoes here,' he said, as two slave girls arrived bearing towels and bowls of scented water. 'Spur's father is Governor Peronius' older brother,' he explained, half-closing his eyes like a pampered cat while a girl washed his hands.

He's enjoying this, Corinna thought, as the girl bent to wash his feet. He loves the attention. She dipped her hands in the water, took a towel from the other girl, and dried herself.

A high-pitched screech split the air. Without waiting for Verendus, she crossed to the far corner of the atrium where swathes of fabric formed a niche. Within stood a wooden upright. 'Poor thing,' she said.

The green parrot squawked in agreement. Eyeing her inquisitively, it shuffled along the perch to which it was chained.

'That creature wouldn't survive a day in the wild,' said Verendus, interrupting her plan to release it. 'Come and eat.'

As a slave drew aside a curtain, Verendus took her arm and they passed by a pair of wooden obelisks as tall as a man. The vast crimson cavern beyond was so luxurious she could almost believe herself back at Castellum Alba. Thick rugs carpeted the floor, statues stood amid potted palms, and a lantern of coloured glass hung from the high, conical roof.

Corinna faltered. She'd been right: other guests were there, reclined on couches around a low table heavy with silver and lamps. Conversation tailed off as they turned to stare. Verendus exchanged greetings; he knew most of those present and introduced her by *praenomen* only, for which she was grateful. The less they knew about her the better.

He led her forward, along the back of a couch, to their places. 'It's only for a few hours.'

Corinna's heart sank. Somehow, she must get through this. She had never dined like this before. Dining in a reclined position was something rich people did. She'd read it required poise and technique. Everyone would see at once that she was a nobody. She glanced around for Eldoran. She hadn't seen him since this morning, although the grumpy decurion was there, perched like a harpy on the side of their couch, sour-faced despite the merriment.

The space between table edge and couch was narrow. Corinna followed Verendus' lead and approached from the lower side of the sloping couch. She sat carefully, trying to be elegant as she manoeuvred, which was tricky as the seat was angled to set the diner slightly higher than the table. Without slipping, she got into a reclined position on the cushions beside him. It felt most improper to be lying so close to him, especially in the presence of others. She propped herself on her left elbow as she'd seen diners in pictures do. Once settled, she looked around to ensure her pose mirrored that of the other guests.

Conversations resumed, the low hum of voices welcome after the hush. Her relief that she was not the only woman amongst the diners evaporated. The other women were metropolitan, professional beauties, vibrant as butterflies in their filmy draperies. As a handmaid, Corinna hadn't cared about clothes and fashions. Beside their glittering jewellery and elaborately styled hair she felt plain.

Verendus leaned closer to whisper that the man on the opposite couch was their host, Spurius Decimius Peronius. Despite a difference in age – Spurius looked well into his thirties, perhaps fifteen years older than Quintus – the resemblance between the cousins was remarkable. Both were tanned and dark-haired, with melancholy, long-lashed eyes. Both handsome and well aware of it.

Plush in his white toga and crowned with a wildflower garland, Spurius reclined imperiously beside a vacant-eyed blonde. With her painted face and silky tunic cinched tight beneath her bust the girl had an aura of maturity, though her smooth, plump features suggested she was fourteen or fifteen. The bejewelled, flame-haired woman beside her was older, more sophisticated. She appraised Corinna with an aloof glance and continued her conversation with Spurius.

Two young patricians and a woman with a laugh that could shatter glass occupied the third couch. The governor's son, Quintus, was squeezed in beside them. He had removed the bandage he'd been sporting for the past few days. No trace of a wound on his neck.

A barrel-chested man, little higher than his recumbent master, stood behind Spurius' couch. Corinna had never seen such a short man before. Curiosity ceded to discomfort when she caught him ogling her, his eyes twinkling like coal, shifty as the beads plaited in his black beard. When she stuck out her tongue, he whispered to Spurius who laughed but didn't share the joke.

A hush descended as two identical slave girls came in, carrying a *situla* between them, straining under the weight of the bucket-shaped vessel that gleamed with silvered images of Bacchus amid grapevines. The twins set it before Spurius and his lazy gaze slid over their tall, well-muscled bodies.

Spurius dipped a ladle into the situla and tasted, sloshing the liquid around his mouth. Satisfied, he nodded approval. The wine was poured into a jug and served. The spectacle continued as the cook wheeled in a huge wooden trolley bearing a haunch of venison. The big, red-faced man had donned a clean apron and, with consummate skill, he carved slices of roast meat. A trio of musicians entered, playing as they walked to the back of the pavilion, where they stood, plucking a jaunty tune. Raising their voices above the melody, the diners paid them no heed.

More slaves arrived and placed little braziers on each table. With a flaming taper, a slave lit the braziers and steaming dishes were set over them to keep warm. For Corinna, accustomed to the Temple's meagre board, the choice was bewildering. In addition to the roast meat, there were cured meats and tiny pies; savoury pastries and sweet pastries; vine-leaf parcels filled with minced veal; snails puréed with garlic and stuffed back into polished shells; the bright orange roe of sea-urchins; whitebait dusted in flour and fried until crisp – each delicacy presented as a bite-size morsel.

With the exception of Bretorus, who sat stiffly upright, all the diners followed their host's example and ate lying down. Slaves refilled glasses and proffered food, using a slender tool with a hook on the end to winkle the snails from their shells. The table was piled with dishes until the air in the canvas room warmed to a heady blend of spices, smoke, and scented oil. Wine flowed and manners waned, though of the men present, only Bretorus appeared disquieted, the odd man out in his mail-coat, his face set so grim Corinna feared it might crack. He looked as uncomfortable as she felt, though she found no solace in that.

In a bid for calm, Corinna began adding up all the different dishes, but kept losing count. With the impression that someone was watching, she glanced at the couch across the table. The attention was directed not at her but at Verendus. The flame-haired woman fluttered kohled lashes and smiled at him. 'Commendator, how lovely to see you. It's been a while.'

'I'm flattered you remember me,' he said politely.

'Hard to forget,' she purred, twisting a curl of her impossibly coiffed hair about her finger.

From her reclined angle Corinna couldn't tell if Verendus smiled back, but the certainty he had bedded that woman crushed her. A flood rose within her, a tide of jealousy. She pictured him beside the woman, stroking that long, silky hair. Surely it was a wig.

Corinna told herself she didn't care what he did. Soon the time would come to ask him to arrange for her to meet the Lignoran named Landren who was resident in Viorum. Composure was required. She would need to be at her most persuasive, though not so eager that Verendus questioned her motives. Until then, she would continue the translation. She suspected her efforts had not disclosed the information he was hoping for. Perhaps that was a good thing. The more he asked of her, the more she could ask of him. How vexing to be a woman, to be under the guardianship of a man and abide by his rules. She had scarcely more agency than a slave.

Last night she had opened the chart on his desk. It had been easy to discover the information. He'd pointed to the miniature city that indicated Viorum; it was then a matter of unfurling the chart a little and memorising the places. She pictured it. Viorum was located on the highway system. No highway ran west directly from the city, just a series of minor roads winding through rough terrain. Lignora seemed further away than ever.

Had Verendus sensed her disappointment? When he'd asked what she was looking for, she had opened the balm in an attempt to distract him. But she had been weak, imagining his embrace as she massaged his arm. His intake of breath told her he'd been thinking of it too.

'I hear the Nemusan was in great haste to leave,' said Quintus, jolting Corinna from her thoughts.

'He had business in Viorum,' Verendus replied.

So, know-all Dorcas was right. Eldoran had departed. Corinna reached for her glass. He hadn't even bid her farewell.

Verendus' revelation raised a murmur of interest. The two young patricians beside Quintus looked up from their food. The louder of the pair, a florid man called Avitus, shredded an asparagus spear with prominent teeth, swallowed audibly, and said, 'Unsociable race.'

Corinna shifted position; she wasn't used to dining on her side. Indigestion stabbed her ribs. The heat in the tent was stifling. She tried to sit, but slid closer to Bretorus who regarded her warily. Verendus pulled her back, pressed closer, his body warm beside hers.

As he stroked her waist, she reminded herself that the arm beneath the folds of cloth bore the mark of the Praetorian Guard. A wolf in sheep's clothing. She should tell him to stop, should push him away. Or perhaps it was better to submit. Upset him, and it would be harder to persuade him to arrange the meeting.

Her thoughts swam, her body floated. His hand slid further up her torso, strayed to the curve of her breasts, waking a pulse between her thighs. His lips brushed her cheek. 'Oh, Corinna, I want to kiss you there.'

Yes... No! How could he tell what she was feeling? But, of course, it was all a game to him. A game he'd played many times before.

She pulled free, swung her legs to the front of the couch, and sat up abruptly. He reached for her hand; she couldn't rise.

'Losing your touch, V?' said Avitus, a smirk on his florid face.

Verendus ignored him, though his hold tightened. Corinna dug her nails into his palm and he released her.

'Now, now, children. Play nicely.' Spurius helped himself to a fig. He took a bite and fed the rest to the blonde. 'You've yet to congratulate me on my betrothal, V.'

'Congratulations,' Verendus said blandly. 'I trust you have a good repertoire of bedtime stories.'

Someone sniggered. There was a moment of awkward silence. Quintus blinked, and exclaimed, 'Here's to Spur and Decimia… and to strengthening the family bond!' He raised his glass and the other men echoed the toast. Bretorus concentrated on his food.

'I'll need to fatten your sister up, eh, Quin,' said Spurius, and slapped the blonde's thigh. 'I thought her thin last time we met.'

'She's been eating like a bird,' said Quintus. 'Wedding nerves.'

'Things will change after we're married.'

Quin's sister? Corinna had assumed Spurius was betrothed to the blonde girl. Clearly, this wasn't the case. An image formed in her mind: the dining hall at Castellum Alba, a skinny girl crossing the floor behind the governor and his wife. Spurius was old enough to be Decimia's father. More than old enough. 'She's a child!' blurted Corinna, and everyone stared. Was no one else appalled by the arrangement?

'And after a night with me, she'll be a woman.' Spurius dabbed his lips with a napkin while he waited for the laughter to subside. 'Married life will be a pleasant change. Viorum's dull and I'm bored with the track.'

'What a shame,' said Verendus. 'You used to have a reputation there.'

Spurius adjusted his garland, patting an errant wisp of hair into place. 'Have I told you about my new chariot horses? Exceptional. All four with coats the lightest grey. You'd be hard pressed to tell 'em apart. They're running in the festival's big race. You must all come and cheer.' He acknowledged the chorus of approval with an expansive wave of his hand, and said, 'Cor-eee-nna…' drawing out the name in an exultant, nasal whine. 'I'll send you my colours – sapphire-blue.'

'I thought you were bored with the track,' Corinna said.

Verendus gave an appreciative snort and slipped his arm around her.

'Too lenient,' said Spurius. 'If she were my woman I'd have her whipped for such cheek.'

'Then it's as well she isn't,' Verendus replied.

Corinna glared; she had no doubt Spurius meant what he said. She eyed the slender winkling-hook, which a slave had left on the table. I killed the last man who threatened me, she thought. Right now, I'd gladly kill you.

If Spurius perceived her contempt, it didn't shut him up. 'Speaking of punishment,' he said, 'allegedly, Legate Sentorus is on his way to discipline the Third.' He brushed a crumb from the blonde's tunic and rested his hand on her breast. She giggled and reached for another fig.

'The Third Gemina?' said Avitus. 'Wasn't that your legion, V?'

The muscles in Verendus' arm tensed, though he didn't reply.

Avitus broke the silence. 'I don't understand why those troops got steamed up about the death of Emperor Domitianus. Whoever dispatched the old goat did us all a favour.' He cast a cool gaze around the tent, challenging anyone to contradict him. No one spoke. 'The Third should have been disbanded years ago.

We're reliant on that rabble to hold the border. One expects altercations from auxiliaries; legionaries should know better.'

Bretorus clanged down his knife. 'Never had any trouble with my lads, sir.'

Guests turned to regard the decurion as though they had only just noticed him.

'Calm down,' said Avitus, amused by the outburst. 'It's a question of heritage, of blood. Your *lads*, where are they from?'

'Mainly recruited in Britannia, sir.'

'Exactly! One can't expect true loyalty from a non-citizen troop of Celtic peasants.'

Bretorus flinched so sharply the couch shook. 'Tell that to the families of my lads what died collecting Rema's taxes!'

'Shut it, Decurion!' barked Verendus. 'Apologies, Avitus, feelings run high at present.' He sat up. Leaning across Corinna so he was closer to Bretorus, he lowered his voice, and said, 'That perfumed turd's not worth wrecking your career over.'

Bretorus mumbled something that sounded like a growl and apologised.

'In future, you'd do well to remember your place, Decurion.' Avitus feigned a yawn. 'As I was explaining before being so rudely interrupted, the Third should be disbanded. Some of those bad apples have been rotting awhile. Legate Sentorus will get to the root of the problem.'

'As a former commander of the Third, he's well-equipped to,' said Verendus.

'Steady, V, you're snarling.' Avitus grinned. It wasn't a confident grin. Like a boy with a stick goading a chained bear, he was safe as long as he didn't get too close.

Verendus wasn't going to play. He turned to the decurion and asked about the morrow's journey. The snub irked Avitus.

He snatched up his glass, drained it in one, and snapped his fingers for more. A serving girl hastened to oblige. Rising unsteadily to his feet, Avitus told her to put down the jug. Then, he grasped her by the waist and hauled the struggling girl over the table.

Quintus laughed. 'Don't think she likes you.'

'She will.' Avitus squeezed the girl's throat. He whispered in her ear, and she lowered her eyes and stopped struggling. He pulled her onto his lap and plunged a hand inside her tunic.

Oblivious, Verendus and Bretorus argued about the journey. No one cared about the girl. Corinna knew she must do something. But what?

She grabbed a fig from one of the serving platters and threw. It smacked Avitus square on the forehead and slid to the floor.

He looked up, face reddening. 'Who did that?'

'I did,' said Corinna. 'Let her go!' Her voice sounded shrill. Around the tent the laughter died. Reproachful faces glared at her.

Clutching the girl's neck with one hand, Avitus seized a napkin with the other and wiped his brow. 'I don't take orders from you.'

Verendus stood. 'Then take one from me. Let the girl go.'

Avitus glowered but had the sense not to answer back. Like a scolded dog eager to please, Spurius glanced from one to the other, and said, 'Let her go. Mustn't upset our guests. Besides, who'll pour the wine?'

Top lip twisted in a sneer, Avitus shrugged and discarded the girl with his dirty napkin.

'Fetch the dancer,' Spurius shouted with a note of desperation.

Bretorus grunted in disapproval as Corinna clambered up. Ignoring the howls of laughter, she dashed past the couches and ran outside. Across the clearing, off-duty auxiliaries sat drinking around the campfire. Someone whistled and called out, inviting her to join them.

Corinna hastened on towards the wagon, the ground rough underfoot. Damn, she'd left her shoes behind. Footsteps followed. The cool night air stung her lungs, but she quickened her pace and didn't turn; she knew that firm, measured step. She broke into a run, but he caught up and overtook, forcing her to stop.

'You forgot these.' Verendus held out her shoes.

As he knelt to put them on her feet, the toga slipped, baring his chest. Trying to keep a straight face, Corinna took the shoes.

'I'll never get used to wearing this,' he said, voice slurred as he pulled up the toga. 'Come back inside.'

'No,' she replied, surprised by her own vehemence. Her head was clearer, the haze lifting. Clarity rushed in. Somewhere, past the line of tents, lay the city they might have arrived at today. Night had shrunk the world to hold them here. 'Why did we have to delay? Aren't you impatient to reach Viorum?'

'Spur's father is a senator of Rema. It would be imprudent to upset his son, especially as I've decided to ask a favour of him.'

'Of the father?' asked Corinna, curious in spite of herself.

'Indeed. He's in Viorum to oversee changes at the Ministerium.' He led her back to the pavilion and beneath the pergola. Music resounded. A slave boy emerged from the atrium and stood attentively. Verendus sent him away.

The music grew louder, people clapping time with the quickening beat. Corinna frowned at the curtained entrance. 'Why did you want me there?'

'Is it not obvious?'

'If you want a woman, I'm sure Spurius can provide one.'

'I prefer your company.' He held out his hand. 'Come back inside. They said you left because we quarrelled.'

'And you heed what they say?' She hated that he cared what Spurius and his horrid friends thought. 'I've had all I can stomach of your world. I don't belong.'

'This is not my world.'

'Whatever it is, it's a cruel place. I want no part of it.' She hugged herself. She didn't need Verendus. Not once they reached Viorum. If he refused to arrange a meeting with Landren, or if Landren could not be found, she still had the purse of coins from Magistra. And she could sell some clothes and the showy earrings. Surely that would raise enough coin to buy safe passage to Lignora, land of her father.

'Would you rather be back at the Temple?' Verendus asked.

Corinna told herself to be careful. Don't say too much. As she formed a response, she realised truth was the best answer. 'At the Temple I longed to be free. I never thought I would miss its walls and doors. There my life had rhythm, purpose. Now I am adrift.'

He considered her words, as if trying to imagine himself in that strange environment. A light came into his eyes. 'No, not adrift. Listen, my father has a maxim: better a fish in the river than one in the pond.'

She pondered this. 'So I'm in the river and must accept that?'

'We're both in the river… but we do not have to swim alone. We could swim together.'

That sounded serious – if only he meant as equals. It could never be so in his world. Not for a woman; not for someone of her class. 'I ask nothing of you.'

His expression of earnest expectancy crumpled, and his hand dropped to his side. In that moment she wanted to tell him of the Seer's prediction, of how Fate's wings had touched her. Wanted to trust him and confess to killing Torvius. Wanted to shed the burden she'd carried since that night at the Temple. How easily the quill had glided in, piercing the centurion's eye, shattering its pale opacity. And then the blood. So much blood.

'I know something is troubling you,' Verendus said kindly. 'Something happened at the Temple. That's why Magistra released you into my care.'

And so he continued, soothing and probing. Corinna shook her head. Her throat contracted as though a noose tightened about it. Her mouth dried. She waited for him to finish talking. And when he did, she said nothing.

'Very well. No more questions. It's too fine a night for conversation.' He steered her into the shadow of an awning and turned her to face him. 'Cara...'

Cara. He had never called her beloved before. He stroked her arm, moving gently upwards, skimming the skin, tracing the line of her shoulder, blurring her body in a flurry of sensations. With the tip of his finger he tilted her chin. Cupping her face in his hands, he kissed her.

She didn't resist. Her body leaned, melting into his, breathing in lemon balm, cloves, and polished leather. A million sparks danced before her eyes and the feeling of standing on the edge of a great precipice overwhelmed her. One more step and she'd fall.

'Cara…' His voice was low, intense. 'Do you know how much I want you?'

'What?' Her vision cleared.

He took her hand and guided it to his loins. She didn't pull away, didn't want him to stop. Beneath the soft wool of his toga, he was rod-hard. His breath deepened as her fingers caressed him. In this moment, she had power over him. But she knew he'd want more. She slipped free and stepped back.

'Cara, what is it? What's the matter?'

She shook her head and tried to push past him.

Face sullen, he blocked her way. 'Well, Corinna, you're quite the tease.' His voice chilled. 'Torment a dog too much and he'll bite you.'

She glared up at him. 'I bite back!'

CHAPTER XIV

The rising sun glowed dimly on the horizon when Verendus emerged from his tent. After an evening of plentiful wine there were several sore heads among the auxiliaries clearing the camp. Piggy Portoc, infamous for being unable to handle his drink, had the pallor of overcooked pork. He got no sympathy from Decurion Bretorus, who told him to fetch a shovel and fill in the latrine pit.

Quintus staggered, blinking into the daylight like a newly released prisoner. Deaf to his pleas to stay and sleep it off, Verendus and Bretorus seized him roughly and hoisted him into the saddle.

Verendus rode at the head of the troop, pounding the highway with the zeal of a homesick recruit on first leave, determined to put distance between himself and the gaudy pavilions. Ahead, a mass of dark cloud hung heavy, weighing down the band of blue sky. The cloud thickened, so low now that it seemed to press his skull.

Woodland ceded to fields and orchards. With traffic light on the highway, the turma reached the next milestone promptly. Verendus reassured himself that the diversion to Spur's villa hadn't cost as much time as he'd feared, for in doing so they had bypassed the busy city of Arausio. Soon they would reach Viorum.

The road climbed, levelled out, and there was the necropolis, the spectre of Viorum looming grey in the distance. In accordance with custom, the dead dwelt outside the city, assigned their own clans and cliques as they had been in life. Tombstones and memorials for soldiers lined the way. The graves were as many and varied as troops in a legion: brightly painted plaques, standing stones carved with an image of the deceased, and a mausoleum of polished marble, the remnants of burnt offerings on the altar before it.

As he rode by, Verendus bowed his head to men killed in the service of Rema and interred here, perhaps hundreds of miles from home. Bones and ashes now. Had they found their way to Elysium?

Those without honour also inhabited the roadside, their gibbets stretched in a stinking row of warning posts along the highway. Verendus usually sped past these horrors, scarcely glancing at the dead and dying criminals hanging there. Today he noticed. Most were hollow-eyed corpses, withered bodies decayed beyond recognition, an easy feast for scavengers. Sporadic wails of agony accompanied the *kraa, kraa* of carrion crows perched upon the crosses. Someone was alive.

The two crosses stood side-by-side – a man and a woman, stripped naked, their blackened arms outstretched and tied to a crossbeam. The letters **FUG** branded on their shorn heads marked the fugitives as runaway slaves. Flies crawled over their sun-scorched skin and swarmed about the bloody spikes that nailed their ankles to the uprights. Head lolling, the woman was almost gone. The man could only breathe by heaving himself up, thereby forcing down on the nails that pierced his heels. This torture would continue until his strength was spent and he sagged into asphyxiation. Lest someone intervene to rescue the pair or hasten their deaths, four soldiers sat breakfasting on a nearby tomb.

Verendus passed by, but could still hear the man's cries. He pondered the young pair's story – absconding lovers, brother and sister, strangers fated to die together? Corinna was right: the world was a cruel place.

The living existed beside the dead, crammed amid the larger tombs and mausoleums in makeshift constructions of crates and sackcloth. The denizens were up and going about their daily business; the greasy reek of cooking fires curdled with the stench of an open latrine.

At the turma's approach, a furore of activity stirred the slum. Filthy, barefoot children darted from the shelters and ran alongside, pleading for coins; pedlars with baskets of trinkets followed, blocking the road and agitating the horses. A sunburnt man in a sweat-stained tunic called out a greeting. As heads turned, he pulled away the tattered sheet that masked the entrance of the hovel beside him. Within, two naked girls sat huddled on a blanket.

'Special rates for soldiers,' the man shouted.

'Eyes forward!' barked Bretorus, silencing the whistles and cries of "how much?"

'High time the authorities sluiced this dump,' said Quintus. 'Flush out the dregs and sewer rats.'

Verendus rode on, glad that Corinna was shut in the wagon. He wished she couldn't hear the noise. Last night she had snapped at him like a wounded bird and refused his plea to return to the pavilion. More in fear than anger, he thought. What a fool he'd been, making advances as though she were a senator's wife at a seedy party. He could blame his fervour on too much wine, but that was a shabby excuse. No, he'd misread Corinna. He'd convinced himself she'd left the Temple because of an illicit liaison with a sentry. Ergo, he had presumed her to be experienced, available. The reality might be different.

Of course, he'd apologised. She hadn't listened. The sorrow in her eyes stung and he didn't know how to wipe it away. He'd escorted her to the wagon and returned to his own tent to drown his disappointment with more wine, and woken early with a rushing sound in his ears and the giddy sensation that the gods were sweeping him along like a leaf in a torrent.

Smoke rising from the workshops and cooking fires of Viorum's outlying settlements distorted the horizon, but the mood of foreboding clung like a sodden paenula cape and his sense of purpose diminished. On reaching the ramparts of Viorum and crossing the towered bridge over the river, the longed for relief didn't materialise. He made the sign against evil and rode on.

Within the city walls, in a cobbled square, stood a temple much like the one he'd visited near Alba. Again, despite misgivings from the small voice of caution that he was ceding to superstition, Verendus halted the turma and dismounted.

After giving thanks for his safe arrival, he asked the priest to bless the day's business. The ritual of sacrifice and black powder that had marked the start of his journey was repeated. This time the powder refused to light. More was fetched. But although this yielded a curl of acrid smoke, the priest's brow remained creased. 'The path is clouded. A storm brews. Be guarded in word and deed.'

Troubled, Verendus sent the turma ahead to the house in the city where Governor Peronius had arranged for them to stay. It would suffice for now.

He watched until the turma passed from view and went to meet Mos. The boy was sitting at a table outside the inn, the plate before him piled with bread and chunks of sausage, which he was dipping in a pot of *garum*.

He stood at Verendus' approach and offered the plate.

'No thanks, Mos.' The smell of fish sauce turned his stomach. 'Did you deliver the message?'

'Yes, sir. There's a reply.' Still chewing, he fished inside his cape and extracted a fold of parchment secured with the distinctive Praetorian Guard eagle.

With a frisson of unease, Verendus snapped the wax seal. The message was brief. Aquinus had an engagement to attend, but if he – Verendus – would report directly to the Castrum Viorum, they could speak in confidence there.

He re-read the message, assessing the risk. If the three Praetorians had pre-empted his arrival and sent word to the castrum, he could be walking into a trap. But Aquinus was an old friend, a trusted ally. Besides, if the tribune was intent on arresting him, that could be done anywhere in the city.

Mos scraped the plate and stuffed the last crust of bread into his mouth. Verendus sent him to ready his mount and went inside to speak with the innkeeper.

The arrangements took longer than anticipated, and Mos was waiting outside when he returned. As they rode off, Verendus explained that when the time came to continue their journey, Corinna would lodge here at the inn. 'If anything befalls me, then you must bring her here yourself. Payment has been made.'

Mos nodded gravely. 'What about Saffi, sir?'

'Saffi, too.'

During the journey, Verendus had rehearsed the meeting many times in his head, going over what he would tell Aquinus

– what to say and what to omit. Even so, he felt a twinge in his gut on entering the fortified building. He remembered the importance of appearing calm, of giving no cause for suspicion. In an effort to look the part, he tied the red satin sash of rank about his cuirass. While he waited in an anteroom, he toyed with the knot. It wouldn't sit right. The sash wasn't meant to be worn with a satchel. He felt conspicuous, but not in a good way. He sniffed his shoulder guards and tunic. Gods, he needed to bathe.

A guardsman arrived to inform him that Tribune Aquinus was absent, called away at dawn. The Principal also unavailable, *Optio* Matellius would deputise. Deciding it would be imprudent to leave now, Verendus followed the guard up a flight of gleaming marble stairs and along a passageway. The office at the end smelt musty, as if it hadn't been used in months. The window was shuttered and a solitary lantern hung from a hook in the ceiling. Sparsely furnished with a wooden desk and a few battered chairs, it looked as unwelcoming as the man who waited there.

Matellius rose, rapped his fist against his chest in salute, and in a tone that conveyed no regret, passed on the tribune's apologies. 'Be seated, Commendator.'

Verendus did so carefully, unsure if the chair was sturdy enough to take his weight. It creaked but mercifully didn't collapse. Matellius' chair was larger and high-backed. He was a bear of a man, with coarse dark hair and deep-set eyes that never seemed to blink. His fingernails were ridged and yellowing. Wiry hair sprouted on the back of his hands and grew thick on his arms. Leaning forward in his chair, he offered – in Aquinus' absence – to discuss whatever business Verendus had.

An outright refusal might arouse suspicion, so Verendus told how the turma had been attacked on the old north road.

As he expounded his theory that the attackers were a horde of escaped Helutti slaves, Matellius listened impassively, interrupting occasionally to verify that the scribe, standing attentively behind the chair, had logged a particular point. Matellius made additional notes, the stylus a twig in his bearpaw hand, the writing so scrawled that Verendus, peering across the desk, couldn't decipher it.

'What news from Auster Grenorum?' Verendus asked. Was this other, bigger threat of Helutti aggression in the north being addressed? 'Has Legate Sentorus reached the Third Legion's base?'

'I expect so,' said Matellius, checking the notes.

For such a grave matter of imperial security, the optio's lack of concern was lamentable. Determined to avenge the assassination of Emperor Domitianus, Third Legion Gemina was on the brink of revolt. Across the river in Barbarian Germania, the Helutti were building boats and calling on neighbouring tribes to fight with them against the Empire.

Last year he had crossed the Rhenus River, risked his life to survey a swathe of Helutti land and gather information. He'd sent warning to Prefect Secundus in Rema and camps along the border. With Secundus now in prison was that intelligence being acted on? 'Do you appreciate how vulnerable the Germanian border is?' Verendus asked, and receiving no reply, said, 'The Helutti are readying their boats. Attack is probable. If the Third revolt, who'll repel the barbarians?'

Matellius set down his stylus. 'No need to concern yourself. Legate Sentorus will have the matter in hand.'

Further questions were countered with the verbal dexterity of a sledgehammer. The optio was just as obtuse over Aquinus' whereabouts 'Rest assured, Commendator, Tribune Aquinus is due back in three days, maybe four.' Matellius snapped shut the tablet. He eased himself from his chair and opened the door. 'How long do you intend staying in Viorum, Commendator?'

'As long as necessary.'

On descending the stairs Verendus realised he hadn't left the address of the lodgings in case Aquinus returned early and wanted to send word. He didn't go back; he didn't trust Matellius with the information.

The priest at the Temple of Janus had foretold a storm. The first gusts were blowing, impeding his progress. He must wait to consult Tribune Aquinus. Only then could he and Mos head east for the Alps to find Fes. It wouldn't be easy. The journey was long and the going rough. It would take many days. Even longer to find Legate Capito and his legionary *vexillation* of a thousand troops. Perhaps he should lie low and weather the storm.

Outside, in the sunshine, Verendus reassured himself he'd weathered storms before. He crossed the forecourt and a weight lifted from his shoulders. He hadn't been arrested. No one had questioned him about the codex. The three Praetorians must have fallen for the ruse and ridden south to Narbo Martius.

'Nothing to report,' he told Mos, who was waiting beside their mounts. 'I have business at the Ministerium. Take the horses to the lodgings and unpack.'

'Yes, sir… which way?'

'North.' Verendus pointed across the forecourt to the gates, where a beggar in a patched grey cloak sat cross-legged in the dust. Hand outstretched, ponytailed head bent, he was spat at or ignored by passers-by in the busy street. A gang of men in grubby tunics loitered nearby, probably labourers hoping for work. A heavy-set, colossus of a man stood in their midst. Despite his proximity he seemed separate, detached from the other men and their discussion. His expression was blank; his eyes were fixed on Mos.

Verendus nudged the boy. 'Come, I'll go with you as far as the baths.'

As they passed the gates, the colossus wiped his nose with the back of his hand and turned away. The beggar raised his hood and disappeared into the crowd.

***

Viorum's baths were reputedly the finest in the province of Gallia Narbonensis, and a dazzling array of plaques in the vestibule bore shining testament to the generosity of local benefactors. In addition to several pools, the vast complex boasted a library and a gymnasium. A garden formed an oasis within where clients who preferred not to break sweat could relax and view proceedings through the arched windows of the *tepidarium* pools. Here, among the palms, business and pleasure met and mingled.

Verendus saw Mos safely on his way, paid the admission fee, and deposited his blades. He'd arranged to meet Quintus at the Ministerium, but it would be good to bathe first.

The place thrummed with noise and purpose. Queues for the food counters and beauty parlours snaked across a palatial atrium bright with white marble and gilded niches. Aromas of spicy food flavoured the air, vying with perfumes and the piquant herbs of the apothecary's booth.

Verendus strode through the crowd, catching glimpses of the mosaic floor as he went: a leaping swordfish here, the twining tentacles of an octopus there. On passing the dispensary booth, he recognised the medic he'd consulted earlier this year about the injury he'd suffered in Germania. The wound from the barbarian sword had been slow to heal, growing redder and sorer as the journey south progressed. The genial Graecian had provided a salve and a poultice of sweet-smelling herbs, which cooled the skin and calmed the pain. Just the person to wean Corinna off that bloody somniferum. Verendus decided to bathe, then return and engage him.

Signage above the triple-arched entrance of the baths denoted where men and women could part to bathe separately, though mixed bathing was also permitted. His pace slowed. Easy to pick up a girl in there, easy for someone like him. Time you reined that in, he told himself. The itch burned regardless. Corinna was no easy pick-up, which only increased her appeal. Last night he'd lain awake thinking about her, about what he'd like to do to her. Being patient was wretched.

At the arches, he glanced around like a guilty child. The heavy-set man he'd noticed at the castrum was standing by the atrium fountain. Verendus avoided meeting his eyes, but was certain the colossus was watching him. A former comrade hoping to scrounge a drink? With his upright stance and his tunic cinched short with a studded belt, the man had the look of a soldier.

No, screamed the voice of caution. *Leave!*

Verendus hesitated. He'd left his blades at the entrance. Collect them now and it would be obvious he was leaving. He passed beneath the mixed-bathing arch. Once out of sight of the atrium, he tipped an attendant to show him to a side door reserved for the establishment's more discreet clients. He emerged in a courtyard and cut through an alley. The blades could be collected later. Pray gods he wouldn't need them in the meantime.

He walked the length of a street lined with stalls selling coloured ribbons for the chariot races, stopping now and then to browse the wares, trying to blend in with the crowd while stealing a glance over his shoulder. Walk too quickly or break into a run and he would attract attention.

It appeared he had eluded the man; nevertheless, Verendus changed course twice before finding the food bar he intended bringing Corinna to. He chose a seat inside, a dim corner, and sat with his back to the wall, facing the open door and the street beyond.

Glaring afternoon sun thinned the crowd along the colonnaded shopfronts where a red-curtained litter waited, its muscular bearers standing idle beside, watching the door of a lamp shop and sweating in the heat. A roadside bar heaved with men slaking their thirst and jeering at a mime artist posing precariously atop a crate on the pavement. Oblivious, an old man and his dog dozed on a bench.

A slave brought a bowl of warm water and a towel. Verendus washed the dust from his face and hands, small compensation for the bath he'd been looking forward to. He gave his order and the waiter brought wine, water, and a basket of bread hot from the oven. Then came the seafood: a platter of golden delicacies – prawns, tiny octopuses, rings of squid – coated in seasoned flour and fried until crisp.

As he sipped the cool, acidic wine, the bearers across the street snapped to attention, hoisted the litter, and moved off. There, in the shade of the colonnade, was the heavy-set man chewing on a strip of dried meat. Shaven-headed, thick-necked, and built like a wrestler, he oozed aggression.

Verendus downed his wine. Whoever had sent this colossus wanted him to know about it. Had the optio reinforced instructions not to leave the city by letting loose this overgrown guard dog?

Verendus crunched on a prawn. It tasted of grit and he pushed the plate aside.

The Castrum, Viorum

'You are disappointed, Matellius. You think I should have arrested him?' said Principal Norvanus.

The optio closed the grille through which his superior had listened from the adjoining room. He maintained a tactful silence and Norvanus continued.

'As yet, there are no grounds. He is an associate of Governor Peronius; we must tread carefully.'

Matellius licked his dry lips; he had this in hand. He took a moment to savour his proficiency. 'Sir, my informant assures me that Verendus is sheltering a runaway handmaid and her slave. From Iolia's Temple of the Flame, no less.'

There was a satisfying intake of breath. 'Assisting fugitives,' said Principal Norvanus. 'A serious offence. That will do nicely, Matellius. Very nicely. Have the arrest warrant drawn up, but don't enforce it until Verendus has spoken with his senator friend.'

'Senator?'

'Peronius' brother, Senator Decimius, is visiting Viorum to oversee inaugurations at the Ministerium. I would wager my toga that's where Verendus will go next. Despite his inherent arrogance, he's uncertain how to proceed. He'll seek advice.' Norvanus took a tablet from the desk. 'Find out what he asks Decimius. It shouldn't prove difficult – the senator is devoted to his family.'

Matellius nodded. 'Decimius will talk.'

'I want to know why Verendus fabricated such an elaborate lie – the fire at the Officers' Club, the massacre of Parhels in the square outside. He's intent on discrediting the Iolian Watch and dragging Tribune Aquinus into his scheme.' Norvanus opened the tablet and re-read the transcript of Verendus' missive to Aquinus – made before Matellius burned the original. He handed over the tablet. 'Don't leave this lying around.'

'Understood, sir.' Matellius considered the words scratched into the wax. 'It's true that Portula Harbour was closed.'

'Indeed. And at such times, rumours abound. But we know the Iolian Gap is clear now and the harbour is open.' Norvanus went to the window. 'For the present, Verendus is under surveillance. There's a bigger fish. Given enough rope, Verendus will lead me to him. And I shall hook them both.'

'He served with distinction in Germania, sir.'

'His allegiance has since shifted. Apparently, his mother descends from a tribe of *Iutum* people from the north.'

'He has the look of a barbarian.' Matellius made a note on the tablet. 'And when you have your fish, sir?'

'It's my intention to present both to Prefect Galenius.'

Matellius' eyebrows rose. 'Verendus is a bigger catch than I realised.'

'Allegedly, he's a Speculator. How I'd relish landing a rogue one. What a terrific coup.' The Principal opened a shutter and glanced outside. 'Have no concern, Matellius, I've arranged that Verendus be followed. He won't escape.'

CHAPTER XV

Even before he reached the side gate, the sound of Murvaro's voice rising to a yell told Mos he had found the right house. He peered through a gap in the planking. The burly auxiliary was supervising drill in the backyard. Glad to avoid him, Mos walked the horses round to the stables – just as the Commendator had said to do. He left them with a stable lad and went to make himself known to the doorkeeper.

The huge Numidian had a glare that could freeze lava, but his hostility melted when Mos handed over the Commendator's note of introduction. Whistling, Mos strode inside. Smart place, too. The walls of the hallway shone with creamy marble and a vast mosaic teeming with exotic creatures covered the floor. Beyond, light flooded an atrium ringed with palms and fig trees in giant pots. A fountain stood at the centre, water gushing from the beaks of stone dolphins.

Two boys hastened from an alcove by the door and helped him off with his sword-belt, mail, and caligae. Mos pulled on the proffered slippers; he could get used to this. Enjoying the sensation of lightness after the weight of the mail, he smoothed creases from his crumpled tunic. With the feeling someone was watching, he looked up and his heart soared.

Saffi was standing by the fountain. At Alba, she had thanked him when he found the copper bracelet she'd lost. Even so, he was surprised when she called across the atrium to ask where he'd been.

'Commendator had business,' Mos said. 'Jupiter, I'm hungry.'

Saffi smiled. Barefoot, in a loose, undyed tunic, her fair hair gleaming gold, she looked like a wood nymph. Or how he supposed a nymph would look.

'There is bread in the kitchen.' Her strong accent didn't have the sweet melody a nymph's might have. It didn't matter. 'Come,' she said, 'I show you.'

To accompany the bread she found ham, olives, and pickles in the larder, and set them at the far end of the long kitchen table away from slaves preparing dinner. She sat on the bench beside him and watched him eat.

'Aren't you hungry?'

'No. How many days are we here?'

'Two or three. Commendator's not one for staying put. He might follow Fes east to the Alps, but I'm praying he'll change his mind so we can return to Iolia.' Mos devoured another pickle. He shouldn't have told her where Fes was heading. He leaned on an elbow, and said, 'Did you see the towered bridge? What did you think? I'm going to draw it. Take a picture home to show my father.'

'I see nothing in that stinky wagon.'

'Oh. Well, there's lots to see in the city,' said Mos, keen to impress. 'It's the opening ceremony of the races today and there's stalls selling rosettes and ribbons. Different colours for different chariot teams,' he explained, when she regarded him blankly. 'The first race is this afternoon. I went to the Forum

– lots of stalls there. And I saw the Atrox Column. Well, it's not the actual site of the Battle of Atrox. That's further south – near Castellum Alba…' Too bad he hadn't been able to inspect the painted battle scenes that twisted up the monument. The moment he'd stopped, a gang of ragged children had crowded round, patting the horses and begging for coin he didn't have. Still, he could go back. He'd ask Saffi to come with him.

She pointed at the brass pendant in the shape of a flaming sun that hung at his throat. 'Why do you wear that?'

'It's Helios, the sun god.'

She seemed confused. 'So you are a Parhel, but you serve the Empire?'

'Mother's Parhel, Father's Reman… I've got a foot in both camps.' Best not tell her how much he was picked on because of it. 'Don't know why my parents married, they argue all the time.'

'Mine are dead.'

'Gods, sorry, I didn't…' He couldn't think what to say.

Saffi sniffed and scratched a red rake down her neck. 'Is there more forest behind the walls?'

'You mean, *beyond the walls*.'

'As you like, *beyond*.'

Mos pictured the Commendator's chart. 'Yes, hilly too. Why?'

Colour flared on her pale cheeks. 'Why can I not ask? Why is everyone unkind?'

Mos apologised. He was always apologising. To make amends, he asked, 'Who's been unkind?'

'Dorcas. She says the catchers will find me.' Tears welled. 'She says they will nail me up…'

'No!' said Mos, and the slaves looked over. He lowered his voice. 'I won't let them near you.' He wanted to tell her it was no idle brag, that he really could protect her. He'd killed that Helutti warrior, the one with the fox pelt, driven his dagger deep into the man's throat.

The memory brought a surge of bile. Mos swallowed and said nothing. Wouldn't be right. After all, the Commendator had killed lots of men. Mos had never once heard him brag about it.

Saffi wiped her eyes. 'I tell Dorcas I am freeborn, but I see doubt on her ugly face. That is why she stole my bracelet.'

'Don't worry, you've got it back.' Mos licked his finger and ran it around the plate, gathering crumbs. 'I'll tell the Commendator about her, he'll deal with her. Dorcas is a nosy cow. She'd want to know the insides of a cat's arse.'

Saffi's eyes widened, and then she sniggered. 'Why would she want to know that?'

'I don't know. It's one of Mother's sayings.' He'd made Saffi smile. Despite the chipped tooth, she had a nice smile. He inched closer.

She plucked a stray olive from his plate. 'Your Commendator, he shouts at me.'

'Shouts at me, too.' Mos remembered his chores. 'I must unpack. Come if you like, we could talk…'

He checked which bedroom had been assigned to the Commendator and went upstairs. Saffi followed him in and closed the door, plunging the room into shadow save for shafts of light piercing gaps in the shutters. She sat on the bed.

'I should unpack,' said Mos, not moving.

'You want me to go?'

Heart thudding, Mos sat beside her. He met her eyes and looked away to stare at the door. If the Commendator returned now… No, he'd gone to the baths; he usually spent hours bathing. But he'd mentioned the Ministerium. Would he come here first? Get changed?

'You do not like me. I smell bad?'

'Course not,' said Mos, though they were both sticky with the dust of the road. Maybe he should have bathed. He picked at his nails. Jupiter Maximus, he was messing this up. He swallowed hard. 'I've always liked you.'

Mos shut his eyes as he kissed her. He put his arms around her – gods, she was thin, but warm, and soft, and kissing him back. Excitement overrode his anxiety. He pushed his tongue into her mouth. Saffi wriggled and he slobbered over her cheek.

'You have not done this before,' she said.

He wasn't about to admit that. 'Want me to stop?'

'Is that what you want?'

Stiff with anticipation, Mos whispered, 'No.'

Saffi cried afterwards. Mos attempted to comfort her; nothing he said helped. She dressed quickly and ran from the room. His fault, he decided. He'd come almost at once, and he knew that was wrong. He had tried to take his time, kissing and stroking. He knew what to do. Sort of. He'd watched the Commendator and the young widow who gave them shelter when they were deep in the Germanian forest, hiding from Helutti scouts who'd crossed the river. Mos, feigning sleep, had spied through the dividing screen, night after night, as the Commendator lay with her.

Mos doubted Saffi would ever let him touch her again. He hoped he hadn't hurt her. There wasn't any blood. His friend Col had had several girls, or so he'd claimed. There was always blood the first time he'd said. Mos had shaped a gruesome image of copious bleeding that had, until now, proved a more effective deterrent than Father's stilted advice on not getting a girl into trouble. Fresh horror descended: if Saffi fell pregnant, the Commendator would flay him alive.

Mos made the bed. He should find Saffi; say he was sorry. Better let her calm down first. That's what Father did when Mother was in one of her tempers.

Mos unpacked. It took ages. Always did. Everything, even the surveying equipment that hadn't been used since the last mission to Germania, had to be checked against the list on the baggage scroll. Every item must be accounted for.

When, at last, Mos checked through his own things, he brought out the leather folder of drawing materials the Commendator had given him. He set everything on the little desk, selected a stick of charcoal, and stared at the parchment. That bridge he'd crossed to enter the city was so impressive. Determined to convey this, he sketched a faint outline. Next, the three crenellated towers, one at either side of the water, another at the centre, positioned to give the sentries guarding the bridge a clear view. Picturing the bridge as he worked, he filled in the rest. The great arched door at the base of each tower through which all traffic passed; the high city wall with its pair of watchtowers, a double portal between them. He added trees and bushes to the riverbank, and a barge to the water. Then some shading and smudging, and his drawing was complete.

Mos frowned at the finished picture, doubtful it was good enough to show the Commendator. Setting the parchment aside, he went to find Saffi.

Blabbermouth Dorcas was lurking on the landing, a pile of bedclothes in her arms. She scowled as though he had crawled out from under a log and told him that the girl was in the herb garden. Without reply, Mos wandered downstairs, through the atrium and out into a vast, colonnaded courtyard with many rooms around it. Rooms he wasn't allowed to enter. He crept on, through an arch and into a garden. The land was divided into plots: chicken coops, beehives, roses, and a vegetable patch. He passed vines and fruit canes and found the herb garden. Only the Commendator's woman was there, slouched on a bench by the wall. Best not bother her, thought Mos, and retreated inside.

Corinna looked up; no one was there. Raddled with somniferum, she slumped on the bench and stared at the sky. Wisps of cloud floated through the blue, drifting and merging in ever changing shapes. The wind found its breath and the pace quickened. A rolling mass split to become a hound: mouth wide, spare body unravelling, it transformed into a winged dragon with smoke at its nostrils, streaking across the sky. Then the blue paled. The sun dipped low and sank behind the wall.

Shadows surged, invading the garden like water seeping into a stricken boat. She drew up her legs and clung to the bench. Far below, in the churning foam, a man floundered against the current. She stuck out her hand, but the distance between them remained. She stretched, couldn't reach him. Silently, he slipped beneath the surface and was gone.

CHAPTER XVI

The Viorum Ministerium was a Travertine marble stronghold of imposing proportions. Beyond the bronze doors, a statue of winged Victory loomed high over an altar where ministers in search of the goddess's blessing could sacrifice before business.

Verendus passed by to join the line for the cloakroom. After returning to the baths to collect his blades, he'd made a couple of shortcuts and double-backs and given the colossus the slip. The journey had taken twice the time it should have done. It occurred to him that the colossus could be one of the three Praetorians who'd turned up at Alba asking questions. None of the men Treseus described had been shaven-headed, but that could be easily achieved with the aid of a razor.

As the rules stipulated, he handed over his blades to the cloakroom attendant before proceeding to the covered atrium that served as an informal meeting place for the city's ministers and their clients. The queue to petition the ministers stretched halfway across the room to a desk piled with scrolls and ledgers, where a fraught-faced clerk and his scribe directed proceedings. Verendus walked by, scanning the faces as he went. Citizens and freedmen in smart bleached tunics, slaves running errands, several heavily swathed matrons. A trio of toga-clad ministers – crusty old men much like his father – turned as he passed.

He found Quintus standing at the foot of the staircase beyond. The young tribune waved in acknowledgement and hastened to the desk. With polite apology, he cut to the front of the queue.

'They'll pass a message to my uncle,' said Quintus, strolling over. He pointed Verendus to a stone bench. 'I signed the forms and left Decurion Bretorus to deposit the taxes. Such a bore having him around, but Father says he's the best thing since bottled garum.'

As they sat watching ministers file from the Chamber, it perplexed Verendus that he overheard no talk of Iolia. No mention of the deadly fire at the Officers' Club, the brutalities of the Iolian Watch, or that the harbour had reopened. Aside from concern for the ongoing turmoil in Rema following the arrest of former Praetorian prefect, Secundus, the talk was mundane. Road maintenance, the price of grain, the need to build better quality housing. Meanwhile, Quin's inane chatter sent the restless part of Verendus' mind wandering. On learning that Senator Decimius was in Viorum, it had seemed a good idea to accompany Quin to surprise him. The senator might have valuable information concerning events in the capital. Might offer his support...

Verendus was deep in thought, for he startled when Quintus nudged him to say, 'Here comes Uncle.'

Verendus hadn't seen Senator Numerius Decimius Peronius for three years. On rising at the senator's approach, it saddened him to find Decimius shrunken in stature and slowed in speech and movement.

'What fair wind has brought the two of you to Viorum?' Decimius said, all charm as he ushered them into a meeting room away from the noise of the atrium.

Despite the smile, the senator did not appear pleased to see them. Perhaps he didn't like surprises. He sat at a marble-topped desk and pushed aside a pile of scrolls. Verendus took the chair across from him; Quintus lounged on a couch at the side of the room and explained they had delivered a consignment of overdue taxes.

Before Quintus could mention the ambush by Helutti slaves, Verendus asked about unrest in Rema.

'Oh, the usual protests over the price of grain…' said Decimius.

Typical politician, evading the issue. Verendus bit back his irritation. 'And the purge of associates of former prefect Secundus. What news of that?'

Decimius straightened a parchment-weight. 'Purge is a robust word to describe a little cleaning up of undesirable opinions. Still, I'm glad to be away from the place,' he said, and asked about their journey.

At this, Quintus launched into a vivid account of the Helutti attack; Verendus interrupted to steer the conversation back to events in Rema.

'It can't have been easy in Iolia these past few months with the harbour closed,' said Senator Decimius, changing the subject. 'Though I'm told that Iolia's governor formed a Watch to keep the peace.'

Verendus felt the blood run hot to his face. A decade ago, he had failed to secure justice for Saxtili villagers slaughtered by soldiers of Third Legion Gemina; soldiers intent on avenging Second Minervia after Saxtili guides led the legion into a

Helutti trap. He'd never believed the Saxtili betrayed the legion. Someone else was responsible. Trouble was, no one listened to him. He must not fail again, must not fail the Parhels as he had failed the Saxtili. The words poured out… 'The Iolian Watch locked scores of out-of-favour officers in a burning building and slaughtered hundreds of Parhels in the square outside. If that's your idea of keeping the peace…'

'My dear boy, I had no idea!' Decimius sounded as pompous as his governor brother. 'Have you reported this?'

'Tribune Aquinus has been informed.' Verendus apologised for his outburst. 'On your return to Rema, would you bring this to the Senate's attention?'

'Something must be done,' said Quintus, sitting up.

Decimius frowned. 'You are convinced of this, er… outrage?'

Hearing scepticism in the senator's tone, Verendus insisted. 'I inspected the aftermath in Regia Square. Most of the Parhel victims were high clan, influential. Without their guidance, it will be easier to subjugate the rest. The Watch is not a force for good.'

Decimius sighed. 'Well, I'll do what I can, though it may be a month before I return to Rema.' He stood to signify the meeting was over. 'I've an appointment to attend, but dine with me this evening and we'll discuss the matter further.'

Preoccupied with the conviction that despite his agreement Decimius would do nothing to help, Verendus reached the bronze doors and hesitated. Had Governor Peronius sent word cautioning his senator brother against involvement? That would explain why Decimius hadn't looked pleased to see them.

Glad he had said nothing about the phixus symbol or his fears of a conspiracy against the emperor, Verendus stepped outside into the sunshine. The clamour of the Forum closed around him. Discordant voices, the stink of the crowd, beggars and touts, slaves and ministers, stallholders selling coloured ribbons for the races. He glanced back at the Ministerium. The colossus was leaning against a column, shading his eyes as he stared across the square. The arrogance of the man was astonishing, no attempt to blend in. This was intimidation.

'Cheer up,' said Quintus. 'You've a face as long as my prick. Let's place a wager on Spur's horses. See, there are booths.'

As he spoke, there was a rumble of caligae and the clink of metal. A column of Praetorians, polished armour gleaming, marched into the square.

'Quin, you'll find better odds along the street,' Verendus said, walking on. He couldn't lose his shadow with Quintus alongside, though he'd make the colossus sweat.

Verendus lengthened his stride and was part way along the street when he realised the codex was still in his satchel. He should turn around – the Temple of Vesta was across the Forum from the Ministerium – but the colossus was following.

'Slow up,' said Quintus. He pointed to a yellow-canopied booth. 'Come on, let's place a bet on Spur.'

At the sight of their uniforms, punters stepped aside and the pair moved to the head of the queue. As soon as the wager was made, Verendus strode off. The street emerged in a colonnaded square, a fountain at the centre and benches on the east side where two old men were setting counters on a chequered board.

'Wait!' said Quintus, catching up. 'This way. Spur's recommended a first-rate bar.'

Across the square, on the other side of the fountain, the colossus stood watching, his pale bulk shimmering in the spray.

The bar, like the drinks it served, was small and expensive. Exclusive, too – if the shadow followed, he wouldn't get past the front door. Verendus resolved to find the back door and slip away. One drink and then he'd make his escape.

He sat on a couch beside Quintus and peered through the fog of lamp smoke and cheap incense at a room all gilt cornicing and black marble. Most tables were occupied, many by officers like themselves. A party of ministers and decorative women had bagged the big table nearest the stage. At the margins, four security men observed proceedings. Verendus knew the type: low-ranking Praetorians who'd served their time but couldn't hack civilian life. More brawn than brain, their sort relished fights, especially with former comrades. They looked as miserable as the underdressed hostesses who sauntered between tables, taking orders for drinks and anything else the clientele desired.

The arrival of a wine jug coincided with the lighting of lamps along the stage, and a murmur of anticipation rippled through the audience. The clear, sweet notes of a lyre drifted from the wings. A golden rope was lowered from the rafters. Someone – a woman, he could see her now the stage was lit – was perched on a platform beside the rope. She rose and made a slow and sinuous descent, her naked, silver-painted body gleaming.

Quintus nudged him and gave a piercing whistle.

Act followed act, each accompanied by more nudges and whistles. Verendus finished his wine and left him in the clinch of a henna-haired hostess.

At the door, someone touched his arm. 'Leaving already, Commendator?' It was the pretty girl who had shown them to their table. 'Buy me a drink?' Her voice was soft, slightly weary.

She wore a smile of invitation that didn't reach her eyes, and a breast-skimming tunic of gauzy muslin, cut so low that as she raised her hand to his shoulder, he caught a tantalising glimpse of dusky areola. 'How about that drink, Commendator?'

Verendus followed her to a table at the back of the room and sat watching as she poured the wine. A dark bruise discoloured her arm. She pulled a fold of muslin to cover it and asked if he was enjoying the show.

When he shrugged, she draped herself on the couch beside him, and said, 'You have beautiful hair.' She smoothed a lock from his forehead. 'That's the first time I've seen you smile. Why are you sad? Did you argue with your friend?'

'Him? No, aside from being an idiot, all's well.'

'Your woman then? Is that why you're here?'

Verendus sat up. Time to go. Beside him, the girl straightened too. She neatened the red satin sash of rank about his chest. 'You're young for a commendator.'

'Perhaps,' he said coolly, flattered nonetheless. 'What's your name?'

'Veturia.'

'Don't you have other customers, Veturia?'

'They can wait.' She downed her drink and leaned closer until her cheek brushed his. 'Would you like to buy something else now?'

Verendus drew back. He'd told himself he wouldn't do this anymore. He would change; things were different now. Except they weren't. Corinna didn't want him. This morning, before sending the turma on ahead to the lodgings, he'd called her from the wagon and apologised again. He'd reminded her about the seafood bar near the Forum, had suggested they attend a race at the Circus too. But she didn't want to go anywhere with him.

He stood. Gods, it was warm.

Veturia stroked his arm. 'Say yes…'

Front of house glamour terminated at the bedroom door. Inside the small red room, the air stank of sweat and stale semen. There was another odour: floral, cloying. He glanced around for a window but found only a cobweb covered vent. A phallus-shaped lamp hung from the ceiling, casting wan light over the stained mattress. With a rare feeling of self-consciousness, he stepped out of his loincloth and sank onto the stone pallet that served as a bed. As he rested his head against the wall, low moans of ecstasy rose from the room next door. A shout resounded; something clattered on the floor above. Sweet Venus, what was he doing in this crimson cell?

The cuirass pressed, cooking him like a lobster. He fiddled with a buckle, but couldn't face the bother of removing it. He tugged his penis. It was as limp as the rest of him.

Veturia stripped to scanty briefs. She knelt before him and moistened her lips with the tip of her tongue. Still nothing – even Priapus had scorned him. *Guilty conscience*, the small voice whispered. *Can't get it up.* Gods above, this had never happened before. Never.

'What's the matter, Commendator?' Veturia squeezed his thigh and stroked a path to his hip and the raw scar above, tracing an outline with her finger. 'Battle scars?'

Last autumn that wound had consigned him to Vetera's fort hospital for a month. He'd feared he wouldn't leave Germania. Pain woke, stinging his flesh. 'Don't.' He pushed aside her hand. The perfume smell was in his mouth, sticky in his throat.

'Commendator?' Veturia regarded him with glassy eyes.

'Forgive me. I need air.'

Verendus dressed, retrieved his blades, and staggered outside. He vomited in the gutter and remained bowed, catching his breath and trying to determine if he was going to be sick again. Probably those prawns.

Something rustled. He straightened, cold now, heart hammering as he gazed around the dingy courtyard. This wasn't the way he'd come in. Late afternoon shade shrouded the far wall where a mangy cat scavenged amongst crates and amphorae. A green couch, tufts of horsehair sprouting from the seat, lay on its side by an archway. An alley stretched beyond.

Verendus slunk back to the club door, fumbling for his flask as he went. He should return to the house, get some sleep. His friend Carbo was right, he was seeing shadows everywhere.

The cat hissed and Verendus turned. A man in a patched grey cloak darted from behind the couch, skidded through the arch, and ran into the alley. Verendus drew his dagger and sprinted after him.

The high, blank walls of *insulae* tenement blocks enclosed the alley on either side, the quivering movement of the street at the end a distant oasis. The cloaked man a third of the way through, Verendus hastened, closed in. 'Halt!'

The man glanced over his shoulder and the hood slipped back revealing a lank ponytail. Surely the same greasy-haired beggar he'd seen sitting outside the castrum.

'Halt, or you'll feel my blade.'

The man kept running.

Verendus slowed, aimed, and hurled the dagger. The moment it left his hand he knew he'd blundered. A weak throw. The blade skimmed the man's shoulder and dropped, useless. No, not useless. The beggar stumbled, almost tripped, a dark stain spreading across his cloak. The dagger had grazed him.

Three more paces and Verendus caught up. He grabbed the beggar and shoved his face against the wall. 'Why are you tailing me?'

The beggar whimpered and struggled like a weasel in a sack. He stank like one too. Verendus shoved harder and repeated the question.

'Ow! You're hurting.'

'Who sent you?'

'The man said to follow you. Don't know his name.'

'Think!' Verendus shoved again.

'Honest. I don't know. He—'

Metal flashed through the air and the side of the beggar's face exploded in a spray of red. He lurched, writhed in agony, and then sagged, a knife lodged hilt-deep in the side of his cheek.

Verendus dropped the body and turned, drawing his sword. He wasn't surprised to see the colossus striding away, pace quickening.

And then he was gone.

Without pausing to wipe the beggar's blood from his face Verendus hastened in pursuit, keeping low so as not to present too large a target. No sign of the colossus. He can't have vanished into thin air.

Verendus neared the place where the colossus had disappeared and saw another alley cutting through the insula block at a right-angle to the first. Closed in by high walls, it was long, even narrower, a few yard doors on either side. No street at the end, just another wall and a pile of crates stacked high. At the edge of the crates a shadow trembled.

Sword in hand, Verendus strode nearer. 'You're too big to hide. Come out and we'll discuss this face-to-face. Why did you kill your weasel? What were you afraid he would tell me?'

A crate shifted, toppled, and smashed on the ground. Verendus sprang back. Another crate fell and the colossus crashed free. His face betrayed no emotion. In one fluid movement he threw back his cloak and drew his sword, a barbarian weapon with a long, curving blade that glided from the scabbard without a murmur. With the confident gait of a professional killer, he strode nearer. Hades, the man was huge.

'Who sent you?' Verendus demanded. 'Why are you following me?'

The colossus answered with a snarl and charged. With no shield to block, Verendus parried the thrust, slipped in a jab of his own, and sidestepped into a yard doorway. The man evaded the jab with an agility that belied his girth. He landed a blow that sliced Verendus' cloak and gouged the door behind, pinning him there.

A dog barked. In the instant it took the colossus to register that the blade had stuck in the wood, Verendus back-kicked the door. It yielded and he staggered backwards, ripping his cloak. He smacked into an expanse of something soft and damp, which slowed but did not stop him. He faltered, couldn't regain his balance, and crashed into a wall.

Splinters of light burst behind his eyes and he slumped to the ground. As he sat blinking, trying to summon the will to rise, he was aware of something beside him. Rank breath warmed his brow, the glittering lights faded, and he was staring into the slavering jaws of an enormous black hound. For one dreadful moment, he thought he'd died and passed over to the next world.

His vision cleared. This was not the Underworld. He was not at the mercy of Cerberus, three-headed dog of Hades. This dog had one head. One very large head.

Straining against the chain about its neck, the dog growled and fixed him with sly yellow eyes. Verendus edged away, mindful that he was splattered with blood and that the dog could smell it.

He struggled free from the line of washing that had broken his fall, flung off the wet sheet, and clambered up. There was nowhere to run. All four of the miniscule windows in the house beside the yard were shuttered, and both doors were obstructed: the house door by the dog, and the yard door by the colossus – the sword in his hand again.

As the dog barked and tugged at its chain, the house door opened. An elderly man peered out. 'Be off with you!' he shouted, and slammed the door.

Verendus glanced at the yard wall. Too high, he'd never get over in his armour. But there was a water cistern; he could climb up. He'd have to get past one-headed Cerberus first.

The colossus gave the dog a wide berth and advanced with the swagger of a champion gladiator, poised for the kill and determined to deliver a crowd-pleasing spectacle. The curved blade flashed. Verendus sidestepped the jab and countered. His sword clanked against metal – he might have known there would be armour under that thick tunic.

He veered away and aimed for a hefty thigh. The colossus parried hard, blocking the blow. Pain pulsated up Verendus' arm, numbing his grip. The sword dropped from his grasp and clanged on the concrete. He groped for his dagger, but it was lying in the dirt of the alleyway.

The sword was just out of reach. He inched towards it. The colossus had him covered and wielded a cautionary swipe to leave Verendus in no doubt that his hand would be lopped before he could retrieve the blade.

With rapid prods, the colossus pressed forward, tramping a trail of filthy footprints across the discarded sheet. Sweat dripped from his brow and he panted for breath as he forced Verendus back towards the dog. Teeth bared, chain digging into its neck, the dog snapped ferociously.

Verendus dodged the next sword blow and ducked the follow-through. Something firm jarred beneath his heel. The washing line. He'd trodden on the frayed end of the washing line. The rope must have broken when he stumbled into it; a short length still hung from the far wall. He put out his arms to keep his balance, stooped low, and snatched up the line. He reeled it in and almost laughed aloud. The iron spike, to which the other end of the rope was tied, had dislodged from the wall.

Verendus checked his grip, weighing the rope in his hand, calculating the distance between him and his opponent. He'd only get one chance.

He swung the rope, released, and sent the spiked end flying. It zipped away and the colossus shrieked as metal smashed his nose. Verendus snatched up his sword and charged. In one precise lunge, he thrust the blade up, under the chin and into the skull. Bone crunched. A jet of blood streaked the air. Eyes bulging, the colossus collapsed.

Chest pounding like a galley drum, Verendus retook his guard, glancing around as he did so. Defiant, alert, ready for another assailant. None came.

He crouched beside the corpse and closed the staring eyes. Another glance and then he searched. A pigskin purse on the man's belt contained several *denarii*. There were no keepsakes, no documents, nothing to identify the man.

Verendus had wondered if the colossus was a Praetorian on his trail or a former comrade hoping to scrounge a drink. The man's skill with the vulgar sword suggested this was no soldier of Rema, but a barbarian for hire. The sort of man the castrum might use for *ad hoc* assignments. No questions asked, no details recorded. *Follow the Commendator. Find out where he goes, to whom he speaks.*

The dog whined. Saliva dribbled from its fleshy mouth.

'Hungry?' asked Verendus, slipping the purse into his satchel. He grasped the colossus by the scruff of his tunic and hauled the body towards the drooling jaws. Soon the pallid face would be unrecognisable.

Verendus closed the yard door behind him and retrieved his dagger. A search of the beggar's body yielded nothing save for a knotted scrap of cloth containing several low denomination coins and a silver denarius – perhaps payment for assisting the hunt.

Verendus set the denarius between the beggar's lips to pay the ferryman, closed the dead eyes, and headed for the baths.

CHAPTER XVII

Yesterday's small triumph of defeating his shadow proved hollow when Verendus opened a shutter to see a red-headed oaf lurking in an alcove across the street. So, the colossus had an accomplice – muscular, menacing, and just as conspicuous.

Controlling the urge to slam the shutter, Verendus closed it quietly. A slight tilt of the head suggested that despite the precaution, this new shadow had spotted him.

Sod the shadow, this would be a better day. After this morning's business at the Ministerium, he would deposit the codex at the Temple of Vesta. His luck would improve once he was rid of the codex; Fortuna would smile on him again. He could taste the relief.

He re-read Senator Decimius' note from yesterday, which regretted that dinner would not be possible, but to come to the Ministerium before the morning session commenced. A senator – and trusted friend – who was to assist in the inaugurations, had arrived in Viorum sooner than expected. And, in the meantime, was eager to hear Verendus' account of the situation. Decimius went on to apologise for his earlier scepticism. His friend had convinced him of the seriousness of the matter.

Verendus slipped the note into his satchel. Decimius had been careful not to name Iolia in the note – an indication he really was taking things seriously. The opportunity to discuss Iolia with two Reman senators, to secure their support, was a gift from the gods.

While Mos set out his uniform, Verendus stripped off his night-tunic and washed. His back stiff after yesterday's impact against the yard wall, he couldn't hasten. Mos frowned at the bruising and suggested Corinna's balm might help. Verendus lay face down on the bed. Shame he had to settle for Mos to apply it.

'Smells nice, sir,' said Mos, rubbing hard. 'Nasty bruise.'

'Indeed.' Verendus couldn't see the injury, but it felt bloody sore. He rose and put on a linen under-tunic, the thin fabric sticking to the balm. 'Remember what I told you about the box in my satchel, about taking it to the Temple of Vesta?'

'Yes, sir. If anything should happen to you.'

Verendus stepped into his best, fine-gauge woollen tunic, splendid with its gold embroidered hem and purple stripes of rank. He smoothed down the fabric. Next came the sub-cuirass of quilted linen to cushion and protect his body from the armour. White leather fringing ornamented with silver-coated strips of steel was attached about his waist and at his shoulders. Then the cuirass of polished iron, the metal shaped to resemble a muscular male torso. Already he felt warm.

When caligae, greaves, belt, and baldric were secure, Mos helped him tie the red satin sash of rank about his cuirass. The boy had mastered the distinctive way of knotting the fabric so the sash draped correctly. While Verendus wrapped on his scarlet cloak, Mos opened a box and brought out a brooch of golden leaves crafted in the shape of a miniature wreath with the stylised head of a horse at its centre. He fastened the cloak at Verendus' left shoulder and straightened the tassel that hung from the gilded edge. Then he fetched the helmet and screwed the red ostrich feather crest into the top. He blew a speck of dust from the cheek-guard and handed it over.

Verendus glimpsed his reflection distorted in the bright metal. It looked like he felt – unsteady, insubstantial. 'Let's get this over with,' he said, more to his reflection than to Mos. 'While you're waiting for me at the Ministerium, make a list of the supplies we'll need for Brigantium.'

'That place in the Alps where Fes went, sir?' The boy sniffed. 'Can't we go home?'

'No.' Verendus didn't explain. Governor Peronius had issued a permit so Fes could travel via the highway to the Alpine village of Brigantium. No doubt the three Praetorians who'd turned up at Alba had discovered that. They would arrange for Fes to be tracked down and brought in for questioning. Questions that would establish why he was travelling to the Alps and whether he was carrying the codex. Verendus needed to find him first. He passed Mos his satchel. 'Carry this. The sash doesn't sit right if I wear the satchel. Don't let it out of your sight.'

Down in the yard, the trumpet sounded. Verendus strapped on his belt, gladius, and ceremonial dagger, and headed for the back door. Mos slung the satchel across his chest and followed.

Second-in-command Perseo was overseeing morning drill. He barked an order and the auxiliaries stood to attention and saluted as Verendus crossed the yard. Outside, the street was busy with racegoers and slaves laden with supplies: food baskets, wineskins, cushions for the stone seats. A father with two young sons hurried by, the green ribbons of their chariot team rosettes fluttering.

One day, thought Verendus, and marched on, the crowd parting before him.

The Ministerium doors were open. To the right, a row of curtained litters waited in the shade. No sign of Hostus. Gods, the dozy auxiliary was supposed to be keeping an eye on the litter. Perhaps it hadn't arrived yet.

Last night, when he'd told her of his plan, Corinna had made her feelings clear – she didn't want to leave Saffi. Verendus insisted. Once his business at the Ministerium was done, he would escort her to the new lodgings. He didn't tell Corinna he'd arranged for the litter to be one of the larger sized models; how much he was looking forward to sharing it with her. Again she told him she would not leave Saffi. Again he explained that Saffi would remain at the house to pack and join her later. Corinna had stormed off then. Verendus hadn't followed. He'd gone to bed and stared at his drawing of her until sleep freed him.

Verendus left Mos in the cloakroom queue to deposit blades and helmet, and went in search of Quintus who had gone ahead. The atrium was abuzz with ministers huddled in discussion or poring over scrolls and tablets.

He couldn't see the governor's son in the crowd, so consulted the visitors' register. The huge ledger lay open, the parchment blank. Verendus turned the page back and scanned the names to check if Quintus had signed in. His eyes alighted on the title Landren of Lignora. For an instant, he puzzled why he should recognise this name. A chill touched his neck and Magistra's words rang in his head: *seek out the Ennean, Landren of Lignora.*

Was it an omen? Truly, the Fates were colluding.

He read the name below: Eldoran of Nemusa. Not so ominous after all. Perhaps Landren was the reason for Eldoran's haste to reach Viorum. With mild distaste Verendus regarded the florid signature beside the Nemusan's name, then turned the page and signed his own in a bold hand.

He stood aside to let the next man sign. Still no sight of Quin. Five tall, powerfully built men marched through the wide doors, hitching up their togas as they crossed the atrium. Undercover Praetorians were so obvious. They stopped at the big panelled doors where a pair of blue-uniformed sentries supervised access to the chamber beyond. Verendus told himself it was routine. They weren't here for him. Stay calm.

Above, on the landing, two more sentries guarded the doors of the public gallery. Someone called his name. His heart jerked. He turned and, thank the gods, it was Quintus, sitting alone on a bench at the side of the room, his hand raised in greeting. Verendus strode over. 'Where is he?'

'Who? Oh, you mean Uncle. He's bound to be along soon, he's known for his punctuality. Or shall I enquire?' Quintus said, not rising, the tension in his bearing at odds with his usual languor.

Verendus remained standing, scanning the atrium.

'I'll need a drink after this...' Quintus broke off as a man with no more than a passing resemblance to Decimius walked by. 'No, no, that's not him. After this is over, let's go back to that club. Did you see the girl I had yesterday? Hair the colour of wine and tits like melons. Come on, let's go back.'

Verendus flexed his left hand and his fingers cramped as though coated in wet concrete. He groped at his neck for the horse-head talisman. Quintus rambled on. Verendus gave up on the talisman and unhooked his flask. 'For luck.'

Quintus grimaced, swallowed, and returned the flask. 'What filthy stuff is this, V?'

Verendus laughed and took a gulp. The sharp alcohol warmed his chest to steel him. As he sealed the flask, a flash of colour intruded on the edge of his vision: two uniformed Praetorians, eyes searching the room as they advanced.

Hairs rose on the back of his neck. He glanced at the chamber doors.

Closed.

CHAPTER XVIII

orinna kept still. Verendus wasn't looking in her direction, but movement might draw his eye. She reassured herself that she was cloaked and veiled. Even if his gaze wandered on across the landing to the corner where she stood – head bent, hands resting on the marble rail – he might not notice her. Then again, he probably would.

She wasn't supposed to be in the Ministerium. She'd been told to wait in the litter; he'd been clear about that. But it was boring waiting there, hot too. The litter's swaying motion and the nerve-wracking jolts as the bearers negotiated the busy street had left her feeling queasy. In the hope of cool air, she had drawn back the curtain and seen Eldoran hasten by and into the Ministerium.

Verendus was staring at the big doors on the landing where two sentries stood guarding access to the room beyond. Perhaps somebody hailed him for he looked away, scanned the atrium, and walked off. Other men stood aside to let him pass, and he strode on, out of view. Corinna wanted to go after him, to implore him to be wary. Though wary of what, she did not know.

A bell chimed, startling her from her thoughts. With impeccable timing the sentries stood aside and opened the doors.

Voices rose: loud, eager, as people ascended the stairs, quickening their pace, pushing and shoving to secure the best seats in the viewing gallery. Corinna turned away. She should fetch Hostus and return to the litter. The big auxiliary had escorted her here, trotting beside the litter like a devoted dog. It hadn't been easy to persuade him to escort her inside; she'd given him a coin. Now he was hunched on a low bench, his head nodding. Some people could sleep anywhere.

Corinna peered over the rail, but couldn't see Verendus in the atrium below. Last night she had tried to be cordial, to work up the nerve to ask him to arrange for her to meet the Lignoran named Landren. She had started by asking about the race at the Circus. Verendus had been dismissive – arms folded, staring at the wall. She knew he hadn't been there. A man does not return from a warm afternoon at the chariot races gleaming like a freshly groomed show horse and smelling of lemon balm and verbena. She knew he'd been somewhere with Quintus, somewhere where there were *lovely girls* – the tribune had a loud voice.

She supposed they had visited the baths. There were bathing facilities at the house where they were staying, but perhaps the girls there weren't lovely enough. Then he had said she must move to new lodgings. Always he was telling her what to do, and meanwhile behaving as he pleased. Corinna gripped the rail. Why should she care what he did? The bitter taste of jealousy remained.

Auxiliary Hostus shambled over. 'I should escort you back to the litter, *domina*,' he said, addressing her courteously. 'If the Commendator sees you in here he'll have my… well, my you-know-whats.'

Corinna surveyed the atrium again. Ministers were filing into the Chamber. She caught her breath – there, in the sea of heads, was Eldoran deep in conversation with two raven-haired companions. All three, beautifully distinguished in gilt-trimmed robes, stood majestic as peacocks in a flock of geese.

The taller of Eldoran's companions turned and looked up. Corinna averted her eyes and stepped back. The man was ascending the stairs, his amethyst robe trailing.

He halted beside her. She was certain he was Ennean, though when he spoke his Latin was perfect. 'Corinna Aurius, I presume. I am Landren of Lignora. May I sit with you?'

Her heart quickened. *Landren*. He had sought her out. Endeavouring to remain calm, she told Hostus to wait outside. She couldn't risk him overhearing and reporting back to Verendus. The auxiliary assumed a protective stance beside her and opened his mouth to protest. She gave him another coin and he nodded and marched off.

Landren indicated a bench and they sat together. He radiated an aura of nobility, the depth of which Corinna had not encountered before. Wisdom pervaded his sharp green gaze, though his long black hair showed no grey and his proud face was barely lined.

'Eldoran believes I may be of assistance,' he said, voice stern and yet melodious. 'We have a short while before commencement. Do you have the ring? I understand it belonged to your father. That he hailed from Lignora.'

Corinna nodded. Eldoran had told her he was due to meet Landren; that he might recognise the ring. She glanced at the stairs. No Verendus. If he arrived now, he would be angry. She unfastened the chain at her neck, fumbling with the catch. As she unthreaded the ring, she wondered what else Eldoran had disclosed about her. Once again, he had kept his distance. At least he was trying to help.

A shadow fell over them. Corinna jumped, but it was only someone passing by to join the queue for the public gallery.

She placed the ring in Landren's hand and studied his face for any clue. He must recognise the engraved crest, he must. His impassive expression told her nothing.

Landren turned the ring in his fingers, making a careful scrutiny of the antlered head of a stag carved in the jade setting. 'On hearing Eldoran's description, I was hopeful.' He returned the ring. 'Alas, I cannot assist.'

'Oh… are you sure?' Tears pricked. 'Isn't it a family crest?'

'No, not a crest,' he said kindly. 'This style of stag's head is popular in Lignora and found on rings and brooches across the land. Yours is made of jade and rather fine, it may have some small value, though I am no expert. My speciality is ancient books and letters – I have a modest collection.' He stood and glanced at the queue streaming into the public gallery. 'It has been a pleasure to meet you, Corinna. It is rare for Enneans to consort with other races. Your mother must have been a remarkable woman.' With a polite nod, he took his leave.

Corinna lifted the veil and dabbed her eyes. This was a set back, not a defeat – she would not give up. Somebody would recognise that ring and be able to tell her about her father.

The sentries were closing the doors to the viewing gallery. Many men had passed by during those minutes with Landren, but she hadn't noticed Verendus, and he was a man one noticed. She opened the purse on her belt and found the sachet of somniferum. Just a flake. It wasn't fair, she'd been counting on Landren's help.

The atrium bell chimed again.

Sunlight cut through the high, narrow windows, blurring the offal-red porphyry walls. She swayed to her feet. Somehow, for it seemed her feet scarcely touched the floor, she drifted across the landing to the stairs. It was hot, close, as if the walls pressed, stealing the air. Someone called out. The words evaporated into steam.

The walls shifted. She stuck out a steadying hand and grabbed at the bannister. Her hand flailed the air. The floor tilted, fell away, and shadows rushed in.

Into the darkness came words, soft and disjointed, the voice familiar. Shapes floated in and out of focus. A hand held hers, a face formed in the fog, and the words became whole. 'Be still, you fainted. Here, drink.' Eldoran pressed a flask to her lips. 'Shall I find Verendus? I was awaiting him.'

Corinna drank a few sips of the honeyed liquor and pushed aside the flask. Eldoran was here, but all she could think was that something must have happened to Verendus. 'Awaiting him? Hasn't he gone in?' The dull band of pain squeezed. 'Where is he?'

'In a meeting room.'

Corinna glanced around. The blue uniformed sentries were watching. One came over. 'You all right, lady?'

Fear sobered her. 'Perfectly well…'

'You certain?'

'I shall see her safely home.' Eldoran took Corinna's arm and helped her to rise. He steadied her at the stairs. 'Slowly. That poison is making you ill.'

'Poison?'

'Somniferum. I can smell it on your breath.' His grip tightened, slowing her descent. 'Corinna, please heed me. Even in the brief time I have known you, your eyes have dimmed.'

At last, they reached the foot of the stairs. As he walked her across the atrium, the doors flew open and eight Praetorians marched in. Corinna froze. Eldoran steered her aside and they waited for the soldiers to pass.

'Would you like to sit?' he asked.

'No. Get me out of here.'

He guided her through the doors and into the sunshine where Hostus stood waiting. The auxiliary stepped forward, but Eldoran insisted on helping Corinna into the litter.

She sank onto the cushions. She was sweating, shaking, a complete wreck. Eldoran was holding back the curtain, looking in. He must have realised Landren could not identify the ring; she was grateful he didn't attempt to comfort her with platitudes.

'Why do you take that stuff?' he asked.

Corinna already knew the answer. 'Because I do not want to feel.'

He regarded her with the same tender concern he had shown on their visit to the Atrox Tower. 'That saddens me.'

And now he pities me, she thought. 'It's no business of yours. Thank you for your help, but I'm better now. No need to wait.'

Eyes shining, Eldoran turned and walked away.

Mos took the ceramic token from the cloakroom attendant and dropped it into his purse. The blades were deposited, there was nothing to do but wait. He could go back to the house and try talking to Saffi. No, too risky. The Commendator might catch him sneaking off. Then he'd be right in the shit.

Best stay put. Blabbermouth Dorcas had scolded him for skulking outside Saffi's bedroom. The girl was proper poorly, she'd said, and his calling out and knocking the door wasn't helping anyone.

The atrium bell chimed. Soon the ministers would get down to business. Mos hesitated at the entrance to the atrium, the great room empty apart from a few men hastening to the doors at the far side, their footsteps clattering on the marble floor. No sign of the Commendator. Beyond the doors he glimpsed a mass of white, scores of toga-clad ministers chattering as they found their seats.

A man in a toga pushed by, too engrossed in dictating to the scribe beside him to notice Mos. The pair crossed the room and went into the chamber. With smooth precision two sentries closed the doors behind them and took position in front, crossing their lances to bar the way.

The atrium fell quiet. Perhaps he wasn't allowed to wait in here. Mos looked for somewhere inconspicuous to sit. Past the stairs, at the side of the room, he found an alcove with a bench. He sat in the corner and set the satchel beside him. Whatever was in that box the Commendator insisted on carting around weighed heavy as a brick.

His stomach growled. Could be hours before his next meal. Something gnawed in his memory. Gods below, he'd been told to write a list of supplies while he was waiting. Jupiter, he'd be for it now. How could he make a list when he'd forgotten to bring a tablet? But of course, the Commendator usually kept a spare tablet in his satchel.

Mos reached for the clasp and his pulse quickened. The Commendator's binder would be in there too. It wouldn't take long to write the list. There'd be time to look in the binder. At Alba, when the Commendator was busy in a meeting, the binder had been lying on the desk. Mos had untied the cords and looked inside. And some of the drawings, those women. Mos flushed, stiffening at the thought.

He remembered Saffi and faltered, his fingers on the satchel clasp. He'd messed up. She'd probably never speak to him again.

Mos unfastened the clasp. Just a peep. As he rummaged in the satchel, the atrium doors burst open and five Praetorians marched in. Three more followed. Mos shrank into the alcove. Looked like they meant business.

GERMANIA INFERIOR

850 AUC (AD 97)

*A decade after the disaster at Grenorum, those Saxtili who re-
main in Germania Inferior are subject to strict controls. Under
Rema's authority, they live crowded in a small settlement on the
west bank of the Rhenus River and are forbidden to own armour
or to bear arms.*

*That spring morning, it was a straightforward procedure for
Sentorus' Twenty-Fourth Legion to march into the settlement and
commandeer Saxtili animals and supplies. The residents were
herded into the town square where a centurion strode along the
lines, selecting – with a tap of his vine-stick – those who would
serve as slaves. Men to toil and carry, women and girls for service.*

*Only the young and fit were chosen. The rest were put to the
sword and left where they fell.*

Chronicles of Imperial Rema

by Marcus Vedius Verendus

CHAPTER XIX

A shaft of sunlight pierced a chink in the shutters to shine a pale stripe across the floor. Verendus raised his head and a barbed knot of pain, burning his skull from the inside, seared through him. The metallic taste of blood soured his mouth. He groaned, slumped forward, but did not fall.

Fear pricked. Where was he? Wherever it was, the place stank: a musty infusion of sweat, urine, and damp stone. He forced himself to look up at the small room. The only furniture was a table, the lamp on its grimy surface fading fast.

Gradually, awareness of his body grew. Hades, someone had stripped him, taken his uniform, his silver wristbands; taken it all except for the thin under-tunic. Bruises mottled his skin. Everything hurt, ached like he'd been tied in a sack and kicked. He was upright, not of his own volition, but restrained, half-hanging, arms wide. Trapped.

He pulled, tried to move, but clanked vainly. His wrists, neck, and ankles were chained, the floor cold beneath the balls of his feet. The left side of his jaw felt numb, sore. Carefully, he ran his tongue over his teeth, checking all were intact.

Had he been fighting? He wasn't sure. He had no memory of coming to this place. Had he been here an hour or a day? Impossible to tell.

He squinted into the gloom and attempted to absorb every detail of his surroundings. The torches around the walls were unlit. Dark flecks splattered the walls and the paintwork was gouged with lines as though scratched, repeatedly, by somebody desperate to escape. Rusty-brown stains streaked the concrete floor that sloped to a drainage hole: a small, metal-gridded square, not much larger than a boot heel, where a draught wafted in.

The lamp sputtered a plume of black smoke that clouded the low ceiling and drifted through the grille of the iron-banded door. A whip hung from a hook on the door: a flagrum whip. It resembled a strange sea creature, plucked from the water and strung out to dry. The thick handle – its legless body – terminated in long, knotted leather thongs, dark tentacles hanging limp. Limp but not innocuous. Wielded by an expert, those thongs could sting like nine scorpions and lacerate a man's skin with the sharpness of a blade.

He stared around, searching frantically for a way out. There was none save the door; the window was tiny.

And what of Corinna, Mos, Quin? Where were they? The codex. Where was the codex? In his satchel? Yes, he'd given Mos the satchel to carry. He'd told the boy to wait for him in the atrium. Was he still there? Mars above, where was Mos? Each new thought unleashed a further concern before he had addressed the last, until his mind whirred.

Verendus shut his eyes, trying to blot out the pain and remember. The Ministerium. He had been waiting in one of the side rooms with Quintus when a clerk arrived to say Senator Decimius would see them now. But Quin's uncle wasn't in the meeting room. Neither was his senator friend. Five Praetorians waited. As the door closed before Quin could follow him inside, Verendus had turned to see three more. They seized him. Eight of them kicking and punching and wrestling him to the floor. They shackled him, shoved his head hard against the tiles, and the room dissolved.

A warrant. Someone had said something about a warrant. He'd opened his eyes to a blur. His head throbbed; his mouth was dry with dust. Someone with a big bear-paw hand had waved a piece of parchment under his nose. Assisting fugitives, the man said. And then question after question. Verendus tried to remember. He hadn't answered any. Or had he? Difficult to be certain. He couldn't escape – too many guards. And then the bear-paw hand socked into his jaw.

They must have brought him to the castrum. *You've had it now*, whispered the small voice of caution. *You should never have come to Viorum.*

'Release me!' shouted Verendus. Must get out. Few men left such prisons intact. Most never left at all. He pulled at the shackles. Where the fuck was Quin and that uncle of his?

No one came. Shouting made his head worse. And now he needed to piss. With his hands restrained, the awkwardness stalled him and, despite the urgency to empty his bladder, at first he couldn't go. When at last he did, the relief was such that he fell asleep.

***

Something was gripping his left hand. Pain speared his finger. Was the bear stealing his signet ring? Verendus struggled and focused bleary eyes on the face before him. It wasn't the bear.

Red-eyed and bloated with a bulbous nose ruddy in the dim light, the man was more ape than bear. He grunted a rasp of stale wine, and said, 'Fucking thing won't come off.'

Verendus coughed, found his voice. 'I am Ericus Vedius Verendus, Reman citizen and Praetorian Guard commendator. I demand to see Tribune Aquinus.'

The man smirked.

Verendus could see him clearly now, a broad-shouldered, mid-ranking optio, a mail-coat over his scarlet tunic and a stained leather apron about his waist. Under his brawny arms, dark half-moons of sweat discoloured the tunic and added a new reek to the cell.

Across the room, under the table, was a large, rectangular basket, the lid secured with two buckles. That hadn't been there before. The lamp on the table had been replenished, the wick trimmed. A pitcher stood beside. 'Water…'

In the shadows behind him, a figure moved. 'You're in no position to demand anything.'

That smooth, sardonic voice. Verendus felt his heart shrink. Slowly, as far as the chain allowed, he craned his neck and met the eyes of Titus Galenius Dax.

Verendus looked away. Memories flared in his mind's vivid gallery. Germania. He was sixteen again, homesick and afraid – his first proper campaign. No, don't think of that. He affected an air of bravado. 'Titus, it's been a while…' His voice sounded thin, lacking the casual air he'd intended.

Galenius crossed the cell. With accomplished ennui, he placed a writing tablet and scroll on the table, straightened his purple cloak, and said, 'Prefect Galenius to you. And still your superior officer.' He unhooked the flagrum from the door and balanced the handle in his grip as though assessing its weight. Swishing menacingly, he advanced.

Even from a cubit away, Verendus could smell the musky oil that soaked Galenius – that same heady scent. Save for a deepening of lines and a heaviness around the jowls, the tanned face with the wide, slate-blue eyes hadn't changed. The full lips were as pink and sensuous as a tart's, the black hair thick and wavy, though perhaps its uniformity was courtesy of the dye bottle.

'*Commendator* Verendus. You've done well,' said Galenius, 'though we both know Fortuna smiled on you. Curious, we seldom run into each other in Rema. Been avoiding me?' He slipped the knotted leather tassels through manicured fingers. 'Not the golden boy today. Pining for your provincial back-water? I was stuck on that rock for three months. Such a relief to return to civilisation now the harbour's reopened. Reassure everyone all's well in Iolia.' He was beside Verendus, their eyes level. 'You look worried, Commendator.'

This is how it would feel to converse with a cobra, to be hypnotised by the suave tone, never knowing when the fatal strike would come. He braced for the flagrum's bite.

It didn't come. With his free hand Galenius grasped Veren-dus' left bicep, wrapping his fingers around the tattooed crest of the Third Legion. He squeezed. 'The Third Gemina,' he said over his shoulder to the optio. 'My old legion, Rectus.'

'Is that a fact, sir? Fine legion.'

'With the odd exception.' Eyes back on Verendus, Galenius prodded the inked crest. 'Never cared for one myself. Rather common.' His nail scraped the muscle, moving up past the pair of scorpions to an eagle clutching a lightning bolt in its talons.

'The Praetorian eagle, too. Very ornate. Must have taken hours. You enjoy pain?'

Rectus sniggered, the keys on his belt jangling.

'Strange how the Fates have set our paths in a similar di-rection.' Galenius' touch softened and moved up. 'A shame that journey's almost over for you.'

On slid the hand, stroking Verendus' collarbone, slipping inside the neck of his tunic to grasp his identity tag. He tensed, skin crawling. Don't react.

'You don't need that anymore.' Galenius tore off the tag. His hand paused, crept back, and drew out the leather cord with its little agate horse-head. 'What's this?' He cupped the precious talisman. 'A keepsake from your dear mater? How is she?'

Was that a threat? Would Galenius have her brought in for questioning? Mother knew nothing of the mission, surely they would see that. But Father… Father knew of it. And his status as a minister would offer scant protection.

'Your parents' villa is very fine, probably the finest on the island,' Galenius said. 'And your mother is so charming. I adored the party.'

So Galenius had visited the Villa Vedius. Was nowhere safe? Verendus clenched his hands; mustn't let the sod know it bothered him. 'I'll speak to Mother about the guest list.'

'But you won't see her again.' Galenius ripped off the talisman and tossed it to the optio. 'Rectus, dispose of this tat.'

The optio gave the talisman a cursory glance and set it on the table. Verendus fought for composure. That talisman had hung over his cradle. Protected him all his life. Now his life hung by a thread, would Fortuna abandon him?

'Hiding anything else?' Galenius grabbed the edge of the linen under-tunic and tore it open.

'I'm an imperial citizen. I demand an advocate—'

The optio forced a wad of tough leather between his teeth, silencing his protest. Rage burned like a fever. This meant pain.

'We can't have you biting your tongue,' said Galenius. 'You must be able to speak clearly to answer my questions. First you need a taste of what will happen if you refuse to co-operate.'

He brandished the flagrum in a wide arc. The knotted tassels whooshed through the air.

Verendus bit down on the leather and its bitter reek filled his mouth. Pain sliced his chest. He bit harder. Again the flagrum struck, slashing through him. Mouth set, he stared ahead. He'd trained for these situations, been taught to endure. Those sessions had been tough, bloody terrifying sometimes, but no matter how terrible, he'd clung to the knowledge that eventually the ordeal would end.

This was different. He couldn't see an end to this. Moreover, he knew Galenius could strike harder. Much harder.

The flagrum struck again. He bit so hard he feared his teeth would break.

Again, and then as abruptly as it started, the flogging stopped. The prefect regarded him with concern and hung up the flagrum. Verendus slumped, shaking, drifting into darkness. A hand clamped his jaw, pulling him back.

'Wake up!' Galenius squeezed and let go. He pulled out the mouth-guard and dropped it on the floor. Tender as a lover, he touched Verendus' chest, stroking a path between the lacerations. The finger glided on, skimming the right nipple, a touch that lingered too long to be accidental.

Verendus tugged the restraints.

The finger found a tear in the skin and pressed, forcing into his flesh. He shrieked, bit down. The restraint had gone. For an instant he feared he'd bitten his tongue, but the burning in his mouth was bile. Coughing, spluttering, he couldn't spit it away.

'Just like old times.' Galenius laughed as he withdrew. He wiped his finger on the torn tunic, smearing blood across the white cloth. 'Rectus, he's bleeding like a stuck pig. Patch him up before he makes any more mess.'

The optio brought needle and thread from the pouch of his apron. Despite his meaty hands, he threaded it at the first attempt. He beamed at his accomplishment and shoved the needle through the rent skin.

Scorching pain drilled Verendus. Sweat prickled, damp on his brow. His vision clouded. He ground his teeth and kept grinding until the optio finished joining the skin.

Galenius leaned in to inspect the damage. 'V? May I call you, V? As your friends do.'

Verendus recoiled but couldn't evade the touch.

'That's going to scar. A new mark to commemorate the occasion.' The prefect circled the stitched and reddened lump with his fingertip. 'Who put you up to this scheme? You haven't the wits to plan it alone. Was it Tribune Aquinus? Are you working for him?'

'My oath is to the emperor. Speak to Aquinus. He'll vouch for me.'

'Aquinus isn't here.' Galenius assumed a purposeful look. 'Why did you go to the Temple of the Flame in Iolia?'

How did he know that? 'I'm a Praetorian officer...'

'Not anymore. You're finished.' He turned away and bent to heave the basket from under the table.

Verendus was in no doubt what it contained. Now, the real torment would begin.

Galenius crouched beside the basket and unbuckled the lid. With the aplomb of a street magician, he flipped it open. Strapped inside was a gradiated row of knives and pliers. Idly, as if unable to decide, he ran his fingers along the handles, then reached inside the basket and brought out a saw. He held it aloft, scrutinising the serrated teeth before setting it on the table.

Verendus stifled a cry. Once, when interrogating a traitor, he'd watched a torturer ply his skills. How slowly the brute had pulled out the toenails, one by one, drawing out the agony – mindful of how much pain to inflict while keeping the prisoner conscious. When no information was forthcoming, the brute had sawn off the man's toes. Again, taking them one by one, careful to ensure the prisoner did not die of shock. Somehow, Verendus had ignored the pleas for mercy. The torturer hadn't bothered with a mouth-guard. Even when the prisoner bit through his own tongue, and blood poured from the screaming mouth, Verendus had not halted the procedure. When one tool failed to elicit a response, the torturer selected another. On and on until the prisoner died without revealing anything.

Shamed, Verendus hung his head.

'It's a while since I've had you in this position,' said Galenius. 'Not since I initiated you into the tribunate of Third Legion Gemina.'

Verendus' skin prickled. Do not think of that.

'As I'm sure you're aware, the Praetorian Guard is under my sole command. I have a warrant…' he held out his hand and Rectus snatched up the scroll from the table and placed it there. With a flick of his wrist, Galenius unfurled the scroll. 'A warrant from Iolia's governor, countersigned and sealed by Centurion Novius Nevoso of the Praetorian Guard, authorising your arrest on charge of treason.'

Treason? The irony. Galenius was the one who should be in chains. The prefect droned on. Fuck him, the bastard was enjoying this.

'Are you listening?' barked Galenius. 'Treason is a serious offence. I have set the date for your court-martial in Rema. Providing you survive long enough to attend.'

'If you wanted me dead you'd have had your henchmen kill me already.'

Galenius dropped the scroll on the table and drew his dagger, bringing the blade to within a parchment width of Verendus' throat. Closer, and the blade touched his skin. He froze at the sting of metal. Stared at the door. Tried not to retch. One swipe of that blade and it would be all over.

'So tempting…' Galenius lowered the dagger and took the tablet from the desk. 'But we mustn't deny our great public the spectacle of your execution. And in the meantime, I shall amuse myself. I have so many questions, and I will keep asking them until I get satisfactory answers. Why were you at the Temple of the Flame?'

'I wasn't.'

'Liar! The watchman you assaulted in the Belvedere yard was most informative.' He consulted the tablet. 'In spite of his broken jaw.'

So that was how Galenius knew so much. Through the fog of memory, Verendus pictured the watchman bending towards him, reaching to unstrap his helmet. He'd given the lad a solid blow across the jaw, but hadn't bothered to check for a pulse. Finding Corinna there had driven everything from his mind.

Verendus attempted to reason things through. Thinking hurt his head. He tried to concentrate, to recall the day he'd left Iolia. He had gone into the Belvedere and climbed the staircase to find Magistra waiting. She'd handed him the codex and told him to take it to Castellum Alba. To hide it in the vault. The watchman was outside; he would not know what had passed within the Belvedere's walls.

Galenius was talking… 'On your return to Iolia last month, you neglected to register at the castrum. How did you sail to Iolia and then flee the island three days later? Portula Harbour didn't reopen until after the Equinox. Ergo, you know a route through the Iolian Rings. Parhel are you?'

'No.'

'Parhel friends?'

'No!'

'And yet three days before Equinox, you were seen sailing towards the island.'

Verendus remembered unloading the boat on the beach in Iolia. The crunch of gravel, the bearded face peering over the ridge. But the coastguard was dead – wasn't he? Hades, how many spies were there?

'A woman reported a boat off the coast of the Vedius Estate,' said Galenius. 'The coastguard sent to investigate never returned. Why?'

'I don't know. I wasn't there.'

Galenius yawned. The deep inhalation invigorated him. 'Liar!' he yelled in a spray of spittle. 'You half-breed fucking liar. The woman saw you put out to sea. Did you dump the coastguard's body there?'

Verendus shrank from the barrage. The beat in his head pounded. Gods preserve him, it was an accident. He hadn't meant to kill the coastguard.

'It's warm in here.' Galenius picked up the pitcher and drank. Eyes closed, full lips puckered, he swilled water around his mouth. He spat into the drain and tipped the pitcher, pouring until none remained. 'Now, I have sweeter fish to fry. In my absence, reconsider your position. I want to know everything that happened at the Belvedere. And you will tell me. Once Rectus gets started on you, you'll be begging to tell me.'

Verendus stared at the stream of water disappearing down the drain at the centre of the floor and didn't reply.

When he looked up, Galenius and his butcher were gone. Alone, Verendus endeavoured to shut out the pain and concentrate. His one clear thought: Corinna. Magistra had placed her in his care. It was his duty to protect her. He had failed. What had she said to him that night at Spur's camp? *I don't belong in your world.* Would she ever?

Though he'd denied it at the time, it was his world, and she had witnessed parts of it he didn't wish her to see. Too late now. It made no difference anymore. He hadn't told Corinna of his belief that Magistra was her mother. Perhaps it was best she didn't know.

Corinna. His thoughts raced. Had she left the Ministerium and returned to the house? Been followed? Arrested? What would Galenius do to her?

***

Verendus blinked at the mellow early evening light. One moment of ignorance and then a surge of distress as he realised where he was and how much everything ached.

He'd been dreaming. That detested dream of the dark house with the twisting staircase. He was almost there, almost at the top of the stairs. His legs were so heavy. Each step required immense effort. Somehow he reached the top, the passageway of many doors stretching before him. Someone was there, a small figure walking ahead. The figure slowed and paused outside a door. *Mos.*

Verendus called to him, but he didn't turn. There were so many doors. Did Mos know that some must never be opened? Verendus attempted to catch up, but his legs were growing heavier, sinking into the floor. He kept shouting, imploring

Mos to stop, telling the boy to take Corinna to safety, telling him over and over, but Mos didn't turn.

Someone screamed, tearing him back to reality. Alert now, ears straining, he tried to determine where the cry came from. The next cell? Or a trick of pipes and drains carrying the sound across the castrum? Incoherent voices echoed. Another scream – a woman. Not that he could help her.

She screamed again and fell silent. The voices fell silent too.

As he drifted towards sleep, something touched him, tickling the raw lines that criss-crossed his torso. Startled, he opened his eyes and pulled against the shackles. A fly. It flew to a nook in the shutters, buzzing in frustration as it sought escape. A moment later, it was back. He shooed the bluebottle only for it to return, again and again, the torment continuing until darkness subdued the creature.

Parched, exhausted, Verendus slept.

CHAPTER XX

The rasp of a bolt woke Verendus. He opened eyes sticky with sleep and gasped at the stale air. Even breathing hurt. He was still here, trapped, chained like a beast for slaughter. Blood had pooled on the floor around his feet. His blood. The realisation made him queasy, as though he was standing on a narrow ledge, looking down from a great height. He knew he should turn away, but continued to stare.

Someone was talking quietly. He couldn't discern the words; that smooth voice was unmistakable.

Galenius unhooked the flagrum from the door and passed it to Optio Rectus. Torches had been lit and the lamp on the table burned with a steady glow. The horse-head talisman was there, the water pitcher stood beside it. There was something else, something familiar. A worn leather cover. The binder. And, if Galenius had the binder, he had the satchel, and the codex. And Mos.

A cold wave of despair smacked over him. He struggled vainly. 'I'm a Praetorian officer…'

'Persisting with that dirge.' Galenius rested his hand on the table. 'You look rough, V. Blood will out – one missed shave and you're looking quite the barbarian. A taint inherited from the maternal branch of the family, I believe.'

Verendus stared at the door. He must not yield. Must stay strong. His Ambrone blood, that *barbarian taint*. That would give him strength.

'We've been inspecting your binder.' Galenius ran his finger over the cover. 'Fascinating drawings. You've some small talent, after all. Tell me…' his voice softened to silk, 'who are all these women? A fine stable.'

Verendus swallowed but couldn't spit the sourness from his dry mouth. Alerted by a cough, he looked over at Rectus. The optio winked and flashed a tannin-stained grin. 'Dirty fucker.'

'Water… I want water.'

'Respect, Verendus, you arrogant shit.' Galenius twitched his hand and stepped back as the optio dispensed a chest-stinging crack of the whip. 'It's *please, Prefect Galenius.*'

He willed himself to comply. What good was pride if he died of thirst? '…please, Prefect Galenius.'

'Answers first.' Galenius took the binder, turned a few pages, and held up a drawing of Drusilla. 'This woman… Drusilla wife of Blandinius, I'd say. Intimate portrait.'

'That's a slave.'

'Liar. Blandinius is an old friend of mine. So you're the dog who's been fucking his wife. He suspected, you know. He'd do well to heed my advice and divorce the miserable bitch.'

The prefect thumbed through the binder and paused at an explicit sketch of Nellis. Verendus shut his eyes and choked back a sob. Poor dead Nel, slain with hundreds of other Parhels in Regia Square. He'd tried to persuade her to leave the city; with the Watch in control, it wasn't safe for Parhels.

'Pay attention!' Galenius slapped him across the cheek. 'Don't cry. I always could make you cry.'

Verendus steeled himself. A rivulet of blood slid down his torso and dripped on the floor.

'Which one is that bit of skirt you stole from the Temple? Don't look like that, I know about her. Abducting a handmaid, that's novel even for you. I can't see an advocate getting you off that charge. The punishment is fitting, too. For both of you.' Galenius turned to the back of the binder. With barely concealed glee, he extracted a piece of parchment and held it up. The body, drawn from imagination, could have belonged to any beautiful woman. The face was Corinna's. 'Lovely. Our missing handmaid?'

Verendus bit back his retort. *Don't react. Beside his right eye, a tiny vein pulsed.* Did Galenius detect this flutter of unease? *The door. Focus on the door. He doesn't have Corinna. He'd recognise her picture if he had, he'd be positively crowing. Don't react. Focus on the door.*

Sudden comprehension set his heart racing. He'll find her. It's my fault. He'll find her.

Galenius smiled. A lip-curling snarl of triumph. 'I'm right! It is her! I can see it in your eyes. Fond of her, aren't you? A shame there's only the one drawing of the little whore. We were hoping for others. I searched… It didn't take me long to find your hiding place.' He peeled back the lining, slipped his fingers inside the binder, and pulled out a fold of parchment. 'This was unexpected.'

If this was an act of theatre contrived to intimidate, it was cruelly effective. Slowly, Galenius unfolded the drawing, his expression pure malice.

For a moment, it baffled Verendus. And then he realised those strange serpents were the ones on the codex clasp. At Alba, when he'd opened the codex, he had made a sketch of the clasp.

'You're shaking, V. Nervous? You should be. I've long had concerns over your loyalty to the Empire. Those serpents are the double ouroboros. Is that a codex beneath? Is this what Magistra gave you?'

'No.'

'Liar! Where is it?'

'Don't know.' Why was Galenius asking? In the fog of his mind, Verendus strove for clarity.

'Let me jog your memory.'

A punch struck his ribs and crashed through his body. The reply caught in his mouth. Acid scalded his throat. The room wavered like mist; black spots glimmered.

'My patience wears thin. Where is the codex? Think!'

Another punch. The spots grew and merged. Verendus didn't understand. Surely, if Galenius had the binder, he had the satchel *and* the codex.

'Did you give it to your Saxtili runt? Did you tell him to hide it when you sent him east to find Legate Capito?'

Verendus realised he was referring to Fes.

'The Praetorians who apprehended Festinus sent me a list of what he was carrying. This included a fascinating missive you wrote asking Capito about a camp on Iolia's Waterside Plain, which you believe to be occupied by troops of the Twenty-Third Legion. What a vivid imagination you have. No mention of a codex, though. Shame I won't have the opportunity to question Festinus in person. He died attempting to escape.'

Fes dead? Verendus couldn't take it in. How could someone so full of spirit be dead? The walls trembled. Thunder growled. He fancied he could hear crowds at the Circus, roaring as chariots hurtled along the track. Or was it the blood pounding in his ears? Consciousness slid into shadow. Fading...

Someone gave him water. Just enough to revive.

'Tip the rest over him,' Galenius ordered. 'He stinks.'

Rectus poured. Verendus raised his head, trying to drink as water streamed down his face. He blinked away the cool droplets. Galenius was watching him, watching the water roll off his naked skin, watching him as a man watches a woman.

'Big boy, isn't he, Rectus?' Galenius leaned closer. 'Do you know what a gelding is, V? All my horses are geldings. Makes them better behaved, easier to control. It's a simple procedure.' Honeyed breath brushed Verendus' lips. 'You wouldn't make it past the finishing post with any more fillies.'

Galenius' hand cupped his scrotum like an overzealous medic. Verendus yelped. His blood chilled to ice.

'Maybe I'll stay to oversee the operation.' He squeezed, digging his fingers into the soft flesh until Verendus screamed. Galenius let go. 'Quiet! There's an easier way. Tell me where the codex is and I'll drop the charge against you *and* the handmaid.' He opened the basket and selected a pair of iron pincers. 'These, I think.' He clanked the hefty claws together and passed the pincers to the optio. 'I hate to do this to you, V. You're one of my special ones, I'd like to keep you whole.'

Verendus gritted his teeth. Was he shaking? He could no longer tell.

A sly look crossed Galenius' face. 'Did I mention the boy?' The prefect sounded pleased.

'What boy?'

'Your attendant and heir Lucius Mostus.'

'How did…' Verendus stopped, furious at the slip.

'How did I know he was your heir? Easy. When I inspected the carnage you caused at the Belvedere, I went to the Temple library and requested your Will. A rudimentary document bequeathing half your assets to Marcus Vedius Verendus the

Third – ha, he must be that cute little boy you have so many drawings of. And the remainder to be divided between Lucius Mostus, Festinus Vedius – too late for him now – and an assortment of freedmen. Then I amused myself by reading the details of your somewhat ostentatious proposed memorial stone. Nice sketch.'

'You'd no right.'

'Nonsense, we're old friends.' He beckoned the optio. 'Rectus, ensure he stays awake. You're capable with a needle – I've another couple of holes for you to darn. Sew his eyelids open. Strong, double yarn. And remove his ring. He's no right to wear it.' Galenius resumed his purposeful expression. 'Back to the rack. I'll question young Mostus again. He's proving co-operative.'

'No!' The last thread of hope broke. Please, not Mos. But Galenius had the binder – of course he had Mos. Dear gods, the boy wouldn't last long once Rectus got started with his toolset.

A smile twisted the prefect's lips. 'You have an hour. Then we'll see what Rectus can do.'

Hot, futile, rage filled Verendus. He knew that smile. Galenius had more than information on his mind, and Mos would suffer for it.

Deep within him a cry rose and grew, rising and pressing until he could contain it no longer. The piercing howl stung his ears and shook his body. It was all his fault. He'd sent Fes off with that bloody message for Capito. Sent him into danger. And now Galenius would butcher Mos.

It was then that his resolve cracked. Verendus felt it happen: a sharp point of pain in his chest that stole his breath. How easy to stray from the path. A slip here, a poor choice there. And he had sunk to this. Eyes closed tight, he began to pray.

CHAPTER XXI

The big Numidian doorkeeper told Corinna that Commendator Verendus had not returned from the Ministerium. He would probably scold her when he did. She had come back to the house without his permission. She was meant to wait for him in the litter so he could escort her to the new lodgings. When he left the Ministerium and realised she wasn't waiting outside, he would be angry. He would be angry with Auxiliary Hostus, too.

Perhaps aware of this predicament, Hostus tramped after her, into the hall, where he stood watching her with doleful eyes. Corinna gave him a coin for his trouble, dismissed him, and went to her room. Somebody had been here: a rosette of blue ribbons lay on the dressing table. The odious Spurius hadn't forgotten his pledge to send her his chariot team's colours. She tossed the rosette onto the floor.

At the side of the room, clothes had been folded and piled on a stool, ready to pack. There wasn't much; she'd see to it later. She removed her earrings and placed them in the little onyx dish. Such a pretty dish. She would pack that too.

She rubbed her earlobes. The morning had been awful: Landren unable to shed light on her father's identity, Eldoran's admonishment over the somniferum. How dare he tell her what to do.

Outside, two pigeons exchanged a strident barrage of coos. Corinna fastened the shutters and fetched the bottle of somniferum. Just one flake. After the disappointment she needed something to help her through the afternoon.

The crystal dissolved on her tongue, filling her mouth with aniseed. She felt the drug's pull and sank onto the bed. Closing her eyes, she floated into oblivion.

The centurion shuddered and fell forward, the dead weight crushing her chest. Ready for me, little rabbit?

A dull thud.

Corinna opened her eyes and sat up, gulping air. Only a nightmare. Torvius was dead. Sunlight sliced through the gap at the top of the shutters. She hadn't been asleep for long.

Another thud, then a groan. Not here, but next door. In her haste, she rose too quickly. Light-headed, unsteady, she staggered out to the landing and tried Verendus' door. Locked. She knocked. Louder when he didn't respond. 'Verendus? Verendus, what's the matter?'

She was on the verge of tears when the door opened.

'Shush!' Mos pulled her inside and shot the bolt.

She looked from the boy's red-rimmed eyes to the jumble of kit strewn over the floor. Something was very wrong.

'The Commendator,' said Mos, voice shaky. 'They've arrested him… at the Ministerium. I'd just got back from depositing his blades and was waiting in the atrium, keeping out everyone's way like he'd told me.' He knelt and stared at the disorder. 'The Praetorians came. They took him and Tribune Quintus. They were chained. What could I do? I didn't come straight to the house in case someone followed. Someone followed us there, you see. I hid a while, then crept round the back and climbed over the wall. You haven't seen me… right?'

Corinna nodded, struggling to take it all in. She had the disorientating sensation of being sealed in a glass amphora: aware of things around her but confined, powerless to act. *Verendus arrested.* She opened her mouth to ask why, then closed it again. It must be because of what had happened at the Belvedere – those guards he'd killed.

Mos concentrated on the kit: folding clothing, opening bags, moving mess-tins and tools from one pile to another. 'You still here?' he snapped without looking up. 'Praetorians will come. Serpents, too.'

Corinna dug her nails into her palms and fought to remain calm. 'Serpents? What are you talking about?'

'Caesar's Serpents! The Speculatores: Praetorian imperial agents.' He flung a tunic onto the pile and jumped to his feet. 'I'm off.'

Magistra had said the Speculatores were ruthless. If they came here, they would question everyone. Then they'd find out she'd killed Torvius. The Praetorians would not let his death pass unpunished, and she would be thrown to beasts in the arena. She must leave. Fetch Saffi and leave.

But she couldn't abandon Verendus. Had they hurt him? Probably. Praetorians were like that. One morning, years ago, when Nonna sent her to the market for bread, a youth was caught stealing. While the stallholder tried to detain him, two soldiers of the Guard came out of a bar. Seeing the struggle, they marched across and took control. Corinna, huddled in a group of bystanders, watched horrified as the soldiers chained the youth, beat him with cudgels, and dragged him away, leaving a trail of blood smeared across the paving. There was a moment of silence, and then the crowd exhaled as one and resumed shopping.

Corinna reminded herself that Verendus was a Praetorian officer, not a thief in a market square. That must count for something. Last month in the Belvedere yard, he had been in the custody of the Iolian Watch, his wrists tied with rope. Somehow, he had freed himself and escaped. She didn't see how he could break free from chains and manacles. It wasn't reassuring.

She picked up the satchel.

'No,' said Mos. 'I'm looking after that. Commendator couldn't wear it with his best uniform.' He snatched at the strap.

Corinna swerved aside. She unfastened the clasp, opened Verendus' satchel, and the scent of him – lemon balm, leather, the tang of cloves – filled her. Blinking away tears, she started her search.

Three cloth pockets divided the interior. Two were crammed with stuff: drawing materials, wax tablets, a scroll case, a tapered stick, a fold of parchment, and a pigskin purse she hadn't seen before. She unfolded the parchment: a note from Senator Decimius asking Verendus to meet him, and another senator, at the Ministerium before the morning session commenced. Had they colluded in his arrest? She must be careful.

In the third pocket she found a cloth parcel tied with cord. This was what he'd taken from Magistra. Perhaps this was the reason for his arrest.

The parcel was heavier than it looked. Corinna set it on the bed and untied the cord.

'Don't touch that!' Mos stood over her. 'I'm in charge of that. Don't open it.'

As she unwrapped the cloth, he leaned closer, huffing and tutting, though he didn't attempt to stop her. He was as intrigued as she was to see inside.

The stitching on the leather binding had been cut already. She eased it apart and pulled a wooden box from the binding. Suddenly, she didn't want to open it. She could be wrong about the contents. It might be dangerous.

No, she was not Pandora. She wasn't about to unleash evil into the world. Carefully, she slid back the lid. Packing straw. She brushed it aside and brought out a white satin pouch, the fabric stretched around an angular outline. Her heart jolted. Surely this was the satin pouch that had hung beside the keys on Magistra's girdle; the pouch Centurion Torvius had hidden under the folds of his cloak. Had Magistra given this sacred thing to Verendus? Or had he stolen it? That would explain his arrest.

Corinna unfastened the pouch and gasped. It *was* the sacred codex. The small book was bound with a golden band and secured by an ornate clasp, elliptical in shape and almost as large as the codex. Two bulbous-headed, ruby-eyed serpents adorned the clasp. Jaws agape, fangs bared, each swallowed the other's tail to lock them in a ring of death.

She stared, blinked, and the image burned a dark spectre of a familiar symbol into her vision. Phixus, sign of the serpents. Now, at last, she understood. Magistra had asked Verendus to take the codex away from Iolia to a place of safety. And all the while not realising that she – Corinna – had the key to unlock it. In her years at the Temple she'd heard the legend about a map of a secret Alpine pass. A map that was guarded by serpents. If that map was here, in the codex, it would be worth its weight in gold.

Beside her, Mos drew in his breath. 'What's that? It's horrible.'

'What did the Commendator tell you to do?'

'None of your business.'

'Mos, we have a better chance of helping the Commendator if we work together.'

'Together?' He frowned. 'The Commendator and me should be on our way to the Alps. Shame I can't get word to Fes, he'd know what to do.'

'You'll have to make do with me.' She re-wrapped the codex; Mos must not know she had the key.

He sniffed and wiped his nose with the back of his hand. 'Commendator told me if anything happened to him then I must take that box to the Temple of Vesta. There's one near the Ministerium. He only showed me the box. I never saw inside.'

'This is the sacred codex of the Temple of the Flame.'

'Sacred codex? Says who?'

She found Verendus' purse at the bottom of the satchel and didn't reply.

'Not that.' Mos pulled her sleeve. 'How will I get by without coin?'

Corinna tore free. 'I have to borrow some.' To have any hope of helping Verendus she'd need all the coin she could get. She opened the pigskin purse. Several denarii. Perhaps it would be as well for Mos to have some. She handed over the purse and he attached it to his belt. 'As for this,' she shoved the box into the satchel, 'this codex belongs in Iolia.'

'But he told me to take it to the Temple of Vesta.'

'Why there? Is that where he was taking it?'

'How would I know? I don't question orders. Him and Decanus Carbo were planning stuff the day we sailed from

Iolia. But they never told me.' Mos kicked a water flask clattering across the floor. 'They never tell me anything.'

'Losing your temper won't help.' Corinna slung the satchel across her chest and went to the small lattice window. The panes were of obscure green glass, save for one clear square through which she peered. The angle was tight, the fraction of street framed below distorted by the thick glass. 'Are you certain no one saw you come into the house?'

'Certain as I can be.'

She tilted her head, shifting the vista, and immediately stepped back. 'There's a man out there. A big, red-haired man, standing beneath the colonnade across the street. He's watching the front door.'

Mos pressed beside her. 'Shit. That's the oaf what followed us to the Ministerium.'

'Is he a Praetorian in disguise?'

'Doesn't look like one. Too scruffy.' Mos turned away and picked at a fingernail. 'The Praetorians will find out where I am. They'll come here. You're better off without me.'

'No, we stay together and help Verendus.'

'The Praetorians would've taken him to the castrum. We'll never get him out.'

'Verendus has coin.' She opened his purse. Plenty of coins, mainly silver denarii and a few coppers. She delved deeper and found an iron key – large enough to be a door key – and three gold *aurei*. Would that be enough? Unwilling to admit she didn't know, she tied the purse to her belt and concealed it with a fold of her palla. 'We'll pay someone to help him escape.'

'Pay someone? Like who? Everyone knows those places are a gateway to Hades. We'd need Orpheus to get him out.'

'So we abandon him?'

The boy's cheeks flushed. 'I'm not abandoning him!' He all but spat the words. 'I'll find Tribune Aquinus. He's the Commendator's friend. I'll ask him to help.'

'Won't that mean going to the castrum?'

Mos explained that the tribune was away, but would be back in a few days.

Corinna's hopes plummeted. 'We can't wait a few days.'

'We could look for Aquinus.'

'Where? Do you know where he went?'

'…no. But I'll find out. You got a better idea?' Mos flinched as the front door slammed.

Corinna went to the bedroom door and listened. Somebody was moving about downstairs, pacing. 'Mos, wait here.'

'No, I told you. I'm leaving.'

'Not without me. Wait here and keep quiet.'

She opened the door a crack and peered out. The pacing stopped. A man's voice drifted up from the atrium. Tribune Quintus. Checking the urge to run downstairs, she crossed the landing. No Verendus. No Praetorians. Just Quintus and the grumpy decurion standing by the fountain. Corinna took several deep breaths and descended.

On seeing her, Quintus strode over. Taking her gently by the elbow, he steered her to a couch. 'V's not with me,' he said apologetically. He sat beside her and launched into an account of the arrest.

Corinna listened, playing her part. She mustn't let slip that she knew about the arrest, mustn't give him reason to suppose Mos was here – she wasn't sure she trusted Quintus. He rambled on, his description of the brutal arrest showed no sign of concluding.

'Isn't there something you could do?' she asked, interrupting him, which was most unladylike.

He regarded her with puppy dog eyes. 'All Uncle's efforts were in vain. The charge is treason. The Praetorians are drawing up a warrant so they can search the house.'

Decurion Bretorus marched over. 'If your father wasn't governor they'd be here already, Tribune.' He turned to Corinna. 'There's nothing you can do, lady. Treason's a capital offence.'

Her heart contracted. If Senator Decimius could not help Verendus, the decurion was right: what could she do? This was even worse than she'd feared. 'Why treason?' she asked. 'What is he accused of?'

'The Praetorians wouldn't say. Gods, they were vile.' Quintus rubbed his bruised wrist. 'Anyone seen Mos?'

'That lad's got the brain of a boiled dormouse,' Bretorus said. 'They'll learn nothing from him.'

Movement beyond the potted palms caught Corinna's eye. *Dorcas.* How long had she been standing there? The slave bustled over and asked her to come upstairs. 'It's urgent, domina.'

Trying not to appear too concerned, Corinna followed. If the meddlesome slave had discovered Mos was here, it would doubtless require a bribe to buy her silence.

They reached the landing. 'What is it, Dorcas?' Corinna raised her voice so Mos might hear and be on his guard.

'It's Mostus, that's what.' Dorcas sped along the corridor.

Corinna raced to catch up. 'Wait! I'm sure we can work something out.' She slipped by and stood in front of Verendus' door.

'It's all his fault.' With a puzzled look, Dorcas walked on, past Verendus' room and around the corner. At the end of the landing, she flung open the door of Saffi's bedroom and stomped to the storage chest. Lifting the lid, she said triumphantly, 'The little bitch has run away. Always knew she would. It's Mostus' fault, sniffing round her like a hungry dog.'

Corinna knelt beside the chest. The few items of clothing Verendus had provided for Saffi were gone, as was the bag she'd carried them in. She'd left without a word. 'When did you see her last?'

Dorcas shrugged. 'Before midday. I expect she heard that them Praetorians were coming here. Put the wind up her.'

Had Saffi been eavesdropping? Surely she couldn't have left so soon after Quintus' assertion about Praetorians coming to search the house. She must have overheard Mos saying they would come. It wouldn't take the Praetorians long to discover Saffi was a runaway slave – not with that **Io** denoting *property of Iolia* branded on her wrist.

If only she'd come to me, Corinna thought. I would have hidden her, kept her safe. Maybe Saffi was still here, hiding.

Dorcas folded her arms. 'Mostus will know. Them two is thick as thieves. Like I said, it's his fault. You should ask him where she's gone.'

'I will – *when* he returns from the Ministerium.'

'That's odd, domina. Could have sworn I saw him climbing over the wall and into the garden. Must've been an hour ago.'

The threat in the slave's tone was clear. Corinna looked her in the eyes and, with all the menace she could muster, said, 'Not a word of this to anyone. Remember, Dorcas, it pays to be discreet. One word, and I'll tell Tribune Quintus to sell you to…' she tried to think of something horrible. 'To the local brothel! Now go away.'

When the slave had plodded off, Corinna searched the little room, but found no clue as to where Saffi had gone. The girl could be anywhere: in the house, in the street, on a road heading out of the city. A road to where? Which direction? Walking or had she hitched a lift in a cart? Maybe she was stowed on a river barge.

Corinna tried to slow her racing mind. To search effectively, she needed to be calm. As she took a sniff of somniferum and her mind slowed, she saw the dilemma. If she searched for Saffi, then she couldn't help Verendus. She must decide. Must choose between them.

She hurried downstairs, through the kitchen and out to the garden. Lizards basking on the path darted into the shrubbery. Corinna hastened on. In the walled garden she found one of the slave boys weeding a flowerbed. She handed him a copper coin from Verendus' purse. 'Our secret,' she said, and explained what she wanted him to do. Together, neither speaking, they walked to the stables and stopped in the shadow of an archway.

A fine afternoon, the off-duty auxiliaries sat outside, ribbing each other as they polished their kit. While she waited out of sight, the boy fetched Hostus. Head down, hand scraping back unruly hair, the trooper ambled across the yard. The slave boy directed him to the arch.

Hostus blinked in the half-light. He stank of horse sweat and manure; there was mud on his tunic and straw in his hair. On seeing Corinna, the look of enquiry faded. 'Domina?' He grinned down at her.

Afraid he might misread her intentions Corinna stared back, expression stern. 'Auxiliary, you're Mos' friend.'

'Yes, domina. The lads are awful worried for him and the Commendator.' He brushed dirt from his tunic. 'I've been mucking out. The decurion told us to act busy and carry on as usual, let the Praetorians see we've nothing to hide. They're coming to search the place.'

'Indeed,' said Corinna, heartened by this show of unity. 'Hostus, I need your help.'

Somebody shuffled nearer. A shadow slinked across the yard wall and onto the arch. 'Anything I can assist with, lady?' A stocky, eager-voiced trooper edged closer and doffed his leather cap. 'Don't bother with that donkey, I'm the one who drives things round here.'

Hostus shoved him away. 'Piss off, Slug. And keep your mouth shut.'

The auxiliary's face looked as downcast as his droopy moustache. 'But I could help…'

'No,' said Hostus. 'Slither!' He turned to Corinna. 'We'll be here all day if Slug pokes his nose in.'

'Do slugs have noses?'

'Never thought about that before.' He laughed. 'Don't suppose they have moustaches either.'

He held out a hand – large, stout-fingered, the lines crossing its surface stained with tack polish. Corinna stepped back. Until this morning, when he escorted her to the Ministerium, she had paid him little heed as an individual: he was just one of the troop. Away from his comrades he was different, less self-assured. He was still grinning, baring cracked and crooked teeth. 'Got kicked in the mouth by a horse when I were a lad,' he said. 'Was me own fault.'

'Forgive me, I didn't mean to stare.'

'Doesn't matter.' He rubbed his hands together purposefully. 'What can I do for you?'

***

Once she had gone over the details with Auxiliary Hostus, Corinna returned inside and ran upstairs to her bedroom. The dish on the dressing table was empty, the jade earrings gone. She pushed aside bottles and jars of creams and cosmetics – she was certain she'd put them in the onyx dish. There wasn't time to search. She gathered up her clothes and crammed them into her bag.

With the bag over her shoulder and a bundle of clothes in her arms, she crept to Verendus' room and knocked softly. 'Mos, it's me.'

He let her in and closed the door. 'I've been waiting ages. Where've you been?'

'Making arrangements.' She dropped the loose clothes on the bed.

'What's that?'

'A place to hide.' Corinna set down her bag, picked up a long blue tunic, and smoothed out the creases.

'No!' He shook his head. 'That's girl's stuff.'

'Shut up and get dressed.'

Mos grimaced but he took the tunic, turning it over in his hands as if he'd never seen such a strange garment before. While he changed, Corinna looked out of the window. The redheaded oaf was still outside. At least there weren't any Praetorians, though they might arrive at any moment. She repeated what Quintus had said about his uncle's failure to secure Verendus' release. As for the senator friend, he probably never existed.

'So what are we going to do?' demanded Mos.

'We'll find Eldoran.' After this morning's disagreement it would be awkward to ask for his help, but where else could she turn. 'We'll start at the Ministerium.' It was the last place she'd seen him.

'The Ministerium closes early today. Everything does because of the races.'

'Hurry, then.'

'I'm not going out in this.'

'Yes, you are. Dorcas knows you're here. She mustn't see you leave the house.' Corinna turned and managed not to laugh at Mos, ridiculous in his disguise, the long tunic tucked in his belt, his tanned, hairy legs on show.

'Stand still.' She untucked the tunic so it covered his legs, threaded the thin belt around his chest, and added two balls of scrunched rag to show the soft hint of a bosom. Then she pinned on a veil that shrouded his face, twisting the fabric to suggest a knot of hair.

Mos fussed with the belt, pushing up his padded bust.

'Leave that,' she said. 'We must go. Auxiliary Hostus is readying the horses. He will escort us to the Ministerium.'

'Great! He'll get to see how stupid I look.'

'That can't be helped. We'll be safer with an escort. We're responsible for the codex and the streets are riddled with thieves and…' She thought of poor Saffi. She hadn't told Mos. He'd insist on searching for the girl and they couldn't risk further delay.

Mos pushed back the veil. 'Jupiter Maximus, I've remembered something else the Commendator said about that codex thing. Only I can't remember all of it.'

'Oh, gods, Mostus! Tell me what you do remember and the rest might follow.'

He looked dubious. 'Commendator said, *if the Empire fails you, seek out the Ennean…*' His brow furrowed. 'It's the next bit, the name, that I can't recall.'

'Do think, Mos. Was it one name or someone of somewhere?'

Mos screwed up his face in concentration. 'Someone of somewhere,' he said, at last. 'It sounded nice. Light. Lignora! That's it. Land of Lignora.'

'*Landren* of Lignora! Was the name Landren?'

'Yes, Landren. He was a last resort. I have to take the codex to the Temple of Vesta.'

'No. I'll answer to Verendus.' Corinna tried to think. Why Landren? Why take the codex to him? She searched her mind. What did she know of Landren? He was knowledgeable, eminent, rich… and a collector of old books. 'That's it!' she exclaimed, a plan forming.

'That's what?' Mos stared as if she'd lost her mind.

Corinna opened the satchel. 'Mos, the Commendator told me you're good at drawing. Draw something for me.'

'Why?'

'Please… Then we'll go to the Ministerium.' It seemed the best place to start.

His face clouded. 'What about Saffi? Is she ready to leave?'

Corinna contemplated a lie, but he'd discover the truth soon enough. She explained what had happened. 'Hostus sent a couple of off-duty auxiliaries to search for her.'

'She won't trust them. I'll have to find her.'

'No! We must go before the Praetorians come,' said Corinna, and found some parchment.

CHAPTER XXII

Corinna waited in the vestibule. The front door was closed, she couldn't see the street, though she could hear it. The shouts and laughter of passers-by, their footfalls resounding on the cobbles, the clip-clop of hooves. Every vibration set her pulse racing. She must leave before the Praetorians arrived.

In the minutes before, she had returned to her room, shut the door, and unwrapped the codex. With no time to question the ethics of what she was about to do, she'd brought the little key from her bag and set it in the keyhole of the securing band. She turned the key and the golden band sprang apart revealing a page of ancient script, the letter alpha set in a gilded square. These were the verses Magistra read before the divination service. No map here. Corinna turned the page. Turned another. She kept turning until she reached the end, then started at the beginning, scanning the words and pictures of plants and animals, but found no map of an Alpine pass. The legend was just a story.

Disappointed, and yet relieved to be free of the extra burden of responsibility – heavy enough already given the sacred texts within these pages – she had locked the codex and hastened downstairs to await the litter.

There was a clatter of feet. She stepped back, heart hammering as the door swung open.

'*Domina…*' The big doorkeeper looked inside. 'Domina, the litter is here.'

With shaking hands, Corinna adjusted her veil to cover her face and stepped outside. It hadn't been easy to persuade Quintus to let her have use of the litter; he'd become cautious since his uncle's message advising against involvement in Verendus' affairs. She had found the crumpled note discarded on the atrium floor and used it to shame him into helping her.

Across the street, the red-haired oaf was lurking under the colonnade. Corinna climbed into the curtained litter and gave a vociferous request to be conveyed to the Viorum Baths. The bearers played their part perfectly, raising the litter slowly so she had time to slip smartly out again.

Corinna waited in the shadow of the porch, willing the oaf to follow the litter, but heard no footsteps. Perhaps he was waiting a moment so as not to be seen following. Perhaps he'd spotted the ruse and was waiting for her. She wanted to check, but was certain he'd notice her. *Wait.* Count to ten. Slowly…

On nine, there was the thud of running feet. He'd fallen for it.

When the oaf was halfway along the street in pursuit of the empty litter, Corinna crept to the side gate. She rapped five times – three quick, two slow – and held her breath. There were five answering raps, the gate opened, and Mos and Hostus led the horses through.

The plan was working. Mos had taken the kit to Saffi's room, which looked out over a yard at the side of the house where Hostus had been waiting below with a ladder. Now, the kit was on the horses and the oaf was following an empty litter to the baths.

Despite her efforts, Mos had covered his disguise with a hooded paenula cape. 'You'll roast,' she said, pulling back the hood to reveal his veiled head.

Hostus burst out laughing.

Still laughing, Hostus led them in the opposite direction to the one taken by the litter bearers. The street opened into a residential square, empty save for two children playing knucklebones, and an elderly matron sitting on a bench in the sunshine. Hostus led Plum across the square. Mos and Pepper followed; Corinna walked behind.

They turned left into a narrow street of three-storey tenements. Washing hung over balconies, lines stretched across the street. A few balconies were decked in blue ribbons, proclaiming the allegiance of the insula block. Corinna glanced back, hoping against hope that Saffi would emerge from a hiding place and run to join them. She said nothing of this to Mos, though he was looking too.

They reached a large square with a fountain at the centre. A distant rumble, like a murmur of expectation, carried on the air. The Circus chariot races would soon be underway, and the square was quieter than she had dared hope. Just a few children rolling a hoop, and a grubby old man hauling a handcart of firewood across the flagstones and into an alley. Many of the shops and bars had closed their shutters, and the rest were clearing their counters.

The lack of people left the little group exposed. Beggars and pedlars came out of the shadows and honed in on the trio, intent on parting them from their coin. For every eager hawker that Hostus shoved aside, another appeared, hindering their progress and vexing the kit-laden horses. Corinna held the satchel close.

How had she become caught in Verendus' web? She was meant to be leaving Viorum to search for her father, not attempting to help a disgraced Praetorian.

The murmur of spectators rose to a steady drone. She didn't know the distance between Forum and Circus, though it sounded nearby. Mos, red-faced and sweating, stopped to hitch up his skirts. Corinna told him to hurry. She tried to calculate how long it would take the oaf to reach the baths, discover the litter was empty, and retrace his steps to the house. Then he would pick up their trail. No doubt somebody had seen the three of them set off. Dorcas probably. For the price of a jug of wine, she would point the oaf in the right direction. He could be following now. Corinna couldn't see him, but that didn't mean he wasn't there.

The drone grew to a roar; the first race was underway. The roar rose and erupted in a great boom that shuddered through her. Mos and Hostus slowed, heads turned towards the noise. Like an incoming tide, the sound had rhythm, an ebbing and flowing, building steadily as each lap was completed.

They passed another fountain. Corinna was certain she'd glimpsed it on her journey to the Ministerium this morning. She hadn't seen much from that curtained box, but she remembered hearing water and drawing back the curtain to see women gathered around a fountain with statues of nereids at the centre. Only a few women were there now, chattering as they washed clothes in the bubbling water.

Her pulse quickened. Almost there. If the doors of the Ministerium were closed, how would she find Landren?

As she turned to tell Mos to hasten, thousands of voices surged like a great wave, drowning her words.

'Bet the Greens won,' he said, shouting against the din.

'Better not,' said Hostus. 'I staked a denarius on Blue.'

Ahead, the bars lining the pavement were crowded with men drinking, voices loud, rough. Head low, Corinna pushed through the crowd and into the Forum. The vast square was seething with people. Those unable to get a seat at the Circus had congregated here, within earshot of the drama. She headed past the Atrox Column and the Temple of Vesta towards the basilica. Huge, brightly painted statues of the gods and the imperial family inhabited niches along the building's upper level, watching over the square with blank gazes. She passed beneath the basilica arches and halted by one of the supporting columns.

At the far end of the colonnade, lawyers and their scribes were packing up for the day, clients and onlookers drifting away. Moneylenders rose from behind their tables, counted their coins into piles, and dropped them clinking into leather pouches. All under the watchful eyes of club-bearing bodyguards.

Across the square, the Ministerium doors stood wide, a steady stream of men emerging.

'Domina, I'd best get back to the house.' Hostus handed over Plum's reins. 'There'll be a proper stink if the Praetorians turn up and I'm not there.'

Corinna thanked him, wished he didn't have to go, but she didn't want him to get into trouble. He wouldn't take any coin for his help, but she insisted – if the search for Saffi proved successful, the girl would need safe lodgings.

'Don't go kissing any strange men,' he said, with a wink to Mos. He trudged off and disappeared into the crowd.

Without the big auxiliary's presence Corinna felt vulnerable, confidence wilting in the afternoon heat. Her fingers trembled, itching to open the somniferum. Plum, who had been calm in Hostus' presence, snorted and pulled at the reins. The stallion could sense her unease.

'When can I change out of this?' said Mos, lifting the veil to scratch his neck. 'You all right?' he added when she didn't reply. 'Want me to go in there?'

But he didn't know Landren. She had to do this. She handed over Plum's reins and told him to wait.

Corinna straightened her veil. With a nod to Mos, she set off, weaving a path across the packed square, endeavouring to avoid the touts and beggars roaming the crowd. Everywhere was noise: a wailing baby, dogs barking, a singer with a couple of musicians belting out a bawdy song. Stallholders selling coloured ribbons for the races vied with merchants, trinket vendors, and a pie-man – all shouting their wares.

Blinking in the sunshine, men filed out of the Ministerium. Corinna slowed as four bearers set down a litter. By the doors, standing a head above them, was a giant of a man: a Herculean doorkeeper, a rod in his hand. Earlier, with Hostus at her side, she had walked in unquestioned. With no escort, the doorkeeper was bound to stop her. She would have to sneak past him.

She edged to the far side of the wide doors and inched nearer, creeping around the stationary litter. Someone pulled her cloak.

'Spare a coin, lady.' A beggar stuck out his hand.

At the same moment, a ragged boy slipped past her and she felt a tug on the strap of the satchel. They were working as a pair. As Corinna pushed the boy away, he made a grab for the satchel. She pushed again, harder. He stumbled backwards, crashing into a wispy-haired minister who was manoeuvring into the litter.

The man groaned, the doorkeeper hastened to assist, and the boy scrambled to his feet and fled, following the beggar into the crowd.

Corinna dodged around them and through the doors. Hugging the satchel close, she squeezed through the departing assembly, past the altar and into the atrium, scrutinising faces as she went. The reek of sweat and aromatic scent took her breath. She jostled a route to the stairs, climbed a few steps, and scanned the atrium. A sea of heads, mostly grey and balding. No glimpse of Landren's raven hair and vibrant robes amid the white tunics and togas.

Boot studs click-clacked on the stairs, and she turned as two Praetorians – a regular and his commendator – descended. Corinna shrank aside. They mustn't notice her, she should look away, but it was cruel irony to see the uniform with the wrong man inside. Perhaps she looked too long, for the commendator, who bore little resemblance to Verendus, met her gaze and smiled. Blood drained from her head and an airless fog rushed in. Unaccompanied, and thus conspicuous, she was taking a risk. He might think she was soliciting.

Corinna felt his eyes follow as she elbowed a retreat to the doors. Men grumbled, stopped to stare. So many people. Too many. She must get out. She reached the doors and knocked against someone. A man in amethyst robes halted abruptly. Corinna's heart leapt.

He glared over his shoulder. It wasn't Landren.

'I beg your pardon.' The man peered down his imperious nose.

'Forgive me,' said Corinna. 'Is Lord Landren here? You were with him this morning. Please, I must see him…'

His brow creased. 'And you are?'

She gabbled an explanation about how she'd spoken with Landren earlier. Was the man listening? Merely being civil? His serene countenance gave no hint. Breathless, cheeks burning, Corinna stopped talking and stepped aside to let a minister pass.

'It was my understanding that Lord Landren could not assist with your enquiry,' said the Lignoran, frown deepening. 'Please excuse me, we are causing an obstruction.'

Corinna followed him outside. He must not get away. 'Please wait,' she called, scurrying alongside to keep up. 'It's not about what we discussed earlier. It's…' No, too soon to mention Verendus. To persuade this man to take her to Landren, she needed to be inventive. 'I have the item he asked about.'

The man stopped and turned to face her. In the bright sunlight he looked older, in his middle-years, the pale skin stretched tight across a fine-boned face, his dark hair streaked with grey. 'What item?' he asked, impatience sharpening his tone.

'Landren told me to inform him as soon as I got it,' she said, embroidering the lie.

'Indeed?'

Corinna stood her ground. 'Landren was most insistent. The item is very precious. We brought it all the way from Iolia.'

'*Iolia*…' His eyes widened and he stared as though she'd slapped him.

'Please. Please help…'

A moment's consideration and then, recovering his composure, the Lignoran bowed. 'My name is Oriedas. Lord Landren departed the Ministerium a half-hour ago. But come, I will take you to him.'

Though not tall he was very upright and walked with a purposeful stride, cutting through the crowd. Corinna caught up and diverted him across the square to the basilica arches where Mos waited. She made the introductions and before the boy could say anything to discredit her lie, added, 'Mos, no talking until we get there.'

With a roll of his eyes, he pulled up the paenula hood.

Oriedas cast a dispassionate glance over the boy sweltering beside the kit-laden horses, and told them to follow. He led the way to a side street near the basilica. Corinna looked back at the square. At this warm, mid-afternoon hour, the crowds had thinned and most of the shops and houses were shuttered. They headed west and the noise of the Circus diminished. Progress through the narrow streets and quiet squares was brisk. She remained alert, determined to observe all she could of their surroundings in case she had to find the route un-aided. As Oriedas led them past yet another drab insula block and row of warehouses, she doubted she'd be able to. Twice he changed direction and double backed as if he knew some-one followed, though Corinna spotted no one on their tail.

He brought them to a large, plain house with an iron-stud-ded door. The shuttered façade was bordered by a high wooden gate on one side and an apothecary's shop on the other. The shop was open for business, jars and miniature am-phorae arranged on the marble counter, bunches of herbs hanging from a rail above. The smell reminded her of the dis-pensary at the Temple, and a pang of nostalgia for a life of peace and order filled her.

Oriedas knocked on the gate and a lad came and led the horses inside. Stables stood on both sides of the yard, and an archway at the end opened on a garden lush with ornamental trees in enormous bronze pots. Oriedas beckoned them through, unlocked the door at the far side, and escorted them along a passageway to a bright atrium surrounded by many doors.

Inside, the house was far larger and grander than the austere façade suggested. Beneath the roof vent, stood a fountain carved with fantastical beasts – half steed, half fish – water gushing from the horses' mouths and teeming noisily into a huge stone bowl.

Mos paused for a closer look; Corinna dragged him on.

Oriedas ushered them into a lamp-lit room where a wine jug, glasses, and a plate of small cakes waited on a table as if someone had been expecting them. He left, shutting the door behind him.

Mos shed the paenula, pulled a rag from the neck of his tunic, and mopped his forehead. He fiddled with the veil, itching to pull it off. Corinna reached for the wine jug.

'Don't!' Mos seized her wrist. 'There might be stuff in it. Poison or something.'

She shook free. 'Really, Mostus, you sound like the Commendator.'

'Good. He said if anything happened to him, then I must look out for you. And he wouldn't want you drinking it, so!'

Sunlight flooded the room. 'I assure you, it is an excellent vintage.' Landren stood at the door, his expression unreadable. 'Please be seated. When the lady Corinna has poured wine for the three of us, do try the chestnut cake.' He arched an eyebrow. 'Mostus, I presume?'

Mos tore off the veil and grabbed a cake.

Landren closed the door and turned to Corinna. 'When Oriedas informed me of your arrival, he said you have the item I enquired about. Was that a fabrication to gain my attention?'

She blushed. 'Not exactly, but I was afraid you would refuse to see me.'

'Well, you are here now, so please speak candidly.'

Corinna didn't know where best to begin, so she told how the Seers' prophecy of a hostile fleet came to pass when she saw strange ships approaching Iolia. As she told of the formation of a new military organisation called the Iolian Watch, which was persecuting Parhels on the island, Mos interrupted to say that Parhels were forced to wear yellow bibs, marking them out as easy targets. 'I saw a boy killed,' he blurted. 'Younger than me, he was. A man smashed in his head with a hammer. People were cheering...'

'A brutal death,' said Landren.

Corinna put a hand on Mos' arm. He sniffed and turned away, unable to continue. She told Landren of their flight from Iolia, how they sailed through the Rings to the mainland, journeyed to the fortress of Castellum Alba and on to Viorum where Verendus had been arrested on charge of treason. She didn't mention the codex – not yet.

Landren listened with polite interest; he made no offer of help. 'After all, if Senator Decimius could not assist, what can I, who am not an imperial citizen, hope to achieve? I have some influence with two or three local ministers, but why would I expend this to help a stranger? Besides, the decision rests with Emperor Flavio. Treason is a heinous crime. If Verendus is guilty, he must face the charge.'

'But he's innocent!' She wasn't certain of this, but she wouldn't back down. 'He'll be executed. They will...' The word *crucify* caught in her throat. It was rare for a Reman citizen to be crucified, but she feared they would make an example of him. Tears stung her eyes. She saw again the row of crosses lining the road to Viorum, the bruised and burnt bodies of men and women hanging there. She heard again that pitiful groan and remembered screaming at Dorcas to shut the wagon door.

Landren was watching her, his face a mixture of curiosity and concern.

'If you won't help, we'll ask Tribune Aquinus,' Mos said, mouth full of cake. 'He's the Commendator's friend, he'll do something.'

Landren raised a hand. 'All you have told me about the situation in Iolia accords with what I suspected. And yet I am unaware of any official report of unrest.'

'Soon as we reached Gallia Narbonensis the Commendator sent word of the strife,' said Mos.

Landren shook his head. 'Perhaps it was to someone's advantage to suppress that information. The only report I heard concerning the island stated that the Iolian Gap is clear and the harbour has reopened.' He set down his glass. 'Tell me about this item which you believe I am interested in.'

In response, Corinna opened the satchel and handed him a fold of parchment.

As Landren inspected the picture Mos had drawn of the codex, a flicker of emotion troubled his face. 'How came you by this?' he said evenly.

'It belongs to Verendus' father. He asked him to sell it in Gallia Narbonensis.'

Mos shot her a look of alarm, though whether he was shocked by her lie or worried she would attempt to sell the codex to Landren, Corinna couldn't tell. She didn't mention Verendus' behest to find Landren – he might demand that the codex be handed over immediately, and she'd lose all bargaining power.

Landren's unguarded expression suggested he wasn't expecting the codex. Though he seemed intrigued by Mos' drawing. If she was careful, if he really was interested, then she might make this work.

'You consider me a prospective buyer?' Landren said, jolting Corinna from her deliberations.

'You told me you collect old books. You're interested, aren't you?'

'I would like to see it.'

Corinna exhaled; she could feel her position strengthening. 'I cannot arrange that without Verendus' permission.'

'Unfortunate.' Landren went to the door.

'Won't this do, sir?' said Mos. 'I drew it careful.'

'You draw well, young man.'

'Commendator taught me. If I were half as good as him, I'd think myself blessed. He can glance at anything and draw it clear as if he'd stared for hours.'

'High praise indeed. And if you have yet to acquire that talent, I surmise that the codex is in your possession.' Landren returned the parchment. 'Given the load your horses bear, it appears you are embarking on a journey. I doubt you would have left the codex behind. If this piece is what I believe it is, then yes, I am interested.'

'We could reach an agreement?' Corinna said.

'Perhaps. But I must see it first.'

He'd outmanoeuvred her. She remembered the codex key, safe at the bottom of her bag. He wasn't getting that. 'Please, grant us a moment.'

'Time does not pause with you.' Landren left, closing the door behind him.

'Can we trust him?' demanded Mos, taking another cake. 'How will he help?'

'I don't know,' Corinna said. 'But the Commendator told you to find Landren if things went wrong. Now we must place our trust in him.'

CHAPTER XXIII

'Wakey, wakey.'

Verendus' eyes snapped open. He hadn't meant to sleep. It can't have been for long.

Optio Rectus busied himself at the table where the lamp burned steadily. Galenius had gone, as had the basket of pain. Dear gods, the sod could be plying those tools on Mos right now. Verendus swallowed, his throat so sore it seemed a rock was lodged there.

Rectus turned, a needle and thread in his fat fingers. Verendus tugged at the restraints. The optio really was going to sew his eyelids open.

'Calm down.' Rectus pinned the needle at his tunic hem and grasped Verendus' left hand. He pulled at the signet ring. 'I'll get this off first, then I'll do me bit of sewing.'

Verendus flinched away and his knuckle popped. 'Rectus, listen to me! The boy. For fuck's sake, get Mostus out of here. I'll pay whatever you ask.'

'Your finger's all puffy. Sorry, mate, I'll have to snip it off.' The grip tightened. With his free hand, he whipped a pair of pincers from his apron pocket. 'Don't fret, I'll make it quick.'

'No!' Verendus tried to pull away. 'Get Mos out of here, I beg you. I've coin. Name your sum.'

Rectus snorted. 'The prefect would have my bollocks in the grinder then, and no mistake. Listen, mate,' he winked a bloodshot eye, 'word of advice, one soldier to another. The prefect's a nasty bit of work. The only way to save that boy is to start talking.'

Nausea swelled, simmering hot inside. Cold sweat prickled his skin. *Concentrate.* A low drone invaded his head. Must shut it out and think. Something stirred in his mind. Something that had troubled him earlier. That bloody droning sound made it hard to concentrate. *Think!* What had troubled him? Something about the binder. Yes, that was it. If Galenius had the binder, then surely, he had the satchel, *and* the codex. And yet he was demanding the codex. Mos must have followed orders and taken it to the Temple of Vesta.

That was good. It would be safe there. Keep quiet and the codex would be safe.

Thoughts of defiance soared and crashed faster than a broken arrow. It wouldn't be long before Galenius got the truth out of Mos and discovered where he'd taken the codex. With Mos at stake, any attempt to play Galenius at his own game was too great a risk. If Galenius wanted the codex, he could bloody well have the thing.

Breathing garlic, the optio leaned closer and slapped him hard. 'You listening, mate? Prefect Galenius is bent as the fucking Circus track. He's not like you and me. It's not just cunny with him. He's got a taste for lads too. Lads like your Mostus. About fifteen is he? That's how Galenius likes 'em. If you don't talk, he'll have that boy. And when he's buggered him senseless, when the boy's no further use...' Rectus sighed and drew a forefinger across his throat. 'He'll get me to do that bit.' He opened the pincer claws. 'Tell Galenius what he wants – for the boy's sake. Now, let's see about your finger.'

'Wait!' screamed Verendus, eyes fixed on the iron claws. 'I'll talk.'

The drone intensified. A sour, vinegary aroma filled the air. 'Knew you'd see sense.'

A sharp whack. Rectus winced, mouth reddening. Bubbles of blood foamed on his lips and spilled over his stubbled chin. He groaned and collapsed. His head struck the floor with a thud.

Verendus squinted at the dark corners across the cell. At the edge of his vision, something moved. He pulled as far as the chains would permit. He hadn't imagined it. Someone was there. A figure shrouded in a hooded cloak, a rod raised in its left hand. Silently, it crept nearer.

Verendus yanked at the restraints. Hopeless. He braced, determined not to show weakness and cry out. Jupiter Optimus Maximus, father of the gods, let it be swift.

The blow never came. The figure straightened and a pale hand shot from the folds of the cloak. 'Quiet!' The voice was as firm and cold as the hand covering his mouth. 'Do exactly as I say and I shall free you. Blink twice to show you understand.'

Verendus met the limpid green eyes that stared from the shadow of the hood, but felt no reassurance. Nonetheless, he obeyed and the hooded man set down the rod. It was a mop. The cleaner? Not with eyes like that. Eyes like Corinna's.

The hooded man bent and unhooked the keys from the optio's belt. He flicked through the bunch, selected a key, and unlocked the shackles. After hours of being chained with only the balls of his feet touching the floor, Verendus was standing unaided, the concrete wet and sticky underfoot.

His knees buckled. He put out a steadying hand and sank down. With a shiver of revulsion, he realised he was slumped in his own blood and waste. He dragged himself clear of the mess, tried to rise, but his legs were like putty. Everything ached. He wiped his hands on his tunic, but there was no tunic – he'd smeared blood across his skin. He closed his eyes. Drifted.

A flask was pressed to his lips. 'Drink.'

A burst of honey, bitter herbs, spices, and then the piquant liquor burnt his throat. Warmth coursed through him, melting his pain. 'Who are you?' Verendus gasped. 'Find Mos.'

'Mos? Mostus is safe.'

Relief surged, rushed to his head, and stung eyes too dry to weep. Doubt sobered him. 'But how? How did you get him out?'

'He is safe – trust me.' From the dark corner beside the door he fetched a pair of semi-circular buckets, the two wood and leather containers sealed with lids and joined by a single handle. He uncovered one and brought out a fabric bundle. 'I am Oriedas of Lignora, aide to Lord Landren. Put this on.'

Landren again. Why did his name keep cropping up? Questions engulfed Verendus. 'Did he send you, Lignoran?'

'No time for questions.'

Oriedas had to help him into the strange garment. A silky sack of a thing with mesh slit-eyes, mitten hands, and a drawstring at the neck and crown. It sheathed his whole body and stank of the sour aroma.

Oriedas pulled off the mop head and stuffed it into the bucket – now it was a staff. He moved the buckets back to the corner, then wrapped Verendus' fingers around the staff. Straining under the exertion, he got him up, past Rectus' body, and across the cell.

While Verendus leaned against the wall and endeavoured to remain upright, Oriedas drew the embedded knife from the optio's neck. Cleaning it on the dead man's tunic, he said, 'Another sentry patrols this wing. Shout for him; see he causes no trouble. Await me here.'

And with that, he was gone.

Verendus edged along the wall until he was behind the door. He probed his left hand inside the coverall. The ring was there, his little finger swollen and flaccid. He'd have to remedy that.

He grasped his finger and set his jaw. Do it!

One quick click. Pain shot through him and he set the joint back into its socket. He wiped his eyes and took a moment to compose himself before raising the staff. He must find the strength to do this. He took a breath and did his best to mimic Rectus' raspy tone. 'Ho, Guard.'

No answer. No sound of feet approaching. He waited, listening intently, trying to gauge how long to allow before trying again. Still no one came. All he could hear was that bloody droning noise. It was coming from one of the buckets. He glared at the lid but didn't open it. He cleared his throat, and shouted, 'Ho, Guard! Help with this.'

'Rectus? What d'you want now?' A guard plodded in and stopped a couple of cubits from the hiding place behind the door.

Poised to strike, Verendus tensed, tried not to cough. The staff shook in his hands. He couldn't see the guard's face, but the stoop of the man's shoulders suggested he was staring at the corpse on the floor. The guard bent closer, reached out… Verendus tightened his grip and brought the staff crashing down.

It took two blows to floor the guard. Even then, the brute rallied, rolled over to face him, and fought to rise, gripping the end of the shaft and trying to shove it back.

Verendus held on. He stamped his right foot on the guard's chest and kept pushing, striving to tighten his grip on the staff, the mitten hands slipping. The guard struggled, grunting as he tried to force the staff aside. They reached an impasse, frozen in time like two figures painted on a vase.

Verendus pressed harder and his left foot slipped on the damp floor. The sole of the coverall lacked the traction of an iron-studded caliga boot. The guard pushed against him. Verendus recovered his balance and kept him down. If he didn't finish this soon…

Gritting his teeth, he found the will, forcing the blunt end down, ever closer, pressing it towards the dip of the guard's throat. As wood met flesh, he sunk his weight behind the staff, pushed with all his might, and the guard's skin punctured with a dull pop. A gush of blood and the staff slid on to jar against the spine.

Verendus exhaled and drew out the staff. He crouched, gasping for air. Get up. Get the keys.

He was unhooking them from the guard's belt when Oriedas returned and tutted at the blood. Verendus slipped the ring of keys onto his wrist like a bracelet. Using the staff for leverage, he rocked to his feet and collided with the table, almost knocking over the lamp. The flame flared and something glinted. Something small and white. A spark of hope ignited, firing him to his senses. He snatched up the horse-head talisman and pulled the cord over his head. Truly, the gods were watching over him.

With the staff and the arm of his rescuer to support him, he staggered out through the cell door and along a torch-lit passageway. A metal gate barred the end. Oriedas set down his buckets, searched through the keys, and unlocked it. As he ushered Verendus through, someone shouted. Hobnail boots clacked on the concrete floor.

'Lock the gate!' Oriedas ran on and around the corner.

Alone now, Verendus swayed, grasped at the bars to steady himself, and fell against them. The gate swung forward. It clanged against the wall and the keys dropped, clattering on the floor. Enough noise to rouse a mausoleum.

He sank to his knees and groped for the keys. Save for one, which was larger than the others, they all looked much the same. He fumbled through the bunch. Each of the smaller keys had a numeral scratched into the bow. If they were the keys to the cell doors, then the large key might serve the gates.

The footsteps were getting louder. Verendus groaned. Must get up. Get up now. Using the gate for support, he clambered to his feet. The mitten hands were clumsy, and it took three attempts to slot the key into the lock. At last, he turned the key and the gate was secured.

As he lurched along the passageway, there was a muffled shriek. Ahead, the passageway turned. He didn't know what had caused the disturbance. If something had happened to Oriedas, the odds of escaping this place would be even grimmer.

Verendus reached the corner and slowed. He adjusted his grip on the staff, preparing himself to fight. He stood, listening, alert for movement or an intake of breath. Not a sound, and yet he sensed someone was there. Cautiously, he peered around the corner.

In the anteroom beyond, a guard's body lay sprawled beside an overturned desk, the Lignoran and his buckets waited beside it. 'What took you so long?' said Oriedas.

Verendus didn't have the breath to answer.

Three further passages led from the anteroom, each barred by a metal gate. Oriedas unlocked the left-hand gate into a wide, dimly lit passageway that stank of sweat and soiled straw. Chains clanked, men's voices grumbled in the shadows. Verendus hesitated. Where was the Lignoran leading him?

'Come,' said Oriedas. 'Leave this gate open.'

He directed Verendus past iron-banded doors and along the passage to a large, cage-like cell. In place of a wall and door, floor-to-ceiling bars of thick iron separated the cell from the passageway. The prisoners within this stinking, multi-occupancy hell were pale shadows, wretches with the skeletal, rash-covered bodies of men who have been left to rot. Only their ankles were fettered and, on seeing Oriedas, several of them clattered nearer, straining against their restraints and stretching scrawny hands towards the bars, though none could reach them. A few rattled their chains. An old man with matted hair and a long beard that reached his gaunt chest, pointed a crooked finger at Verendus. 'You! Yes, you. Listen! There is no escape.' He spoke Latin with the precise accent of a patrician. 'No one gets out alive.'

'Who are you, sir? Why are you here?' asked Verendus, drawing closer.

'Stay back!' Oriedas pulled him away and unhooked the bunch of keys. He removed the largest one and tossed the rest through the bars. The prisoners fell on the keys, scrabbling and fighting in the filthy straw. 'Hurry,' he said, dragging Verendus on.

They reached a gate, which Oriedas unlocked with the big key. They passed through and he locked it behind them. Now Verendus understood. Without a gate key the prisoners could not follow, though they might hamper any guards who tried to.

The passage divided. Bearing left, they passed more iron-banded doors. Verendus stumbled, almost fell. He steadied himself with the staff. How much further?

His head throbbed and the coverall was too hot. They reached another gate, unlocked and locked it behind them. They passed three more doors and the passageway turned. No window, no door, just a solitary torch in a bracket on the wall. A dead end.

Verendus punched the wall and instantly regretted it. 'Wrong way,' he cried, and clenched his teeth to mask the pain. He looked back in the direction from which they had come. He had a key. He'd find his own way out.

'I shall need your help,' said Oriedas, setting down the buckets. The low droning noise started again. Paying it no heed, he brought two wrenches from his cloak, handed one over, and pointed at the floor.

Blinkered by the coverall, Verendus had to bend his head forward to see. Beneath their feet was a metal cover, circular and flush with the floor. He put down the staff, knelt beside Oriedas, and they set to work.

The cover, dark with rust and grime, seemed cemented in place; may not have been lifted for decades. Verendus strained but couldn't shift it.

'Sentries!' said Oriedas.

Footsteps echoed through the maze of passages, impossible to discern how near. Oriedas put down the wrench and uncoupled the buckets. He picked one up and shook it. The drone became a buzz. Verendus grappled with the wrench.

The footsteps grew louder; a gate was unlocked. The buzz, which was coming from a bucket, rose to a shrill vibration. As the guards turned the corner, Oriedas angled the bucket, pointing the top towards the passageway. He flipped up the lid and a dark cluster exploded.

Verendus flinched, but the swirling black swarm massed in the air like a ball of dense smoke. With a piercing whine the swarm whooshed along the passageway, guards fleeing in its wake. Men screamed, begging their comrades for help. Verendus cringed, couldn't shut out the cries.

'More guards will come.' Oriedas knelt. 'We must not slow.'

Still the cover wouldn't budge. A few bees lingered, disorientated, around the bucket. One crawled up his sleeve. Blue-black in colour and bigger than any bee he'd seen before, he dare not pause to flick it away.

'Its sting cannot penetrate the fabric,' Oriedas said. Despite his ordinary looking cloak and tunic, he showed no fear of the bees.

The screams ceased. The prisoners must have fled their cell only to share the guards' fate. Preferable to the cross or being thrown to beasts in the arena, but still a shameful and terrible death. Jupiter Maximus, may his taste of freedom not be as brief.

'Lift!' ordered Oriedas.

Verendus sighed and licked his lips, still tingling with the piquant liquor. A rush of vigour steeled him. He heaved and the metal grated and moved. Again, and the cover slid clear, clanging on the stone floor.

A foul stench, the reek of a thousand public latrines, erupted from the hole beneath. Oriedas rose and seized the torch from its bracket. Together they peered into the murk. Something was moving.

'Rats.' Verendus drew back. 'Oh, shit.'

'Alas, that also.' Oriedas handed him the torch and brought a small sack from the other bucket. He set this over his shoulder and, agile as a monkey, dropped down into the hole.

The steady drip, drip, drip of water resounded from the abyss. Verendus wielded the torch nearer. The hole wasn't as deep as it appeared; Oriedas, hand outstretched, was within touching distance. Verendus passed down the torch and then the staff. He took a long breath. There was no going back.

Eyes watering, the muscles in his arms burning with the exertion, he lowered himself through the hole and dropped the short distance to a ledge, where he crouched, getting his bearings.

The tunnel resembled an enormous drainpipe. Beside the narrow ledge, a river of effluence sloshed into the darkness. Already he was retching. He took the staff and attempted to stand. Impossible. The curving walls of the sewer meant no one over five-and-a-half feet could have stood upright. Moss grew like fur on the walls. Under his stockinged feet, the ledge was slippery with thick, cold slime. He leaned on the staff. Head bent, shoulders stooped, he edged after Oriedas in the direction of the slow-flowing waste.

The rats followed. Squeaking and scuttling, they climbed over Verendus and clung to his clothes. Some plopped into the stinking stream and scrambled desperately against the smooth banks. None touched Oriedas, and those before him ran on out of his path. Ahead, beyond the lamp, the darkness was less impenetrable. A few more shuffled steps and grey light permeated a circular grille. The stream flowed through, though anything larger than the fist-sized holes would be trapped. Only the lower third of the grille was underwater. They would have to wrench it open.

Metal clanked. As Verendus glanced behind, a lantern was lowered through the opening in the tunnel roof, where it hung a moment like a bright, all-seeing eye. Voices drifted down; a pair of caligae-shod feet dangled in mid-air. 'Guards!' he hissed, and sidled on as Oriedas extinguished the torch.

Boots pounded the concrete ledge. A new torch flared. Shadows, huge in the gloom, floated along the walls. 'Halt!' yelled an authoritative voice.

Verendus pressed closer to the wall.

'Deal with them,' Oriedas said, without pausing from loosening the grille. An arrow sped by and jangled against the iron. 'Now!'

Verendus tried to turn, but wobbled on the ledge. He flattened against the sewer wall. He could barely stand, let alone manoeuvre. An arrow whizzed above him and clattered off the wall. Too close.

He jumped into the sewage and turned, sliding. The sludge reached his knees and chilled him to the bone, though incredibly he was dry; the muck had not seeped through the coverall. In the faint light, he could scarcely distinguish guards from gloom. With luck, they were having the same problem.

Another arrow. He ducked, almost slipped, and stepped on a chunk of what felt like rubble rough under the fabric heel. As he clutched the staff and regained his balance, an idea formed.

He raised the staff, drew it back behind his shoulder, and launched it as a javelin. It flew straight and true and thwacked into a guard who flopped backwards onto his comrade, sending both splashing and cursing into the filthy stream.

Oriedas was still grappling with the grille.

'Stand clear!' shouted Verendus. With a burst of energy, he lurched through the sludge to shunt against it. The metal creaked, he shoved again, and the grille dropped out. He toppled forward with it and Oriedas shoved him through.

Verendus gulped like a landed fish and clambered up, marvelling at the leaden sky and a shimmer of pallid sunshine fading in the west. Joy flooded him. He was free and Mos was safe. The gods were merciful. He would never complain about anything again.

The sewer emptied into a river. As he skidded down the slimy bank, a cry echoed in the tunnel. Oriedas climbed through the opening. 'Those guards won't bother us,' he said.

They crept upstream of the waste and stood at the water's edge. Oriedas pulled a length of rope from the sack, then removed his cloak and bundled it inside. He secured the rope about Verendus' waist and gathered up the slack. 'The current is strong. I will guide you. Soldiers patrol the bridge and the castrum roof. Keep quiet.'

Knee-deep in freezing water, they inched along the submerged bank until it fell away and they waded into the river. Weeds wound around Verendus' ankles and his feet sank in mud, but he stumbled on through the foul water until it was deep enough to swim.

The churning current embraced him, tugging his legs and seeping through the coverall until the silky fabric clung like a second skin. Gods, it was icy cold. He focused on the far bank where the pale glow of braziers lit the riverside road. Surely he was getting nearer. Each chill breath squeezed his chest and his limbs ached. If only he could rest. With numb feet, he searched for the riverbed. It had sunk out of reach.

The darkness receded. There, beyond the bend in the river, was the towered bridge he had crossed to enter the city, the scene much like Mos' sketch shown bashfully on an evening that seemed a lifetime ago. Brightly lit, the bridge was thick with soldiers patrolling the length.

The scene shifted. Drizzle misted his vision. A sensation of insurmountable distance, of being on the outside looking in, overwhelmed him. His stroke floundered. Water surged over his head. Desperately he kicked to the surface. Again the water swallowed him, pulling him down, rushing into his nose and mouth and burning his lungs. With leaden legs he kicked again, splashed, and faltered. The old patrician's voice whispered in his head.

No one gets out alive. No one…

No more. No further. He was spent.

The current gripped and dragged him thrashing into its depths.

CHAPTER XXIV

Verendus slipped from a shadowland of glare, gloom, and muted voices into a realm inhabited by creatures of strange ilk. How had he come here? Was this the Underworld? He had crossed a river; that much he remembered.

He was lying on the ground, too dark to tell where. Some-one was whispering. He listened, straining, trying to make out the words. *No one gets out alive. No one…*

Someone touched his chest and pressed hard. He gasped for breath, couldn't rise. Black bees the size of mice crawled over him, six-legged rats ran down the walls and scrambled shrieking across the blanket. They vanished at his swipe, only to reappear moments later.

Again, he tried to rise, but they were there above him, hanging in the air, two yellow snakes, fangs bared. Slithering closer they merged and twined together, each swallowing the other's tail to become a phixus, sign of the serpents.

He must escape, swim back across the river to the land of mortal men. He tussled with the blanket. It was weighing him down; impossible to break free. If only he could lift it. He swiped aside another rat and sank back, exhausted. He was wet. Must have reached the river. Gods help him, he didn't have the strength to swim.

The wagon rocked and changed direction. Water sloshed from the bowl in Corinna's hands, splashing the front of her tunic and soaking Verendus. Kneeling closer to the low bunk, she braced against the motion and dipped her cloth into what little water remained. She squeezed out the cloth and mopped his brow.

She could look at him now. Now that she knew he was alive. When Mos and Oriedas hauled him in: bloated, red-faced, helpless as a giant swaddled baby, she had turned away and fetched the somniferum.

Inhaling the opiate had not calmed her. Panic quickened her pulse and deadened her mind, reducing her to a useless bystander. Thank Fortuna, Mos had cleaned him. Oriedas took charge of everything else. From a box under the wagon bunk he'd brought linen bandages, a jar of salve, and sachets of herbs – some that Corinna could not identify. Briefly but clearly, he had shown her which herbs to mix into an infusion to calm fever and which ones to add to the salve to soothe the cuts and bruises that marbled Verendus' body. There was no need to instruct her how much somniferum was required to ease his pain.

At Landren's house, before the rescue plan was devised, she had told Oriedas of her life in the Temple, how unhappy she'd been. Perhaps because of his interest, she had said more than she'd intended, of finding solace working in the herb garden, and how helping at the dispensary entailed treating ailments and injuries. Oriedas had listened, asked a few pertinent questions, and then nodded thoughtfully and said her skills would be an asset.

After an hour rattling along in the moonlight, Oriedas told the driver to steer the wagon off the road and into woodland. Mos was sent outside to keep watch.

'Must we stop?' asked Corinna. 'What about the Praetorians?'

'If they were following we would know by now,' Oriedas said. 'It is possible the guards on the bridge saw Verendus thrashing in the river and assumed he drowned. The far bank, where Mos and I dragged him out, is poorly lit. With luck, they did not see us.'

Having done his best to ensure their patient was comfortable, Oriedas took over the watch. Mos wrapped himself in a blanket and was soon snoring softly and twitching in his sleep.

Despite a restless night at Landren's house, Corinna couldn't sleep. Verendus knew nothing of the bargain she'd made. She propped his satchel against the bunk and knelt beside. Of course, he might never wake up.

At dawn, the wagon set off. Corinna took a sniff of somniferum and mixed another dose for Verendus. Despite the chill air, he was sweating freely.

'His chest looks sore. Is there anything you can put on it?' Mos stifled a yawn.

'It needs re-stitching,' said Corinna. Amid the lacerations was a large, sour smelling wound. Whoever patched up the gash on his chest had made a poor job of it.

'Do you think Hostus found Saffi? We shouldn't have left without her. She doesn't know Viorum. She won't know where we've gone.'

'Hostus will look after her.'

'If he finds her!'

Corinna didn't reply. There was nothing she could do to help Saffi.

With the rolling gait of a sailor, Mos shambled to the rear of the wagon where Oriedas crouched with the door open on the shadowy road, looking out over the backs of Plum and Pepper who trotted behind. He squatted beside Oriedas. 'Sir, why have we changed course?'

'We cannot chance the highway.'

Mos shook his head. 'But what about bandits and Helutti slaves?'

'A risk we must take. On this road, if the Praetorians follow, Dacoren might lose them before the next river.'

Dacoren, the wagon driver, was a swarthy Lignoran with a permanent scowl. His Latin was basic, though even when speaking with Oriedas in his own tongue his words were few. All that mattered to Corinna was that he kept the wagon moving at a good pace. Though it would never match the speed of galloping horses if the Praetorians closed in.

Drizzle became rain. 'It could be a rough ride for our patient,' said Oriedas, and closed the wagon door.

'He's still unconscious, he...' Corinna's voice drowned in the brisk tempo of a shower drumming the roof.

'It is to be expected.' Oriedas pushed past the pile of kit towards her. 'His eyes opened briefly when I purged him of the river water. Let him sleep.'

'This wound, it's so badly stitched. Now it's inflamed like an ulcer...'

Oriedas wielded the lantern. Light fell on the bunk and lit Verendus' chest. Beneath the translucent surface of the ulcer, the raw flesh was alive with movement. Oriedas recoiled. He brought a pouch from inside his cloak and pulled out a slender blade. 'Quick, Corinna. Bucket, water, cloth. Mostus help me sit him up.'

The wagon swayed. Oriedas shifted his stance and put out a hand to steady himself on the edge of the bunk. With his free hand he plied the blade, using its tip to sever the stitches.

The lump burst. Corinna covered her mouth – the wound was teeming with tiny, wriggling maggots.

Colour drained from Mos' cheeks. 'Yuk! How did they get in there?'

'A fly. The injury was not adequately dressed.' Oriedas worked swiftly, scraping out the stinking mass with a small, blunt-headed tool. 'They have eaten away the bad flesh; it is not deep. I have seen such creatures befoul battlefield corpses, though they seldom afflict the living. I shall re-stitch.'

'He'll get better… won't he?'

'Time alone can answer your question, Mostus.'

In the confines of the wagon, the stench of decay was powerful. Corinna swabbed the wound and pressed a fresh dressing over it. 'Please ask Dacoren to stop. The road's rough and we need air.'

Oriedas tensed and put a finger to his lips. He cocked his head, listening, a frown creasing his brow. He darted to the door and opened it a crack. 'Soldiers! I hear the beat of many hooves. We have but a short time before they sight us. Stay in the wagon.' He tossed the pouch to Corinna, grabbed his kitbag, and whistled as he eased the door open.

Plum whinnied and checked his stride to move closer beside the wagon. Agile as a cat, Oriedas ducked through the door and leapt into the saddle. He untethered both horses and turned Plum towards the trees. Pepper followed.

'Pepper!' yelled Mos. The wagon jerked, bumping along as it gathered speed. 'Pepper, come back…'

The pony cantered away.

'Shut the door.' Corinna kept her tone firm. 'Now!'

Mos slammed the door and stomped over, cursing under his breath. Corinna ignored him. She had a task to complete and his temper was endangering them all.

Within the pouch was an assortment of miniature tools and dressings, gauze sachets of dried herbs and powders. She extracted a needle, lifted the lantern shade, and held its point in the flame. The wagon bounced and she almost dropped the needle. Her hands were shaking; the thread wouldn't go through.

'I'll do it.' Mos took the needle and threaded it at the first attempt. With a look of satisfaction, he handed it back. 'It's me what sees to mending the Commendator's kit, you know.'

Corinna hesitated. She reminded herself that she knew what to do, she'd done this twice before at the Temple – though never to someone she cared about. Already the dressing was soaked with blood.

Verendus twitched as the needle went in. Blood welled on his torso and trickled down his chest. Corinna pushed the needle through, tied the first knot, and cut it with a knife she found in the kit.

She pretended she was darning a ripped tunic, but the smell of blood marred the illusion. No, she was sewing the breast of a boned and stuffed quail. Adept at this delicate procedure, she'd sewn scores of the little birds on feast days at the Temple. Now, by thinking of the quails, she could concentrate on the stitches rather than Verendus' skin beneath her needle. Six stitches followed, each easier than the last, until a red track puckered his chest.

Behind her, Mos rummaged through the kit. 'Where's my bow? Can't find the lucky horse-head neither.'

Without pausing from her work, Corinna said, 'The white talisman? It must be in the kit.' She knotted the final stitch and didn't tell him that the talisman hung from her own neck. She had taken it from Verendus, telling herself she would return it…

As she cut the thread, the wagon lurched and slowed. Into that moment of quiet came the distant rumble of hooves. The knife slipped through her fingers and dropped, stabbing into the floor. She pulled the blade free and returned it to the pouch.

Another bump. The satchel slid across the floor. She grasped the strap, dragged it back, and slung it across her chest.

The wheels rolled onto new, unsteady ground. Mos knelt by the door and flung it open. Rain blew in. 'Jupiter Maximus!' He drew back. 'We'll never get across.'

Blinking against the rain, Corinna squeezed beside him and gasped. Dacoren had manoeuvred the wagon onto a wooden bridge. Trees and vegetation rose like green walls beside the bridgehead behind them. As the sheer bank fell away, gaps in the planking revealed turbulent water below. A wafer to spare on each side, the bridge creaking, he inched the mules on.

Corinna counted each beat of the wagon's measured rhythm on the planking and willed it to keep moving forward across the bridge. Movement on the riverbank caught her eye. A figure creeping through the undergrowth. But the bank was so steep. It must have been the wind stirring the leaves, or a trick of the light.

She focused on the road behind. It was more track than road. Narrow, a few spindly trees ranged along the verge; walls of rough stone enclosed freshly tilled fields. The rain stopped. Sunshine broke through the low cloud. On the near horizon, something glittered. Soldiers.

Corinna jumped up and found her leather case in the kit pile. At Alba, when Verendus gave her the bow, he'd insisted that she keep it secured in the case, clean and dry so the wood wouldn't spoil – but gods, those fiddly buckles. She tore at them and threw open the case. Mos reached across and snatched the bow. He strung it in a flash, grabbed the quiver, and nocked an arrow.

The soldiers were closing the gap, eight riders thundering along the track, their billowing red cloaks stark against the drab earth, the rising sun glinting on their armour.

'Praetorians,' Mos said. 'We've had it.'

The wheels jarred on the rutted bridge, hardly moving at all. The bridge might be fifty feet across. Back here in the wagon, with only a rear view, she had no way of telling.

Hooves pounded. The foremost rider, a spear held high, shouted, 'Halt!'

Now she understood the urgency to reach the river. The trees and dense vegetation shrank the target the Praetorians could aim at. But once they had crossed – what then?

Mos raised the bow and sent the arrow flying low and straight. A horse shrieked, stumbled a few paces, and collapsed, pitching its rider onto the road.

'No! No! No!' Mos lowered the bow. 'Not the poor horse. I never meant to do that.'

'They're going to catch us!' Corinna pinned the door open and pulled an arrow from the quiver. She flinched as a spear split the doorframe and hung there juddering. 'Shoot!'

'Can't,' he cried.

Corinna seized the bow and nocked the arrow. Thank the gods she had practised at Alba. Even so, her hand trembled as she drew the string. She must try. She could do this. Years of working in the Temple garden had made her arms strong.

A spear clanked on the road. Another thirty paces and the guardsmen would reach the bridge. Corinna checked her aim and loosed an arrow. Someone screamed.

'Man down,' Mos said through his tears. 'Reckon you only grazed him though.'

Corinna nocked the next shaft, raised the bow, and loosed again. The arrow cut the air and a Praetorian tumbled from the saddle. 'Oh, hell,' she whispered.

A spear thudded into the wagon, its spike protruding from the wood an inch from Mos' thigh. He sprang back and Corinna slammed the door. She held her breath, waiting for the drum of hooves on the bridge.

A colossal bang shook the wagon. Corinna fell against the bunk and covered her head with her hands. A whiff of sulphur, a moment of stunned silence, and then a dreadful cacophony of neighs and screams. The wagon kept moving. The bridge creaking beneath it.

Mos opened the door a chink. Blue sparks flared across the bridgehead. Smoke and the smell of burning wood drifted in. He opened it further and turned, ashen-faced. 'Bridge is on fire.'

Flames licked the wooden rails. The Praetorians, just visible through the smoke, reined in. Timbers creaked.

'The bridge,' cried Mos, coughing and spluttering against the pungent smoke. 'It's breaking up!'

Corinna pushed past him and shut the door. He grabbed her hand, pulled her close, and they huddled on the floor, clinging to each other, hardly daring to breathe. With a screech of splintering wood, the wagon trundled off the bridge and onto firmer ground.

Mos whooped and drew back. Sheepishly, he turned away and searched through the kit. She left him glugging from a water flask and went to Verendus. He shivered, though his forehead felt hot and his fair hair was dark with perspiration. His breathing quickened. He woke with a cry and stared at her as though she were a stranger.

'Water,' he said, voice barely audible above the clattering wheels.

Mos leapt up and held out his flask. Corinna poured water into a cup and dissolved a pinch of somniferum into it.

'What's that?' demanded Mos. 'Smells horrid.'

'Medicine usually does. Help me to sit him up.'

Verendus, blank-eyed, did not seem to recognise them, and gave no reply to Mos' words of reassurance. After a few sips, he closed his eyes and fell asleep.

The wagon stopped, and Dacoren shouted for Mos to help water the mules. When he'd gone, Corinna drained the cup. It would have to suffice. She couldn't risk a larger dose, not when she was responsible for Verendus. Images seeped into her mind. Blood and maggots and fire. She tried to shut them out. Had she killed those Praetorian riders? No, she told herself. She had winged them, nothing more.

Verendus moaned in his sleep. She slipped the blanket from his grip. In place of the wide metal bracelets, dark bruises circled his wrists. His hands were cracked dry, the nails ragged and dirty, and the little finger of his left hand was swollen. The ring with its miniature engraving of the Praetorian eagle was there. That much endured.

Corinna took his right hand, stroked his palm, rough and calloused from years of service. She held tight, finding comfort in its warmth and weight.

He blinked and opened his eyes.

'I'm here,' she said.

CHAPTER XXV

The wagon jolted. Corinna opened her eyes; she hadn't meant to close them. She squinted into shadow at the same cramped world of yesterday, and the day before, and the days before that.

Despite Mos' insistence that Jupiter himself had struck the bridge with a thunderbolt, Corinna was certain Oriedas had started the fire. Neither he nor the horses had returned. He may have been hurt. When she shared this concern with Dacoren, he said worrying would make no difference.

The wagon slowed. It would soon be dusk, time to halt and set camp for the night. Those long nights in her cell at the Temple, Corinna had dreamed of finding the road to Lignora. Even after her release from the Temple, it had seemed beyond reach.

Her visit to the Atrox Tower with Eldoran marked a turning point, the realisation that her dream was closer than she'd dared to hope. She had confided in someone she scarcely knew, and he had offered his help. His kindness gave her strength, taught her she must not be daunted, but seize every opportunity to make her dream a reality. And now she was bound for Lignora. She wondered if Eldoran knew this. If he knew how much his kindness meant to her and how sorry she was they had not parted amicably.

His voice echoed: *Ennean lives flow to a different rhythm. We hear the song of the forest. Choose your path before it is too late.*

His words troubled her now more than ever.

She had never envisaged it would turn out like this, with Verendus by her side. Would she come to regret his presence? His arrest had allayed her fear that he would discover her secret and hand her over to the authorities for the murder of Centurion Torvius. For now.

If she closed her eyes, she could see the centurion's dead face, the blood-splattered body. Not that she felt remorse; she'd acted in self-defence. But the memory remained. She told herself it was a nightmare, told herself repeatedly, until the edges smudged and it didn't seem real.

Last night, she had asked Dacoren how much longer this crate on wheels would be their home. He'd fixed her with deep blue eyes imbued with an ennui that hinted he was even older than his weather-beaten face suggested, and said, 'Takes as long as it takes to reach Lord Landren's lodge.'

Another jolt. Surely they weren't on the move again; it would be dark outside. She slung the satchel across her chest and rose, body stiff from sleeping on the hard boards. The wagon was smaller than the one she had ridden in to Viorum and contained only one bunk. The smaller size probably made it lighter; Dacoren drove the mules at a fair speed. Night after night of discomfort made her grateful she wasn't a slave, resigned to a life of sleeping on the floor or a mean pallet bed.

She reached across the low bunk and smoothed Verendus' forehead. How long had he been like this: frail, feverish, slipping in and out of consciousness? The stubble on his cheeks was becoming a beard, though she daren't shave him in case he flinched against the blade. She found the cloth to mop his brow, but it was as dry as her throat.

The water flask was empty. She slipped her feet into sandals and, careful not to disturb Mos who lay curled beside the kit, groped past him to the door at the rear of the wagon.

A wedge of moon hung dim in the cloudless sky. She stepped down, tripped on her loose sandal strap, and stumbled against something. No, someone. Opaque pupils stared from puffy eyes. She gasped and shrank away.

'Hush!' hissed Dacoren, coming to stand beside her. He pulled the cover from a lantern at the back of the wagon to shine a sallow patch of light on the wheel where a gagged and bound soldier sat slumped on the ground.

'Praetorian?' asked Corinna, though he wore no helmet and his uniform was unadorned.

'Legionary.' Dacoren dangled a small metal disc before her. It was strung on a cord like a pendant, and she realised it was an identity tag. 'Claims he was on manoeuvres and got separated from his squad. Following us, more likely.' He slipped the tag into the leather pouch on his belt. 'Go back inside.'

'I must fetch water.'

Dacoren shrugged and drew his knife. With his free hand, he jerked back the legionary's head and leaned closer. 'Time we moved on.'

The young legionary whimpered as the blade touched his throat. Corinna gasped and recoiled at the fountain of blood.

Dacoren released his hold and the head flopped forward, blood pouring from the slit throat.

Determined not to cry, Corinna backed away. The wagon door opened before she reached it and Mos peered out.

'Jupiter!' He jumped down to inspect the corpse. 'They'll send a scout when he doesn't return.'

'Indeed.' Dacoren wiped his knife on the legionary's cloak. 'As I said, time to move on.'

Mos glanced at the sky. 'It's dark.'

'I know this road like the palm of my hand. Get in the wagon.'

Folding her arms tight around her body to stop them shaking, Corinna obeyed. Whistling cheerfully, Dacoren harnessed the mules.

Dacoren drove all night, stopping only to stretch his legs and water the mules. Mos and Corinna sat by the open rear door and watched the sunrise. She asked Mos what he knew of Lignora and his face brightened, as it tended to when she asked him something important. Although he'd never been there, the border was perhaps two days away. 'Don't worry, it's not a fortified border like the palisades and watchtowers in the north,' he added. 'Just a few sentry huts and customs barriers on the main roads, but we'll avoid those.'

'How do you know this?'

'Dacoren told me.' Mos lowered his voice. 'He's not so bad once you get talking.'

The road steepened, hugging a tapering course through arid peaks of pale rock. Cliffs towered, overhung, contorted trees clung to slope and crevice until a tunnel cut a pass through the rock. A moment of darkness and they emerged into bright daylight, high on a narrow escarpment. Below, forest filled the valley in a boundless swell of green and it seemed the wagon and its occupants teetered on the precipice of an exotic ocean. Another instant and they would submerge.

On they rolled, down the steep, meandering road and into the green. Huge oaks with furrowed trunks as broad as a man's outstretched arms lined the way. Trees closed around them like an embrace, the fragrant calm a breath held in awe.

The breath exhaled in a gust and fell still. They were inside the forest.

Days passed and merged, blurred like the ever-deepening forest. Dense, dishevelled, choked with brambles, it stretched forever, a smothering shroud of leaves and branches with only the thread of a road to guide them through.

For mile after languid mile, they sank deeper. Time drowned. Was she seeing the past, looking back at scenes that had already happened, sharing a forgotten dream?

The promise of something more, something yet to be revealed, stirred beneath the taut canopy. Anticipation tingled her fingers, surged through her veins, and fluttered her heart. The wagon slowed and rolled onto a bridge, the water below bright and fast flowing. As they reached the far bank, the mules brayed and upped the pace. And she knew then that she had crossed over the border into the land of her father.

The track wound on through the trees, climbing past banks of bay tangled with ivy. Just when she thought they could go no further, the track levelled out and ran straight and wide. Gravel crunched, hounds barked, and the wagon stopped.

Mos opened the door. 'Look!'

He jumped down, grinning as he beckoned her to follow. Mouth open, he stood on the drive, stamping life into his legs as he stared at the lodge.

Corinna stood beside him and stared too. She had expected a small, mean structure, not this turreted fantasy. Unrestricted by the rules governing imperial architecture, the building possessed a bold, organic quality, as though it had chosen this place amid the forest, set down foundations, and grown as it pleased. Not in a distorted way, it wasn't ugly or unbalanced. It had the pleasing asymmetry of a magnificent tree, its three towers rising from a central trunk. The front door, carved from limed oak and banded with strips of iron, was set in an open porch.

Afraid to venture further into this extraordinary place, and unwilling to be parted from Verendus, Corinna and Mos stood together until Dacoren said he would see to the patient and ushered them inside.

The hall was of double-height, its panelled walls veined like the variegated wings of a golden butterfly and gilded with a cornice of leaves and acorns. A staircase of polished wood curved past tapestries of groves and gardens to a galleried landing.

At the top of the stairs, a woman appeared and all other matter melted into the background. Slight, diminutive, she was as exquisite as the bronze figurines in Spur's lararium. Her hair was the velvet black of midnight and tied in a loose braid that reached the daisy-chain girdle of silver flowers that cinched her crimson gown. She lifted the hem and descended with swift light steps.

'Salutations, friends. I am Strixi. My family oversees Lord Landren's lodge. You are welcome to stay as long as you wish. Dacoren will instruct the servants to carry your patient upstairs. We have no slaves here; however, I trust you will find the staff most efficient.'

Corinna thanked her, wondering as she did how Strixi knew about Verendus. She met the shrewd blue eyes but saw no clue, only perplexity. Was she as much a curiosity among her father's kin as she was to her mother's in Iolia?

***

The south-west tower became their home. Beside the ground-floor bathroom a spiral staircase ascended to Verendus' room where a corridor linked the tower to the main stairs and the rest of the lodge. Corinna was on the next floor; Mos in the attic.

Two days after their arrival, as Corinna ascended the main staircase with clean linen for Verendus, she heard a distant neigh. From along the hall, Strixi's voice rang out, issuing what sounded like a series of orders. Two servants hastened across the hall and out through the side door.

Corinna climbed to the little window at the turn of the stairs. Low sun warmed the elms at the end of the garden with a coppery gleam. Down on the terrace, blurry through the thick glass, the two servants were pointing at the woodland. A third figure sprinted by and disappeared from view. Talking rapidly, the pair followed. And though she did not know their language, their tone implied urgency. If only she could understand Ennean.

The side door stood open. No one was about. Corinna descended the stairs and went outside to the terrace. Below, the garden was laid out in three further terraces, cut deep into the slope, and linked by flights of stone steps.

The servants descended to the lower level and raced to the wall that enclosed the garden. The third figure, which she recognised as Strixi, was there, sliding the bolts of a door in the wall. She passed through into the wood beyond. The servants followed.

Corinna waited, feeling a little foolish. She was about to return inside when Strixi reappeared, leading a large chestnut horse. On its back sat a cloaked figure, slumped so low in the saddle that he did not need to bend his head as they passed under the arch of the door. The servants and a black pony trailed behind. Corinna dropped the sheets, shouted for Mos, and ran to greet them.

The reunion with Oriedas was brief. Too exhausted to answer their questions, he handed Plum and Pepper over to Mos – who was babbling joyously – and went to check on Verendus.

The next morning Oriedas left on a fresh mount, though Strixi wouldn't say where he was going. Mos' delight at Pepper's return was still evident that evening, and he grinned at Corinna when she crept in to take his place beside the bed where Verendus slept, half-reclined, pillows supporting his back and head. In the wan light of the bedside lamp, his tan had faded to the same washed-out shade as the vestment the Lignorans had clothed him in.

In their time at the lodge, his condition had improved. An achievement thanks not only to Lignoran expertise and superior standards of hygiene, but also to Mos, who tended his master with staunch compassion. In his search for the horse-head talisman he had started a systematic unpacking of the kit. Unable to bear his distress, Corinna told him she'd found it, caught in a corner at the bottom of the satchel. Mos had kissed the little horse and hooked the cord over Verendus' bedpost.

Mos straightened the talisman with an affectionate nudge and rose from his chair. 'Commendator got muddled again,' he said quietly. 'Kept asking me how I'd got out of the castrum.'

Corinna nodded. Perhaps she had miscalculated that last dose of somniferum. It wasn't easy to judge. Too much and Verendus became delirious, too little and he was racked with pain. 'It's the shock. That will pass,' she said lightly. Mos must not think she'd made a mistake. He had made clear with his theatrical frowns and objections to the smell that he didn't approve of the medicine.

He lingered in the doorway. 'I don't mind staying. I'll sleep in the chair, it's no trouble.'

'Go and rest,' said Corinna. Still he hesitated. She smiled. 'I'll call if I need you.'

This time he left, closing the door carefully behind him. Corinna lit another lamp. The green damask walls shimmered like willows reflected in a glassy lake. She drew closer, studying Verendus with a thoroughness she would not have indulged in the boy's presence. It was only for a few days, just until Landren arrived at the lodge and she could hand over the codex. Until then, she must be guarded. Verendus was too much in her thoughts already.

Today the fever had eased, smoothing the lines on his brow, though his eyes were sunk into grey-rimmed sockets, and his face, half-hidden by his new beard, was gaunt.

If she had understood her vision of the drowning man and told Verendus he was in danger, could she have prevented this? He could have fled Viorum and escaped arrest. The gods had sent warning, but she hadn't listened. This was her punishment, to witness the consequences of her inaction.

Verendus tensed as she untied his vestment and slipped it from his shoulders, baring his chest. That first day when they arrived in Gallia Narbonensis, she had seen him bathing in the sea, had stared at his nakedness. She stared at him now. Even in that brief time, he had changed. A new chapter was writ carelessly across the chiselled surface: ink-stain bruises, crude punctuation, angry scrawls to deface the parchment-sleek torso.

Remember, he is your patient. But she continued to stare, considering him as one might view a map, traversing rugged contours in search of landmarks. The pale scar at the side of his neck was known to her, as were the tracks of lacerations and the ragged line of stitches across his chest. Other markers were less familiar. A raw scar the length of her thumb cut his left side. The ruddy indentation above it was, according to Mos, where a spear point had pierced shield and armour and slowed to stop between his ribs. Though unsightly, all should heal or fade. The crests inked on his left bicep would endure as long as he did.

She reached to pull the vestment over the Praetorian eagle, sensing the warmth of his skin before she touched him.

His eyes opened, the fierce blue undimmed. '*Cara...*' Taking her hand, he pressed it to his chest and she felt his heartbeat strong beneath the compact muscle. He watched her as she had watched him. 'Where are we?'

'Lignora. At Landren's lodge.' Corinna sighed; she'd explained this yesterday. The possibility he might always suffer for what had happened in that Viorum hellhole terrified her.

She pulled free and fetched the kit Oriedas had given her. 'The stitches should be removed. They pull on your skin.' She found the slender blade and carefully severed each one. Then, with the tiny hook on the other end of the knife, she pulled out the wisps of thread. Verendus winced but didn't complain.

'It's sore,' she said, and reached for a jar of salve. She scooped some out and slicked it over his chest.

'Ow! It stings. Did you say Landren?'

'Yes, the Lignoran. Ericus, who did this to you?'

'An adversary of old.' He lifted her hand and tugged the bedcover, drawing it up. 'He's destroyed all I've worked for... stripped me of my rank, my honour. My career is finished. There will be a court-martial.'

She didn't understand what this involved, but tried to sound confident. 'You could petition.'

'Outlaws can't petition. Can't you comprehend? I'm nothing. I should never have agreed to Magistra's demand. I should have told her to find someone else. Why did she have to ask me? They killed her. The Praetorians killed her.'

Corinna slammed down the jar. Magistra had died to protect the codex. Now they would come after Verendus.

He glared at the door. 'What will happen to my family? It's my fault. I've put them at risk. Fes is dead. He was a brother to me...'

'I know. I'm sorry...' He had told her that this morning. She hadn't liked Fes, but it pained her to see Verendus upset. His body shook with rage. Tears welled, overflowed, the sight of his weeping so distressing that she wept, too, holding him close, his head heavy on her shoulder.

At last, he looked up. 'Forgive me,' he whispered. 'I made you cry.'

She stroked his hair. 'It doesn't matter.'

'I did a lot of thinking in that place. I thought how I could have a different life. Thought if I get out of here...' He swallowed and she feared he would break down again, but he drew in his breath, and said, 'But I can't change anything. Not now.'

'Ericus, please stop.' When had she started calling him by his praenomen? She found a rag and wiped his face. In the hope he might say more in his unguarded state, she asked, 'Why do the Praetorians want the codex?'

'Praetorians? They'll come for me.' Teeth bared like a feral dog, he scanned the room with wild eyes. He seized her arm and heaved himself up. 'Is the door bolted?'

'Yes, no… You're scaring me.'

'Bolt it. Now!'

Corinna did so. Anything to keep him quiet.

'A man followed. Followed me in Viorum. He wouldn't talk, so I killed him. And then another followed. They're hunting me.' He threw back his head and groaned.

'No one is following. We're safe here.'

'We're not safe anywhere.'

'But…' She faltered. Arguing wouldn't calm him.

'Listen.' Words slow, exacting, the effort of explaining blunted his tone. 'I killed. I ran away. I am outside the law. No one can help me.'

'Landren is trying to.'

Mouth half-open, he regarded her doubtfully. 'Why would Landren help me?'

'Because I asked him to. He says you're entitled to a trial.'

'And what did you promise in return for this help?'

Corinna didn't hesitate, she'd prepared for this. 'Your gold,' she said coolly, and the suspicion left his face. Good. He mustn't know she'd pledged the codex. Not yet. 'Mos told him you were planning to meet Tribune Aquinus, but he'd been called away. Landren waited in Viorum for his return. He'll ask him to arrange your defence.'

'Yes, yes, Aquinus will help…' He sounded hopeful.

'In the meantime, you should rest.'

'Can't rest. My sword.' He struggled to sit straighter, gasping with the exertion, his right hand flexing impatiently. 'Fetch my sword.'

She restrained him as best she could and persuaded him to drink a tincture of somniferum. He grimaced at the taste and closed his eyes only to open them a moment later. 'Where's Mos?'

'Gone to bed.'

'The box…the box in my satchel…' His eyelids twitched. 'I must talk to him. Know if he did as I asked.'

'About the codex?'

'Yesss…' his speech slurred as the drug took effect.

'It's here, in your satchel. Safe.'

'Where isss…'

'Here.' She rose and hung the satchel on the chair beside the bed.

He reached out and stroked the leather. Closing his eyes, he sighed and fell asleep.

CHAPTER XXVI

The chair had been placed in a patch of sun beside the bedroom window, but despite his thick woollen tunic and the blanket about his shoulders Verendus shivered. Wishing he'd stayed in bed, he picked up his spoon. The broth on the little table before him resembled the watery stew he'd been served at the Pelican on his return to Iolia. It seemed an age ago. In truth, it was only a couple of months. He attempted to calculate the number of days he'd been here at the lodge, but the stuff Corinna kept feeding him to ease his pain made concentration difficult. There was probably a dose in the broth.

'Do drink it.' Corinna was standing beside the desk, a pestle and mortar in her hands. An array of jars and bottles, bunches of herbs, and a miniature set of scales crowded the surface before her. It resembled an apothecary's bench. Smelt like it too.

'I want a proper drink. Where's my flask?' As he spoke, Verendus remembered he'd been carrying it on the day Galenius' troops arrested him. The fine silver flask was probably hanging from some guardsman's belt, the liquor within quaffed. They had taken his cuirass, and the scarlet cloak that was pinned with the brooch his parents had given him as a coming-of-age present.

One day he'd see that golden brooch adorning someone else's cloak. How he would make the wearer pay for its theft. The fantasy cheered him for a few moments until he realised his gladius had also gone; the ceremonial dagger, too. At least he had the standard one. He'd ask Corinna to fetch it.

She was frowning at the contents of the mortar. Perhaps she'd misjudged the ingredients. With luck, she'd throw it away.

Corinna glanced up. 'No wine unless you finish the broth. You need to build your strength.'

Verendus stirred the insipid liquid but didn't drink. This morning, as he slipped from sleep to wakefulness and caught the scent of lavender in the air, he'd thought he was in Iolia, in his own room, lying in his own bed. When he opened his eyes the ceiling was wrong. Not the mural of a starry sky, but a dreary expanse of green. And then he realised where he was, remembered what had brought him to this place in Lignora, and pulled the covers over his head.

Fes was dead. If the correct rites had not been observed at the time – and he doubted they had – then his dear friend might be stranded between worlds. Unable to return to the living; forbidden to join his kindred feasting in the great ancestral hall.

The gods must be appeased. A priest would know how. Fes had his own gods – Saxtili gods – but he had adopted the Reman god Hercules into his pantheon. A priest of Hercules could make sacrifice on Fes' behalf. A memorial could be set up.

The small voice of caution woke. *You'll have to clear your name first.*

Verendus stirred the broth and told the voice to shut up. He'd consult a priest and honour his friend. Fes was the younger brother he'd always longed for. He had taught Fes how to read; Fes had taught him to speak Saxtili. They had toiled together and hunted together. Shared hopes and fears and laughter. Those first few years had been hard. Fes was angry and grieving for his lost family, but eventually he'd learned to trust again and they had become each other's family.

Verendus kept stirring, kept remembering. He was still stirring the broth when Mos tiptoed in.

'Mos, at last! See, I'm up.' He clanked down the spoon. 'Are you here to shave me? If we put it off any longer I'll become accustomed to this damn beard, and I can tell Corinna doesn't care for it.' He didn't care for it either, but baulked at the prospect of a blade against his skin. He could still feel the sting of Galenius' dagger at his throat.

Another memory surfaced. Those long months preparing for the Germania mission when he'd let his hair grow; dark days creeping hirsute and filthy through unending bleak forest; cold nights of despair when he'd feared he would die there, hundreds of miles from home in a land of strange gods who coveted his bones for a trophy. But he had gone on. For Rema. He'd muttered a prayer, touched the talisman at his neck for protection, and crawled on.

And for what? Information no one listened to, intelligence nobody acted on, and the constant, bitter awareness that he was on his own. If he was captured, the Castrum Remana would deny all knowledge of him.

'Sir, I can't find the razor,' Mos said, snapping him back to the present.

Verendus pulled the blanket tighter. Corinna would go soon. Then he'd pour away the broth, send Mos to fetch wine and proper food. She'd never know. He beckoned the boy. 'What news of Quintus?'

'None, sir.' Mos placed a small rosewood box on the table. He lifted the lid and grinned. 'Look, sir, dice and knucklebones.

I thought you'd like to play – you know, pass the time. We're welcome to stay here as long as we choose. There's gardens, and woods, and a training ground, and the stables are the best I've seen. Real luxury. Plum and Pepper won't want to leave.'

'Well, they'll have to. We all will.'

'Finish your broth first,' said Corinna with a determined pout.

Verendus set the bowl slopping on the floor. He had sunk so low. Wrapped up like an invalid and drinking tepid broth. How easy to stray from the path. His career was wrecked. What was it Minister Dalcamus had called him? A peacock in a gilded uniform, "as big and stupid as any of your ilk". He raked a hand through his hair, pushing it from his face. He didn't even have his gilded uniform anymore. Galenius would hunt him down like a wounded beast and make him suffer.

All those long days and sleep-ravaged nights being pitched and shaken in the back of the Lignoran wagon had afforded him time to think about things he didn't want to think about. He had underestimated Galenius. Big mistake. The prefect had deceived him, made him believe Mos was a prisoner at the castrum. If Oriedas hadn't arrived when he did…

The thought chilled him; he couldn't shut it away. Another minute and he would have told everything to save the boy; he'd come so close. He consoled himself with the measly scrap of comfort: Galenius didn't have the codex.

His satchel and the horse-head talisman hung on the back of the chair. Verendus hooked the talisman over his head and took the scroll case from his satchel. Nothing good would come of feeling sorry for himself. He was alive. Clever Minister Dalcamus was dust and ashes.

Verendus uncapped the cylindrical case. Fes had been taking a missive to Legate Capito, commander of the Twenty-

Third Legion. The bid to discover more about the troops of the Twenty-Third – currently camped on Waterside Plain near Iolia's harbour – had failed, and the missive had fallen into the hands of Prefect Galenius.

Nothing could be done about that, but Verendus resolved to make the next move. Options were limited. He was wanted by the Praetorian Guard; he could not return to Viorum and meet with Tribune Aquinus. According to Corinna, Landren had waited in Viorum to speak with Aquinus. Good might come of that, though he mustn't get his hopes up. Relying on others was risky – and he'd never even met Landren.

Verendus weighed another option. Before his arrest he'd been planning to ride east to find Fes. That plan could be adapted. He would ride to the Alpine village of Brigantium, find the legate, and speak to him in person. Capito would know beyond doubt whether the troops in Iolia were his legionaries or there to serve Galenius.

Verendus pulled out his chart and unwound it, opening the parchment across the table until he found the tiny fortress that denoted Viorum. Unfurling the left of the chart, he let the right side curl in on itself and traced his finger westwards along a road of ink. First, he would find Lignora and plan his route east from there.

The table was too small for this. He couldn't find Lignora. The forts and forests blurred and danced before his eyes. Why couldn't he find the place? He'd drawn the damn chart. Mars above, he knew it was bloody well there. The chart furled back on itself and dropped off the side of the table.

He blinked and looked up. The green walls shimmered. So much green, surrounded by green. The curtains, the counterpane, the bed-hangings, the lawn and trees and woodland outside the window. Green everywhere. Like that interminable Germanian forest closing in, choking him. He needed air.

Heedless to the urgency of the matter, Corinna rolled bandages. Mos sat cross-legged on the floor, playing knucklebones and missing tricks as he chattered about the horses. Verendus coughed purposefully; no one turned. 'Mos,' he said loudly, 'open the window, then show me our location.'

'Yes, sir. Can I take Plum out for exercise later? It's no trouble.'

'No. Show me our location. We must depart before the ides.'

'They're past, sir,' Mos said, without looking up.

Corinna's face clouded. 'You've been unwell. Time passed regardless.'

Verendus gripped the arms of his chair. That bloody codex. Somehow, it was important. Important enough to have brought Galenius to Viorum with a warrant for his arrest. But why? He should ask Corinna to finish the translation. Though he'd have to copy out the remaining pages first – she must not know he had the codex.

He checked the thought. Maybe she did know. Hadn't she told him last night that the codex was here, safe? And so it was. Mos hadn't taken it to the Temple of Vesta.

Verendus stroked the hard edge of the box in his satchel. He'd never get the codex open again, not while his hands were too unsteady to pick the lock. Gods, it was warm. 'The window, Mostus!'

The boy jumped up to oblige, then returned to stand over the knucklebones. He had a thoughtful look, as though pondering how much he could get away with. Maybe he'd opened the box. The satchel had been in his care.

'Why did you open the box?' asked Verendus, testing his hunch.

The look vanished. 'The box in your satchel, sir? Wasn't me. I told her not to.'

Corinna turned. 'I was searching for coin to buy your release. The box felt heavy, so I looked inside.' Her voice was calm, matter-of-fact. 'Why do you have the codex? It belongs at the Temple of the Flame.'

Breeze wafted into the bedroom. Even the air smelt green. His mind reeled. Despite all his precautions, Corinna had opened the box. They both knew about the codex, and that knowledge could be dangerous. 'Who else knows?' he demanded.

Corinna blushed. 'No one except us.'

Mos cast her a look of alarm but didn't speak.

'Ensure it stays that way.' Even as Verendus spoke, a fresh concern grated. 'Did you open the codex?'

'No,' they said in unison.

Corinna returned to her potions. Mos picked up the chart, set it on the table, and unrolled it. 'Here, sir.' He pointed to a depiction of three oak trees in a ring with the title *Lignora* beneath.

Verendus nodded and unfurled the chart in an easterly direction. Lignora was many miles from the nearest highway; when the time for departure came, the going would be rough. Before he left for the Alps, he should send a missive to Iolia and warn his friend Carbo about the Praetorians. The pigeons were trained to fly to Naeos' house where Carbo had taken refuge. It wouldn't be possible to send a reply to Lignora – the pigeons weren't trained for that – but Carbo and Naeos could tread carefully. *Praemonitus, praemunitus* – forewarned is forearmed.

Verendus considered how to word the missive. It must be brief – small enough to fit inside a tiny tube of hollowed-out plant stem and light enough to attach to a carrier pigeon's leg.

A shame Carbo couldn't reply, it would have been good to ask him for news of Torvius, to verify whether the centurion had perished in the fire at the Officers' Club. Torvius was a fine soldier – steadfast, honourable – he could be a useful source of information about events in Iolia and an ally for Carbo. If he was still alive.

'Mos,' said Verendus, though his eyes were drawn to Corinna, watching her sprinkle grey powder into a glass. She'd be better off without him. He was putting her in danger. As for a future together, what could he offer her? 'Mos,' he repeated, regaining focus, his gaze on Corinna, 'on the morning we left Iolia, you said you saw Centurion Torvius at Temple Gate.'

Corinna froze. The glass almost slipped through her fingers. She recovered quickly and set it down.

'You all right?' said Mos. 'You've gone ever so pale.'

'Just tired,' she replied.

Verendus repeated his question about Torvius.

'On Equinox Eve? I'm not sure, sir.'

'Think!'

Mos screwed his eyes shut in concentration. When he opened them again, he looked more assured. 'I think it was Centurion Torvius, but he rode past quick, heading for Temple Gate. I'm certain it was a centurion. Oh, and he had a dark beard.'

As does Nevoso, thought Verendus. Perhaps Torvius died in the fire and the oily guardsman had been promoted into his position. Centurion Nevoso had signed the arrest warrant, and was doubtless under Galenius' thumb.

Verendus brought the scytale stick from his satchel. He should write to Carbo. He found his drawing kit, and set an inkpot and a metal pen on the table.

Mos frowned at the stick. 'Sir, the pigeons are in Viorum.'

'Why in Hades didn't you bring them? I need to send a missive.'

'We forgot.' Corinna stirred the mixture, clanking the spoon against the glass.

Mos scooped up the knucklebones. 'It's not as bad as you leaving Saffi behind.'

'We had no choice.'

'We should have looked for her.' Mos flung the pieces into the box.

'There wasn't time! It wasn't my fault she ran away.'

So Saffi had run away. Verendus clutched the horse-head talisman and prayed she hadn't been captured. Mos, his gaze on the clenched fist, mumbled, 'What if the Praetorians catch her?'

Saffi had a slave brand on her wrist. A brand that linked her to both Iolia and the Temple of the Flame. Verendus closed his eyes and was back on the Viorum road, a row of crosses stretching before him, a poor wretch nailed to each. *Fugitive.* 'They'll know she's a runaway slave,' he said.

Mos swore and kicked the box clattering across the room.

'Mostus!' Verendus barked. The boy flinched and straightened to attention. 'Listen, Mos, it isn't so bad.' He explained how the Praetorians would have searched the house in Viorum and arrested all the slaves for questioning. Routine procedure. 'By running away, Saffi evaded them.'

Mos looked relieved. And then Corinna said, 'But we left the house before the Praetorians arrived. If Saffi hadn't run away, she would have come with us and been safe.'

Verendus wished he hadn't spoken. That somniferum stuff was muddying his thoughts. He picked up the scytale stick, turning it in his hand. How would he get word to Iolia? He tried to think, but kept slipping back to Centurion Torvius. Something was missing. Or out of place. Something to do with Corinna. He turned to her. 'Did Torvius visit the Temple on Equinox Eve? That last evening you were there, did you see Torvius?'

'No.' She stared at her hands.

Again Torvius' name had touched a nerve. She was hiding something. Ever since he'd found her at the Temple, he'd known she was hiding something. He just needed to ask the right questions. He pressed on. 'I must get word to Carbo and verify whether Torvius is alive. As the pair of you forgot to bring those bloody pigeons, that won't be straightforward.' He left a deliberate pause, building the tension, though he knew what he intended to say. 'Mos, you will take the missive to Castellum Alba. You can send it from there. You will wait for a reply and return here.'

Mos reddened and stepped back.

'Stop this!' cried Corinna. 'Alba's miles away. Don't make him go there – it's too dangerous.' She exchanged a glance with the boy. 'Mos, leave us, please.'

'I'll stay if you want.'

'Out,' shouted Verendus. 'Now!' Holding Corinna with his eyes, he hauled himself to his feet. Mos ran off, slamming the door behind him.

Corinna picked up the glass of somniferum and stamped over. 'Satisfied?'

He pushed her hand aside. 'Don't give me any more of that stuff. I'm much improved.'

'Perhaps your temper will improve too.'

Verendus took a breath. 'Tell me why Magistra released you.'

'No.' Her voice rose to match his. 'Don't press me.'

'You lied to me. Now I want the truth.'

Corinna gazed into the glass as though contemplating whether to drink it herself. 'It isn't easy to explain.'

Her hands were trembling; mixture sloshed over the rim. He quashed the urge to calm her and hardened his resolve. He must learn the truth. 'So, Corinna, I'll make it easy for you now. Magistra released you after what happened to Centurion Torvius.' The glass dropped to shatter on the floor. 'Leave it! You were in trouble, weren't you? That's why she let you go.' He was feeling his way. Nothing in her reaction suggested he had taken a wrong turn. 'Torvius was going to reprimand you, wasn't he? But something happened.'

Her hands tightened into fists. 'He's dead.'

How did she know? Perhaps she'd witnessed his murder. Verendus chose his words carefully. 'I think you know who killed him. I think you know, but are afraid to tell. Whoever is responsible can't hurt you. I will shield you.' He hoped she didn't see the absurdity of this. At present, he could barely walk.

Corinna shook her head. Her expression confused him. As she stood there – gaze lowered, shoulders slumped – he identified it. *Guilt.*

She looked up, and said, 'I killed him.'

Verendus stared, opened his mouth, but didn't have any words. He longed to comfort her, but stood immobile. Silent, defiant, she stared back.

'Why?' he said, at last. His voice sounded dull, detached.

She buried her head in her hands. 'When I close my eyes, I see his face. His-big-horrid-dead-face.'

He waited for her to deny it. She was confused, hysterical. She couldn't have killed the centurion. And yet...

Slowly, patiently, Verendus coaxed out the details. Torvius had threatened her, behaved like a brute. Corinna had fought back and stabbed him in the eye with a quill. It was self-defence. Magistra had found her, hidden her, and then grasped the opportunity to send her to safety.

Light shone on an image he had long struggled to see – the half-glimpsed had become whole and he had his explanation. Gods, he wished it wasn't so. Torvius was dead, had passed beyond his own powers of retribution, curse him for all eternity.

Verendus drew nearer, but Corinna cringed at the brush of his beard and crouched to gather the fragments of glass. He knelt beside her. 'Why didn't you tell me before?'

'You are Praetorian Guard.'

'What?' For a moment, he didn't understand. 'You thought I would arrest you?'

'I was afraid,' she said simply. 'Fear stopped my mouth.'

'Trust conquers fear. We both know that now.'

She lowered her eyes. 'I should clear this mess,' she said, plucking a shard from between the floorboards. 'Ouch!'

'Let me see.' He helped her rise and, holding her hand to the light, pulled out a splinter of glass. Blood welled like a bright bead.

She accepted his handkerchief and pressed it against the cut. 'He was definitely dead.'

'Then the centurion Mos saw at Temple Gate wasn't Torvius. It was probably Nevoso – they were much alike.'

Corinna nodded. 'I always thought so.'

Something nagged in his mind, a question to bring him closer to the truth. The library. 'Did Torvius often visit the Belvedere library?'

'Only in the last few months.' She twisted the handkerchief. 'I failed Saffi. I should have searched for her.'

'You protected Mos, you saved me. You could not do both.' Verendus steered the subject back. 'Try to remember. When Torvius came to the library, was he searching for something in particular?'

Corinna shrugged. 'He had a scroll. It bore a picture of those serpents. And he had the codex.'

The codex. Sweet Venus, what else hadn't she told him? *Think.* Why would Torvius want the codex? Had Galenius sent him to fetch it? 'Corinna, did anyone else know this?'

'I don't know. I don't want to know.'

'It's important.'

'I believe Torvius had a hold over Magistra. That he coerced her into giving him the codex. Must we speak of it?' Corinna sighed. 'It is past.' Three crisp words. Frost had crept into her voice, halting the thaw.

A giddy sensation of teetering on the brink of an abyss washed over Verendus. One small lie and he could leap across the chasm and reach her. Persist with his questions and the gap would widen beyond hope. Soon, once he could get on a horse, he should leave this place. Leave before Galenius tracked him down. Only a fool would waste the chance of a few days of happiness for the sake of an honest answer.

Gently, he raised her chin and looked into her eyes. 'Yes, it's past.' He pulled her close, breathing in her jasmine scent. Her body pressed warm against his. 'We'll never speak of it again,' he said, though he knew they must.

CHAPTER XXVII

Verendus sat still and focused on Corinna's forehead. Leaning closer, she frowned at his chin and the faint line etched between her brows deepened. He longed to ask whether she was almost finished, but that would entail movement and the razor was at his throat.

'Don't look so nervous, I know what I'm doing,' she said, sweeping the blade over his skin. She swished the razor in the dish of water balanced in her left hand and continued. 'I used to shave my grandfather. Those last few months of his life, poor Nonno didn't have a steady hand. The drink, I suppose.'

Verendus managed not to nod. Hades, he could do with a drink himself. Chilled by the memory of Galenius' dagger at his throat, he gripped the towel, pulling it tight around his shoulders. Focus on Corinna. She had been a long time fetching hot water for his shave; so long that he worried she'd changed her mind.

When at last she returned, she was different, less restrained, with her hair unpinned and her feet bare. The leather belt, which she habitually wore in a masculine style about her waist had gone, replaced by a cord that cinched the tunic beneath her breasts. And yet, there was something else.

As she bent nearer, he knew. The drape of her tunic suggested no confining breast-band beneath, and he felt again that good old stiffening of anticipation he feared had deserted him. He leaned closer and flinched at the sting of the blade.

'You moved!' She dunked the razor in the dish, clouding the water red. 'I was just finishing too.' She pressed the towel against his neck and left him holding it there while she fetched a scrap of gauze and sealed the cut. Eyes widening, she considered him and reached out to stroke his cheek. 'Be thankful I didn't need to shave your head as well.'

This past month the gods had bestowed many indignities upon him, but had spared him the nuisance of lice. Corinna had seen him at his lowest ebb; nevertheless, she remained at his side. He took her hand, pulled her nearer, and she bent her head to his, closing her eyes as he kissed her – a tumbling, plunging, soaring rush. And then the honeyed aniseed of somniferum filled his mouth. Why was she taking that stuff? Sensing his disapproval, she struggled.

Verendus released her. *Idiot.* Take your time. And it had all been going so well.

Corinna took the towel and dried the razor. 'You're staring.'

'I can't take my eyes off you.' It was true enough, and an answer he'd given her before. And yet, something was missing. 'The earrings I bought you, you don't wear them anymore.'

'I lost them…' She bit her lip and turned away, folding the razor into its box.

'Cara, don't cry. It doesn't matter. I'll buy you another pair.'

'I don't want another pair. I won't be in your debt!'

Another lie. Perhaps she'd sold them. He rose and closed the shutters. 'It's getting dark. But don't go – stay with me. Please…'

She didn't reply, neither did she go. Verendus sat on the bed, hoping, willing her to stay, watching in the half-light as she lit a lamp.

'Wine?' she asked, already pouring, filling the glass without adding any water.

When he declined, she drained the glass in one quick draught and poured another, again without diluting it. At this rate, she'd be drunk in a half-hour.

'Ericus…' she remained at the desk, 'may I ask you something?'

'Anything.' He beckoned her. Drink in hand, she came to his side. He took the glass and set it on the bedside table, out of her reach. This would not proceed in a wine-induced haze. 'Well?'

'That night at Spur's camp, did you mean what you said? Could we really swim together?'

Together? Had he said that? He supposed he had, too much wine had loosened his tongue. He lifted her chin. 'Always,' he said, and this time he meant it.

She smiled. A small, knowing smile. 'You should be resting.'

'All I've done is sleep. And now, I shan't be able to.'

She met his gaze. 'Neither shall I.'

Carefully, without touching her, he unfastened the cord and pulled it away. He unpinned the brooch on her right shoulder and the tunic slipped down, revealing a silk strap and a flash of fair skin. She lowered her eyes, and Verendus was alert to a sense of responsibility.

Blood pounding, he unpinned the other brooch. The tunic fell away and, oh sweet Venus, she was wearing the sheer shift. He'd given her that at Alba, one of several items of clothing, though this scrap of silk cost more than the rest put together.

That she had pre-empted this moment and put it on, thrilled him. It was worth every last *sestertius*.

He skimmed the arch of her neck, put his forefingers on either side of her collarbone and traced outwards to the narrow straps, her skin fragrant and rose petal soft. She tensed and glanced at the wineglass.

This wasn't how it was meant to unfold. All those times on the journey when he'd imagined her in his arms, she hadn't needed alcohol to go through with it, she hadn't been afraid. Though, of course, he hadn't known about Torvius then. He'd misjudged Torvius, mistaken him for a man of honour. The centurion was dead, but his shadow hung over them.

Again she glanced at the glass. 'I think you should know, I've never done this before…'

He nodded, glad there had been no one else and shocked how much he cared about something that rarely mattered to him. It was years since his first time, but beside the excitement there were nerves. He hadn't reckoned on those nerves now. He held out his hand. 'See, I tremble too.'

He wasn't literally shaking. Just a feeling inside. But it seemed to reassure her, for she kissed his palm.

Urgency seized him and he tugged the cords of his vestment. 'Help me take this off.'

She leant closer. 'It's all knotted.'

As she picked at the knot, he held her waist, firm under the silk. His fingers slid up, across the pattern of her ribs to her breasts. She looked up, meeting his eyes, and he saw his own desire mirrored there.

She moved his hands and pulled the vestment up and over his head. Heat surged through him. He laid her back on the bed and the shift fluttered, baring her knees. With slow hands, he eased it higher and her breath quickened. He traversed her thighs, ruching the fabric until he reached her briefs, a wisp of silken nothingness, which he touched with a tentative fingertip, teasing at the ribbonned edge before stooping to kiss the triangle of silk.

She gasped, tried to rise.

Verendus sat and placed his hand on her stomach. 'Do you want me to stop?'

'…no.'

She shut her eyes and lay still. His body ached to dive in, sate its thirst, and drink again. *Slowly*, he told himself. Wait. After what Corinna had suffered, her anxiety was natural. Things would improve. He didn't know what Torvius had done to her; he didn't want to know. It was past. It must not overshadow their future.

He shed his loincloth and pressed closer, easing his knee between hers. He touched her face. Beside her mouth was a tiny scar where that brute had struck her. What the hell had the centurion done to her? Hades, if she hadn't killed the bastard, he'd hunt Torvius down and…

And now he was flagging. Gods, please no, not that. He stroked the curves of her breasts. He just needed a few moments.

Corinna's eyes opened, the irises big and green and bright with fear. Unused to such a lack of enthusiasm Verendus hesitated, drew back. He mustn't be disappointed. This wasn't a blow to his ego, this wasn't about him.

He sighed and lay down beside her. 'Sleep now, Cara,' he whispered, stroking her hair. 'Sleep…'

***

Verendus woke to find Corinna beside him. He gently folded back the sheet so as not to wake her. She was naked and curled in a ball, her back towards him, her hair a glossy mantle that reached almost to the base of her spine. He lay listening to the rhythm of her breathing and sketching her in his mind.

He should let her sleep; they'd slept little last night. He'd woken in the night to find her watching him in the pallid light of the bedside lamp. When he kissed her, he'd felt no resistance; when he'd laid her down beside him, she hadn't asked him to stop. Neither had she shown pleasure. He reassured himself this was not unusual. The next time would be better; Torvius' ghost would have no hold over them. But the second time yielded no thaw. He must be patient, winter always warms to spring. And when he held her again, she wrapped herself around him, clung to him, and cried out. He was right, beneath the poise lay passion.

He sat up and brushed aside the curtain of hair. Kissed her neck and the lobe of her ear. 'Cara…'

Frost had returned with the dawn; he could not induce a thaw.

'Aren't you tired?' she said, looking past him.

'Not at all.' He leapt out of bed, bounded three strides, and slowed. He was in no fit state to bound anywhere. He took the next few steps at a sedate pace and threw open the shutters. Sunshine. A tortoiseshell cat padded across the lawn below and crept into the shrubbery.

As he turned, Corinna sat and stretched, her body lean like a gazelle, the skin taut across her ribs. Yesterday evening, sheathed in the sheer shift she had dazzled him; naked, in the clear morning light, she took his breath. He would sketch her before she dressed.

She swathed herself in the sheet, her eyes scanning the room. He realised she was searching for her slip. Finding it first, he picked it up and hung it on the carved fulcrum at the end of the bed.

'Give that to me. I must go before Mos arrives with your breakfast,' she said, though she stared, considering him like a punter assessing a racehorse.

'The door's bolted. He can leave the tray outside.' Verendus fetched his satchel. 'Cara, let me look at you; you're looking at me. Pose for me. Please…'

'You want to draw me?' She blushed. 'No, no, no…'

Despite his efforts to persuade, Corinna refused. It didn't matter; he could sketch her from memory. This time he wouldn't need his imagination.

Even as the thought formed, he regretted it. Thanks to his covert sketches, the two women he cared most about were in danger – Galenius had drawings of Drusilla and Corinna.

CHAPTER XXVIII

Corinna crept from the bedroom and ran downstairs, round and round the twisting staircase. For an instant, she knew she could run on and never stop. She ran into the bathroom and shut the door.

For a long while, she stood cold and naked at the wash-stand, dabbing the bruise on the curve of her breast where his mouth had lingered. Last night she bled after their lovemaking – a speckle of bright drops. There was no blood now; it had only happened the first time. Incarceration at the Temple and Nonna's bitter account of the slow, agonising demise of "poor Attea" had convinced Corinna to accept her lot and be grateful her vow of chastity granted protection from the perils of childbirth which had killed her mother.

That vow had been left at the Temple. Verendus said he'd been careful, but had he?

Corinna had given little thought to such matters before, though in the course of her studies she'd read about ways to avoid conception. The best was purported to be silphium, a plant so rare it was worth its weight in silver. No chance of acquiring any of that. Other methods were rather alarming. Apparently, Egyptians used a pessary made from crocodile dung. Even if such a thing were obtainable here, that was a definite *no*.

Reman methods included a mixture of white lead, honey, and olive oil – she didn't know the ratio, or where she might get some white lead. She recalled reading that Aristotle recommended an application of cedar oil. Perhaps that would be best.

She wished she'd said no. Being with Verendus should have made things better, wiped away the memory of Torvius' grasping hands. Instead, things were worse – more complicated. Already she missed Verendus, wanted to go back. This was wrong; she did not want to feel.

Corinna washed her silks and hung them to dry. Returning to her own room, she fastened the shutters and sat on the bed.

She put a crystal of somniferum on her tongue and closed her eyes.

***

Corinna did go back; she knew she would. When she was with him, nothing else mattered – she had no need for somniferum. After several blissful days and nights in which Verendus made no further mention of leaving the lodge, she dared to hope he was settling to life in Lignora. He slept soundly here, and the speed of his recuperation was remarkable. The place was working its magic on him, just as it had cast a spell over her.

It could not last. Soon Landren would arrive and demand that she honour her side of the agreement and hand over the codex. But she hadn't told Verendus of her bargain. It was never the right moment.

She had even considered taking the codex, but he guarded his satchel like a wolf with a kill. At night, when he couldn't guard it, he hid it. Time was running out. She should confess, while he was in good temper.

In the kit, she found a flask to replace the one he had lost. Not a fine silver flask like the old one, but it would do very well. She filled it with the sweet Lignoran liquor he'd acquired a taste for and brought it to his room.

He was standing naked before the window, moonlight soft on his skin. He didn't turn, so she set down the flask and went to his side. She slipped a hand in his, but before she could speak, he said, 'I've been thinking…' His grip tightened. 'I won't hide here any longer. I've business elsewhere.'

Her thoughts flew. She must stop this before he ruined everything. 'What about your court-martial? Landren could help you prepare.'

He shrugged. 'Perhaps.'

'Wait awhile. Wait for Landren – he said he'd speak with Tribune Aquinus. Let's enjoy the time we have here.' His hold on her eased. She traced a lazy line across his torso and the tension in his bearing tautened to expectancy.

***

Next morning, she left Verendus sleeping and stole outside to the terrace. Another day gone and still she hadn't told him. The shock of cool morning air slowed her and she stopped at the balustrade where the tortoiseshell cat was sitting on a flowerpot, washing its paws. Corinna hesitated. She should return to the room, make Verendus understand that were it not for the bargain she'd made, he wouldn't be here. He probably wouldn't be alive.

She would pick some lemon balm, then go to him and explain. The cat cast an aloof glance in her direction and sprang down.

With the cat slinking behind her, she descended the terrace steps and crossed the lawn. She had gleaned from a brief conversation with Strixi that Lignorans had no temple, no lararium, or wayside shrine. Their peace was here, outside, with Nature.

At the centre of the grass was a small tree, its leafless branches bowed by blooms as lush as overblown lilies, the creamy petals iridescent like the nacre of a seashell. A low wall marked the boundary of the medic garden where beds of herbs and healing plants formed a patchwork of colour and fragrance. Many of the plants were familiar from illustrations in the Belvedere library's botanical volumes. A few were unknown to her. She bent to inspect a moss-like specimen.

'That one is poisonous!'

Corinna snatched back her hand and turned. Strixi stood at the end of the path, her bearing as majestic as a goddess surveying her realm. She stepped into the sunshine and the garden wavered like the painted backdrop of a street theatre stirred by the breeze.

Recovering, Corinna said, 'Forgive my trespass, I was curious.'

Strixi stopped beside her and smiled. She wore a gown of lavender-blue that matched her eyes and her black hair was crowned with a daisy-chain garland. 'I doubt it has teeth,' she said, 'but most plants in that bed are poisonous to some extent.'

Corinna returned the smile and pointed across the lawn. 'That lovely tree with flowers like waterlilies…'

'Amarantia. We planted many in the land that is now called Gallia Narbonensis.'

'There's one at the fortress of Castellum Alba. Broad branched, very beautiful.'

'I am glad it is still there.'

'You know it?' Corinna attempted to read Strixi's expression. The blue gaze glistened like dew on a petal and she saw only her own reflection.

'Some Lignorans refused to leave Narbonensis,' said Strixi. 'We do not speak of that. Much was left behind. Much of our knowledge was appropriated by Rema – glass, mirrors, sophisticated locks and keys. They came to understand these things and were able to make them too – though never achieving our standards.' With a sweep of her hand, she indicated the mossy plant. 'Stag's horn. We use it in a tonic to aid digestion.'

Corinna nodded, the branching stem's resemblance to antlers soft with green velvet plain to her now. 'Lemon balm!' she said, remembering her purpose. 'I wish I knew what these other plants are. Is there a herbal in the library?' As she spoke, she realised such a book would be written in Ennean and thus, for her, indecipherable.

'There is, but it will be pleasanter if I show you. I was hoping for a chance to pass the time with you.'

'And I with you. I've spent most of the past few days indoors.'

Strixi laughed – a high, mischievous laugh. 'As would I in your place. He is handsome. What a shame Reman men are so possessive. They soon bore me. The women too, though their bodies are more pleasing. Oh, have I shocked you?'

'No.' The question left Corinna feeling callow – as green as the stag's horn. She folded her arms and watched the cat, low on its haunches as it stalked across the lawn.

'Did you say your father is Lignoran?'

'I think he is,' said Corinna, though she hadn't confided that belief to her before.

Strixi stepped into the flowerbed and plucked a stem of lemon balm. 'It grows quickly, take all you need.' She rubbed a leaf between her fingers, releasing its soothing scent. 'In your care, Verendus will soon be well. Hurts heal swiftly here. Hurts of the mind and of the body.'

'I sense that. But it can't last, we cannot stay.' Corinna sighed. 'The world outside presses. I sense that too.'

'We are close to the border. You will find deeper peace when you travel further into Lignora.'

'Verendus has other plans. I am bound by his will.'

'How tiresome.'

Strixi reached out and smoothed back a lock of Corinna's hair. It was a simple gesture, accompanied by a smile, and yet unsettling. Self-conscious, Corinna drew back.

'The path Verendus takes may not be of his choosing,' Strixi said. 'Come, I have something for you.'

CHAPTER XXIX

M os set the tray on the landing table and tried the bedroom door. Locked. He didn't knock; the Commendator would only tell him to go away, just as he had done yesterday, and the day before that.

Mos left the tray and climbed the stairs to his own room. He pulled a pair of socks from the pile of kit; he'd need these in Brigantium. Despite his pleas, the Commendator was determined to go to the Alpine village where Fes had been heading. Something to do with Legate Capito and troops from the Twenty-Third Legion. Poor Fes, they'd never see him again.

Mos pictured himself returning to Iolia alone. Joining the resistance under Parhel rebel Kalvos and making a stand against the Iolian Watch. He could see it clearly: his furtive departure from the lodge, his triumphant arrival in Iolia, played out in colourful detail. But the time between these two points, the actual journey, was all fog.

He fingered a sock. There were no holes to darn. The clothes were laundered, the kit cleaned – if only the Commendator would inspect it. Perhaps he'd tire of her soon; he seldom stayed long with anyone. Though he was different with Corinna: too serious, too cheerful, all totally vomit making. He watched her like a sick dog, and in her absence he pined.

Mos hurled the sock across the room. Sod them! What did he care? He snatched up the bow-case and quiver, and ran downstairs and out to the stables.

Pepper nudged him expectantly and gobbled the gift of a carrot pilfered earlier from the larder. 'Just us again,' said Mos, and wiped his eyes. He fetched the saddlecloth and set it over the pony's broad back. 'Come on, Peps. We don't need anyone else.'

A short ride brought them to the woodland that surrounded the lodge. Beneath the trees, Pepper moved into an easy trot. Mos was finding his way around now, drifting in a haven of birdsong, green shade, and the rhythm of hooves on the dry track.

Dacoren said the woods were part of the estate and patrolled regularly. No rogue legionary would get within ten miles of the lodge. Despite this reassurance, on the first outing to the woods, Mos had lost his way and panicked. The possibility that a legionary scout might be lurking in the undergrowth had spooked him, and he'd ridden until hoof-prints revealed he was re-treading the same path. After searching a while he'd allowed the pony its head, and Pepper had brought him home.

Mos dismounted beside an ancient oak and knelt on the rutted ground. The little altar was still there, deep in a hollow of the roots. On his first morning exploring he'd assembled the simple construction of slate balanced on two flat stones. Since then, he'd prayed there every day.

Yesterday's offering had gone. From his purse, he took three breakfast raisins – sticky and squashed together. His mouth watered, but he set the raisins on the slate altar and prayed.

One for his family, one for the Parhel rebel Kalvos, and one for Saffi. Poor Saffi. He didn't think he was in love with her; he wasn't even sure he liked her. She wasn't easy to like. But she was special. What they'd done had been special. Every day he prayed she was safe. He hoped she hadn't run away because of him.

Enough prayers for one day. Mos led Pepper past the oak and along a path through the trees to what he'd dubbed the training ground. Many targets – stationary and hanging from branches – were set at the end of a long gravel clearing. In addition, there was a beam, a swing, and several climbing ropes. Everything was pristine. No weeds or dead branches, no frayed rope or chipped paint, though he never saw anyone tend it.

He hobbled Pepper on a stretch of grass at the side of the clearing and unhooked the bow-case and quiver from the saddle-horn. Guilt gnawed. Really, he should return the bow to Corinna – it was hers, after all. But he couldn't find his. In all the rush, he must have left it in Viorum.

Mos strung the bow, tightening it until the tension was sweet. He retrieved the smooth grey pebble he'd left in the gravel yesterday and set it back another pace from the stationary target of red and yellow rings. He nocked an arrow and raised the bow. So much better than his old one. Corinna probably hadn't noticed it was missing. Too busy in the bedroom with his Commendator.

Left hand steady, Mos drew the string with his right and checked his aim. He loosed and the arrow sped away and flew wide, thudding into the trunk of a tree behind the target. He glanced around. No one except Pepper had seen him blunder. Mustn't give up. Must persevere. After what he'd done to that poor horse, he must improve.

What followed was inconsistent, but a few attempts found the target edge. Perseverance brought improvement, and he found the inner ring. Encouraged, Mos set the pebble back a pace. This new distance mastered, he moved the marker again until the sun climbed past the treetops and his stomach growled.

The Lignorans at the lodge were kind to him and on his return prepared food. The midday meal was quiet; they didn't say much. Alone now, Mos took out his little drawing folder and untied the strap. The Commendator's drawing binder still hadn't turned up. To make matters worse, the Commendator blamed him for losing it. It wasn't fair; he'd been so careful.

That awful day at the Ministerium, the day of the arrest, he hadn't let the satchel out of his sight – not for a moment. And though he'd searched inside for the binder, it hadn't been there. Not that he could tell the Commendator. He couldn't admit he'd opened the satchel – he wasn't allowed to do that. As far as the Commendator was concerned, only Corinna had opened the satchel. And, of course, she wouldn't be punished.

Mos leaned on his elbows and stared at yesterday's sketch of Pepper.

'Is that your horse?'

'Oh!' Mos jumped. Looking up, he closed the folder and pressed his hand on the cover. It was the Lignoran woman. How long had she been standing there? Mos blinked hard. 'His name's Pepper.'

Strixi laughed – a high, clear note that made the hairs on his neck prickle. 'Carrots would be more fitting. He certainly likes them.'

There were no flies on Strixi. She must have seen him take the carrot from the larder. 'Sorry, I shouldn't have helped my-self… but they're Pepper's favourite.'

'I won't tell. I took him one myself this morning.' She winked and picked up the empty dish. 'You enjoyed that, Mostus?'

'I could eat it all over again. And, er, it's only Mostus when I'm in trouble.'

'And when you are not?'

'It's Mos.'

'Then I shall call you Mos.' Strixi smiled. 'Are you as soft as the moss?'

He met her eyes and looked away. Beautiful, captivating, she wasn't soft at all, but honed, sharp as a knife. To touch her would cut. 'Don't know,' he said. 'I try not to be.'

'Be true to your heart, Mos. This is a special place; hurts heal here. Drink in the peace. It will sustain and strengthen you for what is to come.'

***

It was mid-afternoon before Mos completed his chores at the stables. This time he walked to the training ground, it wasn't far and Pepper had had enough exercise for one day.

As he neared, he heard the thwack of an arrow striking wood. Someone was there.

He crept closer. Another thwack. As he peeked through branches into the clearing, Corinna lowered her bow and peered at him with bright eyes he couldn't meet. 'Mos, what are you doing in there?'

'I come here every day. Where's the Commendator?'

'Asleep.'

Mos disentangled himself from a bramble and stepped out to count three shafts bunched at the centre of a target. 'You're good. How far away were you?'

She pointed to the spot. It wasn't that far. Mos made the dismissive huff his mother made if anyone showed off. He prodded a grey pebble with the toe of his caliga. 'Here's my marker. I'm catching you up.' He pointed across the clearing to a target suspended from an overhanging branch. 'Bet you can't hit that.'

Corinna nocked another arrow and considered the swaying target. She loosed and the arrow sliced the air and struck the edge of the inner ring.

'Oh,' said Mos. He wasn't going to applaud. 'That's a fancy bow. Is it Lignoran?'

'A gift from Strixi. Like to try?'

She handed it over and Mos stroked the wood. Longer though lighter than a composite bow, the carved yew was oiled to a sheen and, when he drew the string, the tension hummed. 'Listen. It's singing.' He hesitated, then passed it back. 'I can't. If I do, I'll not want my old bow anymore.'

'*My* old bow.'

'It's not like you need it. You have the Lignoran one now. Besides, I have to train. The Commendator and me, we'll be on the road to Brigantium soon.'

'Brigantium?'

'It's in the Alps.' Probably shouldn't have told her that.

'The path Verendus takes may not be of his choosing.'

'What?' said Mos. She wasn't making sense. 'Sooner the two of us leave the better.'

Corinna sent an arrow screaming into the cluster. Mos pretended not to notice. 'You believe I should remain at the lodge?' she said.

'Well, it'll be business. And somebody must wait here for Lord Landren. You've got to hand over the codex, remember?'

'I know that.'

With the feeling his proverbial barb had hit home, Mos nocked an arrow and eyed the space at the target's centre. He'd show her. He loosed and the arrow flew wide.

'Begin with the fixed one,' Corinna said. 'I wouldn't have hit the hanging target had I not practised.'

Mos wiped his palms on his tunic and grabbed another arrow. Corinna was watching. Maybe she'd return to the lodge. She was usually in the bedroom, had no time to venture outside. 'What if the Commendator needs something?'

'He can fetch for himself.'

'If I knew you were coming out here I would have sat with him.'

'Thank you, Mos. But he's sleeping.'

Mos kicked at the ground, scattering gravel. 'He was awake when I took him his midday tray.' She didn't reply to that. Her face gave no clue, so Mos continued, pressing for a reaction. He'd make her care. 'You're not the only one.'

'The only what?'

'You! Women! You're not the only one. There's one in Iolia. He has me deliver messages to her. First thing he said when we got back last month: take a message to Drusilla. And there are more. Lots more. I've seen pictures in that binder of his. Some are naked. He'll tire of you. He always does.'

Corinna paled and marched off.

Jupiter, he'd be for it now. Mos sprinted after her. 'Wait!' He caught up and she stopped. 'Sorry. I didn't mean it. Please don't tell the Commendator, please…'

Corinna turned and glared, her eyes hard and cold like green ice. 'Things are different now, Mos.'

Raetia

850 AUC (AD 97)

Flush with intent following his vengeance over the Saxtili, Sentorus turned his gaze south to Vetera and converted the Sixth Legion Victrix. Auxiliary forts along the border rallied to his cause, and those that hesitated were soon persuaded.

He left Germania's northern forts depleted, but in the hands of trusted commanders, and marched Legions Three, Six, Nine, and Twenty-Four to Bonna. Here, in the south of Germania Inferior, he won over First Legion Minervia with minimal bloodshed, and moved on to the Twenty-Second in Germania Superior with equal success. Anticipating sterner resistance from the Eighth Augusta at Argentoratum, he left two cohorts building a camp on the banks of the Rhenus, and sent Legions Three, Six, and Nine on around the Alps to hinder imperial forces from the east. With the Twenty-Fourth Legion, Sentorus crossed into Raetia.

On the Raetian border, lives a branch of the Hermunduri tribe, long loyal traders with Rema. Despised and distrusted by their fellow Germani for adopting imperial ways, the tribe enclose themselves behind walls for protection. They call their fortress city Capula.

The Twenty-Fourth camped within sight of the city and Legate Sentorus demanded entry. Alarmed by this show of aggression, the Capulans refused to open their gates. The siege was brief. Capula's old walls could not hold out against the Legion's mighty engines. The gates were breached and Sentorus unleashed his troops.

Their plunder secured, the soldiers helped themselves to whatever else they wanted. Men were slaughtered as beasts; women and girls dragged from their homes and raped; boys and young men of fair appearance, also seized. The old and infirm were put to other use: beaten, baited for sport, and dispatched at will. None were spared, no prisoners were taken. A few escaped to tell of the horror. Sentorus set the city aflame and went in search of fresh spoils.

Chronicles of Imperial Rema

by Marcus Vedius Verendus

CHAPTER XXX

Verendus opened his eyes to the faint glow of the bedside oil lamp. His heart jerked. That rustling in the darkness, he hadn't dreamed it. Silent as a snake, his hand slipped under the mattress and found the dagger hilt. Wide awake now, he sat up quietly, sight adjusting to discern a cloaked and hooded figure, fuzzy in the gloom at the far side of the room.

A light moved fitfully in the shadows. Whoever it was, they were crouched behind the pile of kit – searching. He raised the dagger and aimed. If the intruder would only straighten, then he'd have the thief. Any moment now.

Aware that a quickening of breath could betray him, he inhaled slowly, evenly, as though asleep. He caught a scent of something floral. Jasmine.

Verendus lowered the blade, threw off the bedcover, and sprang across the room. In the same instant the figure turned, dodged, and he crashed into the wall. He dropped the dagger and staggered up, hauling the intruder with him.

A candle fell and guttered on the floor; hot wax splashed his feet. 'Ow! What are you doing?'

'Nothing.' Corinna struggled. 'Let go!'

Verendus scooped her up, thrashing and kicking. He held tighter, felt a surge of arousal – that must wait.

He dumped her on the bed and stood over her. 'I'll ask you again: what are you doing?'

She threw back the hood and started to rise. 'Landren's due on the morrow.'

He put a restraining hand on her shoulder. 'And?' Something told him he wasn't going to like this.

Her voice shrank to a whisper. 'I need to explain…'

Head in hands, Verendus sat on the bed while Corinna related the true price of her agreement. 'The codex? You pledged Landren the codex? You said you'd offered him gold.'

'He's hardly in need of gold,' she said reasonably. 'Where is it?'

'Magistra entrusted the codex to me. It wasn't yours to bargain with.'

Eyes bright with rage, Corinna rose. 'You told Mos, that if the Empire failed you, then he must find Landren. I've done as you asked and saved your ungrateful neck.'

'Landren was a last resort – *in extremis.*'

'The circumstances were extreme! I would have done anything to get you out of that filthy prison.'

Verendus plucked the talisman from its hanging place on the bedpost and gripped the little horse-head. He knew she meant well, knew he should tell her so. Disappointment stifled his apology and she spoke before he found the words.

'In my place,' she demanded, hands on hips, 'what would you have done?'

'The same…' He sighed and touched his chest where the scar from the stitches cut a ragged line. 'You asked who did this and I said an adversary of old. His name is Galenius Dax, Prefect of the Praetorian Guard. He wants the codex. There must be something important inside. Something incriminatory or illuminating. A secret, a map… Whatever it is, the prefect must not get his hands on it.'

She looked to the heavens. 'Of course! Torvius was due to meet with a prefect.'

'Prefect Galenius?'

She considered. 'Yes, that was the name.'

Gods above, she should have told him this earlier. Verendus drew a breath. Don't lose your temper. He hooked the talisman over his head, and said, 'So, the codex and the scroll with the serpent design – the one you told me Torvius was reading – perhaps he was taking both to Galenius.'

'You said we wouldn't speak of this.'

'We must, it's important.' He patted the bed, but Corinna didn't move.

'Judging by his manner it was a coup for Torvius. I don't think the prefect was expecting the codex. Does he know you have it?'

Verendus didn't reply. He marshalled his thoughts, trying to comprehend how Galenius had the binder though not the satchel. When not in use, the binder was kept in the satchel. On finding his drawing of the codex under the flap of the binder, Galenius said it was unexpected. A sobering thought struck. Perhaps Galenius didn't know of the codex at all… *until he saw my drawing.*

The room seemed to grow darker as the seriousness of the matter sank in. Before that discovery, the Praetorian quest appeared to be general not specific, a search through countless ancient scrolls for anything that bore the phixus or those sinister serpents. Now the search had focus. Though if Galenius was searching for a map he would not find one in the codex.

Verendus lit another lamp and pulled his satchel from under the bed. He didn't wish to scare Corinna, but she needed to be alert. He found his drawing kit and a scrap of parchment, closed his eyes a moment in concentration, and began to draw. With each stroke, his pulse accelerated until a face formed on the parchment. The knot in his throat confirmed the truth of the likeness. 'That,' he passed her the drawing, 'is Galenius.'

'It's a distinctive face. Handsome but cruel…'

The mouth was twisted at the corner; the eyes held a cold gleam. A mirror of the real face or had he drawn it that way? 'Do you recognise him?' Verendus asked.

'No.' She set down the parchment and sat beside him. 'Mos was right, you have a special talent. He looks up to you.'

'He'll grow out of it.'

Corinna smiled. 'What did you mean by an adversary of old?'

'Years ago, in Germania.' Verendus tucked the bedcover about his hips. 'It's complicated. He…' The words stuck. Grenorum. Don't think about Grenorum.

Corinna didn't press him. She stood. 'You're tired.'

'Stay. I've hardly seen you all day.'

'I've been with Strixi. I showed her the ring and we searched the library for anything that might shed light on my father's identity.' She shook her head. 'We found nothing. You see, it's not a family crest but a generic design. We couldn't even locate it to a particular region of Lignora.'

'I'm sorry. Generic or not, it looks valuable. Someone will recognise it.' He held out his hand. 'We could make up for lost time.'

'Is that all you want me for?' She pinned him with an incisive glare. 'Whatever happened to your binder?'

That bloody binder. Verendus felt his colour rise. 'I destroyed it.' He swallowed, almost choked on the lie. 'I didn't want anyone to see the drawings.'

'Drawings of women?'

How did she know? 'No,' he said. 'A few.' Wrong answer.

'Drawings of me?' Corinna shut her eyes. When she opened them, he saw fear.

His blood chilled. That last night at the house in Viorum he'd lain awake looking at the sketch he'd made of her. Oh, gods, he must have fallen asleep and dropped the binder down the side of the bed. Galenius would have ordered a search of the room. That's where the Praetorians found it.

He rubbed his brow. Such carelessness could not be explained away. And what of Drusilla in Iolia and the drawings of her. Galenius could cause trouble over those drawings, threaten to show her husband. Verendus cursed and wished he'd never made them. He brought the box from his satchel, unwrapped the codex, and passed it to her. 'Open it.'

'I can't,' she said curtly, the tone at odds with her startled expression. She recovered swiftly, composing her face to neutral like a trooper who thinks he's been selected for latrine duty and then realises the centurion's pointing his vine-stick at a man in the row behind. 'The band can be undone, there...' She indicated a tiny keyhole in the golden band. 'Magistra carried the key on her girdle.'

Verendus prodded the clasp. The golden serpents locked in their ring of death were primordial, like something evil from the tales of his childhood. Again, he wondered at the Praetorian prefect's interest in those interlocked snakes. The double ouroboros.

Verendus brought the cloth roll from his satchel and unfolded his assortment of miniature tools, each secured in its own neat pocket. This time he did not pick the lock – Corinna mustn't know he could do that. If he must hand the codex over to Landren, what did it matter if the securing strap was broken?

'This is what I've been translating, isn't it? What I've been toiling over!'

There was no point denying it. 'You must finish translating before I hand it over to your Lignoran friend.' He extracted the largest pair of pliers and opened them, positioning the claws over the golden band.

'Don't! I promised it in good condition. How did you open it before?'

Verendus swore and threw down the pliers. 'Why the hell did Magistra advise taking it to Landren?'

Corinna puzzled over this. 'Maybe she knew his name from the Belvedere library. He's very knowledgeable, an expert on old books.'

Verendus retrieved the pliers and shoved them back in the kit with the other tools. He would wait for Landren.

CHAPTER XXXI

On the following morning, Verendus ventured outside to the terrace to continue his tentative return to drill. Nothing too strenuous; Corinna was watching. If she thought he was overtaxing himself, she would fuss. She might even withhold favours.

He resigned himself to lifts and stretches. He was lifting the big weight he'd borrowed from the kitchen, raising it above his head, when the blare of a distant trumpet set the dogs barking. Two hounds dashed around the corner and raced towards the front of the lodge. He set down the weight and drew his dagger, taking a stance that left Corinna a clear path to the side door. 'Inside! Now. Bolt the door!'

The trumpet sounded again. Louder, nearer; the hounds yapping like they'd scented blood. Corinna rose from her chair, taking her time, smoothing a crease from her palla. Couldn't she see the urgency? Until he'd established who was out there, he wasn't taking any chances.

Strixi hastened through the side door; servants carrying flasks and towels trailed behind her. She slowed and pointed at the dagger. 'You are not in Rema now, Commendator.' Taking Corinna by the hand, she said, 'Come and greet Lord Landren.'

Verendus thrust the dagger back in its scabbard and marched after them, around the terrace, to the front of the lodge. Mos was there, perched in the bough of a chestnut tree, his legs swinging.

Strixi ordered her staff to line up outside the door. No one spoke. Even the hounds fell silent. Verendus felt a prickle at the nape of his neck, and a rumble like distant thunder stirred the air. This was no storm but the drum of many hooves, perhaps a hundred horsemen advancing on the lodge. He gripped the hilt of his dagger; Strixi had better be right about this being Landren.

Voices and the clink of metal carried on the breeze. On the near horizon, where the track melted into green, light glinted through the trees. Farsighted Strixi, standing on the verge and shading her eyes with her hand, saw them first. She pointed along the gravel drive and a line of black horses appeared, dust rising beneath their pounding hooves so it seemed they splashed through the shallows of a river.

Lignorans. Straight of back and dark of hair, their noble faces impassive. They rode under the banner of the White Hart, its antlers as lustrous as gold. Each black horse, akin to the others as currants on a bush, approached in a synchronised trot, the silver harness pendants jingling.

To the cheers of the servants, the riders reined in beside the lodge. Verendus counted thirty pairs of riders crowded around the entrance. More waited along the drive, chattering in a tongue he didn't understand, the reek of sweat and steaming horses heavy in the air.

He stepped into the porch beside Corinna, her face pensive as she regarded these men of her father's tribe. They were certainly impressive in their polished mail and green tunics. Each carried a bow on his back and a quiver of arrows hung from every saddle.

They dismounted and led their horses to the stable yard. As they passed, he saw his rescuer Oriedas. A jet-haired man walked beside. He wore an amethyst robe draped over his gleaming mail and moved with the haughty grace of a stag in a herd of fine deer.

The last of the Lignoran archers trotted up to the lodge and there, trailing in their wake, were Quintus, Bretorus, and the turma – a straggled line of weary men. Corinna gave a cry of dismay and fled inside. Verendus remained to see what she had seen: the slave Dorcas – crammed amid the baggage in a mule-drawn cart – was the only woman among the riders.

Verendus stared at the auxiliaries. It must be his fault they were here. They had fled Viorum because of their association with him: a wanted man. Or was it a trap?

Guilt flared to anger. Had Galenius let the auxiliaries escape so they would lead the Praetorians here?

He strode through the riders towards Quintus, calling out as he advanced. The young patrician sat hunched, almost asleep in the saddle, and didn't look up. 'Quin!' Verendus shouted to be heard. 'Why are you here?'

Quintus raised his head. 'You might look pleased about it.'

'I'm in a deep hole. I don't want to drag you down too.'

'V, you're a brother to me, I'll do all I can to help clear your name.' He stretched cautiously. 'Feels like I slept on that damn horse.'

Verendus helped him from the saddle. 'Can you be certain you weren't followed?'

Eyes closed in consideration, Quintus pondered the question as though such a risk had never occurred to him. Thinking his friend had fallen asleep on his feet, Verendus grasped him by the shoulder. Quintus blinked, and said, 'Well, we were at first. The Praetorians were on our tail, though we rode hard from Viorum and barely rested. Landren arranged to meet us at a milestone near the border. I could scarcely believe it when we got there to find this lot waiting to escort us.' He gestured towards Lignorans filing through the archway into the stable yard.

'But after that, Quin? Were you followed then?' Verendus was still gripping his friend's shoulder. He released him and stepped back.

'Don't think so. These Lignorans find paths where there are no paths…' He broke off to call Bretorus over.

The decurion marched up, face resolute, though Verendus fancied he saw a twinkle in those flinty eyes as Bretorus saluted. 'Commendator, the men are yours to command.'

On the decurion's order, the auxiliaries dismounted and fell in. Sticky with sweat and dusty from the road, their dark-circled eyes sunken in weathered faces, the troopers stood proudly beside their horses as Perseo raised the standard and Adarius blew a blast on his trumpet.

A lump formed in Verendus' throat and he heard a catch in his voice. 'From my heart, I thank you one and all for this show of support. Your loyalty will be rewarded.' The turma cheered. 'All shall profit when my name is cleared.' They cheered louder.

Verendus spoke with each. He quizzed the scout Dexo about the journey, and thanked Hostus for helping Corinna and Mos leave Viorum. He asked new lad Marinus how he was settling in, joked with old hand Adarius that retirement wasn't far off, and avoided being waylaid by Slug Strabo.

Callenus the medic was next, the sash across his tunic more salmon pink than red after days on the road. Verendus took care to express sorrow at the absence of the wounded auxiliary still languishing in hospital, and even managed a few pleasantries with Piggy Portoc and Murvaro, though he guessed they were here solely in hope of financial gain.

Head bowed, Gallus the Mole stood at the end of the row. When Verendus commended him on making the journey, the auxiliary looked up. He wore a leather patch over his ruined eye, lost to a sling stone in the flight across the river to Combarus. 'Glad to be here, sir. And someone had to ensure we brought those pigeons of yours.'

'You brought them? Wonderful!' Verendus almost kissed him. At last, he could get word to Iolia.

Across the terrace, Quintus leaned against the wall and drained his water flask. 'You twat,' he said as Verendus strolled over. 'I've already promised them fifty denarii each.'

'Sweet Venus. Once again, I'm in your father's debt.'

'He can afford it,' drawled Quintus with prodigal ease. He pulled a handkerchief from the neck of his tunic and wiped his chapped lips. 'That reminds me. You should have taken my tip – Spur's horses won by a length. I made a tidy profit.'

'Good for you, I only bet on Green.' Trust Quin to mention Spur and his bloody chariot team.

'Salutations! Commendator Verendus, I presume.' The distinguished-looking Lignoran, his right hand raised in greeting, came to stand beside them. 'I am Landren of Lignora. I regret to inform you that your levity is misplaced. The tidings are grave.'

The words sharp, the tone hard, had the Lignoran slapped him it could not have stung more. 'What tidings?'

'All in good time.'

Landren's keen gaze appraised him with the adroitness of a scribe scanning a ledger for faults. Verendus winced and wondered how many he'd detected. The possibility that this Lignoran was Corinna's father was disconcerting. If Landren had visited Iolia two decades ago, he may have been Attea's lover before she became Magistra. He calculated the possibility. Landren was probably well into his fifth decade. Subtract Corinna's age, and Landren would have been in his mid-twenties when he came to Iolia.

Verendus realised he was staring, searching for a resemblance. Remembering his manners, he thanked Landren for his help and hospitality.

The Lignoran graciously waved this aside. 'Do not despair. Rumour circulates that you met your demise in Viorum's river. Pending further evidence, or the discovery of a body, your court-martial is postponed. Use this situation to your advantage.'

'I intend clearing my name as soon as possible.'

'A delay could be prudent.' Imperious of voice and, despite the long ride, immaculate in his armour, Landren was taller than most Enneans – close to Verendus' own height. 'Consider my words, Commendator. We shall speak further.' He turned his scrutiny on Quintus. 'Rest now, Tribune. My steward will arrange all.'

Mos jumped down from the tree. 'Where's Saffi, lord?'

'There is no news,' said Landren. 'Though Oriedas searched long for her.'

Mos swore and ran off. Verendus made his excuses and followed. Preoccupied as to what he might say to the boy, he rounded the corner and almost collided with Oriedas. The Lignoran bowed and accepted his gratitude with humility.

'I'm in your debt,' Verendus maintained. 'How in Hades did you get past the castrum guards?'

'My disguise as a cleaner proved effective. No one gave me a second glance.' Oriedas smiled at the memory. 'And my reward is to see you restored to health. For one dreadful moment, I feared the river had claimed you.'

'Were it not for you...'

'And Mostus. You are a large man, Verendus. I did not drag you from the river unaided.'

'Mos never told me.'

'It is not his way. Now, if you permit, I shall examine you.'

Oriedas led him inside to a small, oak-panelled sitting room, and sent for hot water while Verendus undressed.

Oriedas made a methodical inspection of every yellowing bruise and fading lash wound, peering at each with a birdlike intensity. 'You are healing well,' he said at last, and touched the raw line where the stitches had been removed. 'Is it sore?'

'Stings a bit.'

'Regrettably, it will leave a scar.'

'Something to mark the occasion.' Verendus put on his tunic.

Oriedas looked up from washing his hands. 'Alas, the slave Saffi was less fortunate.'

'Landren said there was no news.'

'He asked me to speak with you alone. I was at the governor's house in Viorum when a Praetorian delivered this.' Oriedas dried his hands and brought a pouch of black cloth from his cloak. 'I assumed it belonged to Corinna. The slave Dorcas mentioned that a pair of earrings went missing on the day Saffi disappeared.'

Verendus took the pouch and untied the cords. At first, he could see nothing inside. He delved further and drew in his breath. A single jade earring. It was pierced through something that had the size and texture of a dried and shrivelled apricot, but was as pale as bone. 'Poor wretch.' He dropped the desiccated earlobe into the pouch and threw it on the grate.

'From your reaction, this is indeed one of Corinna's earrings.'

Verendus nodded. There was no doubt. He'd spent a long time choosing them.

'There was no message. It may not be Saffi's ear,' said Oriedas. 'Even if it is, she may be alive.'

'Unlikely.' Gods, what had Saffi told Galenius? How much had she known?

Oriedas sighed. 'The lives of men are brief, yet such cruelties abound.'

'Prefect Galenius specialises in them.'

'Do you think the girl talked?'

'Someone did. Galenius is a snake of the lowest order. He knew things he couldn't otherwise have known.' Galenius would have a full description of Corinna. Verendus fastened his belt. He must stay alert.

He set off in the direction Mos had taken through the garden and followed a path into the woods. Overnight rain had left the path damp, and he soon found the boy kneeling before a hollow in the contorted roots of an ancient oak.

Mos turned at his approach. 'Commendator.' He jumped to his feet and straightened to attention.

'Stand easy.'

Mos sensed something was wrong and remained rigid, fists clenched. 'Saffi's not coming back is she, sir? She wanted to go home.'

Verendus shook his head; Saffi hadn't made it past the city gate. 'We will avenge her. And Fes.'

'When?' said Mos, eyes sparkling.

'I thought I was the impatient one.' He ruffled the boy's hair. 'My father says vengeance is like the grapes on the vine – sweeter for having time to ripen. For now, our focus remains the codex.'

They returned to the terrace, deserted now, and passed the open front door, the polished wood-block floor shining. They walked on, through the archway and into a yard with stables along three sides.

'Impressive,' said Verendus. 'Even that gold tap above the trough looks splendid enough for Caesar's bathroom.'

'Nothing's too good for these horses. Come and see Pepper. I've brushed him to a real sheen.'

'He'll roll in the dust the minute you let him out.'

'I know,' Mos said, leading the way past auxiliaries rubbing down their weary mounts. 'But Lignoran horses are so fine, I don't want him thinking he's a poor relation.'

Pepper was housed at the far side of the yard. Anticipating his customary carrot, the pony stuck his head over the stable door and whinnied. 'There you are, Peps.' Plum appeared at the next-door stable to see what the fuss was.

Mos handed over a chunk of carrot, and Verendus balanced it on the flat of his palm. Plum snaffled the treat in an instant and rubbed his head against him. Verendus rubbed back. 'Yes, I've missed you too.'

Mos stroked Pepper's dark muzzle. 'Commendator, if that prefect reckons you drowned in the river, he's in for a shock.'

'Galenius won't believe I'm dead – not without evidence. We mustn't underestimate him. What troubles me most is that he has my binder. There was a drawing of Corinna inside, so he knows she's important to me. We must be vigilant.'

Mos kept stroking Pepper. 'Yes, sir.'

'I owe you an apology. The missing binder… it wasn't your fault. I was wrong to blame you. Forgive me.'

The boy turned, nodded, but didn't meet his eyes. Troubled by this avoidance, Verendus thought back – he couldn't recall what he'd said on realising the binder was missing. But he'd shouted at Mos, made him cry, that much he knew. It was time to make amends – but how?

Plum blew warm air down his neck and nibbled his hair. The answer was staring him in the face. 'Mos, once you've seen to the pigeons, Plum needs exercise. Would you take him out?'

'Would I, sir?' He grinned and flushed with delight. 'Oh, yes!'

'Don't let him have his head until you reach a clear stretch of ground.'

CHAPTER XXXII

Mos did as he'd been told and kept Plum on a tight rein, managing a gentle trot as he followed the track west through the trees. This was the life. If Plum was his horse, he'd ride around Iolia like an emperor. Everyone, even that gang of boys, even soldiers of the Watch, would stand aside.

He patted Plum's neck and let the dream spin out, filling in the details: the fine armour he'd wear, the gold hilted sword strapped at his side. People would stop and stare in awe. But for all his imaginings, it wasn't for him. If Plum was his horse, he'd ride back to Viorum and search for Saffi. The Commendator didn't know for certain what had happened to her. That was the trouble with growing older, it sucked away hope. It occurred to Mos that if he stopped hoping, stopped looking forward, then one day, he'd wake up as grey and tired and miserable as his father.

The fork in the track where the special oak tree stood came into view. Mos decided to stop at the little altar he'd made and pray for Saffi. The gods favoured mortals who didn't give up. If any gods were listening in the first place. Still, it wouldn't hurt to try. Then he could have a session at the archery targets and be back in time for supper.

Plum had other ideas. On reaching the fork, the stallion refused to slow, and trotted on, bearing north. Ahead, the trees thinned, revealing a stretch of clear ground. Since their arrival at the lodge, Dacoren, the wagon driver, had exercised Plum. It seemed the horse had a favourite route.

As they emerged from the wood, late afternoon sun broke through the cloud, shining so brightly that a field of gold stretched before them. Plum pulled hard, eager as a hound catching a scent. Easing from trot to canter, the harness pendants clanking, Mos sensed the power of the horse and an answering thrill seized him. Faster. Whooping in delight. Galloping now, bending low over the saddle, he leaned in and felt the speed. Wind skimmed his face and smarted his eyes, the beat of hooves drummed in his ears. He was the great Alexander charging into battle on mighty Bucephalus. Enemy warriors threw down sword and shield and fled screaming.

The ground rose, blurred. A wall of green loomed. Trees.

Plum thundered on into the scrub. Mos tugged the reins. He wedged his thighs against the front saddle-horns and clung on. Just in time, he ducked under a low branch. Twigs whipped stinging across his brow. 'Woah,' he cried. 'Woah!'

Plum shuddered to a halt, trees closing around them.

The stallion snorted and shook foam from its mouth. Panting for breath, Mos sank into the saddle and glanced about, trying to get his bearings. He hadn't ventured this far before, might have reached the estate boundary. Something warm trickled down his face. He wiped it away and saw blood on his fingers. The twigs had grazed him. Just a scratch – hopefully. He found a rag in his tunic, but it wasn't long enough to tie around his head.

Mos pressed the rag against the cut, wincing at the pain. Bet I look a right mess. He told himself to stay calm and remember what the Commendator had taught him. Look, listen, feel. That was it.

As he gazed around, the pounding in his head eased and from somewhere nearby came the whooshing rush of water. Sunshine flickered through the branches. 'It's getting late,' he said, stroking Plum's neck. 'We should go back.'

Mos allowed some slack and tried to turn the horse. Heedless, Plum continued into the wood. 'No! Not that way.'

Plum pushed through undergrowth. Ahead, it looked brighter. Lush weeds covered a wide bank that sloped to a river. Plum's huffing breaths and the rushing water the only sound. The opposite shore, some forty feet away, was narrower and bordered by a steep bank of pale stone thrice the height of a man. Weeds and brittle bushes of thorns sprouted from crevices in the rock, forming patches of green amid the flat stones of the shore below.

Mos jumped from the saddle. He led Plum to the river and the horse lowered its head to drink noisily.

'Not too much,' said Mos, scooping a mouthful. He soaked the rag and dabbed his brow, cleaning away the blood. With luck, by the time he got back to the lodge, the Commendator would have retired for the evening. By morning, the scratch wouldn't be so bad.

He splashed his back where the tunic clung. 'May as well go in,' he said, peeling it off. As he hung the tunic on a branch, Plum looked up, ears pricked. 'Listening to me now, are you?' Even as he spoke, Mos knew the horse had heard something else.

Helutti bandits? He froze, tried to think. *Hide.* Must hide.

Upstream, over the river, came the steady clop of hooves on hard ground. Grasping the reins, he dragged Plum into the shadow of the trees and stood quietly, watching and waiting and hoping that whoever it was would turn around. Maybe Dacoren was exercising one of the horses.

Across the river, light glinted on metal. Two cloaked and hooded riders emerged from woodland at the top of the bank and reined in, too far away for Mos to notice much about them. One of them dismounted and made his way down the steep bank, edging in a sideways movement and using the bushes as handholds. He jumped the last couple of feet and squinted across the water. Then he pushed back his hood and splashed his face and dark, close-shorn hair. He wasn't Helutti. Wasn't Dacoren either.

The man was familiar, or perhaps it was the uniform. Beneath the cloak, he wore a short mail-coat over a bleached tunic. It was distinctive with protective fringing at the thighs like the fancy mail that cavalrymen wear. He wore one of those long cavalry swords too. That legionary, the one Dacoren killed, he'd had a sword like that. Mos had said at the time there might be more of them. And now they were here.

Mos edged away. He gripped the sun pendant at his throat. Please don't let him see me. To his relief, the man unhooked a water-skin from his back and bent to fill it. Mos inched backwards towards Plum. He must do something. He should ride for help, but it would take too long. The legionaries must be after the Commendator. They'd arrest him. Or worse…

Without taking his eyes from the crouching legionary, Mos reached for his bow. Slowly, carefully, he unhooked his quiver from the saddle-horn and crept closer, drawing back the bowstring and nocking an arrow. He would wing him;

bring him down so he couldn't climb back up the bank. Then the Commendator could question him. He'd get answers.

Mos took aim. The distance to his target seemed to grow, unrolling like a scroll before his eyes. It was too far. He might miss. Might kill the legionary. Right hand twitching, Mos lowered the bow. Decanus Carbo was right: he was a lousy shot.

The legionary rose and called to the man at the top of the bank. Distance and the roar of the river between them, Mos couldn't make out the words. A moment later, a rope was lowered. The legionary tied it about the neck of the water-skin and his comrade pulled it up. The legionary moved to follow, groping for a grip on the flat rock. Soon he would climb up and be gone.

Mos told himself to try. He raised the bow again, aimed, and sent an arrow arcing across the river. The legionary jumped aside as it struck the ground by his boot in a puff of dust.

Mos snatched up another arrow. He'd been so close. One more try. He was on the shady side of the bank; they wouldn't spot him here. He nocked the next arrow and cursed. Hadn't he left his tunic, his white tunic, hanging from a branch? In spite of himself, he looked. And there it was, plain as a flag.

Suddenly, a spear soared towards him, spinning on its axis as it drilled the air. It thudded into the tree beside the tunic, sliced through bark, and hung juddering. The legionary atop the bank had spotted him.

Mos dropped his arrow and ran. He skidded on damp weeds and almost tumbled as a second spear pierced the earth a cubit from his foot. Plum neighing in protest, the legionary taking aim again, Mos slung the bow on his back, grabbed the reins, and leapt into the saddle. Turning Plum in the direction of the lodge, he dug his heels hard into the stallion's flanks.

The Castrum, Viorum

Principal Norvanus stepped back from the window. He closed the tablet he had been reading and placed it on his desk. 'After all that, it wasn't Verendus.'

'No, sir,' said Optio Matellius. 'I inspected what was left of the body and I wasn't convinced. Plenty of bodies end up in the river, each with their own sorry tale to tell – if only they could.'

'Eloquently put. Of course, Galenius won't find Verendus even if he drains the entire river.'

'You believe he escaped?'

'He's wriggled out of tighter holes,' said Norvanus. 'However, the architect of this plot is unaccounted for. To find him, we must capture Verendus.'

Matellius scratched a pimple on his chin, making it bleed. 'Prefect Galenius has cast his net beyond the river, sir.'

'His methods are remarkably thorough. And he has the Speculatores at his disposal. Set a rat to catch a rat.' Norvanus unhooked his cloak from the peg beside the door. 'Cancel this morning's appointments, it's time I visited the Villa Aquinus to express my condolences in person. A most unfortunate business.' The Principal squared his shoulders and the optio draped the cloak around him. 'And, Matellius, my meeting with the prefect this afternoon – make a note to raise the matter of highway security.'

'Yes, sir.' The optio picked up the tablet. 'Poor Tribune Aquinus. Shall I have your things moved into his office?'

'No rush, we shall proceed with decorum. They say Aquinus offered stout resistance, but those bandits are a ruthless lot.'
'Indeed, sir. Most unfortunate.'

CHAPTER XXXIII

By the time Verendus had completed a brief drill session, the yard was quiet. The archers and auxiliaries had seen to the needs of the horses and left to find their own comforts. The shadows were lengthening; Mos should have returned by now.

Verendus doused himself at the tap. He shouldn't fuss. The boy was no doubt making the most of his ride.

'Oh, there you are!' Corinna hastened through the archway. 'Landren's waiting.'

'Let him wait, I don't take orders from him.' He ran a hand through his wet hair. The exercises had tired him more than he cared to admit, but he stood straight and breathed slowly.

'Please, Ericus. Come.' Her gaze swept over his naked torso. Not the lingering scrutiny he would have liked, but a look of concern. He pulled on his tunic and didn't bother to explain the importance of resuming regular drill. He was still damp and the soft wool of the tunic soaked up the water, releasing the aroma of newly washed sheep.

Corinna handed him his satchel and he slung it across his chest. Resistance was futile. He must honour the agreement and give Landren the codex. Without the Lignoran's help he would be languishing in Viorum's castrum awaiting execution.

Or worse. 'Let's get it over with,' he said, buckling on his belt as he traipsed after her.

Three chairs and a large round table draped in white linen were set on the terrace. With a sweep of his hand Landren invited them to sit facing the garden, the better to appreciate the view. It was a fine one. From the circular fishpond to the grove of apple trees bright with blossom, the garden was a pattern of paths and lawns and flowerbeds as perfect as a mosaic. A high wall enclosed the garden. Woods lay beyond, rising to hills and forest spilling over the horizon in a blue-green blur.

Landren sat with his back to the scenery, his dark hair glossy in the afternoon sun. The side door opened and Strixi came out. Dorcas followed, bearing a tray laden with jugs and glasses, which she set upon the table. Strixi poured the wine, added a little water to each glass, and they returned inside.

'Good health.' Landren raised his glass.

The light in his eyes, Verendus couldn't read his host's expression. He hung his satchel on the back of a chair and returned the toast. 'My thanks, Lord Landren, for your help and hospitality. Albeit, at a considerable price.'

'We shall settle that in time,' said Landren, dismissing the comment with a shake of his head.

The cool tone left Verendus pondering the implications of their settlement. Something told him the cost of his rescue exceeded the codex. More was expected.

'Spring is much celebrated by your people...' said Landren, and sniffed the wine as assiduously as an apothecary checking for poison. 'Alas, the festivities rendered business at the Ministerium both intermittent and slow.'

Verendus could picture the commotion. Crowds flocking to plays at the theatre and races at the Circus, torchlight processions along Viorum's festooned streets, locals and country folk streaming through the city. Thousands of citizens eager to enjoy themselves, plus the usual swarms of pimps, whores, and traders out for a quick profit. Galenius had made good use of festivals to distract the attention of a pleasure-hungry populace. Verendus brushed away a wasp that was circling the wine jug. 'You don't approve of our entertainments, Lord Landren?'

'When you have lived as long as I, it is politic to cultivate tolerance. My capacity for outrage is as keen as ever.'

'Has something upset you?' asked Corinna. She was paler than usual, attempting an appearance of calm, but not succeeding.

Again Verendus searched for a resemblance between her and Landren. Both had the same emerald green eyes and that defiant tilt of the chin.

Landren took a sip of wine and dabbed his lips with a napkin. 'An unconfirmed report claims that troops under the command of Legate Regimius Sentorus sacked the hillside town of Capula and left it to burn.'

Verendus opened his mouth; no words came. Why would Sentorus attack Capula? Furthermore, the logistics were all wrong. Capula bordered the province of Raetia. If Sentorus and his forces had landed on the coast of Germania at the start of the season, then he could not be in Capula. Not unless he'd sprouted wings. Verendus scoured his mind for an explanation, and finding none, said, 'Huh, unconfirmed report. Sentorus is in Germania disciplining the Third Legion. Capula's hundreds of miles away on the Raetian border. And besides, Capula has a treaty of non-aggression with Rema.'

'*Had*,' replied Landren. 'And treaty or not, it was a savage brutality.'

The wasp buzzed over the table and settled on the jug. As it crawled around the rim, Landren reached out and touched the creature's thorax with his fingertip. There was a low whine like a whetstone being drawn across steel and the wasp dropped on the table, dead.

Verendus stared, not sure what he'd witnessed. Had Landren killed the wasp with a single touch?

'It wasn't doing any harm,' Corinna said.

'Had it fallen into the wine someone may have swallowed it.' Landren picked up the wasp by its wings and dropped it into one of the enormous urns which stood on either side of the door.

He retook his seat and turned to Verendus. 'Capula is a wealthy city and Sentorus has troops to pay. Now he can recruit more. Need I remind you both how Julius Caesar increased his army from four to twelve legions, paid for and equipped with the profits of war?'

'Are you implying that Sentorus has designs on Rema?' Verendus demanded. This was a serious allegation with no solid evidence, yet it accorded with his own concerns.

Landren's composure showed no sign of cracking. 'There are legions in Germania spoiling to avenge the assassination of Emperor Domitianus. Unrest could spread to other provinces. There are many imperial outposts manned by auxiliaries armed and trained by Rema which, given encouragement, would revolt against their patron. Others will watch and follow the first sign of success. Emperor Flavio is weak.' Landren paused purposefully. 'The troops may look to Sentorus to lead the cause.'

The Lignoran had a point. Sentorus was the younger brother of Galenius' adoptive father. Rema's Senate had chosen Sentorus to lead the disciplinary force to Germania — surely part of Galenius' plot against the new emperor. For such a plot to succeed, legionary and auxiliary support was essential. Galenius and Sentorus – two snakes scheming together.

Landren was aware of this family connection, so Verendus told him how Galenius had undermined the Praetorian Guard in Iolia, and had doubtless done the same in Rema. Gratified when Landren nodded thoughtfully, he explained that Galenius had helped Iolia's governor form the Iolian Watch, ostensibly to manage harbour closure, though its chief role seemed to be persecuting Parhels. The Lignoran appeared genuinely saddened by his account of the Regia Square massacre. With Corinna present, Verendus kept it brief – she'd wept last night when he told her of the bloodshed.

'Whatever the legate's motives in Capula,' said Landren, 'the consequences will be far-reaching.'

'I must return to Viorum, find Tribune Aquinus. He'll know what to do.'

'Viorum? No, it's too dangerous.' Corinna turned to Landren. 'Did you speak to the tribune? Has he agreed to defend Verendus?'

'Aquinus is dead,' said Landren. 'Murdered by bandits on his way to Avennio.'

The garden faded. Blurred momentarily. Verendus clamped a hand over his mouth, but couldn't stop a sob from escaping. His old friend, the one senior Praetorian officer he trusted. He'd been counting on Aquinus' support in securing justice for the officers and Parhels slaughtered by the Watch – Parhels like Nel. He'd written to the tribune, told him of the turmoil in Iolia. Aquinus would have taken steps to counter Galenius' conspiracy against Emperor Flavio. Would have known which soldiers and senators might stand against Galenius. Known whom to trust…

Verendus groaned. His voice, his hope, was dead. He was a fugitive, hundreds of miles from home – how could he help Iolia now?

'Ericus…' Corinna said gently.

Verendus didn't turn. If only he hadn't diverted to Spur's camp. He might have passed Aquinus on the highway, spoken to him then and warned of treachery in the Guard. This was no murder by bandits. Galenius was behind this.

Verendus tossed back his wine and rose. 'I'll fight my own corner.'

'Sit down!' Landren ordered. 'This is no time for audacity. Your allies diminish. Even the loyalty of your paltry cavalry troop has been bought. And if Britannia's *Pax Remana* crumbles, how long before half of them desert you to return to their beleaguered homeland?'

Verendus remained standing, letting the words wash over him, hearing the truth of them, but unable to absorb any more misery. Sun warm on his face, he stared at the garden – at topiary hedges, and rose bushes, and the tree with the waterlily blooms – until the world outside grew hazy, a distant memory best forgotten.

Corinna touched his arm. 'Don't start a fight you cannot win.'

She was right. He could not stand long, one man against the Guard. Nor could he run forever. He resumed his seat with a truculent thud.

'This decay runs deep,' said Landren. 'With imperial forces stretched by conflict in the Danuvius region, Sentorus and Galenius have planned their bid for power impeccably. I believe events in Iolia and Capula are connected.'

Verendus poured more wine and said nothing. The Lignoran knew more than he'd assumed.

Like a conjurer about to pluck a coin from thin air, Landren adjusted the sleeves of his robe. 'Consider this: if you and I were to trust each other, to work together, we would double our strength.'

'You really would help?' asked Corinna.

'I have my own plans,' Verendus said. Any discussion would be a waste of time. The moment he was fit enough, he'd put the lodge and his enigmatic host behind him, head east to the mountains and find Legate Capito. The sooner the better.

'Think on it,' said Landren, indifferent to his reluctance. 'In the meantime, please honour our agreement and give me the codex.'

The Lignoran stood firm, deaf to every appeal. Corinna intervened to remind Verendus – as if he needed reminding – that without Landren's help, he would still be a prisoner in the castrum. Nevertheless, he couldn't shed the feeling his escape had been bought with an item that should not have been up for bargain.

He took the parcel from his satchel and set it on the table. He had prepared for this eventuality. This morning, in the privacy of his room, he had unpeeled the waxed calfskin and re-wrapped the box in the buff-coloured cloth. Thus, Landren wouldn't see the severed stitches, and the dried glue on the leather, and realise the package had been prised open.

Landren didn't hesitate to untie the cord and remove the cloth. He inspected the pine box within and raised an eyebrow at the stamp of the Cardinal Square greengrocer printed on the side. He slid back the lid, pushed away the packing straw, and brought out a pouch of white silk. As he drew the codex from within and saw a gleam of gold, he practically purred.

'Magnificent.' Landren ran his fingertip over the golden band until he reached the keyhole.

Remembering the wasp, and fearing that Landren would attempt to singe the metal, Verendus said quickly, 'There is a key.'

The Lignoran looked up expectantly.

'Afraid I don't have it though,' he added vindictively.

'I do.' Corinna unhooked the purse from her belt and fished inside. 'Here.' She held out a little golden key.

'Corinna!' She'd had it all along and never said a word. The startled expression, which flashed across her face last night when he asked her to open the codex, made sense now.

Landren regarded them both with bemusement. He took the key and, with careful, almost reverential attention, inserted it into the slot.

Verendus held his breath as the key was turned and the band parted. Landren peeled away the band, leaving a pale stripe across the leather cover. With an audible intake of breath, he opened the codex.

Verendus pointed to the key and, in his best, disinterested tone, said, 'May I?'

Without pausing from turning a page, the Lignoran nodded.

The little key with its ruby-eyed serpents was half the length of his ring finger and weighed heavy in his hand. Verendus couldn't read the tracery of silver script engraved on the shaft and double-edged cleft, though he guessed it was Ennean. That, and the exceptional artistry, fitted his belief that an Ennean goldsmith had made both key and clasp.

He held the key to the light. The tiny snakes coiled at the top of the shaft were identical in all but size to those on the codex, the shadow cast on the white cloth a distinctive phixus.

Landren closed the codex and slipped it back into the pouch. 'Keep this,' he said, passing it to Corinna. 'The codex belongs at the Temple of the Flame. I hope you will return it there one day.'

He had to insist before she took the codex and put it in the box. She thanked him and tied the cloth around it. 'How did you know?'

'I have read of the Ambrone tribe and its exodus.' Landren smiled, smug as a basking crocodile. 'When I saw Mostus' drawing of the codex, I knew the clasp for what it used to be.'

'Magistra said you would. I thought she meant the codex.' Verendus recalled how she had handed him the cloth-covered package. *He will know this thing for what it was.*

Verendus almost mentioned his surprise that Landren had no interest in keeping the leather-bound book, but thought better of it – he would hate for the Lignoran to change his mind. Those discoloured parchment leaves might amount to nothing more than an old compilation of brews and incantations, but Corinna's relief that the codex could one day be returned to the Temple of the Flame was palpable. He was pleased for her. And to think he'd dared hope that the lost Alpine route of his Ambrone forebears was hidden in those faded pages. *Idiot,* said the small voice in his head.

As for the golden clasp, he couldn't guess its significance. Strange that Magistra hadn't separated it from the codex. Why send the fragile codex too?

Landren held aloft the clasp. Turning it slowly, he peered through the thick lens of what looked to be a magnifying glass. Such tools were rare, highly prized, and this was an exquisite piece. The glass, about the size of a sestertius coin, was mounted in a silver ring attached to a chain, which he wore around his neck.

Landren tucked the magnifier back inside his robe. 'Permit me to tell you a story.' He eased back in his chair and rested his hands on the table. 'In the first days when the animals were created – one male and one female to populate the land – all the pairs went about their business. All save one. Of all the creatures, the vainest was a golden snake with eyes as red as rubies. He abhorred there was another snake like him, and fought his mate so fiercely they became locked in a circle, each devouring the other's tail. As they fought, flecks of gold sloughed from their skin. All the gold in the world hails from their struggle. They fight to this day.'

'Like those horrid snakes on the codex.' Corinna said.

'The double ouroboros,' said Landren.

Verendus set down the key and straightened in his chair. Galenius had called the serpents that.

Landren turned the golden band with its serpent clasp, aligning it before him. He closed his eyes, placed his long forefingers on either side of the snakes, and traversed the scaled surface, stopping occasionally to press or to tap. His fingers, moving to an inaudible melody, acquired a hypnotic oscillation like snakes locked in a complex dance that quickened, paused, and quickened again. Metal scraped against metal. As if of its own volition, the clasp rotated three-hundred-and-sixty degrees, stopped, and the golden band fell away. Landren opened his eyes and they glowed with new vitality.

Verendus shifted position. His right hand was clenched in a fist, thumb pressed between forefingers, making the sign against evil. He flexed his hand and glanced at Corinna, her mouth forming into an 'O', though she did not speak.

He endeavoured to rationalise what he'd seen. Had the Lignoran called upon some innate mystical ability? Or was this a performance? As with the killing of the wasp, it wasn't clear.

Curious in spite of himself, Verendus leaned forward. In Landren's palm, and almost of its size, lay a golden treasure. Elliptical in shape, it resembled an amulet, the double ouroboros circling its rim, the two serpent heads looking out in opposite directions. At the edge, no longer hidden by the band, was a catch, which Landren pressed with his fingernail. A click and the clasp sprang open. It was hinged at the centre and sat balanced in his hand like an open clamshell.

There was something inside. Verendus leaned nearer. Whatever it was, it appeared impossibly delicate: a golden cobweb suspended between the two halves.

For several moments, Landren peered at it, his brow creasing as though he was calculating a difficult sum. He nodded to himself and passed the clasp to Verendus. 'What do you see?'

The golden tracery within was as intricate as the skeleton of an autumn leaf, but without apparent pattern or symmetry. He spotted a silver thread and followed its line. And there, like a spider in a gilded web, was a tiny phixus. As he stared, the lines took shape and focused. He gasped. Blinked hard. Could it really be? All that searching through the pages of the codex… and yet it was never in the codex. Here it was, in the palm of his hand. Or was he seeing what he hoped to see?

'What is it?' asked Corinna. 'What's the matter?'

'I… well, I *think* it's…' he couldn't find the words. He nodded, attempted to regain his composure and assume a neutral expression, but it was too late – she and Landren had seen his amazement.

Again Verendus felt the nerves and excitement that had accompanied his arrival at the Temple of the Flame, home of the legendary map and the serpents protecting it. On handing over the box, Magistra had implied that safeguarding the contents might thwart the conspiracy. A vague instruction for something so important. But perhaps she didn't know the secret within, only that those serpents were significant. That would explain why she had given him codex and clasp. The theory accorded with Corinna's account of Praetorian soldiers searching the Temple library, looking through countless ancient scrolls for anything that bore the serpents or the phixus. Always, it came back to that. The sign of the serpents.

This raised fresh questions. How did Landren know the clasp's secret, and why would Magistra think he would know? The ease with which he'd opened the catch suggested he had done so before.

Verendus turned the clasp as he pondered this. He didn't get far with his deliberations, his attention was consumed by the artistry before him. The way the silver thread wound through the golden web; gods, surely he was right. This must be the legendary Ambrone map – the route his ancestors had taken through the Alps. And now it belonged to Landren.

Verendus closed his fingers around the clasp. He should never have agreed to hand it over. Beside him, Corinna stiffened, as taut as a deer attentive to a footfall. 'Don't you hear it? That sound, like a creature caught in a snare. It pains me.'

Landren paled too. Perplexed, Verendus closed the clasp and Corinna exhaled. Sunlight reflected off the gold. Bright, dazzling.

'Excuse me,' someone said gravely.

Landren looked up. Verendus jumped. He almost dropped the clasp, but closed his hand about it and was on his feet in one swift movement, turning to see the stable boy who had helped to saddle Plum. Barefoot, in a grubby tunic and breeches, he resembled a stray.

'Well, what is it?' demanded Landren.

'Forgive me, lord…' The boy stared at Verendus' hand, hoping for another glimpse of the treasure concealed there. He glanced around as a horse neighed loudly.

Verendus patted the boy's arm. 'What's the matter?'

'Commendator…' He shuffled his feet. 'It's the big stallion. He's come back on his own.'

Verendus groaned. He shouldn't have let Mos ride out unaccompanied. Not on Plum. He turned to Landren. 'Forgive me, I must search for Mos.'

With a flick of his hand, Landren discarded the apology. 'My servants will assist you. I doubt he has gone far. One moment…' He tapped the table. 'The ouroboros, Commendator.'

Verendus took a last look at the serpents and placed the clasp on the table. 'You've made great profit from my misfortune.'

'That was never my intent.' Landren reached for the clasp and gasped as an arrow struck the table, splintering the wood a hairsbreadth from his hand. He flinched and shrank back.

'Down!' yelled Verendus.

He shoved the table onto its side and the jug and glasses hit the ground with a crash. Landren and Corinna took cover beside him. He pulled her close, pushed her between himself and Landren, and told the stable boy to get down too.

'This is an outrage,' said Landren. 'Where are my men?'

'That came from the garden,' said Verendus, and was proved right when a second arrow struck the table. Thank Minerva it was carved from sturdy oak and thick enough to shield them.

The lodge door was a few paces away. The table had a single, stout central pillar. He grasped hold and dragged it towards the door, trying to keep the table from rolling to the side as they all shuffled backwards. They reached the big stone urns and stopped.

Verendus fought to manoeuvre the table, but the gap between the column-shaped bases on which the urns were set was too narrow. They could go no further.

He shoved the nearest urn. The plants shook, petals dropped. The urn wouldn't shift – it had probably stood there for decades. He turned to Corinna. 'I'll run to the door. When I open it, get inside. Quickly! Don't look back. We'll follow.'

'Not without the ouroboros,' said Landren. 'Where is it?'

Verendus ignored him and darted the short distance to the door. 'It's locked! Why's the bloody door locked?' He shoved against it. An arrow thwacked into the wood and he dived to the cover of the table. 'Don't worry,' he told Corinna, 'help will come. Until then, we can hold out here.' He reached for his satchel and realised he'd hung it on the back of his chair. Now it was lying halfway across the terrace. It would take a suicidal dash to reach the thing.

The neighing grew louder. Men were shouting; he couldn't discern the words. He sniffed the air. Smoke. This was no random assault, but a well-coordinated attack.

'Fire.' Corinna pointed to a column of smoke rising dark beyond the lodge. 'It's the stables.'

'The horses!' The boy rose. Reaching past Landren, Corinna grabbed his tunic and clung, pulling him down.

The shouts and neighs grew louder. A thud as something heavy fell, and then the whoosh of flames feeding on straw and timber. By the sound of the din everyone else was there, at the stables, trying to put it out.

'It is a trap!' cried Landren. 'We must protect the ouroboros. Where is it? Where is my treasure?'

'I see it.' This time the stable boy was too quick for Corinna. Keeping low, he scampered from the cover of the table and across the terrace.

'No!' yelled Verendus. He peered around the rim of the table. The clasp had rolled further than he'd thought, for the boy was crouching beside the stone balustrade that bordered the terrace.

The boy turned, a grin on his face as he snatched up the clasp. An arrow thrummed, split the air. The grin burst in a shriek of agony. He stumbled and fell, an arrow lodged in his spine.

'What happened?' demanded Landren. 'My treasure! Did he reach it?'

'Verendus? Where is the fugitive Verendus?' The voice was firm, assured, and coming from the end of the terrace. 'Show yourself! Do as I say and no one else will be harmed.'

So, there was more than one assailant. Verendus drew his dagger. He'd deal with this one first, then go after the bowman in the garden. As he moved, an arrow thumped into the rim of the table above Corinna. She gasped and covered her head with her hands. The bowman was nearer than he'd realised.

'Come out from your hiding place and throw down your weapon. By the balustrade, where I can see it. Any tricks and you will all die.'

'No!' Corinna grasped his wrist. 'Don't go. Please, Ericus...'

'Do not yield,' said Landren. 'They want the ouroboros.'

Verendus didn't reply. Were these the Praetorians who had tracked him to Alba? Had they picked up his trail and followed him here? Treseus said there were three men. The third could be hiding, waiting, bow poised ready to shoot. Corinna was still gripping his wrist. He'd never forgive himself if she got hurt.

He summoned his best parade-ground voice, and called, 'As one soldier to another, do I have your word no one else will be harmed?'

Without hesitation, the voice answered, 'You do.'

Carefully, Verendus prised away Corinna's fingers and kissed her hand. He wanted to say something eloquent, tender, but the words swelled in his throat. He threw down the dagger and stepped out onto the terrace. His legs felt unsteady, but he forced himself to stand straight. He would not beg for mercy.

'Good,' said the firm voice. 'Fetch the double ouroboros and go down the steps. Slowly!'

Verendus crossed to where the stable boy lay, blood pooling on the flagstones. He crouched beside the body, lifted the flaccid arm, and plucked the clasp from the boy's hand.

Someone followed Verendus across the terrace. A glance confirmed it was a soldier, sword in hand, his face concealed by a masked helmet that resembled a prop from a gladiator show. His short mail-coat was girded with a wide belt; a layered fringe of leather protected his upper arms and thighs. The armour was standard legionary cavalry kit, the sword a long-bladed spatha. Nothing suggested he was a Praetorian. But that didn't mean he wasn't.

Ahead in the garden, the bowman, anonymous in a cavalry parade helmet complete with silvered faceplate stood, bow drawn, watching. It occurred to Verendus that the men could have taken the clasp themselves, there was no need to involve him. Unless they wanted him, too, and wanted him alive. No doubt Galenius had something in mind.

Verendus told himself to concentrate. He descended the steps, focus flitting between the bowman and the high wall at the end of the path with its stout door that led to the woods. He supposed it would be there, at the door, where the height of the wall made escape improbable, that the pair would bind him before leading him through. Perhaps the third man was waiting with horses on the other side.

Verendus tightened his hold on the clasp, the rigid metal of the serpent scales cold in his grip and slightly raised like the body of a dead fish. He passed the pond and contemplated throwing it into the water. No, they would make him suffer for that.

A change in timbre told him the soldier in the gladiator helmet was on the steps.

A cry. Someone stumbled and landed with a thud. The soldier was down, sprawled on the ground at the foot of the steps and moaning in pain.

Verendus darted aside and vaulted a low wall into the apple grove. An arrow zipped past his shoulder and struck a tree. He kept running, cutting this way and that, through flowerbeds and across the lawn, always moving, always weaving, determined not to be an easy target.

Boots thundered along the path. The soldier was on his feet again. Verendus didn't turn to check. He sprinted to the door and used his momentum to shoulder against it. As he crashed into it, the door flew open – the bolts had been drawn back. Recovering his balance, he ran on into the woods.

CHAPTER XXXIV

A path stretched ahead, snaking through the trees. Verendus kept running until he reached a fork. Hoof prints, distinct in the soft ground, showed that two horses had approached recently along the right-hand path. No sign of the third Praetorian. If indeed these were the Praetorians from Alba. With no way of telling, he decided to refer to them in his mind by the broader term: soldiers. He didn't want to believe they had tracked him from Alba. It was distracting, and he needed his wits about him.

Heart pounding like a smithy hammer, he stepped off the path and into the undergrowth. He hadn't run this hard since his incarceration at the Castrum Viorum. He stopped to catch his breath, the air heady with the sickly sweet scent of wilting bluebells. Black smoke hung ragged in the sky. It appeared the fire at the stables had been swiftly contained. Probably started deliberately to divert attention from the attack on the terrace.

He crouched low in the ferns, kept still, and listened. After the neighing and shouting, the quiet was eerie, just the mournful cries of carrion birds and the distant rush of water. No sound of soldiers, but that didn't mean they had gone. They were out there somewhere, licking their wounds. The one on the terrace was injured. He suspected Corinna's hand in that: she had a good aim.

Verendus fancied he heard the distant clip-clop of hooves. Clearer, getting closer. Now what? Lie low or cut through the wood and find his way back to the lodge. There was the clasp to consider. Perhaps he should hide it. Somewhere safe like the hollow of a tree.

Keeping low, he crept deeper into the thicket, pushing through ferns and nettles, barely feeling the stings. He hunkered down in the shelter of an oak and waited until he could no longer hear the riders. Then waited a little longer before creeping on.

The ground grew damp and lush with weeds. Verendus reached a stream, the water clear and vigorous. He drank, scooping the sweet water in a cupped hand, gulping it down and then splashing his face.

He crossed over, crept on, and stopped abruptly. A path lay ahead. The same, or a different path? Hard to tell. He turned back into the scrub and hesitated. The riders were back. Several horses by the sound of it. The drum of hooves rose to a steady beat. He shrank into the undergrowth. As long as they remained on the path he was safe.

A dog barked. It was answered by another, then another, and soon several hounds were baying. Time to go.

He changed direction, back to the stream and into the water. Gods, it was cold. At least it was only ankle deep. Trying not to splash, he kept walking, the stony bed slippery under his caligae boots.

The stream widened. Deeper here, it lapped at his knees and dampened his breeches. He stopped and listened. The steady churn of water drowned out other noise. There must be a river ahead. He would ford it and put the hounds off his scent.

Verendus pressed on, running now, trampling through weeds, sending a moorhen hissing and clattering into the bushes. The water reached his thighs, soaking into his tunic and slowing him. The stream meandered, doubled back on itself. He waded on, glancing around for a quicker route. On his right, the trees thinned and there was the river. Shafts of sunlight pierced the woodland canopy, dappling the ground and turning the water to a shimmering surge. Beyond, he caught a glimpse of white, vivid against the green.

He waded from the stream and crept through the trees. As he neared, he realised it was a white tunic hanging from a tree. He slid down a slope to the riverbank and skidded to a halt. His heart lurched. Above the tunic, a spear was embedded in the tree. The design of the metal shank and head were Reman; the gash in the bark fresh.

He pulled down the tunic and stood dripping and shivering and turning it over in his hands. It belonged to Mos. That was the bow-shaped brooch he'd bought from the pedlar on the road to Combarus.

'Mos? Mos…' he called, careful to keep his voice low. Verendus searched, afraid of what he might find; going over what may have happened as he scanned the bank. All he found was an arrow lying on the ground. It looked like one of his own.

The sun was sinking towards the treetops. Perhaps an hour remained until dusk – then the chances of finding Mos would plummet. If anything happened to him, if he was hurt… No use thinking that.

Verendus continued his search and found imprints of Plum's big hooves in a patch of mud. The prints went down the weed-covered bank to the river, petered out on the flat stones of the shore, and trailed back again. Beside them were the pits of caligae boot studs – small feet. Mos had small feet.

Verendus returned to the tree. Beneath its branches, the prints were less clear, splodging over each other as if Mos had attempted to pull Plum away from the river. He crouched for a better look and wished again that he'd never allowed him to ride the horse. The boy could be injured, or worse. May have fallen into the water, been swept away.

Leaves rustled. Verendus sprang up, turning, dropping the tunic, and reaching for a dagger he no longer wore. The two soldiers burst from the undergrowth and charged. Between them they were dragging something pale and flowing, raising it as they ran. Verendus dodged aside. The pair turned and advanced again, startling him with the speed of their manoeuvre. They cast the shimmering mesh and it smacked over him. A weighted net. His legs skidded from under him and he fell backwards, landing on his buttocks.

The net tightened. His arms were pinned. 'Help!' he yelled. 'Help!' Not that anyone would heed him. Though somebody might. Gods, please, somebody come.

The soldier in the gladiator helmet grabbed the net. Anonymous in the sleek, masked helmet with its two small eyeholes, he was more deadly *secutor* than lightly armoured netbearer. The fall on the garden steps had injured him for his upper right arm was grazed and he carried it awkwardly. He drew the net away from Verendus' head and grasped his hair, holding him still. As Verendus opened his mouth to yell again, the other soldier shoved in a stinking wad of rag.

Verendus jerked his head free, but couldn't spit out the rag. He thrashed vainly, helpless as a fallen gladiator entangled in a *retiarius's* net. The secutor muttered what sounded like a curse and punched. A flash of white light. Scorching pain. Verendus collapsed, as dazed as a bludgeoned tuna. Darkness closed in.

A jolt jarred him to his senses. The net covered him, the fine mesh stronger than it appeared. He was being dragged, bumping over rough ground. Straining under the weight the pair dragged him up the slope, hauling him in like a fish. Here the terrain levelled to a small patch of clear ground amid the trees where two horses and a mule were tethered. Verendus struggled, tried to roll back to the slope.

The bowman pulled the net tighter and, mindful of the bow strapped on his back, crouched beside him. With its sculpted silver face and head of stylised bronze curls, the cavalry helmet was sinister; the man wearing it more demi-god than human. His eyes, staring through the solid mask, were a vivid blue. He set a dagger at Verendus' throat. 'Keep still or I cut!' His Latin was hard and heavily accented, perhaps Germanic.

The blade bit, cold against Verendus' skin. One twitch and he would feel its sharpness. He should have hidden the clasp while he had the opportunity. Now he had no bargaining power.

The secutor, who had been fetching something from a sad-dlebag, drew his spatha and marched over, gait unsteady. The cut on his arm was bandaged and his suede breeches were ripped. With the tip of the long-bladed sword, he prodded the knuckles of Verendus' clenched hand. 'The ouroboros, Commendator.' He drew the blade across the side of Veren-dus' wrist, cutting a few threads of the net and etching the skin. 'Don't make me take your hand as well.'

Where his wide silver wristband would once have protected, blood welled. Slowly, Verendus uncurled his fingers. He could feel the scales of those snakes indented into his palm.

The secutor bent nearer. With thumb and forefinger, he reached through the split in the net and took the clasp. One of the serpent's fangs snagged the fine mesh, but the secutor tugged and pulled it through. Verendus resisted an urge to snatch it back. The bowman's blade was at his throat.

The secutor sheathed his spatha and straightened to inspect the plunder. The bowman lowered his dagger and rose beside, leaning in to see.

Slowly, very slowly, while their attention was on the clasp, Verendus moved his legs. They were bound tight by the net, he couldn't move them separately, but little by little, he drew them up until he was curled like a sleeping baby.

The pair were still examining the clasp. 'You certain this is it?' asked the bowman.

'It matches the drawing the prefect showed me.'

Drawing? Verendus tried to think. The answer came almost immediately and chilled him to the core. They meant his drawing. The one Galenius had ripped from his binder.

The secutor looked up, listening.

Hounds. They sounded close. Verendus turned onto his back and waited, regulating his breathing and focusing his mind. He must not fail.

Like a bolt out of a *scorpio* weapon, he launched himself feet first and crashed into the secutor who staggered backwards, dropping the clasp. The bowman made a grab for it, but it rolled away, down the slope. The bowman turned and kicked out.

Verendus groaned and the bowman kicked him again, harder.

Verendus lay still. Heat seared his side, he could feel the bruise spreading. The soldiers – had they gone? All he heard was his own ragged breath. Into the darkness came words – angry, urgent. He told himself to open his eyes. Pain blurred his vision, but he discerned their shapes descending the slope. They were searching for the clasp.

This was his chance. The secutor's blade had cut the net. But where? Verendus groped along the mesh. Surely here, near his left hand.

His vision cleared. He kept his eyes fixed on the two soldiers and ran his fingers over the mesh, plucking and pulling until he found the rent. He tugged at it, but the mesh was strong, he couldn't get any purchase. Lying down made the task awkward, but he dare not rise. Not yet.

Hounds bayed. 'Let's go,' said the bowman. 'Can't we leave the thing?'

'And risk the Lignorans finding it?' The secutor swore, voice harsh within the mask. 'We'll have to deal with him.'

'Orders were to take him alive. The prefect made that clear.'

'He'll slow us down.'

Verendus tore at the mesh. The noise alerted the secutor who turned and strode over, hand resting on the hilt of his spatha. Verendus drew back, hiding the tear in the net. The secutor eyed him suspiciously, but before he could investigate the bowman charged up the bank. 'Found it!'

The secutor took the clasp and set it on the ground beside his right foot. Mystified, Verendus looked on. Sunlight glinted on the golden scales and lit the ruby eyes. It seemed the serpents would awake, uncoil, and slink away.

With great care, the secutor raised his foot over the clasp and stamped down hard. A sharp crunch. He stepped away from the pathetic scrap of flattened metal; all that remained of the double ouroboros crushed beneath his caliga boot. The bowman said something about orders being carried out. Verendus could scarcely discern the words. Cold rage gripped him. He had the sensation of being detached from his body, observing all from a distance but powerless to act. He'd carted that bloody thing across land and sea, risked his life to protect it. The clasp had been in Landren's possession for less than an hour and now it was ruined.

A hound barked and the din was echoed by another and another. The bowman fled into the trees. Verendus daren't turn his head, but the distinctive thud of a soldier leaping into the saddle and the beat of hooves told him the bowman was on the move. The secutor watched him go. Then with a bone-melting screech of steel he drew his spatha, raised it two-handed, barbarian fashion, and lunged.

Verendus recoiled, felt a rush of air. The blade gouged the earth in a spray of soil a handspan from his ear. With both hands about the hilt, the secutor pulled out the sword.

Time slowed, stalled. Verendus bit hard on the rag. *Jupiter Optimus, Jupiter Optimus…* he couldn't form the words to pray. He bit harder. Time caught up. *Move.*

Like a landed trout making a desperate attempt to return to water, he flipped his body and flung himself at the secutor, knocking him over. Verendus rolled onto the man's sword arm, holding down the injured limb and using his bulk to block the secutor from reaching the dagger. As Verendus fumbled through the net, trying to reach the dagger for himself, the secutor pummelled him with his left fist.

Verendus shifted his weight, increasing the pressure on the secutor's sword arm. The man yelped, dropped the sword, and kept pummelling. A surge of nausea rose. Verendus swallowed, breathed deeply. Vomit now, with the gag in his mouth, and he'd choke. He strained against the net. Something loosened. Ripped. He thrust his hand through the tear and yanked the dagger from its scabbard. It sliced the net as easy as cutting cobwebs. He was free.

As he clambered to his knees, putting more weight on the secutor's arm, the barking grew louder, rising in excitement. He lunged for the neck, but the secutor flinched and the blade only grazed him, etching a red line across his skin. The man grunted and, with a sudden burst of force, butted him in the chest.

Verendus reeled from the blow and scrambled aside. He pulled the wad of rag from his mouth and spitting blood and soil, lurched to his feet. The secutor rose, too, his sword arm hung limp, but he retrieved the spatha with his left.

Verendus had a heartbeat to adjust his grip on the dagger and aim. The dagger cut the air, skimmed the secutor's right leg, and passed by. The man shrieked and reached for his thigh with his wounded arm, the suede breeches turning red beneath his fingers. With his accomplice gone and the hounds closing in, surely the man would take his chances and flee. But he abandoned his efforts to staunch the bleeding and stepped back to take guard. It would be attack.

An image from the arena flashed into Verendus' mind. The lightly armoured retiarius gladiator bore a trident, a dagger, and a net. Verendus had no trident, the dagger was gone, but he had the net. He snatched it up and stepped back, passing the mesh through his hands, checking his grip. Sword raised, the secutor advanced, hobbling but still formidable.

Verendus swung the net, whirling it round and round. It swished through the air and caught on the secutor's blade –

just like in the arena. Verendus pulled, dragging him down. The secutor lost his grip on the hilt and the spatha dropped. He groped to recover it, but before he could close his hand around the pommel, Verendus kicked him in the jaw – hard but not too hard. He crashed down and Verendus planted an iron-shod foot on his chest. 'Why did you destroy the ouroboros? Speak!'

The man stared. No fear or entreaty, no wrath or defiance in those cement-grey eyes peering through the mask. No trace of emotion at all. Blood flowed freely, seeping through the sodden breeches and dripping on the ground.

'Why did you destroy the ouroboros?' Verendus demanded.

The secutor coughed. 'Water…'

The man was almost spent. If he didn't speak soon, it would be too late. Verendus recalled his own ordeal in the Castrum Viorum, how he'd pleaded for water. He reduced the pressure on the man's chest. 'Tell me why, and then I'll fetch water.'

In the same moment, a mule brayed and something crashed from the undergrowth. It thudded into Verendus, shoving him forward. He stumbled, lost his footing, and fell, face down in the grass.

As he raised his head, a hound growled. A huge Lignoran hound was standing over him. More bounded past towards the river. It occurred to him that these were the hounds he'd heard when first he entered the wood. Friend not foe. But they weren't his dogs. As a boy, he'd seen one of Father's slaves torn to pieces by a pack of frenzied hounds when the lad, sent by the cook to pick mushrooms, strayed into the path of a hunt.

Safer to lie quiet. He could just make out the riverbank, the secutor skidding down to the water, hounds snapping at his heels.

Men shouted, hooves pounded, thundering through the wood. The ground seemed to shake. Oriedas, Dacoren, and a dozen archers followed. Oriedas yelled at the secutor to stop, but the man didn't turn. Two hounds leapt to bring him down, but couldn't get a hold on the mail-coat. One of them sank its teeth into the man's calf. He faltered, hobbled on, and plunged into the water.

Weighed down by his mail, he didn't try to swim and sank beneath the surface. The hounds massed at the water's edge, yapping and snarling.

Oriedas reined in beside Verendus and called off the hound, which was standing guard. The dog obeyed and stood watching, its dark eyes grim. Verendus sat slowly. The clasp had gone. The secutor must have grabbed the mangled remains. Now it was in the river.

Pointing east, Verendus said the other soldier had fled into the wood. Oriedas sent archers in pursuit. Dacoren seized the net and an attempt was made to drag the river. All they retrieved was a drenched and shivering hound.

Oriedas yelled in Ennean and the remaining archers gathered up the net and hastened away along the bank. 'There is a bridge nearby,' he said, helping Verendus to his feet. 'They may have better fishing there. After that the river is treacherous and flows down to the Egelidan Falls.'

Verendus blinked and wiped his eyes. He was alive. Alive and furious. He'd had the secutor at his mercy and then that hound had bounded from the bushes.

'Do you have the clasp?' asked Oriedas.

'No…' A fist of pain pressed his forehead. What was he about to say? Shaking, panting, he sank to his knees. His tunic was torn, his arms and legs bramble-scratched. 'Mos…' he gasped.

And there was the boy, gazing down with wide eyes, his face pinched pale, a ruddy bruise and scratches on his forehead. 'We found him lying in undergrowth at the side of the path,' said Oriedas.

If he said more, Verendus didn't heed. A rushing sound like the roar of waves filled his ears. Everything blurred. The ground ebbed, shifted, and he tumbled into the void.

THE KOSORANS

According to the Illustrious Scribe, in ages past, mighty Hercules travelled far. On reaching the Alps, and with no time to go around the mountains, he used his club to smash a path through the rock.

Centuries later, Reman soldiers paved this legendary path to form a section of the Via Domitia, the great highway that runs through the Alps to Gallia Narbonensis and on to Hispania. As Rema explored the mountains in search of other passes, Alpine tribes rose in resistance.

The fiercest resistance came from the Kosorans. One of the nine tribes of the Ennea, the Kosorans dwelled in the forested foothills south of the Via Domitia. Unlike the Lignorans, this Ennean tribe did not trade with outsiders. Intent on impeding Reman progress through the Alps, the Kosorans used their knowledge of the mountain paths to terrorise Rema's soldiers in a series of audacious ambushes. The intention was both to kill and to capture, for the Kosorans worshiped a twin-headed serpent with a thirst for human blood. It is said that before sacrifice was made, prisoners were branded with the sign of the serpents. When the branded and mutilated body of a senior officer was discovered hanging from a tree outside the Reman camp, reinforcements were sent for.

Rema prevailed. The Kosorans were defeated, their settlements destroyed. Tales of vengeful ghosts and giant serpents abounded.

Soldiers are a superstitious breed, and that region of the mountains remained uncharted.

Chronicles of Imperial Rema
by Marcus Vedius Verendus

CHAPTER XXXV

As Verendus descended the main staircase, his sense of foreboding grew. The same clammy unease that had twisted his gut before the Praetorians seized him at the Ministerium. He glanced at Corinna, but she did not seem to have noticed his disquiet. The hour was late and he was tempted to return to his room, but her insistence he should rest after the skirmish in the wood made him determined to prove his fitness. After bandaging his cuts and smothering ointment on his bruises, she had made him a dose of that filthy somniferum drink to ease his pain. Verendus had poured it into the piss pot.

Odours of smoke and burnt wood soured the air. The gods were merciful and neither man nor beast was injured in the fire, although damage to the stables could take months to repair. With the feeling he'd forgotten something, Verendus patted his satchel. Thank Fortuna, someone had retrieved that, along with his dagger, and returned both to his room. The terrace had been swept and tidied to its usual pristine state after Corinna threw her dagger at the soldier, grazing his arm. He'd slipped and fallen down the steps, knocking over several flowerpots, which had added to the mess.

The satchel felt remarkably light without Magistra's box weighing it down. Verendus missed that reassuring weight. He'd risked his neck trying to protect the codex, and then with one stamp of his boot, that bloody soldier had destroyed the ouroboros clasp. Bile rose, scorching his throat. Why hadn't the soldier just taken the clasp? Why destroy it?

Mos was waiting at the turn of the stairs, staring at the little window though the world outside was dark. He turned at their approach and grinned sheepishly, expecting a reprimand. There had been none, nor would there be. Mos was bruised, nothing worse; Verendus was too relieved to be angry.

Glass in hand, Quintus sauntered from the dining room. On seeing them, he smiled and crossed the hall to the foot of the stairs. 'Better, V? Ghastly things, nets. Caught my leg in one once, got in quite a tangle, but that's another story. Come and have supper. Eldoran's here with news from Rema. He's made good time.'

'What news?' Verendus demanded. Again he wondered if the Nemusan was following him. Though if Eldoran was interested in the double ouroboros, he'd left it too late.

As if taking his cue, the Nemusan came to the door of the library. 'I have been many days in the saddle to bring word to Landren. He will explain everything. But, alas, the news is grave.'

'Ill news travels fast,' said Verendus. That feeling of foreboding had been prescient. Beside him, Corinna tensed. She reached out to grip the bannister rail and didn't let go until she reached the foot of the stairs.

Eldoran greeted them cordially, though his gaze was on Corinna. Verendus pressed closer to her and a tide of jealousy rose inside him. The same vile emotion he'd felt when he first saw the Nemusan watching her in the hall at Castellum Alba.

He knew he was being unreasonable, knew he should dismiss the feeling. Instead, he said, 'We'll bid you goodnight, Corinna. It will bore you to stay up listening to stories.'

'But I like stories. Don't be a grump.'

'Yes, V, don't be such a grump,' said Quintus. 'Let her listen if it amuses her.'

Landren's voice rang out from the library. 'No time for stories. Finish your supper and come in, all of you.'

Bretorus appeared at Quin's shoulder and whispered to the tribune who nodded. 'Oh, I see, there's to be a meeting.' He smiled sweetly at Corinna. 'Men's talk, dear lady. You will indeed be bored.'

'Far from it,' said Corinna. 'Lord Landren said *all of you*. So that includes me.'

'True,' said Verendus, inwardly applauding her spirit despite his objection that she would be in the same room as Eldoran.

'Then please excuse me, I shall fetch my shawl. There's a chill in the air.'

Across the hall, the Nemusan stood in the doorway of the library, his gaze following as she ascended the stairs.

Verendus waited in the dining room. With all the enthusiasm of an imperial food-taster, he picked at the selection of cheese and olives. This news from Rema would be graver than Eldoran implied. The others went into the library, but he remained, pacing back and forth, until Landren's voice boomed from the library, summoning him in.

Corinna was there; he hadn't heard her go in. Convinced that he was walking into trouble, Verendus hesitated in the doorway. The smell uneased him – not the wood smoke from the grate, but an underlying note of parchment and leather that reminded him of his father's *tablinum* and the fateful evening when Magistra's request to take the codex from Iolia was first mooted.

At the centre of the library, the round table was glazed in candlelight and seven high-backed chairs had been set about it. As he neared the one remaining seat the fire surged, casting shadows that leapt across the ceiling to shrink the great room. The table seemed to waver like a coin sinking in a pool. He rested a cautionary hand on the polished surface – it was quite solid. Encouraged by the sight of a wine jug, he hung his satchel on the chair and sat down.

Strixi glided around them, filling the glasses with wine and water before returning with a fresh jug, which she placed on the table. With a bow to Landren, she left, closing the door behind her. Quintus, who had watched the procedure with the look of a ravenous dog, caught Verendus' eye and winked.

Landren straightened the leather folder before him and smoothed the sleeves of his robe. He regarded each person in turn. Oriedas first, impassive on his right, then left to Eldoran, expression pensive though his noble face bore no trace of fatigue after his journey. On the left of the Nemusan sat Quintus, frowning now and toying with his glass. In that moment, he looked old. As careworn as his father the governor. Beside him, Decurion Bretorus also frowned, though his brow creased in irritation.

Verendus watched Landren's gaze slide from Mos – standing behind – then settle upon himself before passing to Corinna, who completed the circle. She had put on the green tunic and palla that matched her eyes bright in the lamplight. Had Eldoran's unexpected arrival prompted this change of attire? The gauzy fabric was fastened at her shoulders and cinched beneath her breasts with a narrow belt of cord. Verendus told himself it would be he, not the Nemusan, who would unpin those brooches and untie that belt. Later…

Reassured, he turned his attention to Landren.

Calm after his earlier distress on learning of the clasp's destruction, the Lignoran spoke with quiet authority. 'A golden clasp of immense value has been stolen, destroyed, and thrown in the river.'

'You accusing us?' demanded Bretorus.

Quintus eased back in his chair and folded his arms. 'Not guilty.'

'Silence, please!' Landren raised his hand. 'Hear me out.'

Murmurs of acquiescence accompanied Quin's apology, and Landren resumed. 'My archers have lately returned. Regrettably, they could not retrieve either the body or the clasp. The river is fast flowing. The thief was swept downstream and over the Egelidan Falls.'

'What of the other soldier?' Verendus asked. 'Did the archers catch him?'

Landren appeared abashed. 'Alas, no.'

Alas, indeed. Verendus asked the question that had troubled him since the attack. 'Why destroy the clasp?'

'That is what I intend to find out,' Landren replied.

Eldoran had that pensive look again. 'Was this theft chance, or did these men know of the clasp?'

'The prisoner's description fits that of the soldier from whom Mostus fled,' said Landren. 'Doubtless, he and his masked accomplice followed him from the river to the lodge and awaited an opportunity.'

Mos gasped as though he'd been struck.

'Don't blame him,' said Verendus, rounding on Landren. 'Those thieves probably tracked you from Viorum.'

'I assure you they did not.' Landren rested his hands on the folder. Despite his serene expression, he clutched the leather. 'Commendator, these hounds have been on your trail since your arrival in Gallia.'

Mos approached the table. 'Excuse me, lord, but the legionary couldn't have followed. Plum and me were the other side of the river from him. And then I fell off!'

Landren sighed. 'The legionary and his accomplice crossed by the Egelidan Bridge and picked up your horse's trail. The mighty Plum has large hooves.'

'Legionary?' Decurion Bretorus spluttered his wine. 'No legion stationed near here.'

'As I stated,' Landren said slowly, as though dealing with an asinine servant, 'three legionaries followed Verendus to Lignora. Dacoren disposed of one of them near the border.'

'What? No one told me!' Verendus controlled an impulse to thump the table. How Landren knew about the three soldiers was a mystery. Somebody, perhaps one of the auxiliaries, had been telling tales.

Around the table conversation resumed. With the feeling he'd missed something important, Verendus tried to think. Despite the warmth of the fire, a chill fluttered in his stomach. And then he realised. A detail was wrong. When Treseus warned of the trio's arrival at Alba, he'd said they were Praetorians. 'How do you know the soldier was a legionary?' Verendus asked.

Landren seemed surprised by the question. 'Dacoren took his identity tag.'

'May I see it?'

'That can be arranged later.'

All very polite, but there was an icy undercurrent. Verendus wasn't satisfied. 'None of this explains how the soldiers gained entry to the garden.' He supposed someone at the lodge had assisted them, bolted the side door to prevent escape from the terrace, and started the fire. 'You should question your staff.'

'No one is above suspicion,' said Landren. 'If the theft of the clasp is associated with events in Iolia—'

'What are you suggesting?' Verendus clanked down his glass and pointed to the folder the Lignoran held so tightly, as though afraid it would float away. 'What's that?'

'Patience, Commendator. First, it is vital that we are all aware of recent events.' Landren gave a brief account of the sacking of Capula and his belief that Galenius Dax and his uncle Sentorus were plotting against the emperor. Again, Quintus and Bretorus were enraged. Again, Landren called for calm. 'You may deny Sentorus' involvement in this plot, but you cannot deny that Emperor Flavio is callow and weak. Rema's legions may look to Legate Sentorus for leadership.' He opened the folder and extracted a mottled sheet of papyrus.

Verendus leaned closer, but couldn't decipher the sinuous lettering.

'This is where it all began,' said Landren, sliding the papyrus away. 'Long ago, when Rema was a republic, its army marched through the Alps, vanquishing local tribes and claiming the mountains and passes as its own. In the south of that region lived an Ennean tribe called the Kosorans. When they dared to stand against Rema, the entire tribe: every man, woman, and child, was slaughtered in their mountain refuge and the settlement was razed to the ground. This historic document dates from what you Remans call the Seventh Age. Permit me to read...'

Like an orator building a speech, he started quietly. '*In a walled city, beside the Kosoran Pass, dwell the people of Kosora, one of the nine tribes of the Ennea. Their territory extends from the Dragon's Peak to the forested foothills of the Minnaeon Mountains…'*

Verendus swigged his wine and wondered where this was leading. He glanced to his right and saw the furrow on the decurion's brow deepen – he was wondering too.

'Minnaeon Mountains?' said Bretorus, stroking his beard as he spoke. 'And where might they be?'

Landren bridled at the interruption. 'Your people call them the Alps.'

'Kosora? Never heard of the place,' Verendus said rudely, and winced as Corinna kicked him beneath the table.

'Neither have I,' said Quintus. 'Sounds a good story.'

Bretorus shifted in his chair. 'I thought there no time for stories.'

'Kosora is no story,' snapped Landren. 'Listen! *This secretive and fierce tribe worships a two-headed serpent god…*' Forefinger resting part way down the parchment, he looked up. '*Their deity is the double ouroboros.*'

Verendus shrank from the Lignoran's gaze. 'Like the snakes on the clasp? Are you saying that thing originated in Kosora?'

Quintus glanced from one to the other. 'What's this snake thingummy?'

'The ouroboros,' said Landren, 'symbolises Time's eternal cycle – life, death, and rebirth. The double ouroboros is formed from two such serpents twisted in a circle, each devouring the other's tail. Like your two-faced god of the first month, these snakes stare out in opposite directions: to past and to future, to beginning and to end. Eventually, they will consume each other and implode so forcefully the world will be destroyed.' He slapped his palm hard on the table. Quintus jumped.

'It is a potent symbol,' said Oriedas.

Bretorus snorted; Quintus opened his mouth but didn't speak. Landren slipped the parchment into the folder. 'The time has come.'

With the distinct impression the Lignoran was directing the statement at him, Verendus reached for his glass. Empty. His heart pounded. Hades, it was stuffy – he should get some air. As he drew back his chair, a voice from the past stirred: soft, barely audible. He hesitated, trying to hear. Magistra's words returned to him, echoing in his head. *If the Empire should fail you, seek out the Ennean, Landren of Lignora. He will know this thing for what it was.* But why?

Everyone was staring, waiting for Landren's reply. He brought the serpent key from the folder and set it on the table. Caught in the candlelight, the golden snakes shone, basking in the glow.

Hot breath brushed Verendus' neck. He turned. 'Why don't you draw up a chair, Mostus?'

The boy stepped back. 'Sorry, sir.'

Landren took the key and offered it to Mos. 'We should all examine it.'

Speculation rose as the key passed from hand to hand. Corinna, perhaps unsure of her standing amongst the men, had scarcely spoken. Now, she sat forward. 'Does any other land use this symbol?'

'I do not think so,' said Eldoran.

'The double ouroboros is synonymous with Kosora,' said Oriedas.

More speculation. Too many voices talking at once. Landren snapped his fingers. 'Listen! An item of great significance was taken from Iolia's Temple of the Flame.' He paused and looked over. 'Would you care to explain, Commendator?'

Verendus shivered. Corinna turned, meeting his eyes in silent entreaty. He nodded, and said, 'By the command of Magistra, High Priestess of the Temple of the Flame, I was asked to deliver a box to a secure location. That box contained a codex of sacred documents.'

'Where is it now?' asked Bretorus.

'Safe,' said Verendus. He'd hidden it in his room. He brought Mos' drawing of the codex from his satchel and passed it to Quin. 'The book was sealed with a clasp. That alone was stolen.'

Quintus grimaced at the picture. 'What an ugly trinket. You're well rid of it.'

'No!' said Landren. 'The legionary gave his life for this so-called trinket.'

'Why destroy it?' asked Corinna, as the drawing passed around the table. 'Is it because of Kosora?'

Bretorus cracked his knuckles. 'Old bones and ruins.'

Landren turned an indignant face. 'This is a matter of grave importance, Decurion. The emergence of this clasp is one ripple in a great tide, a current of discord passing through these lands. I will not stand idle and watch my kindred swept away.'

So that was where Landren was leading – he was worried for his kindred, but lacked the resources to make a stand. If Capula's treaty with Rema had not saved it from a rogue legion, then Lignora was vulnerable too. When the Lignorans signed the Atrox Treaty, they signed away their former homeland in Gallia Narbonensis. In exchange, Rema gave them new land in the forests of Aquitania and a pledge of non-aggression. The treaty was looking as thin as the parchment on which it was written.

Landren was watching him. 'You too have felt this discord, Commendator?'

Verendus attempted to concentrate under the scrutiny, to determine how Father would handle the enigmatic Lignoran. Perhaps it was time to trust this man. Returning the gaze, Verendus said, 'I share your disquiet, Lord Landren. However, all my concerns have been discredited. But I know that Parhels were persecuted, and the Iolian Gap wasn't blocked.'

'But the Colossi,' Mos blurted. 'They blocked the Gap.'

'A deception,' said Verendus, and Mos looked confused. It was understandable. For years the huge bronze statues of Castor and Pollux had stood on either side of the Iolian Gap, marking the entrance to Portula Harbour – galling to think someone had dismantled them. 'The harbour and Portula town were evacuated several days before the Great Storm. Most people were too busy with their *Saturnalia* festivities to question this. I suspect that once the evacuation was complete, piece by piece, the Iolian Watch dismantled the Colossi and took the bronze away. The Gap wasn't blocked. That was an illusion created using weighted nets with a lining stretched taut to give the appearance of solidity.'

A collective intake of breath and everyone else was talking. Verendus steepled his fingers and considered his theory. The old doubts resurfaced. He had no proof of treachery. He hadn't seen inside the nets. His friend Carbo's assertion that the netting was a salvage operation to shore up debris from the statues sounded horribly plausible. The swim to the harbour had yielded no firm evidence, just a Medusa fish sting and the supposition that the netting formed part of an elaborate hoax.

He signalled Mos to pour more wine, and told himself to stick to his argument and state the premise clearly. 'Picture it,' he said, 'a dark shape beneath the water. From the headland, it appeared to be a mound of debris. But this mass had little more substance than a shadow and could be pulled aside to permit the passage of designated ships. With sailing and swimming prohibited, and watchmen in place to enforce the ruling, who would know? Other ships would see the lighthouse warning beacon and stay away. It seems beyond coincidence that both the Watch *and* the ships seen approaching Iolia should carry the phixus on their banners.' He traced the symbol in the air with his forefinger. 'Ten years ago, I saw that symbol carved on the trunks of trees in a sacred grove in Germania.' Time had not faded the memory, the phixus as stark as bone and so distinct it might have been carved that very day.

'Germania?' Bretorus leaned close.

'Near Grenorum.'

The decurion cocked an eyebrow. 'After the Second was lost?'

Verendus made the sign against evil. 'I inspected the site.'

'There was a phixus inside the clasp,' said Landren.

'Can't see it.' Quintus squinted at Mos' drawing.

'You wouldn't,' said Verendus. 'The clasp opened like a shell.'

'Oh, I see. At least, I think I do. What about the codex? Isn't that important?'

'It is,' said Corinna. 'Sacred Ambrone scrolls were bound together to form the codex. It passes from one High Priestess to the next. At some point in its history the serpent clasp was attached.'

'The Ambrone tribe?' said Eldoran. 'Did its leader commission the clasp?'

'No, I suspect one of the Ambrones found the clasp when the tribe trekked through the mountains,' Landren said. 'The work is Ennean. Very old.'

Verendus sat up straight; this was his story. 'My mother's people were Ambrone. When the sea threatened their homeland, they journeyed south through Europa in search of new land.'

'And took what they wanted,' said Eldoran.

'This is not the time to discuss such grievances,' said Landren.

His glare at Eldoran unmet, Verendus continued. 'Even mighty Rema, a republic in those days, quaked before our warrior tribe. But then the tide of battle turned. According to Reman sources, in a matter of hours, the Ambrone teetered on the brink of annihilation. The warriors dead, our women slew their children and then themselves, for they would not be taken as slaves.' He paused respectfully, and said, 'A small contingent remained, separated from the main fray by the caprice of combat. Pressed back, forced ever further away, they won their fight only to discover the battle lost. The last of the Ambrones fled to the Alps where Reman writers state they disappeared. How the tribe reached Iolia is not recorded.'

If the tribe had crossed through the pass and into Italia, the subsequent voyage to Iolia would have been long and fraught with danger. Verendus had formed his own theory that the Ambrones hadn't gone into the mountains, but sheltered in a cave in the foothills. When the legions abandoned the search, the Ambrones continued to the nearest coast, built a boat, and sailed the far shorter distance to Iolia.

He kept his theory private and gave them the Ambrone legend complete with gruelling trek through a desolate mountain pass. 'On realising they had crossed into Italia, the tribe headed south to the sea. That night, their leader Ericus dreamed they should build a boat and sail south west. For days, the Ambrones drifted at sea, lost and afraid they would be captured by Rema's navy or attacked by the pirates who were the scourge of the Mediterraneus. What little food they had was gone. Then the water ran out. Desperate, Ericus prayed for a sign. When he looked to the heavens, a pelican was flying low above the boat. One of his crew fetched a bow – the Ambrones were starving and close to exhaustion. But as the man aimed, Ericus ordered him to set down his arrow. The man cursed as the pelican flew by. Ignoring the protest, Ericus told the crew to change course and follow, for land was surely near. On flew the bird, guiding the boat past the jagged rocks that surround the island and through the Iolian Gap to the shores of Iolia and salvation.

'In gratitude, Ericus decreed the pelican a sacred bird. Once the Ambrones were settled on the island, he built a temple to the flame of hope and gave his oldest daughter as a handmaid. This history has passed through generations of my family. My mother's forebear was that man.'

A fleeting look of incredulity crossed Landren's face, then he nodded politely. 'Your ancestor was a remarkable guide to lead the Ambrones safely through the mountains.'

'Indeed. Though I haven't heard mention of Kosora, only that there was a pass.'

'So the Ambrones found the pass and crossed the Alps,' said Quintus. 'Did they make the clasp?'

'As I stated already, they found it in the mountains. The work is Ennean,' Landren replied. 'Within the clasp was a miniature map crafted from strands of gold. It depicted a mountain range: the phixus on a silver thread in its midst. Exquisite.'

'Phixus?' said Quintus. 'Remind me.'

In the exasperated tone of a tutor saddled with a hopeless student, Landren said, 'The double ouroboros in iconic form.'

'The snake thingummy?' Quintus pursed his lips.

Bretorus jerked to attention. 'Commendator, the sign of the serpents…'

The decurion was right. He'd mentioned that when trekking in the foothills he sometimes saw a phixus painted on the wall of an Alpine cave. The locals called it the sign of the serpents. Verendus met the wide-eyed look of dawning comprehension with a cautionary frown and Bretorus fell silent.

'I believe the symbol inside the clasp marked Kosora,' Landren continued. 'The silver thread is the pass leading through the mountains.'

Verendus' mind raced. Earlier, when he'd stared at the golden web inside the clasp and followed the silver thread running through it, he had supposed he was seeing what he'd hoped to see. There was a moment when he was sure he must be right, this was the legendary Ambrone map of his ancestor's route through the Alps. Years ago, when he'd believed such a map existed, he'd imagined it to be a crumbling old scroll, not something as beautiful as the gold tracery within the clasp.

Conversation returned to speculation over how the legionaries had approached the lodge without challenge. Verendus picked up the key and scrutinised the silver script engraved upon the shaft. 'What does it mean?'

A look passed between Landren and Oriedas. 'Those are sacred words of protection,' said Landren. 'I shall not speak them here.'

It was the evasive response Verendus had anticipated. Prey to a sensation of weightlessness, he held the key to the candlelight. Amid his troubled thoughts, an idea stirred but wouldn't materialise. He stared at the snakes, half expecting them to come to life and slither down his arm. Setting down the key, he said, 'The legionary paid the ultimate price to ensure we don't learn the location of the pass. He plunged into the river so the clasp and its secret might be lost.'

'Aye, dead men can't talk,' said Bretorus.

Like a stray seed on a summer breeze, apprehension drifted into Verendus' mind. He reassured himself that the loss of the clasp meant an end to the problem, but the seed had taken root. Why worry? No one was likely to find the Ambrone Pass. It must be in an inhospitable and uninhabited region.

The thought crystallised. 'Jupiter! They've disturbed the Helutti slaves. Don't you see? Galenius' scouts have already found the pass and want to keep it secret. That's why the clasp was destroyed.' Judging by that look of assurance, Landren had believed this all along and was guiding him slowly and surely to this conclusion.

'We mustn't panic,' said Bretorus. 'As the entrance to the pass lies in imperial territory there's no immediate threat.'

'And what of the ships waiting in Iolia's harbour?' said Landren.

The decurion's jaw dropped and his mouth gaped like a tragic theatre mask. 'They can sail troops from Iolia to Gallia and assail the Alps in a surprise attack. That pass could take an enemy into Rema through the back door.'

'Indeed,' said Landren. 'And Rema dreaming of distant spoils is sacked sleeping.'

Quin and Bretorus arguing the matter with Landren, Oriedas leaned across the table and raised his voice against the cacophony. 'Verendus, how vigilant is Rema regarding the mountains?'

'Extremely. There are several passes, all garrisoned and patrolled regularly. However, the possibility of the Ambrone –

or if you prefer – Kosoran Pass actually existing, has diminished over the years. It's the stuff of legend.'

Oriedas deliberated, his angular features puckering in concentration until he resembled a petulant hawk. 'Legends grow from truth.'

Landren rose and rapped the table. 'The evidence suggests that scouts have ventured into a long-forsaken mountain region. Reports of malevolent incidences across countryside bordering the Alps confirm that Helutti slaves have left their mountain lair and are causing chaos in Gallia Narbonensis.'

'Wait,' said Verendus. The Lignoran was ploughing on when there was still a significant detail to consider. 'We mustn't get ahead of ourselves.' Landren drew in his breath, but Verendus continued. 'At this time of year there will be snow in the mountains. It's unlikely the pass has been fully explored. It may not lead right through the Alps. We only have the legend to go by, and the legend may not be accurate.'

'Good point,' said Bretorus. 'It might be a dead end.'

With the confident poise of an emperor at the races, Landren retook his seat. 'We cannot take that risk. It is possible that Sentorus has positioned troops there in preparation for better conditions. We must seize this opportunity to make our move. We know that scouts have explored the foothills as, in doing so, they disturbed the Helutti slaves.'

'Sentorus is in Germania,' Bretorus said stubbornly. 'Why does this imperial business matter so much to you?'

Landren pinned him with a cold stare. 'Decurion, I am determined to maintain the status quo. Two hundred years ago, my people paid dearly for victory at Atrox – in blood and in land. The Empire is sorely stretched. Spies are everywhere. If the Pax Remana collapses, the consequences will be widespread and terrible. The land of Lignora may be small, but we have a treaty with Rema.'

'It is a poor bargain, much weighted in Rema's favour,' said Eldoran.

'Rema's friendship, albeit on her terms, is preferable to war.'

Eldoran looked unconvinced. 'Capula's treaty with Rema failed to protect it from Sentorus' legion. And now the soldiers who stole the clasp have breached the Atrox Treaty by crossing the border into Lignora.'

Landren frowned at the Nemusan. 'Rest assured, when I next visit Rema to demand an end to the sanctions imposed upon my people, the matter will be raised and addressed. In the meantime, we must make a stand against Sentorus and Galenius Dax. Spring will soon warm to summer. It is claimed that a fleet has sailed into Iolia's harbour and vanished, hidden by the Iolian Watch, waiting until the snows melt and their allies can march through the pass. Rema's legions in the east are stretched, so who will defend the Alps?'

No one had an answer. In his mind's eye, Verendus pictured the legionary bases that stretched across Europa and tried to gauge how long it would take troops to reach the mountains and counter the threat.

'Meanwhile,' said Landren, interrupting the calculations, 'the Helutti in Barbarian Germania are building boats and gathering an army to cross the Rhenus River and attack the Empire. I sincerely hope all legions stationed on that border did not march off with Legate Sentorus. As I said, the Empire is sorely stretched. The Helutti wolves will not hesitate to take advantage of such vulnerability and cross the river. Allied tribes relying on the Third to safeguard the Germanian border will be slaughtered.'

'They might join with the Helutti,' said Eldoran.

Verendus wasn't about to acknowledge such a dire possibility. 'Sentorus won't compromise the border.'

'I hope you are right,' said Landren. He turned to Eldoran. 'And now, another ripple stirs the water. Your tidings from Rema, please…'

The Nemusan nodded. 'There is an unconfirmed report that legions in Germania Inferior have transferred their allegiance to Legate Sentorus.'

'Have you any idea how much it costs to fund a legion?' Verendus demanded.

'Capula was a wealthy city,' said Landren. 'Sentorus would have profited handsomely from its sacking.'

In the ensuing uproar, Verendus rose and marched around the table to Eldoran. 'Which legions have gone over to Sentorus?'

The Nemusan regarded him with cool civility and said the legions were purported to be the Third Gemina, the Sixth Victrix, and possibly the First Minervia at the strategically key site of Bonna in the south of Germania Inferior.

No doubt more would follow. The more troops that went over to Sentorus, the easier it would be to persuade others to join them. Verendus stalked back to his chair. This didn't explain how Sentorus could be in two places at once – disciplining the Third Legion in Germania *and* sacking Capula on the Raetian border. The two were hundreds of miles apart. He drained his glass. The Third Gemina, his former legion. Men he'd served with had broken their oath to Emperor Flavio and gone over to Sentorus. He blushed with the shame of it.

In a bid for calm, he contemplated a wall of shelves dense with tablets and scrolls. So like Father's tablinum. That fateful evening, Father had confided his fears that ships were hidden in Iolia's harbour ready to attack southern Gallia and Rema's harbour at Ostia. Iolia's position in the western Mediterraneus made it an ideal base to launch an attack, while its sheer cliffs and ring of jagged rocks offered a safe haven for retreat.

Voices rose in indignation. Only Corinna remained quiet, her gaze flitting from man to man. As Bretorus stood, red-faced and unsteady on his feet, Landren restored order.

'There is more news from Rema,' said Eldoran. 'Concern grows over the delay of a large shipment of grain from the north of Africa.'

'Rema has gorged on these imports,' said Landren. 'Any suggestion of shortage will panic her considerable populace.'

Bretorus resumed his seat. 'No cause for alarm. Shipments are often delayed.'

'A reliable source informed me that a fort on the frontier south of Carthago has fallen,' said Eldoran.

This was news to Verendus. 'You think this has bearing on the delayed shipment?'

'Probably,' said Landren. 'The balance of power is fragile there. Upset it and you press Rema in the stomach – where it hurts.'

'Rema is hardly dependent on Carthago,' said Quintus. 'We rule the entire coast of northern Africa, you know.'

Bretorus flicked a stray supper crumb onto the floor. 'They'll not starve Rema into submission. This is scaremongering.'

Landren's eyes narrowed. 'This is but the beginning.' His words hung like a knife in the air.

The decurion coughed noisily and turned to Quintus. 'Tribune, may I suggest seeking guidance in Rema?'

'Good idea. I shall go. This should be brought before the Senate.'

'Is there someone we can trust?' said Corinna.

Bretorus sniffed. 'This is business, lady.'

Her cheeks flushed and she turned on him. 'I am here at Lord Landren's request.'

'Indeed,' the Lignoran said decisively. 'Shall we continue?'

'Yes.' Unable to resist forcing the point home, Verendus added, 'She has as much say here as anyone.'

The decurion exchanged an amused glance with Quintus, and said, 'I still say we need guidance. Someone must speak out. I could accompany Tribune Quintus to Rema. We will warn the emperor.'

For someone who had never set foot in Rema, Bretorus had a lot to say about the imperial capital. 'You wouldn't get past his advisors,' Verendus said. 'Most are Galenius' spies.'

'What about the Senate?'

'Approaching the Senate is too great a risk,' Landren said with authority. 'Few men are beyond intimidation or above corruption. Prefect Galenius has undermined the Praetorian Guard in Iolia. I am in no doubt that he has done the same in Rema where his former ally Prefect Secundus is imprisoned, awaiting execution.'

Verendus clasped his hands together and held firm until the trembling ceased. Finally, now his concerns were being taken seriously, he was overcome with nerves. *Speak up*, Father would have urged. Don't lose the momentum. He cleared his throat. 'Galenius must be stopped. With the Guard under his sole command, who will curb him? Not our boy-emperor. I've heard Prefect Galenius is much in Flavio's favour – in and out of the imperial bed.'

Quintus grinned. 'Even so, the Guard doesn't control the Senate.'

'But it holds sway over some of the senators.' Verendus cringed to recall how swiftly Senator Decimius' apathy regarding the crisis in Iolia had changed to support. Surely a ruse. Perhaps Galenius had already bought the senator's co-operation. It would explain how Decimius had afforded that huge villa for his feckless son. He turned to Eldoran. 'Was there news of Iolia?'

'There was. My contact in the city had word that Prefect Galenius Dax would address the Senate.'

So, Galenius was in Rema. The spider was back at the centre of the web.

Eldoran was still speaking. '...when I reached the Senate House, the crowd gathered outside was considerable. I pushed through until close enough to hear the orator on the steps outside relay the prefect's words. Galenius gave testimony that Portula Harbour has reopened and, save for minor shortages, there is no crisis. Then the senators voted to send provisions to Iolia.'

'No troops to disband the Iolian Watch?' said Verendus.

'No troops.'

The Iolian Watch would continue its oppression of Iolia's Parhels. Verendus hid his disappointment.

'The mood in Rema is one of uncertainty; people turn their gaze away from Iolia,' said Eldoran. 'The purge of associates of the former prefect, Secundus, continues. Rumours of Legate Sentorus' alleged coup in Germania and the atrocity in Capula have further unsettled the populace. Galenius assured the Senate there has been no coup. Sentorus is in Germania to discipline the Third Gemina, not to take it over. And, because he is in Germania, he cannot be responsible for atrocities in Capula.'

Landren set down his glass. 'We must act now. What say you, Commendator?'

Again the sharp green gaze fixed him like a cat watching fish in a pond. Verendus didn't care for it. 'I'm sure you have it all worked out, Lord Landren. What do you propose we few do?'

'We may be few, but there is stealth in exiguity.'

Verendus considered. 'Fleas on a bear's back?'

'Deadlier and far more cunning,' said Landren. 'Valour outweighs sheer multitude. Our army is small and I will only call on it *in extremis*, but there are other ways to win a fight. It is my intent to sail to Iolia. I should value your assistance.'

The realisation of where he fitted into Landren's plans materialising in the fog of his brain, Verendus reminded himself to be guarded.

'My voyage must be discreet,' said Landren. 'And I believe you know a way through the Iolian Rings.'

'Presumably you have more than sightseeing on your agenda,' said Verendus. 'Arson perhaps?'

Landren gleamed his crocodile smile. 'We can break a vital link in their chain of attack.'

'Destroy their ships?' said Bretorus without enthusiasm. 'That might hinder them, it won't stop 'em. How many ships are we dealing with? Anyone know?'

'Four were seen,' said Verendus.

'No doubt, there are more,' Landren said. 'We shall do as we are able. With its unique ring of rocks, Iolia is well defended. Those ships may be the first of many, a two-pronged attack waiting for orders: a fleet to transport troops to Gallia Narbonensis and a navy to assail Rema's harbour at Ostia. Our task will not be easy. It is probable that Galenius' allies have not only taken over Iolia's harbour, but also a fort on the nearby peninsula of Chiros. If so, they will have access to specialist military equipment.' He gazed around the table. 'Control Iolia, control the western Mediterraneus.'

Verendus recounted what he had seen of the camp on Waterside Plain. 'Big enough for an entire legion and visible only from a restricted coastal standpoint or from out at sea. It appears Galenius has recruited his own troops and brought them to Iolia under false pretences by passing them off as a vexillation of Twenty-Third Victrix.'

Landren sighed. 'The situation is grave indeed.'

Bretorus rolled his eyes. 'Grave? It's bloody impossible! We don't have the manpower to take the island. And what of the pass? We must send warning. If Sentorus has legions at his disposal, those mountain garrisons won't hold out for long.'

'Or they'll go over to Sentorus,' said Verendus, struck by the sheer nerve and ingenuity of the conspiracy. Sentorus was rallying the troops; Galenius was calming the Senate and people of Rema. He wasn't sure who was the more powerful. Perhaps, like the belligerent snakes of the double ouroboros, that had yet to be settled.

'The pass must be sealed,' said Landren.

'The nearest legion is the Twenty-Third in Raetia. I trained there…' Verendus paused, calculating how long a missive would take.

'Could take a month for word to get to Raetia,' said Bretorus, beating him to it.

'That's what I estimated.' Verendus was still working it out, but the decurion's answer sounded credible. 'This time of year, the going will be hard. If only it weren't so far. But of course,' he said, clapping the decurion on the arm. 'They're already there. The vexillation! One thousand men under Legate Capito's command. He's inspecting the passes.'

That night at Alba when Stanzia told him Capito's wife would not be accompanying the legate's latest posting to the Alps, Verendus had dismissed the information as trifling. Later he'd realised it was anything but. With so many troops stranded on Iolia, how could a vexillation of a thousand more be marching to the Alps? It didn't tally.

Verendus already had plans to search for Capito and ask him if the troops in Iolia were genuine. It was more important than ever that he find the legate.

'The mountains are vast,' said Bretorus, intruding on his thoughts. 'He could be anywhere.'

'On the contrary,' replied Verendus, 'I know where Capito is…' His idea plummeted like a broken arrow. 'Neptune's balls, what good will it do? The bloody clasp is lost. I can find him, but I can't tell him where the pass is.'

To his astonishment, Landren laughed. 'Have you forgotten what was inside the clasp?'

Verendus scraped back his chair, flung his satchel on the table, and pulled out pen, ink, and parchment. Ignoring the clamour of curiosity, he closed his eyes. Concentrate. Try to remember. A few moments later, he opened his eyes and picked up the pen. He began to draw, the nib catching on the parchment in his haste to depict what he'd seen within the clasp. With delicate strokes he drew lines of gold tracery as intricate as a cobweb, the thread that marked the position of the pass running through, the tiny phixus at the centre. In a few minutes it was done. He passed the sheet across the table.

No one spoke as Landren studied the drawing. He nodded. 'You have an extraordinary gift. That range beside the pass,' he indicated it with his fingertip, 'by the shape, I would say that is the range we call the Dragon's Back. See how the mountains curve, decrease in magnitude, and curve again to resemble the spine and tail of a sleeping dragon. That peak there, near the extremity, is Adris.' He gave the sheet to Oriedas. 'Do you agree?'

'Indeed, lord. It is most distinctive, like a pyramid sliced across its apex. This accords with the pass being in the western range and accessible only during the warmer months. The Dragon's Back is one of the higher ranges.'

The parchment was handed around, each person adding their opinion.

'I won't put faith in an old trinket,' Bretorus grumbled into his beard.

'I ask only for your support,' said Landren. 'If the map in the clasp is accurate, then the pass lies south of Mount Adris. Last month Legate Capito and his vexillation travelled east on the Via Domitia; thus, the first pass to be subject to his inspection should be the Hercules Pass, created ages past when the champion smashed a path through the mountains.' He turned to Verendus. 'Earlier, I received a missive from a trusted scout...'

'Trusted spy,' muttered Bretorus.

Landren ignored him. 'The missive reports that, contrary to expectation, Capito and his vexillation left the highway and diverted south east. They set camp in the mountain foothills and have gone no further.'

'Snow can lie thick in that stretch till summer,' Bretorus said. 'They're waiting for better conditions.'

'Or further instructions.' Verendus had been certain Capito would camp near Brigantium. 'Why the diversion?'

Landren glanced at the drawing. 'It places them nearer the Ambrone Pass.'

Verendus sucked in his irritation. The Lignoran had been toying with him, waiting for him to work things out, testing his aptitude for the task ahead. He doubted Capito knew of the pass. No, the diversion would have been ordered by the emperor – at Galenius' instigation. 'I must warn Capito,' he said, and wondered if Landren had anticipated that response.

Quintus regarded him blankly.

'It could be a trap,' said Verendus. 'Capito's under orders to inspect the mountain passes. It appears there has been a change to those orders. I doubt this change mentions the Ambrone Pass. I'd guess that Capito's been directed to a location in the southern foothills and told to await further instructions.' He could see how it might work. He brought a tablet from his satchel and made a note. 'For maximum effectiveness, Sentorus and Galenius will position forces on either side of the mountains. When the weather conditions are right, Capito will be informed of the existence of the Ambrone Pass and told to inspect it. If any Helutti remain in that stretch of the mountain they'll clash with the vexillation, saving Sentorus the bother of flushing the tribesmen out. His troops can then follow and ensure there's no escape for Capito and his vexillation when they reach the far side of the pass to find Sentorus' allies waiting. The vexillation will be trapped like an olive in a press.'

'A most devious plan,' said Landren.

'You must warn him,' said Bretorus.

Eldoran folded his hands together. 'If Verendus writes the missive for Legate Capito, I will deliver it. Verendus' map will help me locate him. I can leave tonight.'

There was no discussion. Verendus didn't object; the offer was generous and in his current state he could not match

Eldoran's pace. Landren thanked the Nemusan and turned. 'Verendus, I propose we act together, in partnership. Will you seize this chance for honour?'

Again, the Lignoran had the upper hand. Again, Verendus felt a creeping foreboding. The small voice of caution woke, whispering that his vow was to the emperor not the Lignoran. He must not lower his guard. 'Honour? Not honour. I wish only to do my duty and clear my name.'

'Noble sentiments,' Landren replied. 'Are we in agreement?'

The serpent key lay before him. Verendus pushed it with his fingertip, setting it spinning. He remembered one of Father's favourite maxims. *Adversity binds strange allies.* Strange indeed. The key slowed, came to rest, and he saw a glimmer of hope. 'I'll need time to consider.'

'Time and tide do not stand still,' said Landren. 'Give me your answer on the morrow. I cannot wait longer.'

Verendus nodded. 'What do you really want from Kosora?'

'Why assume I want anything?'

Again the evasive answer. Verendus didn't hide his frustration. 'So, not an equal partnership.'

Landren stood and picked up his folder. 'No partnership ever is.'

CHAPTER XXXVI

E ven as Corinna reached out, she knew Verendus wasn't beside her. She pushed back the blanket and sat up, rubbing her forehead. Too much wine and not enough sleep – an hour, maybe two. The candle had guttered, embers were fading in the grate, and yet he hadn't come to bed. She should settle down, try to rest, but there were things to discuss – things she needed to know.

Another coal died. She retrieved her night tunic from the floor, pulling it on over her head as she crossed to the window to open the shutters. The moon had arced southward, its pale sheen painting the flowers of the amarantia tree with a luminous glow. She tried to calculate how long it had been since the night at the inn when Saffi was beside her, but she had lost all sense of time. Her eyes welled – she'd let Saffi down. Nothing could change that. Nothing could make it better.

Somewhere outside, a dog barked. Distant voices softened and waned. After the meeting in the library, Verendus had stayed at the table, writing the missive for Legate Capito. He may have fallen asleep there. Corinna found a fresh candle and lit it at the grate.

She took the little mirror from her bag and peered at her reflection, blurry in the candlelight. Her hair hung loose. She wound it into a coil and pinned it atop her head. Such vanity. It would have to do. She draped a cloak around her shoulders, picked up the candle sconce, and crept out to the landing, her hand unsteady as she cupped the flame.

All was quiet. For several moments she waited, alert for movement or footfall. Satisfied no one was about, she tiptoed on. The corridor that linked the tower to the main staircase and the rest of the lodge stretched before her, dark save for a lamp on a table and a solitary torch, its low flame painting the ceiling with quivering shadow. How many paces to the staircase? How many doors must she pass? Rooms she'd never seen inside. Perhaps, this evening, each had an occupant.

Footsteps squeaked on the boards. She drew back and her elbow knocked the wall. The candle swayed, almost dropped. She steadied it and stood still. At the end of the corridor, an unseen hand extinguished the lamp and the steps receded.

How different the lodge appeared at night. She raised the candle, but it scarcely touched the shadows. She should be used to the dark. Even in daylight the Belvedere was shrouded in shadow, all those bleak passageways and dark niches where a sentry might lurk.

She hurried on, past the first door, past the second. Keep walking. Don't look back. Another door and then another. Five, six, seven. She turned the corner and there, a few paces away, were the twisted bannisters of the galleried landing that led to the stairs. Pallid light emanated from the hall below.

Metal clinked on metal – someone was in the hall. She told herself it was one of the servants, told herself to keep going, take the next step. Just a little further, just to the bannister rail.

The clinking stopped.

She reached the rail, glanced over, and her heart leapt. Down in the hall, a lone figure crouched, securing the straps of a pack.

Eldoran. He hadn't left yet.

No longer afraid, Corinna trod softly downstairs. She got as far as the window and he looked up, his face questioning. Sensing his gaze, she descended carefully and crossed the polished floor, past the closed door of the library, to stand beside him. If the sight of her stirred emotion in him, he hid it well and greeted her coolly.

She returned his greeting with what she hoped was comparable poise, and said, 'I am in time to wish you safe journey.'

'You did so earlier this evening.' No hint in his voice suggested it pleased him to see her. 'Though I thank you. I am glad to hear it again.'

Corinna fought to be calm, to think of a witty or perceptive reply. But all she could think was there was symmetry in their farewell, for hadn't they met in a dark hall at Castellum Alba. Remembering how he had amazed her by using a flame to draw a map in the air, she said, 'You have yet to show me how to make a candle drawing.'

'I have not forgotten.' He smiled and the room seemed brighter. 'There is much else I would show you. Perhaps one day?'

'Perhaps…' Tightness in her throat choked the words and the fear she would not see him again struck her chest like a blow.

He bent to fasten the final buckle. His downcast eyes offered no defence to her gaze, his face in the lantern light as smooth and cool and perfect as alabaster. Corinna felt compelled to touch him, to feel beneath her fingers that the sculpted features weren't hard and cold. She reached out.

Behind her, a door clicked open. She snatched back her hand and turned. Light cut like a blade across the floor and a tall figure appeared in the doorway, a scroll case in his hand.

Verendus had the look of a child woken by a nightmare: blank-eyed, the muscles in his face taut, mask-like in the dim light. 'I fell asleep writing that damned message.'

'I came to find you,' Corinna said.

'Well, here I am.' He gave the scroll case to Eldoran. 'For the eyes of Legate Capito alone.'

'Understood.' Eldoran placed the case with his kit, and together they carried the bags out through the side door to the terrace where a horse stood saddled and waiting.

Corinna followed. She set the candle on the garden table and stepped out of the way, resting a hand on the stone balustrade while they loaded the kit, the gelding standing patiently.

Verendus unhooked the flask from his belt and offered it. 'May Fortuna Redux smile on you.'

Eldoran took a draught and returned the flask with a nod. Then he stepped back and placed his hand on the balustrade, so close to her own that she glanced at Verendus to see if he'd noticed. No, he was taking a nip from the flask, eyes half-closed. His lips were touching where Eldoran's had touched. She'd heard some men did that with their women, sharing as readily as they might share a wineskin. The notion had always appalled her. Now she wondered how it would feel to kiss Eldoran, to close her eyes and wrap herself around him. She blushed at the thought.

His hand moved closer, so close she had only to shiver and their fingers would meet. Her pulse quickened. Eldoran's fingertips – smooth, icy – brushed hers. Her heart flipped over and all other matter faded until they, alone, inhabited the evening.

Then he turned and gave a brisk nod. Taking the reins, he sprang into the saddle and rode away, bleary in the darkness as horse and rider melted into the night.

A fox yowled. Verendus glanced towards the wood and slipping a hand about her waist, said, 'Go to bed, I'll join you in a few minutes.'

Corinna had no voice. She could still feel Eldoran's touch, so cold it stole her breath. The moon had climbed out of reach, high above the treetops, and she felt herself shrink beneath the boundless night.

***

Preparations for departure were underway the next morning when Corinna left Verendus sleeping. The flames of torches set along the corridor shuddered – someone must have left the front door open. Two servant girls were pulling towels and bedding from the linen cupboard, packing them into a large leather bag. She nodded to the pair. Strixi had taught her some Ennean, but Corinna shied away from testing out her newfound words. Instead, she made a little theatre of drawing her shawl tight about her shoulders to show it was chilly. The girls smiled back, nodding cheerfully.

Daylight pierced the small round windows above the galleried landing, burnishing the panelled walls and gilded cornice. Last night was another world, a world in which she had acted impulsively. She would think no more of it. Last night was gone, and Eldoran would be miles away.

She gripped the bannister rail. The young Seer at the Temple had foretold this, had said Fate's wings would bind. Corinna doubted she would see Eldoran again, but there would always be a bond between them, a seed buried deep in the cold earth.

A draught rose from the stairwell, swept around her ankles, and enfolded her in an icy embrace. She must not think of him. No reminiscences, no regrets. The Fates would decide.

She descended to the window at the turn of the stairs. Down in the hall, early sun warmed the woodblock floor. Kit and stacks of arrows were piled beside the wall, the shafts tied in sheaves like stalks of wheat. Dacoren and one of Landren's archers were carrying a trunk towards the front door. A gust of wind whooshed in, slamming the big door before they reached it. Dacoren groaned and they set down the trunk.

Outside the dining room, a hound waited, fleshy mouth drooling at the smell of fried bacon. Voices and laughter drifted from the room. The terrace door opened and Strixi dashed inside, cheeks flushed, hair dishevelled, a basket on her arm and the tortoiseshell cat at her heels. Corinna ran downstairs and followed them along a passageway and into the larder.

From floor to ceiling the cold-room was lined with shelves, each filled with waxy discs of cheese, sacks of vegetables, an assortment of bottles and jars. Barrels were stacked in an alcove; bunches of herbs and several chickens – dead but not yet plucked – hung from a rail; an enormous ham rested on a platter ready for carving.

Hunched at a table at the centre of the little room, the slave Dorcas sat chopping onions by the light of an oil lamp. She stilled her knife and looked up expectantly, wiping away tears with the back of her hand.

'Shoo!' hissed Strixi.

Dorcas stared stupidly like a rabbit transfixed by a stoat, then dropped the knife and ran out. After a furtive glance along the passage, Strixi closed the door and set down her basket. She picked up the knife. Using the broad blade as a mirror, she scrutinised her reflection. 'The East Wind will bring trouble.'

'Perhaps,' said Corinna. Its presence was unsettling. 'Whatever's the matter?'

Strixi rolled her eyes. 'Tribune Quintus! He follows me like a lost dog.' The cat meowed and jumped onto the table. Strixi perched beside it, turning the knife in her hand and swinging her suede-shod feet. 'Quin is pretty, no? I thought he would amuse me. But he talks so much – before, during, after. Thus, I know you are leaving on the morrow. I shall miss you.'

'And I you.' How easily her friend had taken the tribune for a lover, choosing him as one might pluck a flower, then discarding it in the morning. With a tinge of envy, Corinna doubted she'd ever achieve such nonchalance.

'Thank goodness for silphium,' said Strixi.

Days ago, when Corinna had asked her for cedar oil, Strixi had guessed why she wanted it and offered silphium instead. Clever Strixi had cultivated this rare type of fennel in the herb garden, and ate both plant and seeds regularly as a form of contraception. The thought woke a memory. 'Oh, I had the strangest dream. Don't smirk. It wasn't *that* sort of dream. I was in a garden, the bushes lush with overblown yellow roses. I plucked the loveliest bloom, held it to my face, but there was no scent...'

'And?' Strixi murmured.

'Something moved. Tiny black insects crawling inside. And the petals were all brown and curled at the edges. What can it mean?'

Strixi nodded sagely. 'A warning: be careful what you choose. The fairest blooms fade fastest.'

This wasn't the answer she wanted. Corinna tried to explain. 'You make it sound simple…' How could she explain what she didn't understand? That small cold seed had taken root. 'But one does not choose love. Cupid's barb is as startling as a lightning strike.'

'And likewise best avoided.'

Corinna sighed. Maybe she was right.

'Be glad,' said Strixi with an indulgent smile. 'We have today. Dorcas can pack for you. We shall ride out this afternoon – bluebells still flower in the north wood.' She set down the knife and took Corinna's hand. 'Do not despair, my friend. I have thought of a way to find your father.'

CHAPTER XXXVII

Verendus opened the door and Corinna flinched. As he went into the bedroom, she stopped mixing powder into a glass and didn't meet his eyes.

He sniffed. Aniseed. 'I thought you were off that stuff.'

She resumed stirring, clanking the long spoon against the glass. 'Why don't you knock instead of barging in?'

'Hardly barging,' he said, and it was his room, after all. He bent to kiss her neck, but she shrank away. This wasn't a good start.

Last night, when he wrote the missive for Legate Capito, he'd abandoned caution – he was so deep in the mire that if he didn't speak out now, it might be too late. Capito was a strict disciplinarian and a pedantic old sod, but he was principled. Having decided to trust him, Verendus included an account of Iolian Watch atrocities: the fire at the Officers' Club and his conviction it was arson, the slaughter of Parhels in the square outside. He explained his belief that Galenius Dax and his uncle Legate Sentorus were plotting against the emperor, and concluded with a few lines regarding the troops camped on Waterside Plain. If they weren't soldiers of the Twenty-Third Legion, they should not be in Iolia. Capito could send warning to the Senate.

Things were falling into place. With Eldoran acting as messenger, Verendus had agreed to Landren's proposal to navigate a team of saboteurs through the Iolian Rings, thus avoiding the harbour checkpoint. Moreover, it would be expedient to return to Iolia. Although Corinna might not welcome the news.

He unfastened his satchel. This first – while she was still speaking to him. He drew out a cloth-wrapped box. 'I've brought you this.'

'The codex?' She put down the spoon. 'Landren asked me to take charge of that. Can't let it go, can you?'

He checked his reluctance and held out the box. 'Here. Open it.'

'Magistra alone is permitted.' She frowned. 'I didn't tie the cord like this. You've looked already, but can't understand it so you bring it to me.'

As usual, she was right. Earlier he had tried again to decode the strange words, but made no progress. 'Corinna, just open the thing.'

Needing no further encouragement, she set the box on the table and untied the cord. Carefully she slipped the codex from the silk pouch. Without the serpent clasp the book seemed naked, and a dark circle discoloured the leather binding.

'Don't you think it odd that Landren opened the clasp so easily?' Verendus asked.

She pondered this. 'Not really. After all, an Ennean made it. Strixi told me their locks and keys are superior to imperial ones. The clasp is a type of lock – a type Landren is familiar with. I expect Magistra knew it was Ennean. That, coupled with Landren's knowledge of old books, made him an ideal custodian for the codex.'

More likely, a choice of the heart. Landren may have been Magistra's lover. Verendus nodded and kept the thought to himself. The possibility that Landren could be Corinna's father was disconcerting. If true, it would make him her rightful guardian. It seemed unlikely the Lignoran would welcome Verendus' interest in his daughter's future wellbeing.

Corinna opened the codex at the page denoted by a strip of ribbon. 'Magistra recites these verses before divination.'

'The Temple is a secretive place, part of its power, I suppose. Will you read to me?'

She scanned the page and turned to the next. 'Another incantation. I should find where I reached in my translation and start there.' She turned back.

'Wait. Start at the beginning. The first page is so faded, I didn't attempt a copy. Try to decipher it… please.'

'Very well.' She turned to the first page where the letter phi in its gilded square resembled a phixus.

Verendus stared at ink grey with age. The familiar letters formed unfamiliar sounds that rang harsh in his head. The words of his ancestors. Sacred words. When he'd opened the codex at Castellum Alba, he had been puzzled that he could not read its Graecian lettering. Later, Corinna had explained that the text was a phonetic form of Ambrone, which Parliel slaves had taught the handmaids to write.

She smoothed the stiff parchment leaf. 'The first word is "Phixus", then "the sign" but I can't make out more than a word or two after that.'

'The sign of the serpents?'

'You're right.' Her finger settled part way down the page. Colour drained from her cheeks, leaving her as pale as the parchment. 'This is clearer,' she said solemnly. She took a breath and read aloud. '*Nothing on earth endures. The Tower will fall and be consumed by flame. The Sea will swallow the land. The innocent will be slaughtered. And lo, the Serpents will enslave us.*'

'But this has happened!' Images filled his head: fire, blood, hundreds of mutilated bodies. How could an ancient book know these things? 'Gods, it's a prophecy. The Parhelion Tower burned down, the harbour at Portula flooded, Parhels were massacred in Regia Square. All these things happened in Iolia…' He faltered, trying to make sense of the final portent.

'The serpents may be the double ouroboros,' Corinna said.

'Maybe…' He searched his mind for a reason to counter this possibility and realised he was clenching his fist. 'The ouroboros is a symbol. A symbol can't enslave.'

'Those who carry its banner might.'

Verendus sighed. It was plausible. 'What else does it say?'

'It's too faint. I can distinguish a few words: *wolf, red moon, sea*. And the last line: *Beware the Serpents.*'

Caesar's Serpents, the Speculatores? Or did it mean the Iolian Watch? Its banner was the phixus: the sign of the serpents.

He peered over her shoulder as she skimmed the pages, pausing at his bidding to translate anything with an illustration that interested him. Recipes for potions filled most of the book. From love charms to curses, from cures to poisons, each accompanied by a simple drawing of the plant or creature that was its chief ingredient. Corinna said she knew enough of herb lore to appreciate the potency. The concoctions designed to kill, would kill. But she found nothing more about serpents.

Verendus opened the door. 'I'm finalising arrangements with Landren.'

'Then we are returning to Iolia?'

'I must do something to help. My Parhel friends may be in danger.' He didn't tell her of his intention to go to Naeos' house.

It wasn't part of the impending mission and he didn't want details getting back to Landren. 'You like Lignora, don't you?'

'You know I do.' She regarded him with suspicion, then closed the book with a thud. 'Are you saying I must remain here?'

'Not exactly. It's been arranged that Dacoren will escort you to Landren's house in Mid-Lignora. It's further west, away from the border. You'll be safer there.'

'I thought we would discuss it.'

'We just have.' Verendus didn't understand. If she was happy in Lignora, why was she upset? He was doing his best for her; if only she would see that. Those years at the Temple had imparted a self-assurance that would scandalise his ancestors. But she wasn't in the Temple now. 'Magistra entrusted you to my care. I am responsible for you, and that means keeping you safe.' As he spoke, his conviction deepened – he was doing the right thing. He marched out into the corridor.

Corinna followed. 'Brute!' she shouted, and flew at him.

He turned, raising his hand to block hers. She screeched and glared up.

'Go on,' he said, head tilted, offering his cheek, 'slap if you wish. I probably deserve it.' He stood firm, steeling himself for the blow as she drew herself up.

'I am not your property.' She lowered her hand but continued to glare. 'You should have asked me first.' Turning on her heel, she ran back into the room and slammed the door.

Someone coughed apologetically, and he looked around to see Oriedas beside a trunk in an open doorway further down the corridor.

'That went well,' said Verendus, stopping beside him. 'Here, let me help.'

Expression inscrutable, Oriedas thanked him, and said, 'Corinna is unhappy with the arrangements?'

'She'll be safer in Mid-Lignora.'

Together they hoisted the trunk and lurched to the staircase. 'Here will suffice,' Oriedas said. 'The archers have devised a system for carrying it downstairs.'

'Hades, what's inside?'

'Landren does not travel light.' The tone implied no details of the contents would be forthcoming. The keys on his belt clanking, Oriedas descended the stairs. On reaching the window, he beckoned Verendus to stand beside him. 'I have much to tell you. Dacoren, Mos, and I have been out hunting for the missing legionary.'

'Mos?' This was unexpected.

'He was riding in the wood and asked if he could accompany us. I had not the heart to refuse.' Oriedas glanced at the window. 'Alas, our man eluded us. All we found were hastily concealed campfire ashes and the prints of hooves heading east.'

'For the highway?'

'After a mile the tracks turned west, back towards the river and the lodge.' Again he glanced at the window. 'It will not be easy for him to cross. The river is fast flowing and the bridge will be guarded day and night.'

Nevertheless, the net was closing. No doubt the legionary, Praetorian, whatever he was, had sent word to his superiors. More would come. Verendus thumped the bannister rail. 'I've stayed here too long.'

'You needed rest.' Oriedas patted his arm. 'But heed me, there is more. We descended to the basin of the Egelidan Falls where we found the body of the other legionary washed up on the riverbank. No,' he said, pre-empting the question, 'we did not find the clasp. The river has claimed it. I sent archers to continue the search, though the body has been carted back here. Mos confirmed it was one of the men he saw by the river yesterday. You are welcome to inspect the body.'

Verendus followed him downstairs and across the hall to a sturdy door, which Oriedas unlocked. Beyond, a steep and narrow staircase of stone descended, a single torch burning high on the wall to light their way. There wasn't a handrail, though Oriedas didn't slow and reached the anteroom at the bottom before Verendus was halfway. With each step, the air grew cooler.

At the foot of the stairs stood two iron-banded doors – both closed. Oriedas unlocked the door on the left and ushered him through. The earthy stench of stale blood and stagnant water brought the bile to Verendus' throat. He coughed and followed Oriedas into a crypt where lamps lit in readiness revealed several stone slabs, two with shrouded bodies upon them, one much smaller than the other.

Oriedas skirted the first slab, bowing his head as he passed. 'Our faithful servant. He was very brave.'

Verendus realised he was referring to the stable boy who had died attempting to retrieve the clasp. He bowed too and stood beside the next slab.

'In life he was a soldier of Rema.' Oriedas pulled back the sheet.

'He fought like a trained man.'

The body, stripped naked save for a leather pouch around the neck, was lean but muscular, and marred with scars and bruises. A warrior's body. The left arm bore the letters **SPQR**: *Senates Populusque Remanus – Senate and People of Rema.*

This was the first time Verendus had seen the soldier without the masked helmet. Beneath the stubble of a beard, the face was pale and bloated from being too long in the water.

And yet there was something vaguely familiar about the man.

Verendus lifted the pouch, the dark leather stained and damp. He loosened the cord and slid out an identity tag.

LEGION XXIII VICTRIX
PUBLIUS PACTORAX

The engraving confirmed the number of the legion. Again, intrigue centred on the Twenty-Third Legion.

'Strange that he is here, hundreds of miles from base in Raetia.' Oriedas frowned at the metal disc. 'Do you recognise him, Commendator? You trained with the Twenty-Third.' He made it sound a simple matter of recollection, not the identification of one face out of thousands.

Verendus stared at the dead face and didn't reply. Gods, he was tired. Stifling a yawn, he put down the tag and tried to think. Nothing would settle. That training was a decade ago, but those fine-hewn features hardened by the chill of too many winters were familiar. As was the name.

He snatched up the lantern and brought it closer, casting a pool of light over the face. Someone had placed a sestertius over each eye, although there was no coin between the man's lips to pay the ferryman. Verendus moved a coin and peeled back the eyelid. In death, the cement-grey pupil had clouded. He replaced the coin, found another in his satchel, and set it between the lips.

A few items of kit and clothing lay at the foot of the slab. Verendus drew the dagger from its sheath. A standard-issue legionary dagger. He squinted along the blade. Strange, the name had been scratched out, but no new one carved. Under the scratches, all he could deduce was the letter: **S**. Equipment was expensive: ownership usually recorded on every last item. He set it down and inspected the rest. Although the mail was good quality cavalry-issue armour, the remaining kit was cheap. Each nondescript item appeared second-hand, like something cobbled together from a consignment of the old gear periodically relegated from legionary to auxiliary on issue of superior equipment. Identity tag excepted, nothing bore the name of its owner, its commander, or the legion in which the man served. Verendus shoved the dagger into its sheath.

He cupped his hands together, forming a window, blocking out peripheral distractions so he could focus on the dead face. 'Think,' he said quietly, willing himself to remember as he stared through. He had seen this face before. And recently. In a city. Somewhere in the shadows…

But, of course, he'd seen the man in Iolia, just a couple of months ago, crossing the courtyard of the castrum behind Prefect Galenius Dax. The soldier had been holding aloft a *signum*: a standard comprising three silver discs on a pole. Instead of the customary spear point or effigy of a raised hand, the pole was surmounted by a phixus: symbol of the Iolian Watch.

He drew in his breath. The man had tailed him all the way from Iolia.

'Are you certain you do not recognise him?' Oriedas asked.

'Certain.' He wasn't about to admit that this man had followed him, wouldn't give Landren the satisfaction of being right. Verendus dropped the tag into the pouch and set it down.

Oriedas opened the purse on his belt. 'This is quite a coincidence,' he said, pulling out another tag.

Coincidence? Verendus frowned, remembering Carbo's words: *I don't like coincidences…*

'Dacoren took this from the soldier he killed en route to the lodge.' Oriedas handed it over. 'It bears the same name.'

The tag was identical. Verendus re-read the name and his blood ran cold. *Pactorax*. Now he knew. This was no legionary. Pactorax was a cover name, one of a dozen or so used occasionally by Praetorian Guard Speculator agents. Hell, he should have realised immediately. The Speculatores, better known as Caesar's Serpents, had picked up his trail.

Bit by bit, he pieced it together and saw what might have happened. By pretending to divert to Narbo Martius, he had been certain he'd lost them. If they had indeed ridden south in pursuit, they may have reported to the castrum at Narbo and been told to stay put and await further instructions. Following his escape from Viorum's castrum, an urgent missive could have been sent instructing the three to ride to the Lignoran border and intercept the wagon. Much of the route from Narbo to Lignora could be travelled via the highway. No highway ran direct from Viorum to Lignora, just a series of minor roads and tracks through rocky landscape. Moreover, the speed of the Praetorians horses would surpass a wagon. Thus, they had caught up with the wagon near the Lignoran border where Dacoren disposed of one of them.

Oh, the irony. In duping the three into riding to Narbo Martius, he had eased their passage to Lignora.

Silent, he stared at the Serpent alias. Unless one was aware of it, there was nothing to connect the corpse with the Speculatores or even the Praetorian Guard. Each item of kit was of the kind a legionary cavalryman might carry.

He reminded himself that Speculatores tended to be lone wolves. Thus he had supposed that the three men who'd arrived at Alba asking questions – and surely the body on the slab was one of those three – were regular Praetorians rather than members of its specialist cohort of Speculatores.

And now they had tracked him here. This went beyond recovering the serpent clasp: this was personal. In their eyes, he had disgraced the unit. There would be glory for the Serpent who brought him in.

'Do you know the name?' asked Oriedas, startling him from his deliberations.

'No.' Verendus handed back the tag. The Serpents had been careless in their preparations. For a moment, he considered confiding in Oriedas and telling him about the Speculatores. *No.* Tell nothing, act at ease. This must not get back to Landren. 'As you say, quite a coincidence.' Verendus stroked the stubble on his chin. 'I should shave.'

'I am sure that can wait.' Oriedas smiled. 'Please accompany me. Mos told me something important was left behind at the Viorum Ministerium.'

Verendus followed him out to the anteroom. The other door stood open now, though he'd heard no one arrive. They went through into a cavernous room filled with rows of wooden shelves stacked with bottles, a small clay tab tied about each neck. Verendus inspected one but couldn't decipher the writing. 'Wine tasting?'

Oriedas shook his head and led on, through an archway. This chamber was larger and equally regimented, modest by Praetorian standards, but a notable armoury nevertheless. Rows of spears, racks of curved composite bows, arrows in quivers of leather embossed with golden symbols and, on the wall beside the arch, the finest bows Verendus had ever seen. As tall as a man, they would require much strength to pull and he wondered at their range. Closer examination showed they were made of polished yew, the arrows as long as his arm.

He stepped back from his admiration and followed Oriedas down a short, torch-lit passage to an archway. Ducking his head, he passed below into a small chamber where Landren stood waiting, a sword of shining steel in his hand.

The Lignoran turned the hilt and the blade glinted in the lamplight. 'Come in, Commendator. I have taken the liberty of selecting a sword for you.'

Verendus drew nearer and regarded the sword with a trepidation he hoped his face did not betray. His gladius had been lost during the arrest at the Ministerium, but there was a spare in his kit, he didn't need another blade. Especially not this one. But when Landren proffered the hilt, he accepted. Ingratitude would be both impolite and impolitic.

The carved contours of the grip fitted perfectly in his hand. Verendus had expected the hilt to be too small; it might have been made for him. Both sides of the double-edged blade were etched with a scrolling script he could not read. The sword was longer and narrower than the regulation gladius. Similar in length to a cavalry spatha. But it weighed light. Surely too light for vigorous combat.

Landren noticed his confusion. 'Verendus, this weapon is crafted from the finest Lignoran steel. It is called *Oragious, bringer of storms*. Since the Atrox War, it has slept, awaiting a new master. Do not permit prejudice to quash judgement.'

'…er, no. My thanks, Lord Landren. It's splendid.'

In addition to the sword, Landren furnished him with a shirt of mail, a pair of silver wristbands, and a grey-plumed helmet with silvered runes and sleek shape that rendered the legionary model as crude as an old tin bucket.

The mail hung from a hook chained to the ceiling. Accustomed to wearing mail when duties sent him across imperial borders, he was eager to compare this to his own armour. He reached up and prodded the links: an intricate mesh of double-layer, tightly woven rings. Impressive.

Even so, mail was less effective than a cuirass in withstanding a strike and had fallen from favour with the legions where articulated iron was preferred. Again, he reasoned it would be polite to accept the gift. Prudent too – most of his Praetorian Guard uniform was gone. He lifted the mail, anticipating it would have the weight that equals strength. Like the sword, it was light.

Oriedas laughed at his indecision. He took a broadsword from the shelf, motioned him to step aside, and smote the empty mail a clanging blow.

Verendus ran a finger over the metal rings. Unscathed.

Landren acknowledged his thanks with a nod and they discussed arrangements for the mission. Verendus had hoped that by leaving for Iolia he would draw further threats away from the lodge. In light of what Oriedas had said about tracks heading back towards the lodge, he feared it wasn't enough. The Speculator could send for reinforcements and return with more troops. The sooner Corinna left for Mid-Lignora the better.

***

Laden with kit, and with the Lignoran blade strapped to his belt, Verendus set off to find the place Mos called the training ground. Thus far, resumption of daily drill had been confined to the lodge, but Mos' enthusiastic account of the well-equipped training ground in the woods left him determined to try it. The walk gave him a chance to think through what he'd seen in the crypt. That scratched out name on the dagger, surely an error. The assumed name should have been carved in its stead. Perhaps haste was to blame – haste to adopt a false identity and start the pursuit.

The track forked, doubled back on itself, and dipped to a stream traversable via two broad steppingstones. Verendus adjusted the kit pole. A month's near idleness had left him surprised by the weight of it. He hoisted it onto his shoulder and crossed over. Do you good, he told himself.

He reached a clearing that fitted Mos' description of the training ground and put down his kit. With no temple in which to purify the swords, Bretorus had chosen this place for the ceremony before departure on the morrow. Later, the decurion would summon his men and anoint the turma's White Horse Standard and each blade and spear with incense. At present, the clearing was deserted. Only the distant groans and footfalls of auxiliaries jogging along a woodland path resonated through the trees. Verendus couldn't discount the possibility that an auxiliary had started the fire at the stables to assist the attackers. Over the coming days, he'd be keeping a close watch on them.

Verendus hung his cloak over a branch and stripped off his tunic. He unsheathed the Lignoran sword and swung it in a great arc, cutting the air with a satisfying swish. He was trying an over-arm cut manoeuvre when Mos and Bretorus arrived, loaded with kit. Mos set down the large wooden post he carried and wiped sweat from his brow.

'Did you send the missive?' asked Verendus. Last night, after writing the message for Legate Capito, he had encoded a missive for his friend Carbo, warning him that Galenius had called in the Speculatores, and asking that he get word of this to Marcus. Verendus had begged his father not to speak out against Galenius – the risk was too great. Before departing Iolia, he had repeated his plea in a note describing the fire at the Officers' Club and the probability that the Watch was responsible. If only Father would heed the warning.

'Went at dawn,' said Mos. 'The pigeon should be well on its way to Iolia.' He saw the Lignoran sword and his mouth opened in a wide O. 'Jupiter!' He hastened over. 'You have it! It's beautiful. What are these runes, sir?'

'Haven't a clue,' said Verendus. 'Perhaps Oriedas will enlighten me. And thanks, Mos. Your hint to Landren got me this blade.'

Bretorus snorted and propped a wicker *scutum* shield against a tree. 'Blade that length will be difficult to wield in close combat, Commendator. Even with your height.'

'It's no longer than a spatha,' said Verendus, irked by such contempt, but determined not to show it. 'There's no lack of power for the reduction in weight.'

'Looks flimsy. Lethal as a spear of asparagus.' Bretorus unharnessed the tool bag from Mos' back. 'Test it in one of my drills, Commendator.' He opened the bag. 'Look lively, Mostus. Let's get this post struck.'

He set out the tools and together they hammered the post into the ground until it stood vertical to the height of a man. Bretorus gave it a shove. 'That should hold. Ready, Commendator?'

'First, I shall tell you my plan.' Earlier, when he'd informed Bretorus of his decision to assist Landren's mission to Iolia, he had been heartened by the decurion's willingness to help. But there was more to ask, of him and of Mos. Verendus beckoned them nearer. 'Landren will charter a ship and anchor at safe distance from Iolia. From there I shall lead a select squad to the island. We'll navigate the Rings and destroy the traitors' ships in a covert attack. I'd value the assistance of you both. I hear you're a capable sailor, Decurion.'

Bretorus cracked a rare smile. 'Hailing from Britannia's south coast, I've done a fair bit. Aye, count me in.'

Beside him, Mos looked fit to burst. 'I can go home?'

'No,' said Verendus, loathing himself. 'You'll remain with the boat. You know the Rings, Mos. If I fall, it's up to you to ferry the others back to the ship.'

'Yes, sir.' The boy's bottom lip trembled.

'It's Lord Landren you need to watch,' said Bretorus. 'He was the picture of diplomacy at last night's meeting, but I'll wager there's more on his mind than the status quo. He's up to something. You'll have to be vigilant, Commendator – for all our sakes. There's a storm brewing.'

Verendus nodded, he'd heard such words recently. 'A storm indeed. If this news of Legate Sentorus is true the implications are grave.'

'Rumour,' Bretorus muttered into his beard. 'How could Sentorus cover so much ground? March through Germania, win the loyalty of the Third Legion, *and* sack Capula. He can't be in two places at once.'

Verendus had been puzzling this too and kept reaching the same conclusion. 'Therefore, he departed Britannia and sailed to Germania before the emperor and Senate ordered it. Sentorus has little respect for either. He knows as well as we do that the support of the army carries more weight.'

The decurion kicked a grey pebble out of the gravel. 'Landren has no proof about Capula. He's cast a hook into the pond and is watching the ripples spread.'

'Those ripples could grow to become a wave.'

'Time will tell.' Bretorus pulled a wooden sword from the bag and tossed it over. 'Back to basics, Commendator.'

Verendus caught the sword. The wooden training sword with its lead-filled pommel weighed thrice as heavy as Oragious in its gilded scabbard and felt clumsy in his hand.

Bretorus pointed to the wicker scutum propped against a tree. 'Don't forget that, sir.'

Verendus hefted the cumbersome shield, adjusting his hold on the cross-grip. 'So, Decurion, put me through my paces.'

'I don't pull any punches, mind,' said Bretorus. 'Still, it will do you good, sir. Word is the only thing you've exercised these past few days is your prick.'

CHAPTER XXXVIII

The raps and thwacks of wood striking wood beat a steady tempo, calling Corinna to the training ground. She heard their voices before she reached the clearing. Bretorus: loud, strident. Verendus: low, slightly breathless. They didn't heed her approach, and she settled in the shade of an oak to watch.

Instead of his usual gladius, Verendus wielded a wooden sword. Moving with an easy rhythm, he attacked a stout post in a series of slick manoeuvres. He had stripped to calf-length breeches. With his smooth skin shiny and fair hair falling across his forehead, his muscular grace had an equine quality that held her gaze.

'You'll do.' Bretorus handed him a towel. 'Rest a while and we'll try you with the Lignoran blade. Then an archery session. Mos tells me he's been practising. Just as well, too. He couldn't hit an elephant from six paces.'

Corinna stepped from the shade. 'On the contrary – he's very good.'

Verendus turned. 'How long have you been there?'

'Long enough.'

Bretorus glowered. 'Lady, this isn't a performance. Come on, Mos. Let's get some grub. Commendator, we resume in an hour. Don't wear yourself out with her.' Mouth set in a dour line, he saluted and marched off. Mos nodded to Corinna and followed.

Verendus threw down the wooden blade and rolled his shoulders, flexing his muscles as he watched the pair depart. 'Miserable sod,' he said before the decurion was out of earshot.

Corinna drew closer. 'He disapproves of me.'

'None of his business.' He towelled himself roughly.

'He makes it his business. But I didn't come out here to quarrel.'

Verendus grinned and the towel slipped from his hand. 'Good, I don't have to train all afternoon.'

Trust him to misinterpret her motives. 'I'm here to talk. And then I've arranged to ride out with Strixi.'

The grin faded. He picked up his sword-belt and strapped it on. 'Not without an escort.'

'Very well,' Corinna said, with no intention of complying. She lowered her voice. 'Ericus, please listen. I deciphered another of the portents in the codex. It says the wolf will come. Last night, at the meeting, Landren said the Helutti tribe in Barbarian Germania is gathering an army to cross the river and attack the Empire. He called the Helutti wolves.'

'It's true, they are readying their boats.'

Corinna's mind raced. She endeavoured to recall what she knew of the vast imperial province of Germania Inferior and its settlements of tribes allied to Rema – tribes that had grown accustomed to the security provided by the legionary bases on the west bank of the river. 'Without legionary protection how will the settlements withstand a Helutti onslaught?'

Verendus ran a hand through his hair, pushing it back from his face. 'As I said last night, Legate Sentorus won't compromise the border. Even if he has marched south to Capula, he would not leave the Germanian border vulnerable.'

'Landren said Emperor Flavio is weak, that Rema decays. If Legate Sentorus has the support of several legions, he could march on Rema. Have you chosen the right side?'

'My vow is to the emperor.'

'But is he worthy of it?'

Verendus screwed up his face as though tasting something sour. 'Worthier than civil war. Besides, what can I do? It's out of my hands.' The terror that had plagued his fever burned in his eyes. His voice dropped to a whisper. 'They're after me. I told you Praetorians would come.'

No, he was muddled. She stroked his arm and spoke softly. 'Mos said the drowned soldier wore a legionary tag.'

'Indeed.' Verendus laughed – a high, wild laugh. 'Don't look like that, I still have my reasoning. I saw the tag this morning. His name was Publius Pactorax – same name as the man Dacoren killed.'

'What?' She didn't understand. 'It's just a coincidence.'

'It's a false identity, a speciality of the Speculatores. Some names are used time and again.' He sighed. 'One gets to know them.'

'Speculatores!' Her mouth dried. Caesar's Serpents. Praetorian Guard spies and assassins. Thoughts reeled, wouldn't form into words. She didn't want to believe, and yet she saw the truth of it. His lies and evasions, the missions to Germania. Now, at last, she understood. 'You are a Speculator?'

Silent, he stared into the distance. His rigid stance told her she was right. She knew this should appal her. Speculatores were vile, cruel, ruthless. She couldn't make sense of her feelings; he was none of those things.

She clutched his hands. 'The man's dead, the clasp is lost. They'll leave you alone. Won't they?'

'I'm a wanted man. One of the Speculatores is still out there. More will come. I must leave to draw them away from the lodge.'

'You're safer in Lignora. Don't go, Ericus. Please don't go.' What could she say to make him stay? It was no use, that resolute expression told her he wouldn't yield.

'Cara, don't.' He pulled free. 'This isn't easy for me either.'

'Then let me come with you. You said we'd swim together. Let me swim beside you.'

'In all things save this.' He stood as grim as the day he'd found her.

Once, when they first met, she'd asked him why he had become a Praetorian. His answer had been weary, slightly flippant, something about not having the head for a career in law. It wasn't hard to see why he'd grasped the opportunity to join the Guard, everyone knew guardsmen were well paid and served a shorter term than men of the legions. But the Speculatores, those insidious Praetorian snakes. 'Why?' she said. 'Why are you a Speculator?'

He shrugged. 'Because the emperor requested it. And one does not refuse the emperor.'

Corinna nodded. That was good, wasn't it? He hadn't chosen this path, he'd been coerced into it. Her resentment remained. Even if he was no longer a Speculator, he had been part of that infamous unit. Somehow, she would have to accept that. And accept that he had taken a new path.

There was a moment of complete stillness. The birds fell silent and she could no longer hear the distant shouts of auxiliaries at their drill. Cloud obscured the sun, darkening the ground where Verendus stood, clothing his naked torso in a cuirass of shadow. An urge to hit out surged, and she prodded his solid chest. 'You're just as hard inside.'

'That's unfair. I'll come back to you.'

'Empty words! You don't know that.' Her resolve to hold her emotions in check faltered. Each fear spawned another. Her throat tightened. She had tortured herself already over the risks he would face by returning to Iolia. If the Serpents were after him, then those risks were even greater. Hot tears stung her eyes. She tried to pull away, hating that he'd made her cry and wanting him to share her distress, to feel her pain. 'Can't you see how afraid I am?'

'Of course I bloody well can! I'm afraid too.'

She stopped struggling. 'Truly?'

'Yes! It's easier for me to do what I must in Iolia, if I know you're safe.'

He made it sound so reasonable. Always he had the upper hand. 'But don't you understand,' she said, determined to ensure he would, 'we play by your rules.'

'Yes, I see that,' he said warily. 'But I won't change my mind.'

Sun returned to light the glade. The shadowy cuirass vanished and the scars and wounds that patterned his chest were vivid in the sunshine. She counted the tracks left by the stitches she'd sewn to mend his skin. Her thoughts slowed. Forced by circumstance to address her fear, the release of tension in confronting him, despite his refusal, was considerable. By the relief on his face, he felt this too.

Light flickered through the branches. His hand strayed to the hilt of his sword. He gripped the pommel, freeing the blade from the scabbard before easing it back. 'I must go. I will make my stand in Iolia.'

CHAPTER XXXIX

Mos knelt on the rutted ground beside the ancient oak. This morning, there hadn't been time to visit the altar he'd made in the hollow of the roots. Oriedas had asked for his help to search for the missing legionary. They hadn't tracked the man down, but they'd found the body of the other one on the riverbank. It was the legionary he'd seen at the river yesterday, the one he'd tried to bring down. If only that arrow had hit, then they wouldn't have stolen the clasp.

Mos took four raisins from his purse and set them on the slate altar. Father would say no point worrying about what happened yesterday, but it was hard not to. Mos said a prayer for his family, a prayer for the Parhel rebel Kalvos, and one for Saffi. Then he prayed for Fes. He wasn't sure how to word the prayer, but he said something about hoping Fes was in the great hall of his Saxtili forebears.

Low sun warmed the glade. Soon be time for supper. Mos rose and touched the sun pendant that hung at his throat. On the morrow, they would start the journey to the coast and Iolia. Somehow, he must find a way to get home.

On retiring to his bedroom that evening, Verendus was relieved to find Corinna waiting. She led him from the pile of kit and polished mail, upstairs to her own room where glasses and a jug of wine were set upon a table.

Each intent on the other, the lamp left burning at his insistence, they slept little that night and, as darkness brightened to morning, made love one last time.

Yawning, he stretched. He'd catch up on sleep when they set camp tonight.

He had to steel himself to leave. *You're getting soft*, Carbo would have said, and he'd be right. Outside these walls, there was no room for vulnerability. A lapse of attention, a moment's hesitation, could mean the difference between life and death.

And then the sickening dread, the not knowing whether he would survive, descended with an intensity he'd never felt before. Thank the gods Corinna would soon travel to the haven of Mid-Lignora. She would be safe there. He wished he didn't have to go. He may not make it back to her.

Enough, he must remain focused. For Rema.

It had been Corinna's wish to bid farewell in the yard. Verendus declined. He wanted their parting to be private, to picture her as she was now, lying naked on the bed, her body flushed and warm from his embrace, her unbraided hair an aura of coppery-gold. He blinked, imprinting the image into his memory.

Slowly, like mist rising from a lake, she rose and embraced him, kissed him tenderly on the lips. 'My heart goes with you.'

'And mine is ever with you…'

Verendus turned, unable to say more. He pulled on his tunic. Mos would be waiting to help him on with his kit. Then they would pray together, a plea to Fortuna Redux goddess of safe return.

Verendus opened the door. He didn't look back. If he did, he'd never leave.

As he closed the door behind him, a door in his mind closed too, separating Corinna from his present self and from what he must do.

Corinna dressed quickly, wrapped a shawl about her shoulders, and went to stand before the arched window at the back of the lodge. Below, the courtyard was noisy with purpose as auxiliaries checked tack and horses ready for departure. Decurion Bretorus was there, tapping his vine-stick against his thigh as he oversaw the loading of packs, trunks, and two huge cooking pots onto a mule cart.

She couldn't see Verendus. Maybe he was with Landren at the front of the lodge, where – according to Strixi – the archers would assemble separately. Already, there was division between the two forces. The auxiliaries – outnumbered four-to-one – would probably suffer most.

As the troopers lined up beside their horses, it was evident how their numbers had decreased since that first morning at Castellum Alba. Corinna hugged herself, chilled by the bitter inevitability that many of these men would not return.

Bretorus ordered the auxiliaries to attention, and Verendus strode through the archway into their midst. He wasn't wearing his distinctive uniform. The scarlet cloak and red feather crest had ceded to muted shades of slate and silver like a bird in winter plumage about to fly to distant climes. Mos followed, head bowed, leading Plum and Pepper.

Corinna abandoned her intention to watch them ride off. Now Verendus was due to depart she couldn't bear to see him go. As she turned away, a white feather floated down. She turned back and watched it drift, glide, and come to rest on the windowsill. The Seer's third feather.

Thrice Fate's wings will touch you. One will break. One will bind. And one will kill.

It had come to pass. Torvius was dead. Eldoran had come into her life – there would always be a bond between them. And now, Verendus was leaving. That must be break. She shivered and drew the shawl tighter. The prophecy had been fulfilled.

Perhaps it was better this way, to part before things grew stale, before the yellow rose wilted. But however many times she told herself, she didn't believe it. The pain cut too deep.

She must have stood there a while, for when she looked again, the courtyard was empty though she hadn't heard them ride off. With trembling fingers, she opened the purse on her belt. Even as she found a sachet of somniferum, Strixi's words rang in her head: *I have thought of a way to find your father.*

Possibility stirred, focusing her mind. Strixi had offered to arrange everything, and the plan was so simple Corinna wondered why she hadn't thought of it herself. Now, as she would not be returning to Iolia, she could join Strixi in the search.

Corinna tucked the somniferum back into her purse. She must seize this opportunity and follow her own path, as

Verendus must follow his. If Fortuna smiled on them, those paths would cross again. The gods had not finished with Verendus yet.

REMA

850 AUC (AD 97)

In Rema the portents were grave. A midwife reported the birth of a two-headed baby; a vast flock of ill-omened birds circled high above the city and swooped down to perch upon the Senate House; a priest at the Temple of Jupiter Optimus Maximus witnessed tears fall from the eyes of the great god's statue.

That same day, a dispatch arrived at the Imperial Palace to confirm the rumours: an unidentified legion had cut a swathe of destruction across Raetia and disappeared. The whereabouts of Legate Sentorus unknown, word spread swiftly that legions guarding the border of Germania Inferior had broken their oath of allegiance and were marching on Rema.

Chronicles of Imperial Rema

by Marcus Vedius Verendus

TO BE CONTINUED

Dear Reader,

Thank you so much for reading the second book in *The Serpents of Caesar* series. If you enjoyed **Codex**, please let people know. Your review means a lot to me. I would really appreciate it if you could leave a review (as brief as you like) on **Codex's** Amazon page, and / or on BookBub or Goodreads.

Thank you for reading.

With warm regards,

Thea

P.S. If you enjoyed **Codex**, why not join the **Verendus Readers Club**.

On joining, you'll receive **Tribunus**: a free and exclusive eBook prequel to *The Serpents of Caesar* series set ten years before **Codex** at the start of Verendus' military career, plus other exclusive content, musings on Ancient Rome, and news about the next book in the series: **Inferno**.

For more details, please visit my website:
www.trburgess.com

AFTERWORD

Rome, but not as we know it

Codex is a blend of history and legend, speculation and imagination. In this alternate first century world, myths endure – Remus has killed Romulus to found Rema, and the ancient tribes of Europa live a tenuous existence alongside their imperial neighbours. Protagonists Verendus and Corinna are descendants of the factual Ambrone tribe: Jutland migrants annihilated by Roman troops. This novel adopts the premise that some Ambrones escaped to the fictitious Mediterranean island of Iolia, which has since become part of the Empire.

The Emperor, the Praetorian Guard, and the Legions

Ancient Rome's Praetorian Guard began as a select unit of troops that served as an elite bodyguard force. The Guard's original remit, along with its numbers expanded over time. During the reign of Domitian, it is possible there were ten cohorts (an infantry formation of six centuries), each perhaps a thousand strong. Three cohorts were based in Rome; the rest were billeted in neighbouring towns and places of special importance, such as the Mint at Lugdunum (Lyon, France) and the port of Ostia (Italy) where much of Rome's grain supply arrived. I have developed this concept and created small satellite castra to house these cohorts – one of which is located in Iolia, another in Viorum. Similarly, I have expanded the role of the Speculatores – covert conveyors of secret dispatches, gatherers of information, expert assassins – and devised the rank of Commendator (a senior officer rank) for Verendus.

Of the Roman Legions mentioned, most are based geographically in accordance with historical evidence. Legions II Minervia, III Gemina, XXIII Victrix, and XXIV Germanica are creations, as are most of the characters in the novel. A few notable exceptions include Emperor Domitian (ruled AD 81-96), and Praetorian Guard Prefect Titus Petronius Secundus.

History records that Domitian's son died in infancy. In the novel, the boy survives to become Emperor Flavio, and would have been about seventeen-years-old at the time *Codex* is set. Thus, the renowned era of the 'Five Good Emperors' has not begun.

The Auxiliaries

These non-citizen troops served as both cavalry and infantry, and received citizenship at the end of twenty-five years of service. While it is possible that a unit called the Fourth Brittonum existed in the Roman Empire, the name is used fictitiously here. Many of these fictional auxiliaries of the First and Second Cavalry Turma of the Fourth Brittonum are recruits from the island province of Britannia, a relatively recent addition to the Empire.

Roman Time & Distance

In Ancient Rome the natural day was divided into twelve hours from sunrise to sunset; night was divided into four watches. This was subject to seasonal variation: in summer, when the period of daylight was longer, the twelve hours of day were correspondingly longer and the hours of the watches shorter. The classification AUC (*ab urbe condita* – from the founding of the City, i.e. Rome – traditionally 753 BC) is used to date the extracts from Marcus' *Chronicles*.

Only major highways such as the Via Domitia are shown on the Gallia Narbonensis Map; however, these main roads had junctions with other roads linking them to towns not on the highway. In addition, there were many minor roads. An imperial Roman mile is estimated to be approximately 0.92 miles or 1.48 kilometres.

Tribes and Locations

In the late second century BC – perhaps due to prolonged periods of flooding – thousands of men, women, and children of the Ambrone tribe left their Jutland homeland. Along with two neighbouring tribes, they migrated south through Europe in search of new land. In 102 BC, after years of steady advance in which no permanent settlement was secured, the Ambrone tribe was defeated by the Roman Army at the Battle of Aquae Sextiae (Aix-en-Provence, France).

The fate of the surviving Ambrones is unclear. In desperation, many may have killed themselves. The rest were probably massacred, or captured and enslaved. In the world of *The Serpents of Caesar*, a small contingent of the tribe escaped into the Alps. Here, imagination steps in and, via the (fictional) Ambrone Pass, the tribe reached the coast and sailed to sanctuary on Iolia. Independence was brief. Rema coveted the island and, unable to withstand the invasion, the Ambrones yielded. Reman veterans settled on the island, married Ambrone women, and Iolia became an imperial province.

Although there is evidence of an Alpine tribe that worshipped a snake god, little is known about these people. Some of the tribes in the novel – the Helutti, the Saxtili, the Parhels, and the nine tribes of the Ennea – are creations. As are some places, including Iolia, Viorum, Lignora, Castellum Alba, and Grenorum. However, most of the places mentioned existed in the first century. The Temple of the Flame is drawn as a cult similar to that of the Vestals in Rome.

The Parhels

The Parhels were the first inhabitants of Iolia. They built a settlement beside the natural harbour on the site known now as Portula. Over time, they explored the coast and discovered routes through the Iolian Rings.

The Parhels embraced a simple lifestyle. They did not trade with outsiders, but cultivated the island, fished the teeming waters, and lived a peaceful and austere existence. They were ill-prepared for the arrival of the Ambrones. Though outnumbered, the northern tribe conquered and enslaved the Parhels. Power was fleeting, for Rema coveted the island. Unable to withstand the invasion, the Ambrones yielded and Iolia became a province of Rema. Reman veterans settled on the island and married Ambrone women.

The Parhels were less acquiescent. They kept their old ways and spoke their own tongue. The refusal of the monotheistic tribe to worship Reman gods caused further resentment.

The Saxtili and the Helutti

Some ten years before the series begins, the Saxtili and the Helutti tribes gained notoriety in Rema when scouts of Third Legion Gemina discovered the remains of Second Legion Minervia at Grenorum (Germania Inferior). Verendus – a young tribune at the time – was one of several officers sent to inspect the carnage. The mutilation of the bodies suggested the legion had been ambushed by Helutti warriors. Rumour spread that guides from the trusted Saxtili tribe had led the Second Legion into the Helutti's trap. In an act of vengeance, soldiers of the Third Legion marched to the nearest Saxtili village and razed it to the ground.

As war engulfed the region, Rema punished both Germani tribes for their perceived part in the ambush. A decade of imperial wrath enslaved thousands of Saxtili, not only from the communities that fled across the river to Barbarian Germania but also from the colony that remained within the Empire. These Saxtili live in a settlement near Auster Grenorum and are subject to strict regulations.

As for the Helutti, those living on the west bank of the Rhenus River left to join their kindred in Barbarian Germania. Intent on retribution, Rema made regular sorties across the river where payment was taken in the form of blood, plunder, and slaves. Remans value Helutti slaves for their strength and resilience. The best male specimens are sold to amphitheatres to be trained as gladiators. Others are put to work in fields and mines where life is also brutal and short. Many Remans fear the Helutti will cross the river to exact revenge.

The Ennea

In this alternate world, it is said that Enneans descend from the union of the wood sprite Nemusia and the youth Lignorus. Nemusia bore Lignorus nine children and, when they came of age, each went forth into the world. Thus, the Ennea began. The Reman Empire has largely displaced the Enneans. Of the nine tribes of the wood, perhaps five endure. Sources claim that as Rema's hunger for territory grew, so the tribes fled to sanctuary in forests beyond the Germanian border where men live in greater awe of these mystics and let them be. Only the Lignoran tribe remains within the Empire, its small realm constrained by imperial borders and a tenuous alliance set out in the Atrox Treaty.

Ennean influence has myriad and widely enjoyed benefits including medicines, such as the opium-based analgesic somniferum, superior locks and keys, and higher standards of hygiene than evidenced at the time.

The Atrox Treaty

As the Second Century BC drew to a close, Roman forces moved ever westwards through the Alps and into Gaul. By 121 BC, a swathe of prime Mediterranean land (later part of Gallia Narbonensis) was claimed by Rome.

In the world of *The Serpents of Caesar*, this land was home to the Lignorans: one of the nine tribes of the Ennea. When their borders were threatened by the Ambrone tribe, the Lignorans entered into a military alliance with Rema. The allies routed the Ambrones at the Battle of Atrox; however, Rema's Senate declined the agreed payment of Lignoran gold for its services and refused to withdraw the army. More troops arrived to persuade the Lignorans to relinquish their homeland.

Given the choice between conflict and compromise, the Lignorans ceded to Rema's demands and signed the Atrox Treaty. In exchange for new territory in the forests of Aquitania and a pact of non-aggression, the Lignorans moved west and their land was taken by Rema. Some two decades later, the Ambrones made another attempt to settle in Gallia Narbonensis and were defeated again.

Relations between Lignora and the Empire worsened. Following the death of Emperor Domitianus, Lignorans renewed appeals for the reform of the Atrox Treaty and the return of their homeland. His successor has yet to address these issues.

The Ouroboros

Time's eternal cycle of seasons is symbolised by the ouroboros snake, which devours its own tail in an act of rebirth. Here, the double ouroboros embodies a more sinister meaning. This pair of twisting serpents devours each other's tail in a struggle of equal but opposing forces. Eventually, each will consume the other, causing an implosion of such force the world will end.

DRAMATIS PERSONAE

<u>Emperors</u>

Domitianus: known today as Emperor Domitian (ruled AD 81-96)

Flavio: Rema's young emperor, son of Domitianus

<u>On the road to Viorum</u>

Commendator Ericus Vedius Verendus: Praetorian Guard officer on a mission

Corinna Aurius: former Temple handmaid who longs to find her Lignoran father

Dorcas: slave also known as Blabbermouth

Eldoran: enigmatic, silver-haired Nemusan

Mos: Lucius Mostus. Verendus' attendant. Half-Parhel, half-Reman, unsure of himself and where he belongs

Quintus: pleasantly vacant only son of Governor Peronius

Saffi: slave from the Saxtili tribe

<u>Auxiliaries of Fourth Brittonum</u>

Adarius: trumpeter

Bretorus: dry, capable decurion of the First Turma

Callenus: medic

Cico: lanky young recruit

Dexo: scout

Gallus: auxiliary whose nervous expression earned him the nickname Mole

Hostus: big, shaggy-haired auxiliary

Marinus: flame-haired Briton, new to the turma

Murvaro: brutish, big-headed bully

Nonus: third-in-command

Perseo: second-in-command, honoured bearer of the turma's standard

Portoc: chubby-faced auxiliary known as Piggy

Strabo: obsequious auxiliary known as Slug

Tadius: new recruit in debt to Murvaro

Treseus: softly spoken decurion of the Second Turma

Treseus Rufus: younger brother of Treseus

Praetorian Guard

Aquinus: Praetorian Guard Tribune of the Gallia Division based in Viorum

Galenius: Prefect Titus Galenius Dax, chief of the Praetorian Guard

Matellius: optio based at Castrum Viorum

Nevoso: guardsman promoted to centurion following Torvius' death

Norvanus: principal based at Castrum Viorum

Rectus: optio and torturer at Castrum Viorum

Secundus: Titus Petronius Secundus: actual Praetorian Guard Prefect AD 94-96

Torvius: centurion (deceased)

Residents of Iolia

Carbo: decanus. Big, gruff, and extremely tidy

Drusilla: Verendus' coy mistress

Fonattea Concordia (Attea): Magistra, High Priestess of the Temple of the Flame

Jaecinth (Jae): daughter of Naeos. Selective mute who always gets her point across

Kalvos: activist fighting for Parhel rights

Marcus Vedius Verendus: Verendus' father, minister, author of *Chronicles of Imperial Rema*

Naeos: wily old Parhel

Nellis: sometime lover and model for Verendus. Murdered by the Iolian Watch

Residents of Castellum Alba

Dalcamus: efficient and meticulous minister (deceased)

Decimia: daughter of Governor Peronius and Stanzia

Peronius: Decimus Canius Peronius Maximus governor of Narbonensis Province

Stanzia: wife of Governor Peronius

<u>Lignorans</u>

Dacoren: wagon driver

Landren: Ennean lord of the Lignora tribe

Oriedas: Landren's resourceful aide

Strixi: Landren's capable lodge-keeper

<u>Others</u>

Avitus: opinionated friend of Spurius

Capito: legate, commander of Twenty-Third Legion Victrix

Decimius: Senator Numerius Decimius Peronius. Older brother of Governor Peronius

Festinus: Saxtili aide and friend to Verendus

Paullus Regimius Sentorus: legate leading the disciplinary force against Third Legion rebels in Germania

Spurius Decimius Peronius: Senator Decimius' extravagant son

GLOSSARY

AUC – *ab urbe condita*: from the founding of the City (Rema) traditionally dated 753 BC

aureus, aurei – gold coin(s) worth twenty-five silver denarii

auxiliaries – non-citizen troops serving as both cavalry and infantry. Received citizenship at the end of twenty-five years of service

Bacchus – god of wine

Brittonum – of the Britons

caliga(e) – hobnailed military footwear

castrum, castra – military base(s)

centurion – commander of a century

century – legionary unit of eighty soldiers

cohort – military unit, e.g. a legionary unit of six centuries

commendator – fictitious Praetorian Guard rank between centurion and tribune

decanus – commander of a squad of ten

decurion – commander of an auxiliary cavalry unit

denarius, denarii – silver coin(s) worth four sestertii

domina, dominus – mistress, master

Ennea – the nine tribes of the wood

Fortuna Redux – goddess of safe return

fustuarium – extreme punishment meted out with cudgels or clubs by fellow soldiers

garum – fish sauce

Gemina – Twin, legion title

gladius – sword

haruspex – person who makes divinations by interpreting entrails

Hispana – of Spain

ides – approximately the middle day of the month

insula(e) – apartment block(s). Ground floor usually used for shops and businesses

Iutum – Jutland Peninsula

lararium – shrine of the household gods

legate – general in command of a legion

legion – military unit of approximately 5,000 soldiers

maenads – aka Bacchantes. Female followers of Dionysus or the Roman wine god Bacchus

mansio, mansiones – inn(s) for travellers on official business

Minervia – devoted to the goddess Minerva

Ministerium – local government meeting house

optio – centurion's deputy

paenula – hooded cover-all

palla – woman's mantle worn over a tunic

Pax Remana – from **Pax Romana:** Roman Peace

Phi – 21st letter of the Greek alphabet

phixus – symbol for the sign of the serpents

plumeus – feathery, composed of or filled with feathers

praenomen – personal name, usually used only by family and close friends

prefect – commander (or joint-commander) of the Praetorian Guard

Priapus – god of male procreative power, guardian of gardens and vineyards

retiarius – 'net-man' gladiator who fought with a weighted net, trident, and dagger

salvete – a greeting: be well / healthy

Saturnalia – December festival in honour of the god Saturn

scorpio – torsion siege engine and field artillery weapon

scutum – legionary's rectangular shield

scytale – tapered stick used to create and decode ciphers

secutor – 'pursuer' gladiator who fought the retiarius. To protect him from the trident prongs, his helmet – save for two small eye-holes – covered his entire face

sestertius, sestertii – low denomination brass coin(s), around 3cm in diameter

signum – military standard carried by a signifer

situla – a bucket-shaped vessel

somniferum – opium-based analgesic

spatha – long, double-edged cavalry sword

speculatores – elite agents of the Praetorian Guard

tablinum – study where documents and records are stored

tepidarium – warm-room at the baths

tribune – senior officer acting as aide to the legate

turma – unit of thirty auxiliary troopers under the command of a decurion and his second officer

vexillation – military detachment usually consisting of 1,000 infantry and / or 500 cavalry

Victrix – Victorious, title awarded to a legion

BIBLIOGRAPHY

In researching this novel I have consulted too many sources to list here. These are the principal books I have relied on:

Bingham, S. *The Praetorian Guard: A History of Rome's Elite Special Forces*. I.B. Tauris, (London, 2013).

Bishop, M.C., Coulston, J.C.N. *Roman Military Equipment*, 2nd edn., Oxbow Books, (Oxford, 2009).

Bromwich, J. *The Roman Remains of Southern France*. Routledge, (Oxon, 2005).

Campbell, B. *The Roman Army, 31 BC-AD 337 A Sourcebook*. Routledge, (London, 1994).

Cowan, R., and Ó'Brógáin, S. (illust.) *Roman Guardsman 62 BC-AD 324*. Osprey, (Oxford, 2014).

Croom, A. *Roman Clothing and Fashion*. Amberley, (Stroud, 2010).

Cruse, A. *Roman Medicine*, Tempus, (Stroud, 2004).

De La Bédoyère, G. *Praetorian: The Rise and Fall of Rome's Imperial Bodyguard*. Yale University Press, (London, 2017).

Gilliver, K., Goldsworthy, A., Whitby, M. *Rome At War: Caesar and his Legacy*. Osprey, (Oxford, 2005).

Parker, P. *The Empire Stops Here: A Journey Along the Frontiers of the Roman World*. Pimlico, (London, 2009).

Rankov, B. (Dr.), and Hook, R. (illust.) *The Praetorian Guard*. Osprey, (Oxford, 2008).

Southern, P. *The Roman Army: A Social & Institutional History.* Oxford University Press, (New York, 2007).

Tacitus., Mattingly, H. (trs). *Germania.* Penguin Classics, (London, 2009).

Webster, G. *The Roman Imperial Army*, 3rd edn., A & C Black, (London, 1981).

ACKNOWLEDGEMENTS

This novel would never have reached completion without the help and support of my writer friends, especially Jane Shufflebotham and Rosalind Tate, and my indispensable team of Beta Readers. A few of the team suggested that a map of Gallia Narbonensis would be a useful addition. Many thanks to Gianpiero Mangialardi for transforming my working sketch into a beautiful map.

Alongside the writing there is the maintenance of a website to provide more information about *The Serpents of Caesar* series. My thanks to Tina Key of SPRK Design for her help and expertise.

Of all those involved, the biggest thanks must go to my dear friend and writing buddy Robyn West, whose wisdom, encouragement, and humour have been invaluable. And to my husband John for his incredible support while I have been working on this book.

And many thanks to you, dear reader, for joining Verendus in his quest.

Thea Burgess, Britannia, 2024

ABOUT THE AUTHOR

Thea Burgess hails from the Roman city of Aquae Sulis (modern day Bath, England), and has long been fascinated by the history of Ancient Rome.

In addition to working on *The Serpents of Caesar* series, Thea also writes short stories with a Roman theme and has been long-listed for the Historical Writers' Association, Dorothy Dunnett Short Story Award three times.

The Fates have brought her to a village near the beautiful Roman city of Noviomagus Reginorum (modern day Chichester), where she lives with her very patient husband and several angelfish.

For more information about Verendus and *The Serpents of Caesar* and news of *Inferno*, the next book in the series, please visit: **www.trburgess.com**

9 781739 129835